Praise for May McGoldrick's Novels

"Love triumphs in this richly romantic tale." *—Nora Roberts*

"May McGoldrick brings history alive, painting passion and intrigue across a broad, colorful canvas."*—Patricia Gaffney*

"Enchanting tales. Not to be missed." *—The Philadelphia Inquirer*

"Impressive…a splendid Scottish tale, filled with humor and suspense." *—Arnette Lamb*

"May McGoldrick writes with warmth, emotion, and an excellent essence of period detail."*—Heather Graham*

"Well-paced and convincing." *—The Romance Reader*

Over two million
May McGoldrick books in print.

Heart of Gold

May McGoldrick

Complete Book List as of 2015

Writing As May McGoldrick:

THANKSGIVING IN CONNECTICUT
GHOST OF THE THAMES
DREAMS OF DESTINY
CAPTURED DREAMS
BORROWED DREAMS
THE REBEL
TESS AND THE HIGHLANDER
THE PROMISE
THE FIREBRAND
THE ENCHANTRESS
THE DREAMER
FLAME
THE INTENDED
BEAUTY OF THE MIST
HEART OF GOLD
ANGEL OF SKYE
THISTLE AND THE ROSE

Writing As May McGoldrick & Nicole Cody:

ARSENIC AND OLD ARMOR (LOVE AND MAYHEM)

Writing As Jan Coffey:

ROAD KILL
MERCY
AQUARIAN
BLIND EYE
PUPPET MASTER
THE JANUS EFFECT
CROSS WIRED
SILENT WATERS
FIVE IN A ROW
TROPICAL KISS
FOURTH VICTIM
TRIPLE THREAT
TWICE BURNED
TRUST ME ONCE

MACPHERSON BROTHERS TRILOGY BOOK 2

MAY MCGOLDRICK

Heart
OF
GOLD

First Published by Topaz, an imprint of Dutton Signet,
a division of Penguin Books, USA, Inc. 1996

Printed in the United States of America

Cover Art by Dar Albert. www.WickedSmartDesigns.com

*For Pat Teal, Leah Bassoff,
and Constance Martin: three women
who have provided the wings
that make flight possible.*

Prologue

Field of Cloth of Gold
The English Possession of Calais
June 1520

The two knights collided in a shower of sparks, their metal-tipped lances exploding into splinters.

The snorting chargers rushed onward, carrying the men past one another, and Ambrose Macpherson glanced back over his shoulder in time to see his opponent bounce unceremoniously onto the soft earth of the lists. A roar went up from the French courtiers in the grandstands, but the Scottish warrior didn't acknowledge the cheers until he saw the squires of the downed English knight hoist the angry fighter to his feet.

Ignoring the glare of the King Henry's defeated champion, Ambrose stood in his stirrups and waved his shattered spear to the noisy and colorful crowd of spectators. Trotting over to the special box where Francis I, King of France, sat beside Henry VIII, King of England, Ambrose lifted his visor and saluted the two most powerful monarchs in Europe.

"Once again, well done, Sir Ambrose," the French king shouted. Turning to the burly king beside him, Francis clapped Henry Tudor on the shoulder and whispered confidentially, "This is the Scot you should have killed at Flodden, Henry. Not that we think you didn't try, seeing that scar of his." France needed more men like Ambrose as allies, Francis thought to himself. It was rare to find brains, courage, and power all in one man. "He's making the most of his opportunities here, don't you think?"

King Henry tried to look bored as he glanced down at this warrior-diplomat who'd been defeating his best fighters all month. Henry studied the hard lines of the man's face. The Scot's features were handsome enough, were it not for the deep scar crossing his brow from the top of his open helmet to his eye. The mark of a fighter, Henry thought somewhat wistfully, wondering vaguely what he himself would look like with such a scar. With a curt nod of his head, Ambrose wheeled his charger and galloped off toward the barriers.

"Aye, Francis," King Henry conceded. "But he has yet to ride against our man Garnesche."

"Come, Henry. With a lance, this Macpherson is the best horseman in Europe."

"Nay, these are empty words."

"Well, England, we have this golden ring set with a ruby the size of your eye that says he'll defeat your Garland—"

"Garnesche. Sir Peter Garnesche." Henry glared at his regal rival and removed a huge emerald ring from his finger. "Very well. This little trinket should hold its value against yours. Sir Peter will unhorse this Highland jester on the first course."

This friend of France is of hardier stock than all of England's fighters put together, Francis thought. Perhaps we should up the wager. Calais, perhaps. Nay, we'd only end up fighting to take possession of it, anyway. "We'll just see if this champion of yours can remain in his saddle any better than the others. If he keeps his seat after five courses, Henry, the wager is yours." Handing the ruby ring to the nobleman standing behind them, the French king smiled wryly. "Would you trust our Lord Constable to hold the bet, or would you prefer to have one of yours do the honors?"

Henry glanced over at the stern-faced Lord Constable, then back at the broad, pale face of his ambassador, Sir Thomas Boleyn, standing attentive and eager at his shoulder. With a shrug, he tossed the ring to the French official. "You trust the worthy Constable with your kingdom...we think he can be trusted with a bauble. Sir Thomas, tell Sir Peter to arm himself."

The pale blue sky was warm, and Ambrose leaned his weary body back against the barriers, sipping water from a ladle while his squires attended to his mount. Looking across the open ground toward the grandstands, he thought to himself what a wasted opportunity this month had been for each of these two fiercely competitive monarchs. A wasted opportunity for each country.

These great princes had come to the Golden Vale to discuss peace. To settle the differences that had kept their countries at odds for the past hundred years. Instead, they had spent the time trying to outdo each other in wit and shows of strength.

Thank God for their arrogance, Ambrose thought. Thank God for the incredible personal competitiveness that drove these two men. Thank God for the individual pride that had—so far, anyway—kept them from finding a way to come to an accord and forge an alliance that would seriously jeopardize Scotland's future, as well as the future of all Europe.

Ambrose smiled grimly, thinking of how these two kings so often acted like two spoiled adolescents, each trying to surpass the deeds and wealth of the other. Indeed, once, in the middle of the month, when Henry had suggested wrestling and laid his heavy arm on the French king's neck, only a massive diplomatic effort had stopped the two from going to war after Francis deftly tossed the English king to the ground.

And the Scottish knight had to make sure these two rivals would remain just that. For the good of all, the balance of power had to be maintained.

Ambrose scanned the fields outside the jousting lists. The rolling meadows were covered with the peaked tents and banners of the French and English nobles and their entourages. In planning this occasion, thoughts of expense had been discarded. And everything was for show. Covered with the golden tents and royal pavilions, erected to house the ten thousand lords, cardinals, knights, and ladies of each court, the sight was visually dazzling. It was intended to be. Even the fountain that stood by the great hall spewed wine instead of water. This was diplomacy at its most opulent, at its most futile.

Ambrose took in the sight with a twinge of disgust, for his eyes also took in the hungry peasants being held back by soldiers beyond the grand gate on the far side of the field. Tents of gold cloth were being used by the nobles for these few short weeks, while many of these hungry villagers and their children begged for food and slept year round in the open air. Politicians are largely blind men, Ambrose thought in disgust. And it's true everywhere. In England, in France, and even in Scotland. Once, years back, he'd thought the best course was to distance himself from politics. But along the way, he'd learned it was the profession he was best suited for.

On the surface, Ambrose Macpherson was a warrior without peer and the trusted emissary of the Scottish crown. He was a man of action and a man of learning. Though educated at St. Andrew's and the university in Paris, Ambrose had mastered the arts of war fighting beside his father and brothers in the turbulent years of civil unrest that divided Scotland during his youth. Returning to the side of King James IV when war threatened with England, he had fought valiantly beside his king when Scottish blood was spilled on the fields of Flodden. That had been seven years ago, and Ambrose had received land, position, and fame for his continuing acts of valor and devotion.

But that hadn't been all. Being a free spirit, Ambrose had sought adventure and challenge. That had led him to every court in Europe. Renowned across the continent for his diplomatic achievements and his physical prowess, Ambrose Macpherson was respected as a man of honor in a world of treachery.

The sound of the heralds' trumpets brought Ambrose's attention back to the lists. These would be the final jousts of the day and of the tournament. Tomorrow he'd be riding to Boulogne, and from there sailing on to Scotland. He was looking forward to being home for the christening of his new nephew.

But first he had to ride against the Englishman Garnesche—formidable opponent, Ambrose thought. He'd seen him unhorse every knight he'd jousted with. The man was strong as a horse and as lithe as a cat. Ambrose moved toward his horse. The final joust of the day.

The two knights faced each other as the sounds of the drum roll and the blasts of the trumpets filled the air. Peter Garnesche wore a cloak of cloth of gold over his full armor. Ambrose Macpherson was finely appointed in black satin and velvet. The razor sharp blade of a Highland dirk couldn't cut the steady heat of their gazes as each opponent studied the other.

The crowd fell silent as the jousters made their way to their respective sides of the tiltyard. As he passed by the grandstands, Ambrose let his eyes roam the glittering rows of nobility dressed in their colorful finery. He saw the waving kerchiefs of the many young women who'd been beating a steady path to his tent these warm nights. He knew the ways of bringing pleasure to those he bedded. And, thus far, he was free of the scourge of pox that was running rampant. Having that reputation had made Ambrose a most popular courtier wherever he went. But lately he'd found himself somewhat bored with the selection of willing ladies at large. They all seemed the same. Too experienced and all too willing. There was no challenge. There wasn't even a pre-tense of innocence.

Ambrose shook his head to clear his thoughts of such nonsense. Concentrate, he thought to himself. Here he was, a moment away from facing the most challenging of his opponents, and he was still thinking from the proximity of his codpiece.

About to steer his courser toward the field, Ambrose was caught by the unwavering gaze of a young woman standing at the end of the seats. There was an air of power, of assurance in her glance. So much for being bored with the selection of the available ladies, he thought. Aye, some new blood, a new spirit.

Ambrose lowered his lance, saluting the unknown maiden, and wheeled his black stallion.

Elizabeth Boleyn blushed at the champion's sudden attention. And the heads that turned in her direction caught her quite off guard.

Since this was the French king's challenge, the English queen held her kerchief aloft, and Ambrose and Peter Garnesche waited like two great bulls, straining at their tethers in their impatience to do battle. Once more the heralds sounded their trumpets, and as the notes faded away, a deadly stillness descended upon the yard.

The kerchief fell, and the two warriors spurred their steeds into action.

As they thundered down the stretch, Ambrose began to lower the tip of his long lance. With a motion that had grown as familiar as a wave of his hand, the Highlander pinned the end of the lance against the side of his chest with his muscular upper arm. Watching the onrushing knight lower his lance, Ambrose realized immediately why the English fighter had been so successful. Garnesche's lance wasn't completely lowered; the metal tip was pointed directly at Ambrose's visor.

Fighting the instinct to raise himself in his saddle, Ambrose kept his spear pointed directly at his foe's heart.

With a deafening crash, the two warriors collided, the Englishman's lance exploding on Ambrose's shoulder, above his shield, while the Scot's weapon splintered in the direct hit to Garnesche's protecting shield. It took all of Ambrose's strength to remain on his horse as they passed.

The sounds of the cheering crowd rolled across the field as the two fighters turned and rode back to their positions, replacing their spent weapons.

"He cheated, m'lord," the young squire blurted out as he handed Ambrose the new lance. "He lowered his lance late!"

"Aye, but it just confirms the Englishman's reputation." Ambrose looked reassuringly at the lad. "I should have expected such tactics."

The two warriors faced each other once again, awaiting the signal. The heralds blared, the kerchief dropped, and the men flew down the course.

Leveling his lance early, Ambrose raised himself high in his saddle as the horse galloped on furiously. The crowd gasped. Despite the enormous weight of the cumbersome armor, the Highlander held himself and his lance rock steady as the courser raced toward the charging foe. Standing in his stirrups, the Scottish champion was sure to be unhorsed by the impact, or beheaded by the lance of his opponent should his strength falter.

Garnesche sneered through his visor at the oncoming Scot. The fool was finished.

An instant before the men closed, Ambrose sat hard in his saddle. The Englishman's lance was now aimed high, directly at his face. Leaning into the attack, Ambrose never flinched at the oncoming blow.

The impact of the lance against the center of his foe's shield resounded clear across the tiltyard, while the tip of Garnesche's lance whistled past Ambrose's head.

Raising his visor as he reined in his steed, Ambrose dropped his shattered weapon and turned amid the roar of the spectators to see the English knight sprawled flat on his back.

Cursing loudly and viciously, Peter Garnesche grabbed at the hand of his squire and pulled himself abruptly to his feet, glaring all the while at the Scot.

Ambrose's blond hair spilled freely over his shoulders as he removed his helmet. Dropping the metal armor into his squire's hands, the young warrior turned and trotted his stallion toward the grandstands and the royal box. He smiled at the grudgingly appreciative English crowd and gave a small salute to the cheering French. The two kings each greeted the champion, though Francis was clearly in the better humor.

"These are the finest of warriors, Sir Ambrose," the French king called out. "And you have vanquished every one." He motioned for the Lord Constable, and took his winnings from the minister's open fist. Holding up the Tudor king's emerald ring to the light, he looked at it admiringly for a moment before handing it over the railing to the young knight. "I should have gotten England to wager Calais!"

Francis and Ambrose exchanged a smile while the surly English king looked on unamused.

With a nod of his head, the Scottish warrior turned away from the royal box and steered his horse down past the rows of French courtiers. Acknowledging the adulation of the still ex-cited throng, he searched the crowd. He saw the women leaning forward in their seats, hoping for a chance to capture his attention. But his gaze swept over them all.

And then he saw her. She stood where she had been before. She hadn't moved.

Elizabeth studied the image of the warrior. He was all power, all elegance. She had seen enough. She was ready to start. She could feel the tingling, the excitement—in her hands, in the tips of her fingers. The sight of the man as he sat on the magnificent horse, watching her, would remain emblazoned in her memory.

Ambrose had never seen eyes as beautifully dark as hers. They were riveted on him. Studying him. He felt her gaze boring through his shield, roaming his body, studying him. She wanted him, he could tell. He would have her in his bed. Tonight.

Drawing his sword, Ambrose placed the great emerald ring on the razor-sharp point and extended it toward the young and beautiful maiden.

Elizabeth held out her hand as the knight deftly placed the token in her upturned palm.

The crowd fell silent as they watched the exchange. Then a thousand wagging tongues came alive with gossip.

Chapter 1

Her mind raced but her hand was slow to follow.

Elizabeth dipped the brush in the paint mixture and once again raised it to the canvas.

"What are you calling it?"

"The eighth wonder of the world!" Elizabeth murmured as she took a step back, studying her latest creation. *The Field of Cloth of Gold.* She had captured it. The sweep of the rolling countryside outside Calais. The grandeur and the majesty of the royal processions. The unadorned lowliness of the gawking poor. The blue skies overhead and the green fields of late spring. The thick, gray clouds darkening the distant skyline. The gaudy liveries of scurrying servants. The competitive thrill of the joust. The conquering knight. Her best work so far.

Mary shifted her weight on the couch as she stuffed more pillows behind her head. "May I see the ring?"

Elizabeth turned in surprise and looked at her younger half-sister. This was the last thing Mary needed right now, with this illness that was plaguing her. As if the sores from the pox were not bad enough, Mary had been unable to hold down any food for the past week. This once beautiful and robust young woman lay on Elizabeth's bed, exhausted and spent. Elizabeth held back her pity and her tongue. After all, what could she say to this seventeen-year-old who had already endured more pain than others might bear in a lifetime? Elizabeth's mind wandered vaguely to thoughts of her other sister, Anne, and she wondered whether the youngest sister had been the source of Mary's knowledge about the afternoon's incident. The thirteen-year-old Anne was, for most part, Mary's eyes and ears these days.

"Where is the ring, Elizabeth?"

"I don't have it anymore."

"For God's sake, don't pity me." Mary turned her face away, speaking as much to herself as to her sister. "He took my innocence. He slept with me. He used me. So what if you are the one that ends up with his ring?"

"You slept with the Scot?"

"Don't be funny, Elizabeth. You know what I'm talking about."

It was no secret that Mary had been the mistress of Henry, King of England, for several months. The affair had begun immediately after Mary and Anne were summoned to England and to the court by their father only four months ago. From what Elizabeth had been able to gather from Anne, their father had clearly encouraged Mary to respond in kind to the handsome young king's amorous advances, and Sir Thomas had even gone so far as to arrange private meetings in the hunting lodges away from court...and away from the queen. It was common knowledge that the king had long ago grown tired of the woman who could bear him no son.

Ten years back, after death of his wife, Sir Thomas Boleyn had sent Mary and Anne to France to be brought up in the company of Elizabeth, his daughter from an earlier liaison. Growing up together in France in the household that their father kept in the court of Queen Isabel, the bonds had grown strong between the three young siblings. Elizabeth, then ten years old, was only three years older than Mary. Nonetheless, from the start she had taken on the role of guardian and had looked after and offered guidance to her newfound half-sisters.

It was a joy to have them. As a young child, before her sisters' arrival, Elizabeth had been an extremely lonely child. With no parents and no friends, Elizabeth had found other ways way to capture the magic she missed in her life. The little girl had a God-given gift. Elizabeth Boleyn had the ability to see and depict beauty in the darkness around her.

She could still remember what it had been like the night of her mother's death. Dry-eyed, sitting by the burned-out hearth, she had held a fistful of warm ashes in one hand, a charred twig in the other. Using stick and ash, the young girl's small fingers had quietly, desperately swirled and traced a lifeline of patterns. Standing and moving to her mother's cold, lifeless body, Elizabeth had touched her mother's face, as beautiful in death as it had been in life. She left smudge of ash on the high cheekbone.

Elizabeth had only wished the ash could make her warm.

The rest of her childhood was spent drawing on boards, floors, and walls—using whatever subjects she could find and then letting her imagination fill the void.

Years later, she began to paint. As long as Elizabeth made no trouble for her new guardian, she was allowed to run away from the confining prison of her quarters and spend countless hours with the craftsman and the artists that visited Queen Isabel's court. None of the men had ever minded or questioned the bright-faced child who sat silently watching, her knees pulled up to her chest, her eyes intent on their every move. With apprentices bustling about, some of the painters had, in fact, shown interest in the little girl and, as she quietly told them of her interest, provided her with precious scraps of canvas or pigment for paint. She had watched the artisans fashioning their brushes, gazed with wonder at the mixing of paints, and studied the planning and the steps of each artist's technique.

Elizabeth had practiced all she learned. While other young children of the court might fear and avoid the dark corners of the grim castle keep, Elizabeth had taken sanctuary in them. Though the dark stone walls exuded dampness and cold, Elizabeth herself radiated the glowing vibrancy of life. The bold colors that she used in her paintings shone with sunlight and warmth. The lively detail of her work evoked smiles in the few who shared her secret.

And then her sisters had arrived.

As time passed, the three black-haired daughters of Sir Thomas Boleyn had soon attracted the roving eyes of courtiers and knights from France and from many different countries. Of the three, Mary had always been the one drawn to the glamour of that fashionable life. Something in Elizabeth's sister had always cried out for the fawning attention of the court rakes, but nothing unfortunate had ever occurred. Not while Mary had been under Elizabeth's care.

Four months had now passed since her sisters had left. During the years Mary and Anne had been with her, Elizabeth had learned to discipline her creative urge. She would only paint when time allowed and when her siblings didn't need her. After their departure, it had taken a long time to overcome her loneliness for them. But as time passed, Elizabeth had actually grown fond of her newfound solitude. It allowed her time to paint. With no disrupttions, no one to baby, soothe, or look after, she was tasting the first fruits of freedom. But freedom was short-lived.

Suddenly Elizabeth found herself unexpectedly summoned to Calais by Sir Thomas. On arrival, she'd found Mary sick and bedridden. Her sister had contracted the dreaded pox.

She knew what it was. The scourge of every court in Europe. A miserable disease that attacked a lover's body first, and then attacked the mind.

Elizabeth tended to Mary with loving care. There was no need for scolding the younger woman. If the syphilis didn't kill her now, then Mary could look forward to a lifetime of suffering.

Though she herself had always shunned the allure of the court and its shallow inhabitants, something within Elizabeth kept her from condemning Mary for becoming the love interest of the most powerful man in England—the man who held their father's future in his hands. After all, Elizabeth had always had her talent, her painting, her secret life, and her hopes of becoming a great painter. Those dreams offered all the passion that Elizabeth sought in this life. They made her independent, even as a woman. Lost in her art, she needed no man to look after her, to protect her. But Mary was different. She needed attention. She wanted glamour. As Elizabeth strove to be the observer and to capture the image, Mary had always taken pleasure in being the object, the observed, the center of all attention.

Elizabeth thought now of the price her sister was paying. She picked up the brush and started to paint puffs of clouds scudding across the clear blue sky.

"Anne told me everything that happened today at the tournament," Mary whispered, watching the smooth strokes of her sister's brush. "I have to warn you. He is a womanizer."

"You know him?" Elizabeth asked without breaking stride.

"It is hard not to notice him. That Scot is a good-looking man. But don't worry, sister. He is clean. I haven't slept with him."

The crash of the jug against the floor jolted Mary to a sitting position. She looked down sheepishly, trying to avoid the blazing temper of her older sister.

"I warn you!" Elizabeth took a step toward the cowering creature. "If I hear you even one more time belittling yourself as you have been..." She took a deep breath to control her anger before continuing. The walls of these tents were too thin for her liking. "You cannot hold yourself responsible, Mary. If someone should to take the blame, it is that king of yours for giving this god-awful disease to a mere child."

"Then you believe me that he is the only one I have ever slept with?"

"Of course I believe you."

The soft tears that left Mary's eyes did not go unnoticed by her older sister. Elizabeth moved quickly to her and gathered the young woman in her arms.

"Henry doesn't. He hates me. He called me ugly. He said he never wants to see my sickly face. The night before you arrived, I went to him. I was delirious with fever. He wouldn't even let his physician tend to me. He called me a..." Mary clutched at the neck of her sister and wept.

"Hush, my love. That's all in the past. That's all behind you now. Just think of the future. Of a beautiful future."

Elizabeth clutched Mary tightly in her arms—holding her, rocking her. She knew her words lacked conviction. She bit her lips in frustration as she thought of the cold and selfish king. But men were all alike in that respect. Born free to do as they wished. Free to take what they claimed was theirs by right, but never abiding by any civil rules.

"Oh, Elizabeth!" Mary wept. "What future? They once called me the fairest girl in France. Every man at court was after my affections. You know how popular I was. Now see what I've become. No man will ever want to look at me. I'll never have any place in society. No one will want me not even as a friend. I'm already shunned. I just want to die."

"Stop your foolish talk, Mary. That will not happen."

"Why not?"

"Because Death has to face me first before he gets to you."

"You think you could scare him off the way you scare me?" Mary asked with a weak chuckle.

"Of course!"

Mary closed her eyes and took comfort in the protective embrace. She should have asked Father to bring Elizabeth here sooner.

Everything would get better now that she was here. Elizabeth would take care of her, the way she always had. She would never be alone. And she'd get better. Her sister had said so. Elizabeth had already sought the assistance of the French king's physician in examining her illness. The man had been here twice and was coming back this afternoon. He'd sounded quite hopeful last time.

The gentle footstep outside the tent separated the two. Elizabeth moved quickly to her painting and threw a sheet over it.

"Why don't you want me to see it?" The young girl stood in the opening of the tent, watching her eldest sister with a pout on her pretty face.

"Anne, you should not march in on grown-ups as you do. It is not proper." Mary whispered in her weak voice from the couch. "You know very well that Elizabeth doesn't want anyone looking at her pictures."

"I am not anyone. I'm her sister. And what you say is untrue. I saw her show her paintings to the Duc de Bourbon!"

"She saw what?" Mary turned to her older sister in surprise. Elizabeth had sworn Mary to secrecy years back. No one was to see her pictures. No one was to be told. Mary knew it was Elizabeth's greatest fear—that if people discovered her paintings, they would be taken away. After all, it wasn't proper for a young woman to pursue such hobbies to the extent that Elizabeth did. Mary had been shocked in seeing that some of Elizabeth's paintings actually portrayed nude men and women.

"I saw her with my own two eyes," Anne broke in before Elizabeth could respond. "In fact, I saw her accept a bag of gold coins from the duc and leave one of the paintings with him."

Mary jumped out of her place and flung herself at her older sister. "My God! You did it. At last! You sold your work. Which one? How did you convince him to buy one of your paintings? A woman's painting! How did you approach him? How much did you get for it? What made you do it?"

Elizabeth looked up and captured the gaze of her excited sister. She couldn't relate the truth. Not all of it. After all, she had done it for Mary herself. To pay the French physician's fee. But she couldn't let her know.

The Duc de Bourbon, for the past couple of years, had been a persistent pursuer of Elizabeth's. An admirer, true, but Elizabeth knew the duc loved to pursue every young woman who rejected his advances. The nobleman hated to be denied, and he surely thought that she, too, would fall to his charm and wealth—all the young women eventually succumbed. She knew the man had many mistresses. But that was a situation Elizabeth couldn't accept. She was simply not interested in becoming an ornament, tucked away and brought out from time to time for some man's pleasure as her mother had been so many years ago. She had let the duc know her feelings on the matter. But the man wasn't giving up. In their most recent encounters, the duc had been most devious in his efforts to seduce her. She'd been regularly infuriated by his persistent antics and his pathetic tales. So now Elizabeth thought with some satisfaction of how she had earlier today been able to mislead the young nobleman over the painting. She had made up stories that were too unbelievable, but the duc had accepted her tale.

"Tell me, Elizabeth," Mary asked again, "how did you convince him to buy your work?"

"I lied. He thinks he's become the patron of a very talented, though as of yet unknown artist. An unknown *male* artist. He thinks I was just playing the part of the kind-hearted liaison."

"I would have thought he'd be a jealous monster at the thought of your acting for another man."

"I don't see why." Elizabeth sighed as she cleaned and put away her brushes. "My relationship with the duc has never been anything more than one of innocent acquaintance...at least on my part. I've never been attracted to him, and I've never led him on."

"No? Do I have to remind you how men think?" Mary moved back to the couch and sat down. This topic was one in which she had a great deal more expertise than her older sister. "It doesn't matter what you say or what you do. The fact is, Elizabeth, you don't belong to any man. So you are fair game."

"*Oui*! I know the poems...we women are the 'tender prey' for these overgrown, 'love-struck' boys. Well, I'm not. Though I guess I may have embellished the story to take that into account. I did tell him the artist is a crippled nobleman with leprosy who hides himself away in a priory and never sees visitors." Elizabeth removed her apron and tucked it away. "I suppose after hearing that story there was no reason for the duc to feel challenged."

For all her words, though, Elizabeth hoped she wouldn't cross paths with the French nobleman for the rest of her stay here. With the heartache of her sister's ailment, she was in no mood to deal with a persistent courtier.

"Father wants you, Elizabeth." Anne's voice had the singsong quality of a child who knows a secret. The other two women both turned to her in unison.

"Father? What does he want?" Elizabeth had seen her father only from a distance since arriving in the north of France. There was nothing extraordinary in that, however. From the first day she had—as a child—entered Sir Thomas's household, their relationship had never been anything more than politely detached. In fact, unless it was due to Mary's illness, Elizabeth had no idea why her father had summoned her, a daughter he had always seemed intent on ignoring.

"I'll tell you for one of those gold coins."

"No chance, you brat," Elizabeth said curtly, her eyes twinkling. Taking the sides of the painting carefully, she moved it to the back wall of the tent. "I'll find out on my own."

"Perhaps," Anne responded. "But I'll get one of those coins yet." As the words left the girl's mouth, she leaned over and grabbed a couple of Elizabeth's brushes, bolting for the tent's opening.

It took Elizabeth only a moment to realize what Anne had done. She turned and ran after her.

"You spoiled, greedy monster." The older sister chased Anne into the bright afternoon sun. There was no sign of the girl. She was as good at disappearing as she was at appearing.

Elizabeth's eyes roamed the setting before her. There were people everywhere. Squires and stable boys, soldiers and servants, some people dressed in finery and others in rags. Horses and dogs, dull gray carts and brightly painted wagons. The very air was vibrant with action. The gold cloth of the tents reflected the rays of the sun. It looked as though the ropes had captured that celestial orb, holding it down. Elizabeth made a mental note of that. Another touch for her work.

"I have to admit, lass, that I'm offended."

The soft, masculine burr of the accent made Elizabeth turn slowly in the direction of the voice. It was the Highlander. Uncontrollably, she felt her heartbeat quicken at the sight of the giant warrior, dressed in a Scottish tartan now standing only a step away. His deep blue eyes were unwavering as they gazed into hers.

His long, blond hair streamed over shoulders that were wide and powerful. Like a great cat he stood, lithe and balanced and, she thought, ready to pounce.

Ambrose was stunned. She was even more beautiful up close than he had thought her to be. From the grandstand, where he'd first seen her, the young woman's presence, her confidence, her unwavering eyes had piqued his interest. But now, seeing her like this, he was taken aback by the full lips, the high sun-kissed cheekbones, the long luminous lashes, and the incredibly large black eyes that stared back at him in surprise. It was her eyes, black as coal, that had first captured his attention. She was taller than most women, but even in her unattractively sensible clothes, she was quite graceful.

"I'm Ambrose Macpherson. What's your name, lass?"

"Why did you say you were offended?" Elizabeth's mind was racing. Her next painting had to be of this man in his kilt. The sight was definitely too impressive to go uncaptured.

Ambrose smiled.

Elizabeth's heart skipped a beat.

"You were giving this dirt-packed alley more attention than you gave to the joust earlier today." Ambrose took a step toward her, allowing a horse cart to make its way past. He noticed that she didn't retreat from him. But he did see a gentle blush spread across her perfect ivory complexion. As her eyes wandered away from his to the groups of people moving by, the young warrior's eyes continued to roam the young woman's body. She had her hair hidden under a severe-looking headpiece, but from a loose tendril that lay against her forehead he could tell she was dark-haired. The dress, discolored in spots, was rolled up to her elbow and untied at the neck. The tease of what lay beyond the next tie was tempting. She had the stance and the boldness of a noblewoman but the appearance of a maid. Ambrose let his eyes fall on her lips again. They were full, sensuous, inviting.

"You fought an exciting match." She caught his eyes on her.

"I had an exciting audience."

"I thought them dead," Elizabeth teased. "You surely deserved a better reception than what they gave."

Ambrose looked at her with a half grin. He'd thought the French reception quite enthusiastic, at least among the feminine members of the crowd. "Is it safe for me to assume that you were impressed?"

"By them? I prefer the living. The dead don't impress me much."

"I don't mean them." Ambrose frowned in jest. "I was trying to bring the discussion back to me."

This time Elizabeth looked at him appraisingly. "You think well of yourself, don't you?"

Ambrose laughed in response. Oh, no. He wasn't going to make himself a target by answering that question. Studying her closely, he tried to remember if he'd encountered her before today. He was quite sure he hadn't. This one was different. Beautiful, but different from the others. It was something in the way she held her head, slightly cocked, her eyes clear, alert.

"I haven't seen you before. Did you just arrive today?"

Elizabeth didn't seem to hear him. He was handsome, incredibly so. But not proud and aloof. "You could have broken your neck at the joust, standing in your stirrups as you did."

"French or English?" he asked. She had watched from the French section during the joust, but the tent she had walked out of moments ago stood in the English quarter of the camp.

"Did you get that scar pulling a stunt similar to the one you pulled today?" Elizabeth studied the deep mark on the knight's brow. Though his loose blond hair covered some of it, it was clearly a badge of honor. She had to add this touch to her painting later.

"You are not married, are you?" he asked. She didn't seem too willing to answer his questions—not yet, anyway.

Elizabeth turned her eyes back to the activities in the alley. "There is so much more to see here than at the tournament field."

"Any jealous lovers?"

"Real people, in their element." She hid a smile. "They are so interesting to watch."

"Would you come to my tent? Perhaps tonight?" Ambrose reached out and took her hand in his. His thumb gently stroked the soft skin as he lifted her fingers to his lips. She wasn't wearing the ring he had given her earlier. "I will make it interesting."

Elizabeth shivered involuntarily at the feel of his lips against her skin. Their gazes locked. He was so beautiful and so openly sensual. And here she was standing in the midst of all these people, flirting with him. This was so unlike her. Besides, her father was waiting.

"I have to go." She pulled back in haste and, without so much as a backward glance, ran down the alley in the direction of her father's tent.

Chapter 2

...the root, roasted and mixed with hog's lard, makes a gallant poultice to ripen plague sores. The ointment is good for swellings in the privities. Indeed, the best of the Galenists hold that once those afflicted with the pox expel the evil humors by lying with the virgin, the decocted root will cure the pustules with nary a scar...

> *--Camararius, <u>Hortus Medicus,</u>*
> *"On the treatment of the Pox"*

The bloodied squire landed in a heap at her feet.

Elizabeth started, suddenly aware of the commotion she had walked into. She'd been intent on making herself presentable to her father. Now the dress ties and the condition of her hair were forgotten.

Pressed along the sides of the alley between the tents, spectators were taking in the activity wide-eyed, but with no intention of becoming involved. Elizabeth could see blood pouring from a gash above the lad's ear. She stared at the young man, who was groggily dragging himself erect, and instinctively put a hand out to help him up.

A voice filled with malice thundered from the center of the alleyway. "*Don't touch the lazy bastard!*"

Elizabeth's eyes flashed at the knight lurching ominously toward her. "He needs care," she shot back. "He—"

"*You!*" The knight stopped before her. His eyes had the glazed look of one either drunk or mad. Yanking the squire away from her, Sir Peter Garnesche's glare became a sneer. Casting the lad to the side, he spat his next words over his shoulder, never taking his eyes from Elizabeth's face. "Go lick your wounds, boy. The Scot's lady wills it."

Elizabeth looked with loathing on the huge warrior. Like everyone else, she knew him to be among the English king's friends, but she also knew him as the man who, four months ago, had escorted her sister Mary to England—and to a lifetime of suffering. She turned away; she had no desire to converse with him.

"Wait, m'lady," the knight sneered, calling loudly as she walked off. "Perhaps you or your sister can give my squire the name of a good physician."

Elizabeth felt the prickly heat wash over her as she hurried from the ugly scene. The onlookers' laughs pounded in her head. Something brutal hung in the air around the man like a venomous cloud. She had to take Mary away from these vile people. She had to convince her father of that.

Though she was half-English by birth, Elizabeth Boleyn had good reason to feel no shred of loyalty to England or to its people. France was the country of her birth, and for Elizabeth, it was home.

Not that her childhood had been awash with sunlight. After her mother's death, and before Mary and Anne had joined her, Elizabeth had spent long, regimented years under the loveless supervision of her English nanny, Madame Exton. With the exception of the moments when she'd been able to escape to her painters, Elizabeth would prefer to blot this period from her memory. From early on, this manipulative woman had given her young charge a bad taste of English ways, particularly regarding the use of intimidation in child rearing. Even though Madame Exton had continued to run Sir Thomas's household in France through the years, life under the woman's iron rule became much easier to endure once the three girls had faced it together.

Sir Thomas Boleyn's tent was clearly marked with the banner depicting the family coat of arms, and Elizabeth paused before approaching the attendant standing outside. Running her hands quickly down her skirts to straighten her appearance, she thought through what she wanted to say to her father and wondered once again why he'd sent for her. She knew him to be a hard man whose ambitions had taken him high in the government of the English king, but he was also her father. And he had always provided for her.

Taking a deep breath, Elizabeth entered her father's tent.

"You don't know her, Thomas," Sarah Exton countered, never looking up from her needlework. "She won't do what you want simply because you command her. You must work her to your will."

Sir Thomas Boleyn stopped to glare at his cousin and then continued his pacing, pulling irritably at his gray speckled beard as he crossed the room. "This is no girl's game, Sadie. We are talking about the fortunes of this family. About—"

The shadows at the tent's opening stopped him, and he looked quickly at the attendant and the young woman who entered his spacious quarters.

Elizabeth's direct gaze captured the older woman's. The once-over look that her father's cousin gave her was clearly disapproving.

"Good afternoon, Sir...Madame." Elizabeth curtsied and stood quietly.

"Come here, girl, and sit." Her father waved at the chair by the woman and gestured for his squire to let them be. The elder man made no show of affection for the daughter whom he'd not seen in more than two years.

Obediently, Elizabeth seated herself by her overseer, who now bent over her work, seemingly ignoring all around her.

Sir Thomas paced the room, looking carefully at his daughter's intelligent, flashing eyes, at the strong set of her mouth and chin. Just like her mother's. But as Catherine had been gentle and forgiving when it'd come to him, Elizabeth was fierce and avenging. From the time he'd taken in the young girl when her mother died, Sir Thomas had never cared to be alone with her. Even as a child, she'd been able to turn his charity to guilt. Even now, her very presence was enough to prick sharply at his conscience, at the festering wounds that he tried to bury deep. Though Thomas Boleyn had been the one to walk away from Catherine, the pain of losing Elizabeth's mother still ached within him. It was a hurt barely contained beneath the layers of tough skin. An anguish ever-present, no matter how hard he tried to conceal it.

Elizabeth was tall, her complexion clear and healthy. She was not a voluptuous beauty, Sir Thomas thought. Not like Betsy Blount, Henry's first mistress, nor like Mary or any of the others.

"I don't know what he..." The courtier paused, his irritation turning to outright anger. "Oh! the hell with it! Who can understand such things?"

Elizabeth noted the furtive shake of the head that Madame Exton directed toward him. She sat quietly as her father turned and stalked to the table littered with official-looking documents. Sir Thomas lifted a tankard of ale and drained it, banging it on the table before turning back to her.

"Elizabeth, I have always been good to you, haven't I?"

"*Oui*, Sir Thomas—"

"Speak no French with me, girl!" he exploded.

"Y—yes, Father," she stumbled, surprised at the ferocity of his manner. She stared at him as he visibly contained himself, and when he spoke again, his voice was calm, controlled.

"Elizabeth, it's time you took your place in the world." The diplomat paused, turning his black eyes on her. "The point is, you have caught the eye of one who will raise you to the uttermost heights of society, and you will take...you would do well to take that place."

The young woman cursed the Duc de Bourbon under her breath. She should have known better than to be sociable with the nobleman this morning. The man had certainly stooped low. Now he was trying to force her compliance through her father. No chance, she thought.

"Father, I have to explain." Elizabeth paused, trying to gather together the words that were eluding her. "I have no wish to—"

Her father's glare silenced her. He was standing directly before her, his fists planted on his hips. "Girl, this has nothing to do with your wishes. This has to do with duty."

"Duty?" she exclaimed.

"Aye. Duty."

She blurted out the words before she could stop them. "What duty do I owe to a lust-infected nobleman?"

The power of the man's slap knocked the young woman from her chair, sending her sprawling into the middle of the room. There was a sharp pain in her head, and then numbness, ringing, and the taste of her own blood. She crouched before her father, her shaking hand pressed to her face.

"You will never, hear me, *never* again speak of your king in such terms."

"My *king*?" Elizabeth's eyes widened in disbelief. She glanced involuntarily at Madame Exton in her attempt to understand. The older woman's head never lifted. Her father's words brought her attention back to him.

"The king desires to take you into his bed, Elizabeth."

"*No!*" the young woman gasped, her hands clutching desperately at Madame's skirts. The tears rushed down her face uncontrollably. "No...he has...no...he has only seen me but once. This morning at the joust. It was only from a distance. This can't be. He has given his illness to Mary, Father."

"I know that!" Sir Thomas shouted. There was nothing he hated more than hysterical women. "She wasn't pure enough. He liked her well enough, but she wasn't pure enough to cure his pox."

Madame Exton laid her hand on Elizabeth's arm. "The king's doctors have told him that he must lay with only the purest virgins to rid himself of the disease." She looked at the young woman reassuringly. "It will bring great honor to you and to our family."

Elizabeth stared at the woman in horror. She was speaking so softly. No emotions. No excitement. Elizabeth could hear the words clearly. "It is a small sacrifice, Elizabeth. And as Sir Thomas says, it is your duty."

"I cannot. *I am not!*" she exclaimed, casting about in desperation for some answer, some reason that might halt this madness. "I am not pure. I've been raised in the French court. I've been with many m—"

The older woman's hand closed on Elizabeth's mouth roughly, smothering the words that were tumbling out. "Don't lie, Elizabeth. You are forgetting your company. If Mary were sitting here and speaking these words, I would have believed every one of them. But this is you. The pure and innocent Elizabeth. The one who has always hidden away from the glamour and from the temptation. The one who skipped even her own presentation at court." Madame Exton took Elizabeth's chin in her scrawny hands and jerked it upward. Her voice was as sharp as a dagger's edge. "I've watched you for many years, my girl. Don't waste your breath with lies. Just do as you are told. You owe that to your family."

"You have no option, girl," Sir Thomas added. "And just think of it, if you bear him a boy child, it'll be so much the better for all of us, and for you."

Elizabeth slowly raised herself unsteadily to her feet. Her legs were shaking, and she wondered vaguely whether her knees would support her own weight. But then the look of disbelief on her face changed to something else as the terrible reality of her situation set in.

"But I—" There was anguish in her voice.

"There's nothing more to discuss, Elizabeth. Now go and prepare yourself. When the king's entourage leaves for Calais in the morning, you will leave with us." Dismissing her, he turned back toward the table.

The world had gone gray around her, its heavy mists swirling damply within. Her only sensation was the cloudy weight that was settling inexorably on her mind, her body, on her very soul. "But...what of Mary?" she asked in a daze.

Her father half turned to answer, his voice rough, his words clipped. "She'll go back to Kent. To the convent near Hever Castle. Don't you concern yourself about her. Go. *Go now!*"

Chapter 3

"You have the power to make your own future."

As Elizabeth hurried along the torchlit alleyways through the camp, Mary's words kept reverberating in her head. From a small knoll, she glanced across the tented field at the great dinner hall that had been erected out of canvas painted to look like stonework. Its glamour was only a veneer. At the approach of a roving party of men, weaving and lurching their way along, Elizabeth pulled the dark cloak low over her face.

"Hey, you pretty thing! Hey...there goes a woman!"

Elizabeth panicked at the sound of the drunk courtier and lengthened her strides. She wouldn't let them know she was afraid. She wouldn't be their prey. But then she thought of what she was about to do.

"This is insanity," Elizabeth murmured to herself. She could hear the anguish in her own whisper. "I've gone mad! The whole world's gone mad!"

The young woman put a hand to her face. The swelling had hardly subsided. She could still feel the ache that had made her eyes tear for so long after she'd returned to her tent. But it wasn't the physical pain that had torn at her heart; it was a pain that ran far deeper. She'd been sold out by her own father. Traded for...what? For another man's vile use.

When Elizabeth had returned, Mary had been there, waiting for her. Offering comfort, guidance. Coming here, at this hour of the night, had been Mary's idea. Her younger sister had given her the weapon that Elizabeth had desperately needed. Mary had shown her a way to fight their father.

The Scottish warrior's shield hung beside the tent's entryway.

Elizabeth stepped inside.

Sinking deeper into the warm water, Ambrose closed his eyes to the red glow of the coal brazier that had been used to heat the bathwater.

She had not come. He had expected her to. But then, he was no longer one to keep a vigil over any woman. Even one as fascinating as this one was turning out to be, he thought, glancing over at the table—at the emerald ring that he'd given her earlier.

Lying there, soaking his bruised and tired muscles, he let his thoughts drift back over the events of the day, of their political importance. He thought again about the letter of false promises that had been signed by the two kings just a short while ago.

It was common knowledge in diplomatic circles that Henry had come to this meeting with the intention of breaking down the Auld Alliance between France and Scotland. The English king's chancellor, the crafty Cardinal Wolsey, had left no path untried in his maneuvering to gain some hold on the French king, in his search for some wedge to drive between Francis and the troublesome Scots.

But Ambrose had been successful in disrupting all hope of any real trust between the two monarchs. For, in a private meeting just before the signing, the Scottish nobleman had managed to convey to King Francis proof that his enemy the Holy Roman Emperor Charles was waiting to meet secretly with Henry in Calais. On hearing this, Francis had been ready to confront the treacherous English king on the fields. But with the Lord Constable and Ambrose's intervention, they had been able to restrain the French monarch from immediately embroiling himself in a war with England. In fact, Ambrose had been able to persuade him to go on with the show of signing the treaty with the double-dealing Henry, while pursuing a different course—a waiting game—and meanwhile trying to gain some inside information regarding the details of Charles's and Henry's upcoming meeting.

Ambrose had done what needed to be done. Based on the information he'd had, secret envoys of the Roman Emperor had met with the English king earlier today. Now it was up to the Lord Constable's contacts to reveal the details. There was one thing that was certain, though: The Auld Alliance between Scotland and

France had survived the Field of Cloth of Gold. The Highlander had done his job.

Ambrose opened his eyes and reached contentedly for the tankard of ale that sat on the small stool beside the tub.

She was standing just inside the tent.

"I'm offended once again!"

Elizabeth hid a smile as she gave him a quick glance. Consciously turning her full attention back to the emerald ring that sat on the small table, she continued to stifle her urge to study his naked body. "You are far too sensitive for a man your size."

Ambrose's eyes traveled the length of her as she untied the dark cloak and let it fall to the ground at her feet. "I would have hoped that my present vulnerable condition might have attracted a bit more attention than that ring."

"I don't think there are too many things in this world that would attract more attention than this thing." She picked up the ring. The emerald caught the dim light of the brazier and lit up.

"If you were that fond of it, why did you give it up?" Ambrose watched her long, slender fingers, the tilt of her beautiful chin. Her midnight-black hair was gathered on top of her head. Stray tendrils curled against her perfect profile.

Elizabeth could feel the heat of his gaze on her skin. She wouldn't turn. She couldn't.

"How did you get it back?" she asked, though she already knew the answer.

Ambrose gazed at the lass. She was no maid-in-waiting. He had found that out earlier. And she wasn't used to answering questions. She asked her own. "Three of the Lord Constable's men dragged a poor village priest in here. He was caught trying to sell it to get his mistresses separate rooms." Ambrose grinned into his tankard as he quaffed the ale. Her sidelong glance was quick, but he saw it. "They thought he'd stolen the ring from me."

"I hope you made sure they dragged the wretch all the way to Guisnes Castle."

"I certainly did." Ambrose paused and then stood in the tub.

Elizabeth turned her back to pick up her cloak. Busying herself with folding the garment, she tried to ignore the image of him stepping out of the water.

"But not before I made him confess the truth." Ambrose tied the towel loosely around his waist as he moved behind her. She smelled of lavender and the fresh summer air.

"You wanted to know the whereabouts of his mistresses?" She could feel his breath on the back of her neck. He was standing far too close. She leaned over and placed the ring on the table. Elizabeth found herself suddenly fighting the urge to recoil, to run away. After all, wasn't this why she had come here? To lose her virginity?

"Hardly." Ambrose let his lips brush against her skin. It was as soft as it looked. He felt her body go tense. "Why did you give the ring to the priest?" he asked softly.

"Why did you offer him so much gold to take it back?"

"So you've seen him since." Ambrose let his finger run seductively down her back. He smiled as he saw the obvious shudder that ran through her.

Elizabeth clutched her cloak tight in her hand. She knew she had to relax. She had to let this just happen. She had to admit it had helped to get some glimmering of the kind of man this Ambrose Macpherson was...from Friar Matthew. This afternoon, when the priest had returned to her tent with word of Sir Ambrose's generosity, Elizabeth had listened closely to his story. She had known Friar Matthew for a long time, and she'd given him the English king's ring, knowing that many would benefit from it. The ring certainly had no monetary or sentimental value to her. Elizabeth had earned what money she'd needed for Mary's physician by selling the painting earlier. And if only for her sister's sake, she knew it would be far better if Mary's eyes never chanced to fall upon it.

And then the priest had come back, telling her—to Elizabeth's astonishment—that the Scottish nobleman had bought the ring from him. The young woman had never expected the priest to approach him. What must he have thought, learning that the ring he'd given as a token had been handed over to someone else the same day? But then, it had been too late to worry about such things.

Sitting there in her tent, beaten and fairly certain of what course she would take, Elizabeth had been surprised to hear that the Scottish knight had asked about her. And then the priest had told her of the man's generosity and compassion.

After hearing all that, Elizabeth had agreed with Mary, that this was the right course, that this man was the one to come to. After all, she would never see him again. Never.

Ambrose reached up and pulled the pin that held her hair in place. The sliding mass of black curls tumbled caressingly over his hand. He breathed in the heavenly scent, wondered at the silken softness. He ran his hands down her shoulders, thinking back over what he'd managed to pry out of the priest. There was so much that fascinated him about this woman.

"Considering his tongue-flapping profession, your priest friend is not much on talking when he doesn't want to."

"That's very curious, coming from a diplomat." She watched as his hands confidently encircled her waist. She tried to hide her own trembling hands and hesitantly dropped her cloak on the bench.

"Hmm, so you know about me," he crooned, his lips a breath away from her ear. His arms pulled her tightly to him.

"Of course. You are the most charming courtier ever to wield a lance." Her soft voice carried just a touch of irony. "Your name is on the lips of every lady in France. They tell me that wherever you pass by, your squires have to sweep up the swooning maidens that are left in your wake."

"Oh, is that so? And are you feeling a wee bit light-headed, as well?"

"Of course. Well, I'm feeling something." She looked down as his hands roamed the front of her dress. Gently moving up to cup her breasts. "But thinking of it now, it may just be a touch of gas."

"We must be eating from the same pot." Ambrose chuckled as he turned her in his arms. He tensed. Even in the dim glow of the brazier, he could see the swollen cheek that she'd been keeping away from him. Immediately his brow darkened.

"Who did this to you?" his hand reached up to feel the lump, but she turned her face away, not wanting his sympathy.

"I had to fight my way through legions of women to get to you." Elizabeth winced as his hands framed her face and turned it to him. She reached up and tried to remove them but to no avail.

"You must tell me who beat you this way." His voice was sharp.

"So much like a knight," she said with a sigh, trying to lighten the mood. "But I think she is even too tough for you. Rotund. Middle-aged. With a very strong right arm. But she may still be outside."

Ambrose looked at her askance. "That is no answer, lass."

"In fact, I think I might have suffered a blow to the head. My memory is a bit vague right now." Elizabeth tried to avert her eyes so she wouldn't have to look into his intense and beautiful blue eyes. Talking came easy to her. But looking at his handsome face made something inside her go soft. This close to him, she could smell his good, clean, masculine scent. She was very conscious of the chest that her arms rested against.

"Let me help. I know who you are." Ambrose knew a lot more about her than the priest had divulged. And he wasn't fooled by her quick tongue. Someone had hurt her, and he planned to find out who. The Highlander lifted her chin, forcing her to meet his gaze. "You're Elizabeth Boleyn. Eldest daughter of Sir Thomas Boleyn, King Henry's ambassador to France. Born of Catherine Valmont. You've spent most of your life in the French court. Not surprisingly, your beauty and brains are well spoken of. And, as the Duc de Bourbon knows, you are not one to share your bed openly with just anyone."

"He told you all of this?" she whispered. "I'm flattered, m'lord. You must have gone to a great deal of trouble to learn all these things. The truth is, I'm not what one might call 'well known' at this level of society."

"Did someone hurt you because of my gift to you? Because of my attention to you at the joust?"

Elizabeth thought back to the encounter she'd had with her father earlier. It was curious that Sir Thomas had not mentioned even a word about the attention she'd received from the Highlander at the joust. He'd been there and witnessed it, as everyone else had. She still shook her head in response. "It looks a lot worse than it feels. I'm fine, m'lord."

"Whoever you are trying to protect does not deserve you, lass," Ambrose took a half step back and looked at her from head to toe. She was a striking young woman, radiating beauty, charm, and something more. Confidence. Even in her disheveled condition. "If you would allow me, I'd take great pleasure in teaching the man who did this a few lessons on how a woman should be treated."

"Please stop!" She took his hand in her own. "I didn't come here to discuss this...this minor mishap."

"Then why did you come?" Ambrose asked as he lifted her fingers to his lips. He paused as he gently kissed them. "Did you come to punish him?"

He turned her hand in his and stroked the soft palm before bringing it once again to his lips. The streaks of colors on her fingers caught his attention.

"Perhaps!" she whispered, coiling her hand and placing it in the folds of her skirt.

"Well, how far must your vengeance take you?" He stepped toward her, pulling her again into his embrace.

"My ven—" the words died on her lips as he leaned toward her. She felt his mouth possess hers. All at once hard and soft, demanding and giving, seductive and playful.

"How much does he need to suffer?" He whispered the question, tilting her head and deepening the kiss. Her mouth was soft, pliable, warm. Her sweet taste was intoxicating. Suddenly, he couldn't get enough of her. With a silent roar, desire swept through him, desire for skin against skin, body against body. Ambrose knew it should matter that she wasn't there solely because she wanted him. But somehow, he simply didn't care. He knew that when the night was done, when their passion was—for the moment—sated, she would feel differently. Next time, she would come wanting him.

Elizabeth found herself short of breath. She could feel the hammer of her heart in her chest. She had not expected this. So quick. The kiss, this man's mouth, was undoing her, melting her. She felt herself going limp in his embrace, her mouth yielding to his mouth, her body molding to his body. She raised herself on her toes as her hands instinctively encircled his neck. She felt rather than heard his groan of pleasure as her body pressed involuntarily against his.

"Tell me, how much does he need to suffer?" Ambrose's hands worked their way through the laces of her dress front as his lips bit and teased her neck, her jaw, her lips.

"Endlessly!" she whispered.

Chapter 4

Elizabeth had expected it to be quick, painful, and done with.

How could this happen? Her senses, now inflamed by the attentions of Ambrose Macpherson, cried out for release. And as far as she could tell in the amber haze that was swirling in her brain, she was still a virgin.

Elizabeth opened her eyes as Ambrose worked her fingers gently from their death grip on the sheets. She looked up into his passion-filled eyes as he kissed her palm.

"Hold me, Elizabeth. Don't be afraid. Touch me."

She watched in dismay as Ambrose lowered her hand and let it trace downward over the hard muscles of his abdomen. Her fingers played a dance of wonder over his skin. He shifted his weight off of her, to give her better access. She froze. He was naked, Elizabeth realized with a jolt. And so was she, nearly.

She had been so consumed with the magic of this man's beguiling touch, of his hands, his mouth, his searing kisses, that she had hardly paid any attention to her own circumstances. They were gone...forgotten. Elizabeth had only the vaguest awareness of his strong arms removing her dress, lifting her off her feet, and carrying her to bed. After that, she'd been lost to everything.

Now, looking down at her open chemise, her exposed breasts, she yanked her hand out of his grasp, trying to cover her flesh. But he was too quick for her.

"Not so fast." He lifted her hands above her head, trapping them there with one hand. "You have the most beautiful body of any woman I've ever laid eyes on. I want to savor every moment. We can't rush this." Ambrose's eyes lowered to the full breasts. To the raised aurora that invitingly beckoned his lips. He bent down and kissed the soft curves of the valley between her heaving breasts. Then moving on, he tenderly suckled her rose-colored nipples.

Elizabeth groaned uncontrollably in response. She wanted him. He was making her insane. But somewhere inside her head she knew she had to stop. She had to stop the rhythmic dance that was taking over her body, had to stop the liquid heat that was rushing through her. She couldn't go through with this.

Ambrose tried to control the pounding roar of his heart. He was losing control fast. She was incredible. Her beauty, her sweet taste were driving him wild. He wanted to take her now. But more, he wanted to extend this sweet torture. For his own selfish reasons, he wanted Elizabeth to remember him, to remember this night as the best lovemaking she'd ever had. Ambrose felt her hands work their way out of his grip and work themselves into his hair. She pulled at him. He rolled and brought her on top of him, stripping her of the open chemise as they rolled.

Elizabeth gasped as she found herself looking down at the handsome warrior. Her breasts, still tingling from his kisses, rested heavily on his chest. She was afraid. Afraid of her own body's responses. Something inside of her was taking over. Something she couldn't control. His hands were working across the skin of her buttocks, working their way toward the juncture of her legs. Against her judgment, against her very will, she thrilled to this act of love-making. She was ashamed of herself. But she could not deny it.

Ambrose couldn't hold back. Elizabeth's cascading waves of black silk framed her angelic face. Her cloudy eyes searched his face with curiosity, uncertainty. Her full lips, swollen from his kisses, drew his eyes. He wanted those lips on his body. He wanted to teach her things that her French lover obviously had not. The foolish man. He lifted her by the waist.

Elizabeth sat up slowly and watched as Ambrose's hands brushed her hair gently away from her breasts. Then he shifted her weight. Elizabeth looked down as she felt the throbbing member against her. Throbbing to enter her.

No, she thought in a panic. No! She had to get away. She couldn't go through with this.

Everything a blur around her, she leaned backward suddenly and, with a thud, fell heavily into the rushes on the floor.

Ambrose peered over the end of the bed at Elizabeth, shocked to see the naked beauty scuttling backward away from him.

His voice had a touch of humor when he spoke. "I've made more than a few women wild in my time, but I don't think I've ever driven one stark-raving mad."

"I'm not mad," she whispered, modestly turning to hide her exposed body.

"Here, lass," Ambrose called sharply, sitting up. "Watch out for the brazier!"

Elizabeth scrambled to her feet just before upsetting the coals.

"What's wrong?" Ambrose stood, taking a step toward her.

"Don't!" Elizabeth shouted, raising her hand pleadingly. "Please don't." She looked frantically about for her clothes, grabbing at the first things she could find. "I'm sorry, m'lord...I—"

"I'm not going to hurt you," Ambrose said, his tone soothing. She was scared. He couldn't believe it, but in an instant she'd gone from the heights of passion to the depths of cold desperation. He needed to calm her fears. "I don't know what that man has done to you. But, that's him. Not me."

Elizabeth fumbled with the oversized shirt as she tried to pull it over her head. "What man?" Her head just *wouldn't* go into the sleeve.

"You are young, beautiful. In fact, stunning. Any man would be a fool not to want you as his own. To treat you better."

"I am not just a rose sitting about, waiting to be picked, m'lord. I'll decide for myself what I want. I'll make my own choices." Damn, she thought, hearing the shirt rip.

"Then why do you stay with one who abuses you? Hasn't someone ever told you that you deserve better than that?"

Elizabeth's head finally appeared through the collar opening. Her hair was in total disarray. "If my well-being is truly a concern to you, then I have to inform you that I am quite self-sufficient."

Ambrose's eyes traveled the length of her as she tried to close the open collar. She looked wonderful in his shirt. "You might think yourself as in charge, lass. But clearly you are not. Just look at you. You are a woman. A beautiful woman who—"

"There is nothing wrong with that." Elizabeth snapped.

"Let me finish," he growled, silencing her with a glare. "You are a *stubborn*, beautiful woman who obviously has not been told the difference between what she should tolerate and what she should not. You will never be in charge, Elizabeth, until you are able to recognize and act on that difference."

Elizabeth's head pounded with the thought of all that still lay ahead. "Simply, m'lord. Could you please tell me in simple terms...W*hat the devil you are talking about?*"

"I'm talking about you and your lover, my thick-headed English—"

"Don't you dare call me that, you...you... *What* lover are you talking about?" My God, she was losing her mind. Elizabeth's brain whirled as she tried to make some sense out of all that was happening. Then her eyes widened as her gaze fell on the Highlander's imposing arousal. "I...Never mind. I have to go."

"The Duc de Bourbon. I should have known." Ambrose reached down grabbed his tartan, and tossed it to her. "The man nearly went wild when I asked him about you this afternoon. The filthy knave. I can't believe I was so blind. It was he."

Elizabeth paused, gaping at the warrior. Bourbon?"

"Aye. The coward Bourbon. I should have flattened his face before he did this to you." Ambrose ground his fist into his palm. "When did he do it? Was it after I questioned him? Did he come to you after I left?"

Elizabeth gaped at the nobleman. "I don't know what it is you are talking about, but I don't need anyone to defend me. I can tell you right now that I will kill, with no hesitation whatsoever, any man who raises a hand to me again."

"Aye, lass. That's the spirit. And it's about time."

Elizabeth stood for a moment longer, now totally confused. She had no clue whether their discussion had reached its conclusion. In fact, she wasn't even sure if she'd heard half of what was said. She shook her head. She *had* lost her mind. "Good night, m'lord." Elizabeth turned as she pulled her hair back and tied it with a thong.

"Where are you going?" Ambrose asked. Though there was something comical in seeing her wearing his baggy shirt and ankle-length kilt, his belt wrapped twice around her, there was also something quite arousing in the picture.

"I'm going in search of my sanity and perhaps even justice," Elizabeth murmured as she swept toward the tent's opening. "And my future. That's my only chance."

Ambrose stood by his bed and watched her leave. This had been, by far, the strangest encounter he'd ever had with any woman in his life.

Looking down at his still erect member, Ambrose thought about his would-be lover, even now wandering through the Field of Cloth of Gold, appareled in some very fine, albeit large, men's clothing.

Elizabeth Boleyn was, indeed, a strange creature.

Chapter 5

The drunkards roaming the Golden Vale that night never imagined that the Scottish lad walking among them was a woman.

From the cloth great hall far off across the field, the sounds of merrymaking and music broke in gentle waves over Elizabeth's consciousness. Vaguely, she glanced across the knolls to the glow of the bonfire that lit the huge tent from within. With unseeing eyes, she continued on past huddling couples and men lurching about in various degrees of inebriation.

But as she strode through the torchlit alley, Elizabeth's attention was focused inward. Suddenly it was the noise of her own shoes padding along the dirt way that pierced her thoughts.

Twenty paces from her father's tent, Elizabeth stopped short. A cold wave washed over her as she considered what lay ahead. For the past quarter hour, she'd been arguing repeatedly with her father and had been able to convince him to rescind his earlier demands. Tomorrow, Elizabeth would return to France with Mary, where she could care for her sister and they would all forget what took place. Looking at the dimly lit tent, Elizabeth felt suddenly limp and tired. The problem was that their productive exchange had taken place only in her head.

The two reeling knights who now knocked Elizabeth to the ground didn't even cast a glance at the toppled woman.

"Watch where you go, lad," one of the men growled roughly as they continued on their way.

Elizabeth peered up at their retreating backs in amazement. Rising, she shook the dust off the Macpherson tartan.

She stared down at the garment in her hands. At the plaid kilt. At the shapeless shirt draped over her torso. Lad! They thought her a man. She gazed back at the now-deserted alley and then back at her apparel. She'd walked through groups of them and not a soul had said a thing to her. These were the same hungry men who—in their present condition, at least—equated women to meat.

Shaking off the thought that was edging into her brain, Elizabeth turned her attention back to the confrontation that lay ahead. Dread flooded through her at what she thought might be her father's reaction. But what other choice had she left? Elizabeth stared at the attendant nodding beside the open entrance of the tent. The English soldier lifted his head and looked at her blankly. Not finding her stance a threat, the man nodded back to sleep.

Elizabeth took a deep breath and started for the opening. The die was cast; she must carry this through. Noiselessly, she slipped past the guard into the tent.

Sir Thomas sat at his table, a lamp flickering at his elbow. A few papers were spread before him, but nearly everything else had been packed up and stacked near the door for his departure the next day. Standing in the deep shadows, Elizabeth studied her father for a moment. Whatever her mother had seen in him, those many years ago, nothing remained that Elizabeth could discern. Though he now lacked any semblance of gentleness or feeling, she knew he once must have been different.

Sir Thomas was the younger son of a wealthy country squire. Hardly noble and in no position to inherit, he learned early that a man needed to use every resource at his disposal to get ahead in life.

Apparently a man of great knowledge and charm at his younger years, Sir Thomas had used his father's connections to enter King Henry VIII's service. Knowledgeable in several languages, Sir Thomas had taken his first diplomatic mission in France, where he'd met and perhaps loved the young and beautiful Catherine Valmont.

The noble lady's lineage was long and impressive, and her parents' horror at the thought of a penniless young Englishman in the family had forced their ultimatum: If she chose to marry him, she would forfeit all claim to her rank and wealth. Catherine had accepted the condition without a moment's hesitation. After all, she loved him, and that was all that mattered.

Then, to almost no one's surprise, Sir Thomas had walked away from Catherine, but not before he had planted his seed.

Catherine Valmont, cast out by her own family, was left alone, bereft and with child. Nine months later Elizabeth had been born.

For Sir Thomas, love was a condition that could not be allowed in the way of his own upward mobility. Marriage was a contract that allowed the committed parties the ability to improve their social position. Without her family, Catherine had nothing to offer him. So Thomas caught hold of a daughter in the noble English family of Howard. And by that union he attained the Earldom of Ormonde, a title far above anything he'd ever dreamed possible.

Marriage had been a joyless state, but it had produced the results Thomas had sought: wealth, position, and power.

Despite the glamour, Elizabeth knew that her father had paid the price. He had never been loved by his young bride as he'd been loved by Catherine. And after his wife's death in childbirth, the Howard family had made certain he knew he was an outsider. He didn't belong.

From what Elizabeth could gather, it was then that her father had set his course with the king. This grim man standing before her had shut out everything in life besides his mission as a diplomat and a servant to his king. It was all he had left. They were words that defined him, for he never seemed to exist beyond that. Diplomat and servant. Outside of the presence of King Henry, Sir Thomas Boleyn became a hollow, miserable, bad-tempered old man who seemed to take very little pleasure in life.

Her father's hands rested flat on the table, his attention focused on a moth fluttering about the base of the lamp. Elizabeth could read no expression on his pale face. His eyes were black and empty.

Without warning, the man's hand flashed in the lamplight, and his wide palm smashed down with a thunderous bang on the unsuspecting moth. Lifting the lifeless insect by one shattered wing, Sir Thomas inspected the creature carefully. Then, with an expression of clear disdain, he dropped the moth's carcass into the flame, watching with renewed interest as it flared and sizzled before crumbling to ash.

Elizabeth stepped closer to the circle of light.

Sir Thomas's eyes darted toward her, and Elizabeth saw him master a quick look of fear that flashed across his face as he peered into the darkness at the Scottish attire.

For ten years Thomas Boleyn had been working to drive a stake into the heart of the Scottish and French alliance. Learning his craft under the Tudor kings, Sir Thomas had found that the handshakes of diplomacy were rarely effective without the sharp edge of a dagger visible in the other hand. Indeed, his position had often called for duplicity and ruthlessness, and Sir Thomas had long ago proved himself a master of the craft. But as a result, Thomas Boleyn was a man with enemies.

Elizabeth watched his hand go directly to his waist and to the short sword she knew he would be wearing.

"Who is it, there? And what's your business with me?" His tone was sharp and commanding, his face now hardened and bloodless.

"It is I, Father." Elizabeth watched the confusion muddle his stern expression. "It is Elizabeth."

Sir Thomas sat back in his chair and glared across the table.

"Eliz— Why are you here, girl?" His eyes swept over her. "What are you doing wearing those foul weeds?"

Elizabeth glanced down at her clothes and hid her trembling hands behind her. Fear shot through her like bolts of lightning, but she needed to go through with this. Now, while she was alone with him, without Madame Exton present. Sir Thomas, despite his crafty ways, hardly knew Elizabeth well enough to question her word. But Madame would know.

"Speak, girl," the man roared. "Where have you been?"

"I've been to the Scot."

Sir Thomas sneered in disdain. "You've dined with the devil. Hasn't anyone told you how much I hate their entire race? They are worse than animals. They are mindless scum, cluttering our land."

"I've done more than dine with him."

The man's voice was cold and deadly. "What the devil have you done?"

"I'm no longer a virgin." She looked him straight in the eye. Her words were sharp, quick, and piercing. "No longer."

He gasped, staring. "Nay. Don't lie to me." Placing his hands on the table to support his weight, Sir Thomas stood. "Do you think me so simple?" Without taking his eyes from her, he shouted for his squire. "John!"

The young soldier stumbled at once into the tent. His sleepy eyes traveled from his master to the young Scot.

"Go to Madame Exton. Tell her to come here immediately." Seeing the boy hesitate and begin to draw a sword on Elizabeth rather than retreat, he shouted. "Damn it, boy. This is my daughter. And make no pretense of duty now. She passed your sleeping carcass to get in here. Now *go!*"

Elizabeth felt panic seep quickly through her body. Her scalp was prickling with fear. There was no time left. She had to convince him of this lie before her cousin's arrival. The older woman would be able to see the truth. Elizabeth knew Madame Exton all too well. She would stop at nothing. She would probably examine Elizabeth herself before believing her words.

She watched the squire disappear out the opening of the tent.

"Look at me," Elizabeth snapped, scorching her father's downturned face with her own unrelenting gaze. She waited until the older man's eyes focused on her, and then she continued. "I'm wearing the clothes of your enemy. I accepted his favor after the joust today. Hundreds witnessed it. *You* witnessed it. Ambrose Macpherson invited me to his tent. So tonight, I went to him. Your men saw me go. Every man in this Golden Vale saw me go. I went willingly and I slept with him." Elizabeth paused, making certain that every word left its mark. "I lost my virginity. And I'm glad of it. I enjoyed it. Do you want to see the proof now, or would you care to wait for your dear Sadie's arrival? We both know she is far more experienced in dealing with your daughters. But perhaps you should see the blood of lost innocence first."

Elizabeth reached inside the belt and began to draw out a kerchief.

"Hold!" Sir Thomas breathed heavily where he stood. His eyes were wild and bloodshot. His fists clenched tight. "How...how could you? No better than a common whore. How could you defy me this way?"

"Because my purity was not yours to sell. Damn it, <u>I'm</u> not for you to sell!" Elizabeth's eyes never left his face. As her voice had earlier conveyed a calm and resolute chill, it now bore her full fury. "I did what I had to do. To save myself. Now I am no good to you or your king."

"*My* king?" he stormed, sputtering as he careened around the table toward her. "You—? With a filthy Scot?"

"Aye," she said, standing her ground. "I was willing to sleep with your enemy rather than allow you to give me over to that syphilitic goat."

With a roar, Sir Thomas lunged at his daughter, grabbing her by a long, thick lock of hair as she turned to evade his attack. Wheeling about, he smashed her face against the sharp edge of the table, and as he yanked her back again, Elizabeth saw her own blood flying in droplets into the darkness beyond the circle of light.

Sir Thomas turned her around in his rage and glared wildly into her bloodied face. His one hand still held Elizabeth by her mane. "Do you know what happens to those who defy me?" he rasped.

"Kill me," she spat, her blood running in rivulets down her face and spreading on the pure white shirt. "No one is going to stop you. Kill me!" She fought back the tears that stung her eyes. "And I tell you now, I welcome this death. But then again, that shouldn't surprise you. After all, I'm my mother's daughter. But remember one thing. She preferred death to being away from you. But I...I *long* for the next world to get away from you."

Elizabeth's eyes teared in anger. Wiping her hand across her bloodied cheek, she smeared it on her father's doublet as he stared at her. "People said she took away her life with her own hands. The truth is that the stain of her blood, the guilt for her suicide, lies with you. And it has marked you for life. So go ahead. Kill me. Add another chain to the bonds that await you in hell. Go ahead, murderer. *Kill me!*"

Repulsed, Sir Thomas shoved Elizabeth away from him. His hands moved up to his temples as he tried to stop the pounding in his head. He still remembered that grim day so long ago when he'd walked away from his beloved Catherine. She'd stopped him by the door, a sword in her hand, and had begged for him to end her life. She loved him truly. Looking into her tearful eyes, he had known that for certain. But he had simply taken the sword from her trembling hand and walked out the door. Three years later, her servant had found her dead in the same room, her wrists slashed. And Thomas Boleyn knew—he had always known—that Catherine Valmont was the only woman who had ever loved him.

Elizabeth stood a step away. The pain and burning in her face didn't come close to the hurt and anger that she felt in her heart.

"Draw your sword. Kill me where I stand." Her body shook as she moved toward him, reaching for his sword. "Come, I'll die with a smile. I welcome death over the future you planned for me."

"*Get away from me!*" he screamed, pushing her away again.

Elizabeth stumbled, righting herself as she saw the tent flap push open.

Madame Exton and the soldier stared, astonished by the sight before them. Before they could react, Elizabeth ran past them, pushing her cousin into the stack of boxes by the door.

Out into the night air she bolted, running blindly as her eyes adjusted to the darkness.

"*Stop her!*" Elizabeth heard the hysteria in her cousin's shrieking voice. "*After her, you fool!*"

Pressing her hand hard against the gash along her cheekbone, Elizabeth raced down the alley. The shout of the squire and Madame Exton's raging screams rang out behind her, but she never paused as she ran. She could feel the blood running through her fingers, but she dared not stop to tend it. Flying along the torchlit way, Elizabeth glanced back, catching sight of the soldier chasing after her. Turning corner after corner, she raced frantically in the direction of the clusters of French tents.

She couldn't let them catch her. Despite all that she had tried to do, Elizabeth knew if she was caught, Madame Exton would make sure Sir Thomas's plans were carried out. Elizabeth knew, with a certainty that seethed in the pit of her stomach, she would be lying with King Henry before the next sunset. She knew her guardian would see to it.

Panic swept through her as Elizabeth realized that her father's squire was gaining on her. A grove of trees beyond the next line of shimmering tents marked the division between the rival countries' courts, but Elizabeth suddenly felt weak, fearing she wouldn't make it to the tents beyond. She could hear the soldier's rasping breaths and pounding footsteps closing in.

Rounding a sharp bend, Elizabeth ducked between two large pavilions. They were deserted, but both were too well lit with torches to provide a hiding place. Pausing, she listened to her heart pounding so loudly she thought it would surely give her away. At the sound of the pursuer's footsteps, she held her breath and listened as he passed by. Then, by the light of the rising moon, she worked her way along the back of two more tents until she found herself at the edge of the wooded grove. Stepping into the shadows of the overhanging trees, Elizabeth paused to catch her breath.

Assessing her situation, she peered down in the dimness at her bloody hands. Her entire body ached. Her lips were puffy and sore, a good match for the swollen cheek her father had given her that afternoon, but what really concerned her was the stinging, throbbing cut that continued to bleed profusely. She would have a scar, she was sure. He'd marked her. Her own father.

Elizabeth looked up at the moonlit sky. Her problems were just beginning. She needed to get away from this place. But how? Everything she possessed was in the tent that she shared with Mary. All her worldly possessions, she thought, her derisive chuckle turning quickly into a wince of pain. Which meant her paints. But Madame Exton would be waiting for her. Elizabeth was certain of that. The only chance she had was to get a message to Mary. If she could just get her sister to meet her in secret.

The sound of raised voices somewhere nearby startled Elizabeth, and she crouched low in the covering darkness. Whomever the voices belonged to, they were not far from where she'd taken refuge. Elizabeth's first thought was to back out of the grove, but then a familiar voice caught her attention. Creeping forward through the underbrush, she soon spotted the flickering beam of a covered lamp. Following the glimmer of light and the murmuring voices, Elizabeth found herself on the edge of a small glade, and in the middle stood two men, one much larger than the other. He was speaking, and she recognized him instantly. The lamp shone faintly on them from a nearby stump.

"How dare you question me now?" Peter Garnesche growled angrily. "After all this time. Years."

"Then tell me what was said," the other man's voice broke in. "You cannot suddenly begin keeping things from us. We know your king met with the envoys of Charles. I need the details."

"I don't know what was said."

"You can find out. Don't play games with me, Garnesche. We know your tentacles reach into every corner of that English court."

"My sources provided nothing. I could find no information." The man's voice lowered to a dangerous drawl. "You will just have to accept my word for it."

"Your word?" Elizabeth knew that sneering voice. He was a Frenchman. She wracked her brain. From court. Elizabeth remembered. The Lord Constable! The French king's counselor.

"You doubt me?" Garnesche scowled. "Do I have to remind you that it is in your best interest to continue relying on me? After all, who else could you find with such a wealth of useful information as I provide?"

Elizabeth watched as the Lord Constable studied the giant before him.

"I must admit what you say is true. We have been able to count on you in the past. And yes, we have watched you cut your own countrymen's throats. Naturally, that has occurred only when it suited you. When it improved your own stature with your king." The accusation was clear in the man's tone.

"I know what you're referring to." Garnesche glared menacingly at him. "The Duke of Buckingham was a pompous fool who spoke against me before the king in the Star Chamber. He was going to pay for that anyway. It just happened to be his misfortune that his claim to the throne was as good as Henry's."

"A circumstance that you were delighted to use to put his head on the chopping block." The Lord Constable's voice dripped with cynicism.

"And that bothers you, suddenly? You gained more out of that than I did." Garnesche paused, but hearing no response from the Frenchman, continued on. "It was Buckingham who was pushing the hardest for an alliance between England and the Emperor Charles. It didn't take much prodding to make Henry think the two were in league together to take the crown away from him."

Elizabeth's mind flashed back to the year before, when the shocking news of the English nobleman's execution had swept across Europe. It had been the talk of every court in Christendom when the English king had imprisoned the mighty Duke of Buckingham on the charge of plotting to take his crown by force. Henry, lacking a legitimate heir, was acutely sensitive to any hint of revolt against his right to wear the crown. She recalled hearing the details from the endless stream of diplomats passing through her father's house: the accusations, the questionable witnesses, the trial by his peers, the finding of guilt despite his proclamations of loyalty. She recalled most clearly the talk of Buckingham's grisly execution. And now she knew what was behind it all. Now she knew who had caused it to come about.

"How you must have smiled to see Buckingham's neck go under the executioner's ax."

"His conviction for treason set back the alliance between England and the Holy Roman Empire two years, Constable. It was what you and your king wanted, and it was what you got. Why, even now the Emperor Charles must tread lightly with Henry. And it is due to me."

"Yes. It was due to you." The Lord Constable's stony gaze was unwavering. "But we have watched how your friendship has recently blossomed once again with the English king, and it makes us lose confidence in your willingness to deal with us. In so many words, there are some among us who don't trust you."

"Don't generalize, you coward. What you mean is that *you* don't trust me!" Garnesche snapped. Elizabeth watched as he drew himself up to his full height. "You and I both know, *you* are the only one who knows of my dealings on your behalf."

"I don't have to trust you. I employ you and I pay you to do our bidding." The Lord Constable's voice was cold, his tone bordering on disdain.

Garnesche paused, silently considering the other's words.

Elizabeth stood as still as a statue, all her own problems now totally forgotten. From what she could gather, Sir Peter Garnesche's employment by the French government was no short-term affair. Though she certainly had no love for England or its king, this was treachery of the vilest kind.

"I've told you that the king is going directly to Calais to meet with the Emperor Charles. Of what happened earlier, I can't say. But if you wish to see your precious treaties with England honored, then you had better move quickly and keep that alliance from happening."

"What do you expect me to do, attack your king?" the Lord Constable snapped. "I know you are low, but I tell you, we will not dishonor ourselves by killing anyone under a flag of truce. Even if he is the King of England."

"This is all a farce." Garnesche took a step back. "Constable, I grow sick of you and your whining demands. I tell you what must be done, but do you ever do it? Nay, you lack the stomach for real action. Barbaric. Inhumane. Low. That's all I ever hear. Frenchman, you are a spineless coward."

"You are just a dog biting the hand that feeds him." The French nobleman stepped closer to the English knight and lifted his fist. "You are forcing me to put you in your place, and I, too, am growing tired of this game. Don't forget what happened to Buckingham. Treason. It cost him his head. The same could happen to you. But where the charge against him was false, yours will be well deserved."

"No one can bear witness to such an accusation. No one knows—"

"No one, but me, traitor. And that's enough."

"Henry won't believe you."

"Fool, you have forgotten my connections."

Garnesche's hand came up so quickly that the Constable was lifted off the ground as the knight's viselike grip closed over his windpipe. The abrupt gurgling sound that the Frenchman emitted was quickly lost in his thrashing struggle for release.

Grasping his foe's wrist with one hand, he struck at the Englishman's face with the other. A cut opened on the bridge of Sir Peter's nose, and the Lord Constable struck at it again and again.

But the knight was not to be undone, and Elizabeth watched in horror as Garnesche slid his dagger easily from its sheath and drove the point upward into the bowels of the struggling Frenchman.

Unable to cry out, the Lord Constable writhed in silent agony as the knight twisted the blade about, tearing the life from the nobleman.

Elizabeth took a step back as she watched the final twitching moments of the most powerful counselor in France. The bile climbed into her throat as she espied the cruel, maniacal grin that crept across Sir Peter Garnesche's dark and bloodied face. He was mad.

Stepping back again, Elizabeth looked about her in the darkness. She had to get help. As she began to push through the undergrowth, the dragging hem of the kilt caught on the splintered branch of a fallen tree. She could see the giant murderer through the foliage, glancing about him as he lowered the Lord Constable's corpse to the ground. Panic struck at her heart as he wiped the blood from his flashing blade on the velvet cloak of the dead man. What if he came her way? What if he found her here?

Yanking at the kilt, Elizabeth stumbled backward as the cloth gave way with a loud ripping tear. Garnesche's head whipped around as she sat motionless and silent amid the soft green ferns. But she didn't sit for long.

The knight took a step in her direction, and Elizabeth was off through the woods, scrambling on all fours through the undergrowth. Bramble bushes and young saplings slapped at her face as she struggled to her feet. Throwing wild glances over her shoulder, she ran frantically through the dark glade. Flashes of light from a dying moon mixed in swirling confusion with the dark of the passing trees. Chaos had taken over her world, and Elizabeth felt her energy slipping away. Valiantly, she fought hard to keep down the sobs she felt rising in her chest. They were robbing her of her power to run. But on she ran anyway.

She could hear nothing from behind her over the sound of her own pulse, pounding thunderously in her head. Then, as she turned to look for her pursuer, Elizabeth suddenly found herself tumbling in air, only to land with a sickening thud in the soft earth at the bottom of a diverted streambed.

She couldn't move. She couldn't breathe. She was lying face-down in the blackness of the hollow. Short, velvety leaves were brushing against her face, and her eyes were gradually focusing on the spears of dark grass that rose up and limited her field of vision. One ear was pressed to the ground, and she thought she could hear the dull thumps of receding footsteps. But, convinced briefly that she was in the last moments of life, she thought it probably the sound of her own failing heart.

She couldn't die. Images of her two sisters flickered in her brain. What would happen to them? With a massive effort, Elizabeth tried to take a breath. Painfully, the air pushed into her lungs as she rolled slightly to one side. Her left arm, she realized, was stretched out above her head. It was numb, though she only knew it when the dull pins-and-needles feeling started to creep into the limb, spreading gradually and more sharply from her shoulder to her fingers. Pulling herself slowly to a sitting position, Elizabeth lay her head on her upraised knees and attempted to take deeper and deeper breaths. Slowly, her senses returned to her, and only the throbbing in her shoulder remained. Flexing her arm, she knew nothing was broken, but she felt as if she'd been kicked by a mule.

Then she looked about her. The wooded glade was eerily silent and dark as death. She thought briefly of the Lord Constable. Of Garnesche. Her panic had disappeared, but a cold fear remained in the pit of her stomach. Pushing herself to her feet, she cocked an ear in the direction she thought she'd come, but there was no sound. Carefully, Elizabeth clambered to the top of the embankment and quietly pushed through the shrubs until abruptly she found herself standing on the worn path between the French and English encampments.

A young pageboy eyed Elizabeth curiously as he passed. The sky to the east was just taking on the deep, purplish blue that preceded dawn, and the air had the sharp tang of an early summer morn. Elizabeth looked up and down the path. A few late revelers were wandering along, and she stood a moment, undecided as to which way to go. Finally she made up her mind and started hurriedly down the path, looking over her shoulder at the graying canopies of the morning camp.

But she'd only taken a few steps when she slammed into the human wall that blocked her way.

Peter Garnesche stood before her.

Chapter 6

Elizabeth recoiled in shock. Her breath caught in her chest.

Peter Garnesche silently watched the battered woman before him. He reached out and took a hold of her chin. Despite her flinching response, he turned it to the light of the nearby torch. Elizabeth Boleyn's face was covered with blood. From the gash on her cheek that still oozed, he was certain her injury was recent. Looking down at her garment, a menacing sneer crept over the man's face.

"I'll have to remember to congratulate the Scot." Garnesche let his hand drop. "He is a better man than I thought."

Elizabeth tried not to look back at him or at his attire. In her mind's eye she could still see the Lord Constable's blood spilling darkly on the ground. She was sure the man's doublet must be spattered with it. She wondered if the hand that a moment ago held her chin was stained red as well. The smell of death permeated the air.

"I like this," the man continued. "Humility at last from the biggest prude in Europe. I never imagined that you liked it rough."

Elizabeth took a small, hesitant step back. Another group of drunken soldiers was approaching them, working their way back to their camp. Suddenly it occurred to her that the English knight had not connected her with the crime he'd committed moments earlier. She took another half step back, but Garnesche's hand shot out and grabbed her by the tartan, checking her retreat.

Elizabeth's blood ran cold in her veins, and the young woman glanced quickly and cautiously at the man's face. His eyes were not on her. Even though it looked as though he were conversing with her, his gaze was searching the faces of those passing by. But the men passing hardly gave them a second glance, and Garnesche looked back down at her, a foul gleam in his eye. Her blood ran colder yet.

"This is getting better and better." He smirked, pulling Elizabeth roughly to his chest. "Who would have thought that I could take a lesson from the Scot?"

Elizabeth turned her face at once as the man's foul mouth tried to close on hers. Instead of a taste of her lips, Garneshe's mouth roughly descended on her open cut. She cried out in pain. "Let me go," she whispered through clenched teeth.

"Where, my pretty?" His hands grabbed at her breast through the baggy shirt. "We're just getting started."

Elizabeth struggled to get out of the man's grasp. "I'm...I'm his leftover, damn it. You don't want me."

Garnesche pushed her roughly against a nearby tree and moved after her. "Oh, I do want you, you arrogant bitch. In fact, I've always wanted to feel you writhe beneath me. I just can't see why I've waited so long."

"He'll kill you." Elizabeth moved to the side and escaped the madman's clutching grip. Turning quickly, she now had the path to her back. But she knew her speed was nothing compared to the English knight's. "I belong to Ambrose Macpherson. I slept with him. I'm his. Do you hear me?" She retreated as she spoke, but the man continued to follow. "He'll kill you if you touch me."

"That is, if he's alive after I'm done with him," a voice growled.

The sound of the man behind her jerked Elizabeth around. The Duc de Bourbon stood a step away, his eyes blazing with anger.

Elizabeth stopped dead. She'd never been happier seeing anyone in her whole life than at this moment. But the nobleman's grim expression stopped her from showing any sign of it.

"How interesting." Peter Garnesche moved in behind her. "So much chivalry over a fallen maid."

Elizabeth stepped aside as the Englishman put a hand on his great sword. She was relieved to see five of Bourbon's men appear suddenly behind the young man. For one thing, the Duc de Bourbon never traveled alone, Elizabeth knew that from the past encounters. She remembered someone once telling her that a number of husbands had hired a band of fighters and put a prize on the handsome nobleman's head. It was about that time that the duc had started traveling with an entourage.

"She left the Scot's bed. I'm next in line." Garnesche leered in Elizabeth's direction. "When I'm finished with her, I'll send her to you. But I can promise you that it won't be for quite some time."

Elizabeth started to back away in small steps from the group and in the direction of the French quarter.

Bourbon ignored the Englishman altogether.

"You look a bloody mess, Elizabeth," he said. Pain showed in the Frenchman's handsome face. "Was I too gentle? Is this what you were after? A brute? Someone who would abuse you?"

Elizabeth shook with anger, pain, fear. How could she explain? She was alone. No one believed her, nor trusted her. She could tell Bourbon of what the Englishman had done, about the Lord Constable's body, but even the six of them might prove no match for this giant and whatever soldiers he could call for. If they failed to take the knight, he would know it was she who had witnessed the crime and heard the discussion of his treachery. But it was not only her own life that she feared for now. It was Mary's and young Anne's. Both would be prey for this vindictive madman.

"So you have nothing to say?" Bourbon's accusing voice cut in on Elizabeth's thoughts. "Will you just stand there and admit that you've been nothing more than a common whore?"

Elizabeth looked from one hardened face to the next. The Englishman stood a step away from the duc. The same distance he'd stood from the Lord Constable before cutting him down.

She took one last look at the duc. Her throat was tight as she straightened before his angry glare. "You are nothing to me. I don't have to explain a thing to you. Just leave me be." Elizabeth turned and ran. Ran as fast and as far as her tired legs could take her.

The Franciscan friar Father Matthew shook out the straw from his gray habit and rubbed his face to make sure he was awake. This is unbelievable, he thought, as Elizabeth ceased speaking. He must still be dreaming.

Beneath the loft where he sat, the horses crowded into the shed were shuffling hungrily. Unfolding his long, lanky frame, the friar tried to ignore the rumbling in his own empty stomach and concentrate on the story he'd just been told. This poor child needed his help, and he knew he'd be needing all his faculties to help her.

He looked tenderly at Elizabeth's troubled and battered face. Washing the dried blood had not improved the looks of things. He cringed to think that she might need a needle to close the gash on her cheek. She would be scarred for life. Friar Matthew had known this generous young woman for a long time. Why, he still had the leftover gold from the ring she'd given him in the pouch bumping gently against his thigh.

Beatings, a father prostituting his own daughters, treason, murder. It was too unbelievable. He'd helped his flock in the area outside Paris with many problems in his many years as a priest—the hungry farmer who poached the king's deer to feed his family; the apprentice boy who got the landlord's willing daughter with child; the girl caught learning to read against her father's wishes; and, a thousand other matters—but never had he been called on to deal with issues of this enormity, of this magnitude. Silently sending a prayer heavenward, he took a deep breath and let out a sigh.

"First, my child, we must decide if you are in any immediate danger." He sat down again on the straw. "Is there anything that you left behind that could lead the Englishman to you?"

She shook her head. "No, I don't think so, Friar." Gravely, Elizabeth thought for a moment. "Nothing that has to do with the murder."

"Thank God for that much, anyway."

"We have to let someone know about the Lord Constable," Elizabeth whispered as she stood and moved to the shuttered loft window. An odd breeze had picked up outside, rattling the wooden shutter. "We must expose Sir Peter as the murderer."

"I don't see how we can. At least not right now. That would certainly be the end of your life." Father Matthew paused and then blurted out his concerns. "It is not just Garnesche that you will need to watch out for. Think of all his friends and allies in the English court. They will readily believe him when he says you are accusing him falsely. And then you'll be their target. You—and your family—will be the enemy. We must consider the risk to your sisters."

Surprised, Elizabeth turned toward the friar. Looking at the man's somber expression, she had to agree. Who was she, after all? She was more a member of the French court than the English. Born of an unwed French mother, raised so far from London. Everything Friar Matthew had said was true. Who would listen to her? Who would protect them? She couldn't trust even her own father. "I could send a message about the murder. No one ever need know whom it came from."

The priest shook his head in disagreement. "You don't know much about the king's justice, my child. The Lord Constable's death will undoubtedly be blamed on some passing beggar. Anything you say will be ignored right now because King Francis does not want war with England. So no Frenchman would dare accuse an Englishman of the murder of the Lord Constable without absolute proof."

Elizabeth returned to where the friar sat. "How can we let an innocent man's death go unavenged?"

Friar Matthew moved quietly, taking hold of her hand and nodding toward the Golden Vale.

"Out that window ten thousand wealthy men and women are sleeping comfortably in tents made of cloth of gold. But look beyond the vale, as I know you have, and you can see a million peasants and villagers living in the squalor of poverty. You're safe here, right now because no one even imagines that any noblewoman would dirty her shoes in the muck of this stable."

Friar Matthew lowered his eyes and continued. "Elizabeth, the Lord Constable was no innocent. He was brutal and indifferent to the suffering of the poor. He was one of the worst. Everything he ever did was for the benefit of his fellow nobles. I believe he cared nothing for the real France."

Elizabeth thought back over the few passing encounters she'd had with the Lord Constable. She'd really never known much about him. "Are you telling me his death will cause more celebration than grief?"

"Perhaps, my dear. Though he was no champion of the people, I think the peasants of France would celebrate his death only if they thought one of their own had done the bloody deed." The friar smiled grimly at her. "But you and I both know that is really beside the point. What the English knight did was treacherous and evil."

Elizabeth gathered her knees to her chest and rested her pounding forehead against them. At this time yesterday, her problems had been so much simpler. Other than thinking of a way to raise money for Mary's doctor, Elizabeth had been in control. What a mess things had become, she thought. "What am I to do?"

Father Matthew racked his brain—and his heart—for some inspiration, for some guidance. "First we must get you out of here. There must be someplace in Paris where you can go. Your father's house, perhaps."

"I can't." She shook her head violently. "I can never go back. He'll be waiting for me. I'm sure by now Madame Exton has convinced my father that everything I said was nothing but a lie. I just can't go back and wait to see whom he will try to sell me to next."

"What about your mother's family? There are certainly plenty of those left with enough money to feed the whole country."

Elizabeth shuddered at the thought of putting herself at the mercy of strangers she'd never met in her life. They had thrown her mother on the street with a babe in her arms. She could never ask them for help. "Never. I'll never ask for their charity. That's out of question."

The friar paused. This was becoming difficult.

"The Duc de Bourbon! How about him?"

"I think he would probably take in a stray dog before he'd give me shelter." Elizabeth sighed quietly. "But that's probably for the best. He's always wanted something more than friendship from me, but now I'm sure we can't even be friends." Though he'd often tried, Bourbon had never become intimate with her. She had never allowed it. The closest they'd ever come was after a banquet last summer, when the young duc had tried to kiss away her defenses under a moonlit sky. She had escaped his attentions then and never allowed him so close again. He was a friend and nothing more. But tonight, during those brief but incredible moments in Ambrose Macpherson's tent, Elizabeth had for the first time tasted the sweet, dizzying nectar of passion.

"Your choices are becoming more limited, Elizabeth," the friar pointed out, patting her hand. Then he brightened. "What about Sir Ambrose. He seemed to be interested."

Elizabeth blushed. She hadn't told the friar just how interested the Scot was. She also had carefully avoided telling him just how close she'd come to giving her virginity away. Elizabeth shivered unexpectedly at the thought of the man who had awakened feelings in her that she'd never before experienced. How tenderly he had caressed her. She could even now feel his lips upon her skin.

"You never told me how you came to be wearing his clothes."

"I...I borrowed them." She had not told Friar Matthew of visiting the Scot before going to her father. "I took them from his tent. It was much easier traveling through the encampment dressed as a man." Well, that was partly true.

The friar looked directly at the young woman. She was not telling him everything about the Highlander, but that wasn't what they needed to focus on right now.

"Then why not go to him for help? He's a generous man with a noble heart. And he has the resources to protect you from your father and Garnesche."

If life were a dream with no guilt and no consequences, Ambrose Macpherson's side would be the very place she would go. But the world she lived in was one in which the outcome of such a fantasy would undoubtedly bring betrayal and unhappiness. It was the way of the world. Elizabeth's hand unconsciously moved to her face. She didn't have to see her wound to know she was disfigured for life. The Highlander wouldn't even look at her. No man would want to look at her.

And then it occurred to her that this suited her plans. Quite nicely, in fact. The young woman straightened. Gazing down at the kilt that she still wore, Elizabeth brightened.

"Then you agree." The friar clapped his hands, seeing his young friend's face shed its grim expression.

Elizabeth bounced to her feet and moved to a bundle of worn clothing the friar had dropped in the corner of the loft. "I'll go to Italy."

"Who is in Italy?" the priest asked, watching in amazement as the young woman unfolded each item and held it against her frame.

"Some of these will fit!"

"Those are twice your size." The holy man leaped to his feet, moving quickly toward her. "Wh—what are you planning to do, Elizabeth?"

She ignored his question as she continued measuring the clothing. "But no more than twice. And some are quite...hmm."

"Young woman..." He didn't like the look in her eyes.

Elizabeth reached over and put her hands on the priest's shoulder, turning him toward the ladder. "Please get me a very sharp knife and some water."

The man dug his heels into the soft straw flooring. "I'm not going anywhere unless you tell me what you are up to."

"I will not tell you anything unless you go and get me those things." Elizabeth looked the priest squarely in the eye.

The friar stood a moment longer. Then, realizing he simply hadn't the heart to add to this innocent child's troubles, Friar Matthew grudgingly gave in and climbed down the ladder of the loft, muttering a complaint at every rung of his descent.

Chapter 7

The man needed his face rearranged.

As the first rays of light crept across the roof of his tent, Ambrose pulled his traveling clothes out of the leather pack. Wrapping his kilt about him, he found himself getting angry again at the thought of the abusive Duc de Bourbon. The bloody bastard. Why was it that so many fine women put up with such treatment?

He had lain awake for what had remained of the night after Elizabeth left his tent. His thoughts had centered on her. Ambrose Macpherson had spent his entire life not wanting to get tied down to any place or to any woman. He liked his life. He enjoyed his independence. He could come and go. And he could pick and choose among the best, the bonniest. Ambrose enjoyed sampling, taking, and pampering the women he crossed paths with. But like a bee approaching any delicate flower, he liked to taste and then move on. After all, the world was filled with them. And why should he settle for one, when he could have so many?

Last night, though, had been bothersome. Ambrose forced himself to admit that Elizabeth's broken condition had been the cause. Damn Bourbon, he thought.

The Highlander slammed his fist into his palm, then made a conscious effort to shake off the emotion. Such thoughts did no one any good. But perhaps before leaving for Boulogne, he would pay a visit to the amorous duc.

"*Macpherson!*" the French voice shouted angrily from outside the tent. "Come out, you dog!"

Ambrose stiffened, recognizing at once Bourbon's voice and the challenge in his words. Striding quickly across the tent, he threw open the flap and stepped out into the windy morning. The duc and five of his men were standing in the empty alleyway.

When the French nobleman saw the Scot, bare-chested and unarmed, come out of the tent, he quickly unbuckled his sword and tossed it to the retainer standing behind him. It was bad enough that Macpherson had bedded Elizabeth, but roughing her up the way he had was beyond endurance. And marking her face. He would pay dearly for that. The rage that had been seething, building within Bourbon since she ran, suddenly boiled over as the duc moved across the alley.

They were both large men, and when they collided in the middle, the ground shook with the impact.

Ambrose connected solidly with the nose of the duc, and Bourbon's head snapped back even as his fist fell like a hammer on the ear of the Scot. Either blow would have felled a lesser opponent, but the two men hardly flinched as they continued to attack each other with a violence so sudden and so unrestrained that it surprised even the trained fighters looking on.

The fury continued unabated, the warriors battering unmercifully at one another until suddenly the duc was lying dazed on the ground, blood spewing from his flattened nose. Ambrose stood over him, a raging pulse pounding in his brain. "Get up, you coward."

Bourbon looked up at the giant warrior through a haze. He pushed himself groggily to a sitting position. "I'll kill you before I ever let you touch her like that again."

"You are the one that needs to die, knave." Ambrose took a step back to give the man the room to stand on his feet. He wasn't done with him. "How does it feel to get a taste of your own treatment?"

The French nobleman stood unsteadily and took a swing at the Highlander's face. "You cut her. You marked her for life, you animal."

The man's fist went wide of Ambrose's face by quite a distance, and then Bourbon once again lay flat on the ground.

In an instant the Scottish knight was standing on top of the Frenchman. One of Bourbon's men took a half step toward the two, but then backed off at the threatening glare of the Scot.

"What do you mean, *I* cut her?" Ambrose put his boot squarely on his adversary's chest. "You're the one who beats her for nothing."

Bourbon grabbed the boot and threw Ambrose to the ground. Scrambling on top of him, he grabbed the Scot by the throat. "Me? I've...I've never laid a hand on Elizabeth. Do you hear me? Never.

I've admired and respected her since the time she was only a girl. I've even hoped to have her hand in marriage. We French take care of our women, you mountain pig. We don't beat them."

Ambrose pushed the man off of him and leaped nimbly to his feet. In an instant, Bourbon followed suit. Suddenly Ambrose had a gut feeling that his adversary was speaking the truth. "She came to me with a swollen face." He ducked, avoiding another punch thrown by Bourbon. "I was perfectly justified in assuming it was you who did it. Have you forgotten how angry you became when I asked about her earlier? I thought you had punished her for my attentions."

"If you knew her better, you scoundrel, you would understand that she is not one to be owned or punished or made use of in any form. She is a woman of character and talent. But before I grind you into the dirt, just tell me why did you do that to her. You slept with her. Why did you have to cut her?"

Ambrose reached out and grabbed Bourbon on the throat. "I did no such thing, you blackguard. She left my tent in the same condition as she arrived."

"She wore your tartan!"

"So she did."

"Then you admit you slept with her!"

"That is none of your business," Ambrose growled.

"I'm making it my business!"

"No one has given you the right." Ambrose increased the pressure on Bourbon's throat. "Where is she now?"

Bourbon pushed the Highlander's hands away. "There is no need for you to know where she's gone. You've used her as you use all your women. Just move on and throw out your line for the next catch."

"I'm asking you a question." Ambrose once again moved toward the Frenchman. "Where is she?"

"She's no longer your concern. Not that I think she ever was!"

"Listen to me, you pigheaded dandy!" Ambrose shoved Bourbon back a pace and walked threateningly toward him. "Someone beat her up pretty badly before she came to me last night. And you are telling me that after she left here someone cut her face. You claim you didn't do it. Now try moving your brain from your codpiece to your head and think. She could still be in danger. Whoever did these things to her could do even more harm. Now, where did you see her last?"

Bourbon's thoughts went back to his last encounter with Elizabeth, his anger toward the Highlander dissipating like a morning fog. My God, he'd been so stunned by the words that he'd heard her say that he'd paid no attention to anything else. She wasn't just standing with Garnesche; she'd been trying to get away from him! And she had gotten away, he remembered.

Ambrose watched in silence as the nobleman's eyes cleared, finally comprehending the meaning of what was being said.

"Do you have a drink in there?" the Frenchman asked quietly.

"Aye." Ambrose nodded, leading a pensive Bourbon into the tent.

Chapter 8

She had nothing to lose and everything to gain.

Well, she had to lose her name, her identity, her family. And most important of all, she had to lose her hair.

As Friar Matthew looked on aghast, Elizabeth sliced off her ebony locks in chunks, talking quickly as she worked.

Elizabeth laid out her plan for him. She would go to Florence. The Medici family was back in power and stability had returned to the prosperous city of art and culture.

She would find a place, working as an apprentice, or as a laborer if need be, with one of the great artists who resided there. Brilliant, old Leonardo was dead, but perhaps with Raphael. Or with the young genius Cellini. Perhaps, if the heavens smiled on her, she might secure employment in the shops of the great painter and sculptor Michelangelo Buonarroti.

As she talked, Friar Matthew recalled that his order was building a church on the outskirts of Florence. Elizabeth told him she would need a letter of introduction to the friars there so that she could show her talents—her ability to paint.

She would travel there under the guise of a man, she would get work as a man, and she would live as a man. She could do it. Elizabeth knew she could.

Friar Matthew looked at her with incredulous eyes. Elizabeth talked as if she had prepared this masquerade for many years, and he told her his thoughts. Elizabeth admitted that what he said was true. She had dreamed of doing this, many times before. But all that planning, all that preparing, had only been a fantasy. A wonderful, unattainable dream.

The friar knew very well about Elizabeth's paintings. Over the years, she had worked so hard to become the proficient artist he knew her to be. He had seen so many of her works, and he knew she was good. More than good, he admitted. She was exceptional. It had been a pleasure to be her accomplice in supplying the poor village churches around Paris over the past two years with the magnificent religious portraits signed only "Phillipe."

Like any other artist, Elizabeth had needed an audience. A group that would respond to her choice of subject matter, to her composition, her color choices, and her uniquely individual style. Without a master that she could learn from, Friar Matthew's tidings had been an indispensable learning tool.

"I can't watch any more of this, Elizabeth!" Friar Matthew cried. "It's unnatural, I tell you!"

The black hair slipped in silken cascades to the floor of the loft.

"I'm almost finished," she said, casting an adventurous eye around at her friend. "I need you to tell me how the back looks."

"You look like a...like a boy...God help me!"

"Come, now, Friar. You're acting like an accomplice to murder."

"Well, that's exactly how I feel," he moaned. "I feel as if I've just helped murder a lovely young woman who came to me for help."

"Such foolishness," she scolded gently, standing and straightening out her well-worn attire. She pulled an oversized cap over her newly cropped locks. Spying the friar's look of shock, she removed it for the moment. "Friar, this is nothing compared to what is yet to come. I'm just starting."

"I heard everything you just said, Elizabeth. But what we've done with your paintings is far different than what you are asking now. It is one thing to take a beautiful piece of artwork and hang it in a church for everyone to admire. But cutting your hair, dressing in these men's clothes, traveling God knows where...it's just too...well, too drastic! When I was encouraging the development of your talent in the past, my conscience was at ease knowing that you were protected from exposure. I knew you were in no danger so long as you were under your father's roof. But this has already gone too far."

"I see. You heard my plan, but you think I shouldn't go through with it." Elizabeth looked him challengingly in the eye. "What choice do I have, Friar? You've always told me that we must look beyond the trials of our lives. That we must forge ahead."

"I suppose I should have known better." The friar rolled his eyes. "Now I'm at the mercy of my own words!"

She scowled fiercely at her friend. "Well, do I look convincing?"

"Well, you sound convincing," he murmured under his breath.

"That's a good start, anyway!"

Matthew looked at the transformation before him. Elizabeth truly looked like a young man. The layers of baggy clothes covered her feminine curves, and the black tresses now fell in handsome waves to a point above her shoulders. Her bruised and swollen face, now a bit cleaner, lacked the whiskers of a man, but the cut on her face would leave a scar that no courtly woman would wear openly— uncovered and unpainted. Even the way she was standing! So confident. So self-sufficient.

"Walking all the way to Florence. Living the life of a man." Friar Matthew shook his head gravely. "I tell you again, young woman. It's unnatural."

Elizabeth laughed. It seemed to her that it was the first time she'd laughed in a hundred years.

The priest sat heavily on the straw, thinking over the journey that lay ahead of her. He weighed his responsibilities. Who needed his help more, right now—his flock or his troubled young friend? Thinking of whether it would be possible for him to accompany her, he vacantly picked up the Macpherson plaid that lay neatly folded beside him. The wet shirt lay beneath it. She had used the remainder of the water he'd brought to wash the crimson stains out of the blood-soaked garment. Her blood, the friar thought, shaking his head. Elizabeth had asked him if he could somehow return these to the Scottish nobleman. But knowing the man's generosity, Friar Matthew wondered if it wouldn't be better just to give away the clothes to a needy family.

"So, then. You think if I walked out in the open, dressed like this, the Florentines would think I'm a man?"

Hearing no answer to her question, Elizabeth turned in the direction of the friar. He was sitting with the Macpherson plaid in his hands, his face devoid of all color.

"What's wrong?" Elizabeth asked, hurrying to his side.

Friar Matthew held out the kilt that she'd been wearing earlier. "Do you know where this happened?"

Elizabeth stared at the torn hem of the garment. A large section of the plaid was missing, and she knew exactly where it was. She raised her eyes to meet his.

"In the woods, right after the murder. It was dark. There was a tree branch. You don't think he'll go back?"

"If he does, and if he finds the plaid, then he'll recognize it for sure and remember who was wearing it." The friar's face was grave. "And when that happens, Elizabeth, he'll come after you."

Elizabeth stared as her heart sank like a stone into the pit of her stomach.

"That means I have no time. I have to go." Elizabeth's eyes darted to the friar's face. She twisted the cap in her hands as she wrestled with her feelings. "But first I must warn my sisters. Would he harm them to get to me?"

"Only if he thinks you are in contact with them."

Below them, the horses in the stable were becoming perceptibly nervous and active. The whinnying caught the attention of the two friends, and then Elizabeth caught the scent that was being carried along on the strengthening wind. Fire.

Pushing against the stiff breeze, Elizabeth opened the shutter, and the two looked out. Over the encampment across the Golden Vale, black smoke was billowing up and racing across the tops of the tents. Something was burning, and Elizabeth felt a cold fear drive sharply into her belly. She and the friar exchanged a quick look, and then they turned hurriedly toward the ladder. Scrambling down from the loft, Elizabeth was off at a dead run with the friar hot on her heels.

"Wait! You can't forget this," Friar Matthew called before Elizabeth could slip out the door.

The young woman paused an instant, and the friar handed over the large hat. She pulled it hurriedly on her head, yanking it as low as she could over her eyes.

"We have to be careful. This could be a trap," Matthew cautioned, and Elizabeth nodded. Then together they dashed out into the early morning light.

Working their way through the horde of peasants now awake and moving about, the two hurried around the stockade barrier of the tournament field. Scores of poor still sat huddled against the wooden fence that for the past month had separated the peasants from the nobility.

Certainly no one could be left sleeping in the encampment, Elizabeth thought. In spite of the late-night revelry, everyone, it seemed, was awake and active in the face of the raging fire that appeared ready to engulf the entire English sector of the Field of Cloth of Gold.

Elizabeth and the friar ran past the companies of soldiers, already hauling water in buckets of wood and leather. Some were even using steel helmets—anything to slow the crackling flames that the warm, dry breeze was pushing along.

The smoke became thicker as the two worked their way into the throng of gentility milling about in the alleyways. Nearing the source of the conflagration, Elizabeth looked wildly about at the panic-stricken crowds scattering before the hot sparks and thick, black smoke that was engulfing the area on the currents of the shifting wind.

"Mary!" Elizabeth gasped as they pushed through the mob. She looked ahead at the half dozen blazing tents. "She was in my tent. That's my tent." Her hands tried to open a path, pushing at the people ahead of her. She needed to get closer. But they were pressing in from all sides. Someone shoved a bucket into her hands; it was full of water. She held it tightly. A man in front tried to pry it away, but she wouldn't budge. Elizabeth knew she had to get to the front. "Mary!" she called at the top of her lungs. The shouts of the jostling men drowned out her words. She felt the crowd move. They were moving closer to the fire, and she let herself become part of that moving mass. Glancing around her, Elizabeth saw the friar a short distance behind.

One instant she was blocked by a wall of human bodies all around, the next she was in the front row, preparing to throw the water on the burning blaze. It was her tent. The heat from the blaze was scorching the skin of her face, and the roar was deafening. Throwing the water on the flaming material, she took a step closer, then put an arm over her face as she prepared to run inside. Above her, she could see the fiery roof of the tent flapping in the grip of the wind. Beside her someone was chopping at one of the lines that held the shelter up.

If the tent collapses, Elizabeth thought wildly, Mary will be trapped in the flames. She started forward.

A hand from behind gripped her arm, holding her back. She cringed at the pain that suddenly shot down her arm from her injured shoulder. She squirmed, yanking herself free. The hand took hold of her again. She turned her head to see the one holding her. It was the friar. He was shouting, but Elizabeth could not hear him at all. Following his eyes, though, as he turned his head, she could see the cloaked figure standing amid the crowd of onlookers.

Mary.

Elizabeth let him draw her back into the crowd. Working her way toward her sister, she gave one last look in the direction of what remained of the tent. Mary was alive. Elizabeth rejoiced at the thought, wondering in the next moment how her sister had escaped. But as they pushed through the crowd, a lump rose in her throat at the idea of having lost so much. Glancing at the burning tents around her, she considered the losses that others were suffering. And she wondered if this had all started because of what she'd witnessed.

Nearing the place where Mary was standing, Elizabeth was opening her mouth to call out to her when a massive arm struck her brusquely on the side of the head.

"Make way," the rough voice shouted as the giant knight cleared his own path through the swarm of humanity.

Elizabeth stumbled to the side as Peter Garnesche passed by. She stopped dead, gaping after him. Sir Peter strode to a group of three soldiers who were busily surveying the faces in the crowd. Nodding his head curtly as he spoke, he said something to them that Elizabeth, though only a few paces away, could not hear. Then, turning sharply, he shoved his way through the crowd to another group of his men. His face was dark and smudged with soot, and his hard eyes darted from one face to the next as he went.

They're looking for me, Elizabeth thought in a flash of panic as she exchanged a quick glance with Friar Matthew. The priest's brow furrowed with anxiety.

Elizabeth tugged the hat down further over her eyes and peered over to where her sister stood. As she did, she saw Mary, the cloak of her hood pulled low, turning and melting into the crowd beyond.

Elizabeth saw Garnesche's men approaching. They were everywhere, searching the faces of everyone they could lay hands on.

It was then that Friar Matthew took charge. "Pretend you can't breathe, Elizabeth. Your sister is safe. Now we have to get you out of here."

She looked at him wide-eyed.

"Double over."

Seeing the soldiers only a few paces away, Elizabeth followed the friar's order instantly. She knew the ploy of dressing as a man might not work with the Englishman's cronies. After all, Sir Peter had seen and recognized her wearing the Highlander's clothes the night before. And the fresh wound on her cheek was sure to give her away. Garnesche had seen that cut, and Elizabeth was certain he would have mentioned it as an identifying mark for his men.

"Clear the way. Out of the way, there," the friar shouted as he put his arm around her, pushing his way through the oncoming men. Elizabeth held on to her friend's cloak, all the while keeping her head down and allowing him to lead her. Anytime Matthew came across an immobile knot of people, Elizabeth gasped for air and emitted the most heart-wrenching cough she could muster.

Within a few moments, Elizabeth could tell they were leaving the dense throng for a more open area. With the exception of an occasional brush of a passing shoulder, she could no longer feel the press of bodies all around them. Still, she dared not look up, for fear of being recognized.

"I think we've passed the immediate danger," Friar Matthew said quietly, coming to a halt. "I want you to go back to the stables."

"I have to find Mary. She is out there...vulnerable." Elizabeth looked around; there was no sign of her sister. They had stopped at a crossing of alleyways, but they were still in the English sector of tents.

"I'll go after her," he replied. "I saw the direction that she went. You go back, and I'll bring her to you."

"But—"

"This is no time to argue with me, child. By now there are probably a hundred English soldiers looking for a woman with a freshly cut face. You'll be safe among the peasants. They'll never think to search among the poor French wretches." The friar looked about him cautiously. "I give you my word I'll bring your sister to you. Now go."

Chapter 9

If only I *were* a man, she thought.

Pushing against the streaming mass of humanity, Elizabeth moved down the cloth-walled alleys toward the open fields and the stable. She hardly dared to look up at the oncoming faces, for fear of being discovered. She knew she had to leave for Italy. It was her only escape. But she had to convince Friar Matthew that she could survive on her own. The friar's last words as they'd run toward the fires had been that he wouldn't allow Elizabeth to go alone. Even if he could bring himself to believe she would be able to protect herself on the arduous road to Italy, he believed that she would need fellow travelers, with a female especially among her companions. He was certain that would improve Elizabeth's chances of traveling successfully in the guise of a young man.

But Elizabeth didn't want to disrupt any more lives. She and the friar both knew that finding a trustworthy, female companion who would want to travel to Italy right now was nearly impossible. The friar didn't have to mention it, but Elizabeth knew that, in spite of all that was happening, he was already considering going with her. She'd seen it in his face. In fact, he probably was thinking of finding her a safe place—not in Italy, but rather in some remote French convent.

That wasn't the answer. She couldn't remain in hiding the rest of her life, idling away her time and letting someone else take care of her. She couldn't sit, a silent observer, while the world moved on without her.

Elizabeth looked up as a young peasant girl banged into her side. The girl murmured a word or two and continued on. But something in the innocent face of the child washed away the thought of her own problems and reminded Elizabeth of her youngest sister, Anne. She wondered where she had gotten to in the midst of the fiery chaos. Mary obviously had been able to escape Garnesche's wrath, but would the man stoop so low as to bring his fury to bear on a defenseless child?

Anne was smart, though. Even at her age, she was capable of outwitting those around her on nearly every occasion. Elizabeth knew that the young girl had already made a place for herself at the English queen's side. And she had a way with their father, as well. No, Anne would be fine. Elizabeth could let her mind rest on that score. But Mary was a different story.

Glancing across the alley, she saw him first.

Ambrose's eyes roamed the crowd before him. Suddenly he spotted a figure traveling against the tide. For an instant their eyes locked. Then she looked hurriedly away and disappeared into the surging throng.

The Scottish warrior leaped into the alleyway, pushing across the current till he reached the other side. Far off, he saw the large, floppy hat ducking along the edge of the path, and he quickened his long strides, cutting the distance between them in no time.

Rounding a bend, Ambrose saw her throw an anxious look over her shoulder, but he had nearly caught up to her. So with a quick lunge, the Highlander grabbed the shoulder of his scurrying quarry. Elizabeth pulled hard against his grip, trying to free herself, but the Scottish knight wasn't about to let her go.

Pulling her with him, Ambrose backed into a small gap between two tents.

"Let me go!" Elizabeth struggled against him, but he only tightened his hold on her.

"Nay! I'll not let you go. Not until you tell me who it is that you are running away from."

"That's my business, not yours." She looked up just in time to see a mixture of sadness and anger flicker across his face as he studied the wound on her cheek. She could feel the heat of his gaze wash over her skin.

"Who did this to you?"

Elizabeth felt the viselike grip of his fingers dig into her shoulders. She could hear the strong note of anguish in his voice. Then she turned her head, hiding the ugly gash from his stare. "It doesn't matter. Please let me go."

"I won't!"

Ambrose's fingers gently moved up from her shoulders and framed her face. He turned her head until their eyes met. He felt the tremble that coursed through her. "You're frightened."

Elizabeth shook her head, trying to deny it. But the welling up of tears in her eyes spoke the truth.

"Seeing what he's done to you...I can understand why. You are frightened. Tell me who it is. Let me help you, Elizabeth. Let me protect you."

She felt the caress of his thumb against her skin. Protect you. The words drifted about her in a haze of emotion. Her skin was burning at his touch, and she felt the heat shoot downward until it washed over her heart.

She fought to keep her mind clear. What was it about this man that gave him the power to wash away all the troubles that surrounded her, all the tribulations that were, right now, threatening her very life? "I'm marked forever."

She didn't know why she spoke those words. It wasn't like her. But Ambrose's attention made her feel vulnerable. Exposed. She didn't have to look at herself to know what her wound must look like to a man. He had to be appalled, disgusted. After all, women were to be pleasing to the eye. And clearly, she was not. No, she would never be.

"We are a perfect match." He reached down and took hold of her fingers, raising them to his own forehead.

Elizabeth let her hands trace lightly over the scar.

"You are beautiful, Elizabeth." Ambrose reached up and pulled the cap off her head. His jaw dropped. "The devil...what have you done to yourself?"

"My lacerated face you find beautiful, but my shorn hair you do not?" she challenged.

"The first, I know, is the result of some brute's vicious act. But the second...this must be self-inflicted." Giving in to his impulse, he ran his hands through her short tresses. He actually liked the feel of them.

She shook off of his unrestrained touch with the backs of her hands. "Why do you do this if you find it so unattractive?"

"Who says I find it unattractive?" Ambrose's eyes fell on her full lips. "My problem is I find everything about you absolutely fascinating."

She didn't have to follow his gaze to know that he had every intention of kissing her. And that he did. Thoroughly.

All Elizabeth wanted to do was yield to him. And that she did. Utterly.

She parted her lips. The sound of the men and women rushing by, the roar of the fire in the distance, even the imminent danger of Sir Peter Garnesche, all faded away. Nothing else mattered as Elizabeth took refuge in his caress, in his touch, in his kiss.

Ambrose felt every muscle in his body harden as Elizabeth's hands rose to encircle his neck. He dipped deeper into the richness of her sweet mouth, and his arms brought her tight against his body. He remembered what lay beneath. The incredibly beautiful body, the full breasts, the intoxicating taste of her skin.

Elizabeth pulled away from the kiss. She felt weak at the onslaught of this man's attentions. She placed her head against his chest and tried to still her trembling knees, her pounding heart.

"How can I feel this way?" she whispered, fighting to keep her voice calm. "So quickly, I mean. I hardly know you."

"The passion that two people feel for one another cannot be explained in terms of time or place." Ambrose looked down and captured her gaze. "We are good together, Elizabeth. I can feel the passion that is raging inside you. Come with me. I'll never let him get close to you. Never again. I'll protect you. We'll find our own place...Scotland, perhaps. I'll take care of you. We'll find a corner of eternity for just the two of us. Think of the pleasure we could bring to each other. The passion we could share."

She paused, looking deep into his eyes, and then shook her head. This was an offer much like one she'd expect from Bourbon. But there was a difference here that made her hesitate. She would go to her grave before accepting the duc's offer; Bourbon was at best a friend. But Ambrose Macpherson's invitation carried a far greater temptation.

No. She shook her head resolutely. How could she even consider it? Had she already forgotten her mother's fate? Is that what she wanted? How long would it take Ambrose to tire of her? Where would she go once that happened? She was disgusted with herself for being even momentarily tempted by the man's words. "Please don't ask that of me. I can't."

Ambrose gazed silently into her deep, dark eyes. He had never made this offer to anyone. He had never sought a mistress that he might keep for any period of time. There were dangers in that. Dangers of getting attached, of getting caught up in a lengthy relationship. Of giving up one's freedom. But despite it all, he had made the offer. And she'd rejected it. This woman was so different from the others. Different from any woman he had ever been with in his life.

But Ambrose knew women, and he thought for a moment of pursuing the advantage he sensed he had right now. Ambrose Macpherson was a master of the powers of persuasion. Particularly when it concerned women. He knew if he tried again, if he set his mind to it, she would agree. But for the same reasons that he'd never asked another before her, he held back. Something inside told him he wasn't ready. Not yet.

Elizabeth searched for the right words. She didn't want to hurt him or seem ungrateful for his offer. But how could she explain to him that becoming someone's mistress wasn't the life she could accept? Even if that someone was as attractive and alluring as the man standing in front of her. Elizabeth looked up into the Highlander's handsome face. She could see the hint of disappointment in his eyes. But then her eyes were caught by the small gash along the line of his jaw.

"Was this self-inflicted?"

Ambrose caught her hand as she tried to probe the small injury on his chin.

"Nay, lass. This was a good-morning kiss from your French courtier."

"Bourbon? You two fought?"

Ambrose let his hands fall to his sides. Even though the two knights had resigned themselves to the fact that neither was responsible for Elizabeth's injury, Ambrose still wondered if perhaps the duc was the reason Elizabeth rejected his offer. She had changed her mind and walked out of his bed last night. Well, fallen out of his bed. He wondered now if her willing attitude had not just been a way to make the handsome French nobleman jealous enough to propose marriage. Women! Ambrose wanted to banish this new thought from his mind, but even as he pushed it away, he felt it taking root. He still remembered the Frenchman's words. Someday asking for her hand in marriage. *Someday.* That had been the emphasis. The Highlander didn't want to think she was simply trying to push things along.

"Aye," he replied. "We fought. But perhaps it will distress you to know that your friend got the worst of it."

Elizabeth smiled. "Hardly. It's about time someone caught up with the snake."

Ambrose gave her a suspicious glance. "The gentleman seems quite fond of you."

"The gentleman is fond of all women, regardless of their wit, shape, or rank." She leaned down and picked up her hat. "But that's what drew me to you. You are not like that, are you?" she asked wryly.

"Of course not!" He was quick to answer.

"Of course not!" Too quick, Elizabeth thought. She placed the hat on her head and pulled it down over her eyes. "Well, I have to go."

Ambrose's hand shot up to her elbow. "Where to?"

"Paradise!" she whispered dreamily.

"With him?" Ambrose asked shortly. It wasn't Bourbon, but it had to be someone else. She must value the man greatly to continue guarding his identity from both the duc and him. "What he has done to you still has not convinced you to get away?"

"Aye, it has." She stretched up on her toes and kissed him quickly on the lips. "I'll always remember this Field of Cloth of Gold." She tried to turn toward the crowded alleyway.

Ambrose caught her by the elbow and pulled her toward him. "This was yours to keep."

Elizabeth looked down at the large emerald ring that the warrior placed in her palm. "I—"

"Think of it as a keepsake, lass. Just remember me by it."

As she gazed up into his eyes, Elizabeth closed her fingers over the gift. Then she turned without another word and disappeared into the throng.

Chapter 10

Dawdling is the thief of time, Friar Matthew thought.

"I'd been waiting for you, Elizabeth. Then you didn't come, and it was getting so late," Mary explained. "I must have dozed off." The dark-haired young woman gazed out into space as she recollected the events. Elizabeth sat beside her, holding her hand, while the lanky priest stood by the shuttered window, waiting less patiently for her to continue her tale.

Elizabeth urged her on. "And that's when you heard the voices?"

"Yes." Mary nodded. "Just outside the tent—beside my bedding—they were talking. There were two or three, I think. But I heard one of them clearly. He was giving commands to the others."

She looked from her sister's face to the friar's.

Matthew followed the young woman's gaze. How interesting that Mary hadn't once asked about how Elizabeth had come by the gash on her cheek. How typical of her.

"He said, 'Silence her,'" she continued. "'Cut her throat, or smother her, but don't let her cry out. And whatever happens, don't let her live.'"

Elizabeth shuddered at the moment of fear Mary must have experienced.

"So *how did you escape them*?" the friar exploded. "For God's sake, Mary!"

The young woman looked up in shock at the exasperated cleric. "Really, Friar. I'm telling you everything as it happened."

"Please, Friar Matthew, give her time," Elizabeth pleaded, as she watched the priest throw up his hands with a sigh. "Go on, Mary. What happened next?"

The young woman collected her thoughts and gave the priest another quick look before continuing. "Well, when I heard that, I jumped out of bed. I assumed they'd be coming in the front, so I grabbed for my cloak. It was then that I knocked over the brazier. The hot coals spilled right across the floor of the tent." She looked at her sister. "The rushes on the floor lit up like one big torch. The flames and the smoke were everywhere...in an instant."

"Were you hurt?" Elizabeth asked quickly, glancing down at the ivory skin of her sister's hands.

"No. I ran!" she answered. "I scrambled as fast as I could to the back of that tent and slipped under the cloth wall."

"So no one saw you escape?" the friar asked shortly, turning then to Elizabeth. "It's just possible that if they don't find you in the encampment, they might decide you perished in the fire. That would be good for us."

"They were after *me*, Friar Matthew," Mary asserted. "Why would anyone want to hurt Elizabeth? Most of these people don't even know who she is."

He tried to hold his tongue, but he couldn't. "Why would anyone want to use violence against a vain and silly ornament like you?" Friar Matthew scolded. Other than their similar complexions, the two sisters had nothing in common. And Matthew was losing patience with Mary. "After all, what use would there be in anyone coming after you? One just doesn't cut willow branches when there is a house to be built."

Perplexed, Mary looked up to her sister. "But I like willows."

Matthew shook his head. Brilliant she was not. But right now there was a much bigger problem at hand. While going after Mary, he'd heard from some peasants about a reward for anyone who could bring news of the whereabouts of Elizabeth Boleyn. Perhaps they did think she perished in the fire, but perhaps they did not. Friar Matthew knew that Garnesche was not a man to just sit and wait. From what Matthew had heard, the father of the girl was pretending to be heartsick over her disappearance, and Sir Peter Garnesche had taken the lead in the search for her. What liars, he thought. Clearly, the most important thing was to get her out of here...now. As good as many of these commoners were, to them Elizabeth could mean nothing more than a possible reward, and they all had empty stomachs and families to feed. She wouldn't be safe here for long. "Elizabeth, I've already arranged for you to leave here on the hour."

Elizabeth looked up at her friend. There was no sense in arguing or in trying to find the whereabouts of the place he was sending her. She had to leave this camp. Once away from it, she could take control of her own destiny.

Elizabeth flinched as Mary's nails dug into the skin of her hands. She looked at her sister. The young woman sat, her face devoid of all color. Her eyes had welled up with tears, and as she watched, the glistening drops overflowed and coursed down her pale cheeks.

"I need to talk to you, Elizabeth." Mary's voice broke, and she threw a glance at the friar. "I need to talk to you alone."

Elizabeth turned to the friar. The man shook his head and took a step toward them. He had to stop Elizabeth from allowing her frivolous sister to continue using her. The elder sister had finally realized the value her father put on her. Why was she being so blind to the younger sister's manipulative ways? He opened his mouth to speak, but Elizabeth shook her head, stopping him. At his next attempt to intervene, Elizabeth frowned in response. He shrugged and turned to go, pausing by the ladder. "You're leaving in an hour, Elizabeth."

The two women watched as the friar disappeared.

"Elizabeth!" Mary broke into sobs, throwing her arms at once around her sister's neck. "You can't leave me. Please, don't. You promised to take care of me. You know how ill I am."

Elizabeth held back her own sadness, but reached around and hugged the young woman to her. "I'm not leaving forever, Mary. I'm just going in search of a place and work that I can do—yes, work. Once I find it you can join me there, wherever it is. I remember my promise. I'll take care of you."

"But whatever is going to happen to me?" Mary hiccupped as she straightened up, drying her tears with the backs of her hands. "My life is in danger, you know."

Elizabeth knew that there was no point in telling Mary that the assailants were not after her. By explaining the events to her sister, she would just put Mary in the same danger that she herself was in. In addition, Elizabeth knew that in her sister's highly dramatic and imaginary world, Mary might very well relish the idea of a life in jeopardy, without really understanding the ramifications.

"Sir Thomas mentioned yesterday that he'll send you to Kent." Elizabeth tried to be convincing. "That won't be bad for the short term. Before you know it, you can leave and come and stay with me."

"Oh, Elizabeth..." Mary hid her face in her hands and broke down. Her cries this time were heart-wrenching. "I can't go to Kent. I can't go with Father. And I thought I could count on you. But now you tell me that I can't. I have no one. I should just take my life with my own hands and be finished with this misery."

Painfully, Elizabeth watched the suffering young woman weep. "That's not an option, Mary. So stop talking rubbish." She took a deep breath and tried to think things through clearly. It was her own fault. If she hadn't been, for so many years, so supportive and caring when it came to her sisters, she would be on her way to safety right now. Elizabeth knew the problem very well. For years now she had not simply been the older sibling, she'd been the only mother figure, the only nurturer that her sisters had known.

Mary saw her sister pause as she considered the situation. The young woman realized that she had to tell Elizabeth everything— before her sister had a chance to come up with some rational solution for the dilemma at hand. Mary didn't want to chance that. Elizabeth had to know the truth. "The French physician had some additional news when he examined me last night."

Elizabeth stared at her sister. Mary's face in an instant had gone from deep despair to utter happiness. She was sometimes difficult to keep up with.

Mary tucked her legs under her and sat like an excited child. "Don't you want to know what he said?"

"I do, but perhaps not at this moment."

Elizabeth had less than an hour left to decide on a plan that would be acceptable to her younger sister. She couldn't think, though, while Mary chattered away. "Can this wait?"

"Nay, Elizabeth. It can't." Mary sulked. "I don't care if you want to know or not. You're the one who brought that physician to me, and you're the one who will share my secret."

"Secret?"

"The upset stomach, the nausea, the endless naps...all those things were not a new stage of the pox. They've been happening because I'm...I'm..."

Elizabeth's eyes widened. "You're what, Mary?"

"I'm pregnant!"

"You're *what?*"

"Pregnant. With child."

"With child!" Elizabeth repeated, her head whirling with this news.

"When a man and a woman lie together, that's often the outcome." Mary looked into her older sister's astonished face. "You could be pregnant, too. I mean, now. As we speak."

"*Me?*"

"Aye, you." Mary nodded knowingly. "You slept with the Scot, didn't you?"

Elizabeth shook her head to clear it of all she was hearing.

"Was he as good in bed as everyone claims?"

"Stop!" Elizabeth yelled. "Stop this nonsense. Let's go back to what you said earlier. You said you were pregnant."

"I am. I'm carrying Henry's child." Mary turned on her tears once again. "I'm carrying the king's son, and I can't even come out into the open for fear of my life."

"The king's son? Mary, don't talk that way." Elizabeth scolded. "First of all, if you *are* pregnant, you don't know if you are carrying a boy or a girl. But that's not really important, anyway. Is it?"

"Of course it is. Just think of it, Elizabeth, if I had a boy..." Mary smiled dreamily. "He'd be the heir to the throne of England."

"Don't be ridiculous! The way you've been treated, you'd be lucky to have him recognized as Henry's bastard. And even if he is accepted as that, he'll never be heir to the throne. Not Cardinal Wolsey, nor the church, nor the noble families would stand for that."

"Stop being so perverse," Mary snapped petulantly. "You're supposed to be on my side."

"I am, Mary." Elizabeth turned away, shaking her head. Her problems were getting more complicated with each passing moment. Clearly, she had to get her sister out of here, too. Mary hadn't a clue how much trouble her wagging tongue could bring. To herself, and to her unborn babe.

Elizabeth sighed. As much as she would like to deny them, Elizabeth knew deep down that there were a few traits Mary had obviously inherited from their father. Being an opportunistic social climber was one of them.

She glanced back to see Mary eyeing her sulkily once again.

"You know, Elizabeth, if you would stop taking my head off and give me a chance, I could explain everything," Mary said.

"I'm sure you can."

"I have it all figured out." She looked hopefully at her older sister. "This is the way it'll work." Elizabeth sat silently while Mary hurried on. "I'm pregnant, but not everyone should know. Not yet, anyway. You can stay with me during my term. I will need you to look after me. The physician said yesterday that as long as I'm well cared for, I could have a perfectly healthy child. You can take me back to France, and we will stay there until my son is born. Then I'll send for Henry, and after he comes for us, I'll ask him to give you permission to paint. You won't have to hide your work anymore, Elizabeth. You might even get a chance to paint the portrait of the next King of England. A portrait of my son in his mother's arms. Isn't that exciting?"

All Elizabeth could do was stare at her sister. It was too early a stage for the pox to be affecting her mind.

"Mary, if this is your plan, then why don't you take it to Sir Thomas?" Elizabeth could hear her temper becoming shorter. "This is so much in line with his thinking that I'm sure he'll go along with any condition you would set."

Mary brightened before another thought crossed her mind, darkening her brow. "But...there are problems."

"Oh, there is more?" Elizabeth asked incredulously.

"I went to see Father already. This morning. He says he doesn't believe the child is Henry's. He says no one else will believe it, either. That dreadful cousin of ours, Madame Exton, told him that I couldn't have been pure when I lay with the king. That the child must be someone else's." Mary didn't want to tell Elizabeth everything that had been said in their father's tent earlier. It hadn't been a very genteel scene. Sir Thomas had refused to believe her and had told her in no uncertain terms that if Mary was pregnant, she would be sent away to some cloistered nunnery where she could be separated from all who knew her. Mary had walked off, stunned, confused, and angry, but Friar Matthew had found her and brought her back to Elizabeth. Mary looked into her sister's face. "But I know Henry will believe me. I was a virgin, after all. He'll remember that. I will be giving him the son that he wants so much."

Elizabeth waited until Mary finished speaking and then started for the steps. "Friar!" she called, looking over the edge of the loft.

"Where are you going?" Mary asked, her eyes wide with alarm.

Elizabeth glanced back at her sister. "<u>We</u> are going to Italy."

"Italy! But I've never been to Italy." Mary looked about her helplessly. "What happens if I don't like it? Elizabeth? Elizabeth, I don't want to go."

Elizabeth turned sharply and, crossing the floor, knelt directly before her sister. She would help her in spite of herself. "You *will* go to Italy, Mary. That is your only way out of this mess. So you'll do it. And you *will* like it."

Chapter 11

Chapel del Annunziato; Florence, Italy
Four Years Later—April, 1524

Art is long, life short. For man, his days are as grass, as the flower of the field, so he flourisheth...

The sound of Pico hurrying up the ladder disrupted the painter's thoughts.

"Phillipe, hurry! He'll be here soon!" The handsome young sculptor looked anxiously over the top of the scaffolding at the painter and then scurried back down the ladder and across the room to look out the empty window of the newly constructed chapel. Two hours earlier, the room had been bustling with tradesmen of many crafts—carpenters, glaziers, stonemasons, and others—but the last few had left a short time earlier, cheerful with the easy camaraderie of those who work hard and who take pride in their skill.

"Don't worry so much, Pico. The master knows our work will be finished in time." The painter, lying back, cast a critical eye on the scene. The face on the angel directly above was smiling, but there was a sense of strain in the smile. The artist sighed aloud. I should be happy, Elizabeth thought. Why can't I be happy?

She gazed up at the fresco. Certainly the painting wasn't the cause of her melancholy. The colors were brilliant and true. The depiction of the angels bursting in shimmering streams of light through the summer clouds had turned out well. The thin coat of plaster was nearly dry, but it didn't matter...the painting was done.

Elizabeth Boleyn had a lot to be proud of. She considered the process for a moment. Frescoes presented some of the most challenging work done by the artists. Because you were painting on wet plaster, you had to work quickly and with a steady hand. Working on a wall was difficult enough, but lying on your back to paint ceiling frescoes was the most difficult of assignments, and only the two or three best painters in the studio were given those tasks. The old master was very particular about these works. Oh, yes, Michelangelo was very particular, indeed.

And that made Elizabeth feel especially good about being the one the maestro chose the most often. But still, she was living a lie. The maestro had picked Phillipe, the French painter. A likable young man with an exuberant talent and very little social life outside of his work. But in reality she was nothing more than a fraud. A deception. A man's exterior masking a woman's soul.

"He's coming, Phillipe," the man cried, clambering up the ladder. Elizabeth turned her head to see Pico's head appear, then disappear as he missed a rung, then reappear. "I don't like heights."

"Calm down, Pico," she said, chuckling. "I'm ready for him."

"But it isn't just the master. *His Highness* is with him!"

Elizabeth sat up on her elbows and began to edge quickly toward the ladder. "Don Giovanni? With the master?" This was a different story. Giovanni de Medici rarely came out in public anymore, so she knew this visit must be an important one for Michelangelo. She glanced once more at the fresh painting, and prayed that the powerful ruler would find it pleasing.

"Quick, Pico!" she called, scrambling down the ladder after his friend. "Help me pull the scaffolding into the corner."

Two years earlier, Elizabeth had suggested that the scaffolding they used for the ceilings be built upon wheeled platforms, and right now, as she and Pico succeeded in their struggle to push the apparatus aside, she thanked God Michelangelo had seen the value in her suggestion.

She had used her brain, and the master greatly approved of that. Starting as an apprentice, she had learned quickly that she lacked the physical strength that many of the other young men had. And not wanting to spend her time doing the physical labor that gave her the strength required, she saw immediately that she needed to make use of her ingenuity and invention. That had been the key to being recognized early on.

The sound of the heavy oak doors swinging open brought the two students to a halt. The aging master and the ruler of Florence entered the chapel with a train of several dozen men in attendance.

Elizabeth looked about in amazement as the room appeared to fill instantly. There were faces everywhere, and their attention focused on the work, not the worker.

Because the new stained-glass windows were not yet installed, streaming bars of golden sunlight washed the room with a radiant glow. Around the small central rotunda, rows of graceful columns rose straight to the ceiling, branching and bending like willows into an arch far above the resulting gallery. At the point where the pillars divided, Pico's decorative stone carvings adorned the supports in a petrified pattern of leaf, vine, and flower.

And at the center of it all, far above the floor, Elizabeth's angels appeared to burst downward through the dome, revealing a vibrant blue sky and the fair-weather clouds of a benevolent heavenly sphere.

Giovanni gazed upward at the breathtaking scene, enraptured by the sight of celestial creatures so real it seemed they might sweep down beside him.

"Michelangelo!" the powerful ruler murmured. "My friend! How could such a thing of beauty be wrought? What mind, what hand could conjure and execute such figures?" His voice trailed off as he stared upward in wonder.

"Don Giovanni," the aged master responded deferentially, trying to keep the pleased expression out of his voice. Glancing around the room, he spotted Elizabeth and Pico standing unobtrusively beside the scaffolding. "We have only provided what you have asked."

"True, but with such exquisite mastery of color...of space..." The Florentine raised his arm and pointed as he spoke. "The face of that one. Look at how he looks into our eyes. And look at the rippling muscles on that other one. Surely strong enough to wrestle with Jacob. Ah, Michelangelo," he said, glancing at the artist. "This work ranks easily with your work in Rome."

The maestro pulled at his graying beard as he gazed critically at the painting. Elizabeth held her breath as he studied the work. With a smile, he turned back to Don Giovanni. "My friend, you honor a humble sculptor with your words. For this is the work of a young and talented artist. A man with the heart and the soul of a painter.

The one I spoke of earlier, but let me introduce him. He stands here in the shadows. Phillipe, my boy, come here."

Elizabeth felt the knot quickly form in her stomach. She had known for some time now that her paintings spoke in a new and different language. She knew she had a gift that captured more than the exterior of her subject. She had the ability to seize the feelings within. Sadness and tears, joy and laughter, anger and greed. She had a gift; she could perceive the very essence of what she beheld—and it traveled through her fingers. It became alive in what she drew, in the colors of the paint. She knew, but never, never before had she heard her work praised so publicly by someone as important as he who stood with the maestro in the chapel.

Entering the rotunda, Elizabeth approached the group. Stopping before the two men, she bowed and dropped to one knee as Giovanni held out his hand to her. As the young painter kissed his family ring, the ruler appraised the lad before him. He had a small build and frail, delicate hands. The lad was fortunate to have the talent he did, since if he had to make a living by any other means, he wouldn't be long for this world. Then the lad looked up and gazed straight into his eyes, and the Medici padrone nodded approvingly. The young man had the brightest and most intelligent eyes he'd seen in a long time. A quite handsome face—almost beautiful—but for the pasty complexion and the puckered red scar along the high cheekbone. Giovanni raised him up and smiled, waving his plump, jeweled fingers at the ceiling fresco.

"Is it possible that a man so young as you could have produced such a masterwork?"

Elizabeth blushed at the compliment, turning her face skyward.

"He *is* a master," Michelangelo said proudly. "In my studio, Phillipe is the youngest of the ten masters. He will be the finest." The maestro paused and put his arm around Elizabeth's shoulder. "Someday, he'll be another Raphael, Don Giovanni. This young man has the potential to surpass even the great Leonardo...God rest his old bones. You wait and see. It won't be long."

Giovanni de Medici smiled encouragingly on the young painter and turned away. "What other marvels do you have in store for me today, Michelangelo."

And as quickly as they had entered, they were gone, leaving an excited Pico gazing admiringly across the chapel rotunda at Elizabeth.

"How can you stand there so calmly?" The young man ran over and snatched Elizabeth's hat off her head and teasingly threw it into the air. "Look up there, Phillipe. Your angels are smiling at you."

Elizabeth looked up, but all she could see was a smirk.

"This calls for a celebration!" Pico caught the hat and placed it firmly on his friend's short-cropped hair. "I'll run and get the others at the studio, and we'll meet you at the baths off the Piazza del Duomo."

"Pico, you know that I don't—"

"Come on, Phillipe! This is a special occasion. It isn't every day that Giovanni de Medici, the Duke of Nemours, gushes over your work. Come on!"

Elizabeth looked up at the handsome Genoan apprentice and smiled. She'd been working with him for two years, and he'd never even guessed that she was a woman. Pico was a young, squarely built man with large callused hands that showed the signs of his trade. From the first moment when they'd met, the young sculptor had taken the task of looking after the frail, boyish-looking painter. Elizabeth knew it would have been much easier for Pico just to call her weak and to ignore her as some of the other artists in the master's studio had done early on.

But he hadn't. In fact, Pico had often been the shield behind whom Elizabeth had been able to hide during these very public years. He had the strength; she had the talent. He protected the young man he knew as Phillipe. And she shared with him a sensitivity for art that elevated him in the skills of his trade beyond his imagination. She spoke of the softness, the elegance, the way each curve of a sculpture must relay feeling, emotion, a story, even. These concepts of art had been foreign to Pico until he'd met up with Phillipe. And the two artists understood one another in a way that was nearly spiritual.

"My sister is expecting me, Pico. Why don't you go on without me?"

"I won't," Pico said adamantly, turning on the surprised painter and planting his fists on his hips. "Phillipe, how long must this go on?"

"What are you talking about?" Elizabeth asked, raising an eyebrow at the vehemence of the young man's tone.

"You have the right to live your life as much as she does." The sculptor paused. He hadn't intended to speak so brusquely to his friend. "Phillipe, everyone is talking about you two."

"Talking?" Elizabeth face flushed angrily. "Who is talking that has any right? No one, Pico. No one has any right to speak about Mary or about me. I have never given anyone reason to."

Pico grabbed Elizabeth by the shoulders. "Listen to me, my friend. I'm about to tell you things that you should have heard long ago."

"I don't want to hear." Elizabeth tried to turn and shrug off the man's grip on her shoulder, but Pico's large hands held her securely in place.

"It's too late, Phillipe. You must listen to what I have to say."

Elizabeth pushed away the man's hands and walked to the scaffolding, turning and sagging heavily against the ladder.

Following her and leaning against one of the columns, Pico looked down into the sad, black eyes of the young painter. So talented, but so naive. For the entire time he'd known Phillipe, he'd never once heard him speak of any kin other than his sister and her child. It was true that the three lived in the modest villa of Joseph Bardi, the wool merchant. But Joseph and his wife Ernesta were not kin to Phillipe. From what Pico had gathered, the lonely older couple had taken in the three as tenants at first, and from what Phillipe had said, they'd become close over years. But what Pico needed to say to Phillipe wasn't something that those two people would have any knowledge of. No, there was no one else who would do this. Pico knew it was up to him.

"What I have to tell you regards your sister."

"You're about to badmouth her. Because she rejected your advances."

"I don't know what she tells you every night, but your sister didn't refuse my attentions. It happened quite a while ago, and it was wrong, I know. But I slept with her, Phillipe, as more than half of

Florence has." Pico held up his hand as Elizabeth shot to her feet and began to interrupt. "Wait, my friend. Hear me out."

The sculptor watched as Elizabeth stopped, averting her eyes. "What she did reject were my half-empty pockets. But this was after..." Pico paused for effect, "*after* she came to my bed."

Elizabeth sat down on the pedestal at the base of the column and took her head in her hands.

"My friend, you have to put a stop to this. It is no secret that you are the highest-paid apprentice Michelangelo has. With the wages you make, you should be living in comfort, with a servant to attend to you. Instead, where are you? Still living under someone else's roof. You could marry and have a woman and children of your own. But instead, all you do is work. And for what? For wages your sister spends."

Elizabeth felt a knot in her throat, but she knew she wouldn't cry. Even if she were alone, she knew she wouldn't. She'd forgotten how to cry.

"Everyone in the studio knows that you are doing outside work. Everyone knows you need the money."

Elizabeth looked up in surprise. She had worked hard to keep her outside commissions a secret.

"Yes, the portraits. Everyone knows. Including Michelangelo. And don't be so surprised. Your style, your brushwork—it is so obvious, Phillipe. You can call yourself what you want, but everyone knows who you are." Pico looked earnestly into Elizabeth's face. "And tell me, Phillipe. What do you do with that money?"

"I keep what I earn."

"No, you don't. We see your sister spending it."

"Why are you doing this to me, Pico?" Elizabeth's face reflected the pain in her heart. "Why now?"

"Because I am your friend. Your only friend. Phillipe, what just happened here today is nothing you can simply ignore, nothing you can just forget." Pico had to get his friend's attention. "The word will be out in no time. Everyone will want you. You'll have opportunities, commissions far more grand than any you've yet had. But she could ruin it all. You need to put her in her place. She has to curb her...excesses. You need to talk to her. It's your right because you're her brother, and because you support her and the little one. You can order her to stop. Or at least to be more discreet."

Elizabeth had known for a long time about Mary's wildness. But there wasn't much she'd been able to do about it. Mary was twenty-one years old. A grown woman. Elizabeth couldn't lock her away, and she couldn't put her out on the street. Neither option was acceptable.

So all she did was divert what free time she had to Mary's daughter. Jaime. The three-year-old Jaime was the only bright spot that Elizabeth had outside of her work. Truly, the young child was the reason Elizabeth put up with all she did. Elizabeth had loved her sister once, but now she wondered if her love had not turned into an emotion closer to pity.

"She made a scene the night before last."

Elizabeth looked up.

"At the Palazzo Vecchio. Your sister was there...mingling with all the friends of the Duke of Urbino. From what Gino told me, her dress alone must have been worth half a year's wages."

Elizabeth knew Pico's friend Gino. The son of one of the wealthiest families in Florence. She doubted he ever paid for anything in his life. What could he know of the value of money?

"There were also a large number of foreigners there. Guests of the duke. From what I hear, your sister took quite a fancy to an Englishman. They danced and spent most of the evening together. Gino didn't know what happened or what was said between them, but suddenly Mary was screaming at the man to leave her alone. It was quite an embarrassing scene. The duke was mortified, and she left before anything more could be said. Gino said she was as pale as death, Phillipe. I don't think she'll be welcomed back there." Pico fell silent.

After a moment Elizabeth stood and walked toward the door. "I'm sorry, Phillipe." Elizabeth turned and looked at the sculptor. "I'll talk to her," she said quietly, before disappearing through the door.

Pico stood alone in the rotunda. Above him the faces of angels looked on gloomily as the evening's encroaching darkness began to settle on the room.

Chapter 12

Don Giovanni waited for the strolling musicians to move on before continuing his conversation with Ambrose Macpherson, Baron of Roxburgh, Lord Protector of the Borders, Ambassador and Special Emissary of His Majesty, James the Fifth of Scotland.

"I tell you, my friend, the French king has an eye on Florence. My sources bring news of him moving his troops east."

"What makes you think it is your land that he is after?" Ambrose pushed back his chair and looked at his host, Giovanni de Medici, the Duke of Nemours, perhaps the wealthiest man in Europe, and the uncontested ruler of the flourishing Florentine city-state. "You know it is more likely that he would be after the Emperor Charles. Francis's feud with him far exceeds any ill will he feels toward you or your family."

Giovanni paused, looking down into his jeweled goblet. Ambrose had arrived just two nights ago, after spending a week with Francis. If anyone could offer insights into France's intentions, that man was Ambrose Macpherson.

"It's true. Francis would be a fool to move into Italy, turning his back to Charles. This could work to my advantage. After all, the Holy Roman Emperor is the greater threat of the two. Just think, if Francis is busy fighting Charles, he might leave Florence alone."

"Except that Charles has a large number of troops guarding the Pope in Rome." Ambrose looked at the duke straight on. "Just remember, whatever happens this summer, *don't* let your guard down."

The duke's face creased with a smile. "What is this I hear? First you talk me out of my worries; now you fan the flames of my concern. So much for the politician I have learned to admire. You speak as though Scotland, Francis's oldest ally, is at last taking sides with me. Does this mean that you'll help the poor Florentines, my friend?"

"You are pushing your luck, Giovanni!" Ambrose stretched his long legs out before him, while a servant refilled his goblet. "I'm just making you think out loud. There is sometimes more than one way out of a predicament. You and I have known one another a long time—"

"And I know you to be a man of integrity," Giovanni interrupted.

"The obligations of friendship never outweigh the obligations of duty and honor."

"You can't change who you are, Ambrose. But I have heard some interesting news, lately. Of Francis giving you yet another title to add to your property."

"You know I care very little about titles," Ambrose interjected. "And don't forget, my well-informed friend, I paid for my estate there with Macpherson gold. Many years ago."

"I know, my friend. Everyone knows the truth. You can't be bought. All of these things—friendship, duty, honor—they all reside within you. They are not separable from you. They are the qualities that make you who you are. You know how much I've wanted you and Scotland on my side. Fight beside me. Help me."

Ambrose brought his cup to his lips and then, without drinking, placed it back on the table. "You continue to survive in these unsettled times because you are a sharp-witted, practical man. Scotland, however, is in a different position. We have a twelve-year-old king who needs all the alliances he can get. Most of all, though, James needs France. Our nations have been allied for centuries, and we are positioned such that we can keep England between us. But you, Giovanni, you need neither me nor my country. You will remain capable of defending yourself, my friend, so long as you remember never to trust an armed man who gazes longingly at your neighbor's fields. Now stop pestering me and use your brains."

The duke's dark eyes bore into the Highlander's. "Let me see if I hear you correctly." He paused for effect. "In a few weeks, depending on Francis's whim, he may be standing at my door."

Ambrose looked about the huge hall and let his eyes take in the series of sensational paintings that graced the room. Together, the works formed a series depicting the history of Florence and the triumphs of the Medici family. Before them six huge statues representing the toils of Hercules seemed almost trivial.

The Medici ruler held up his hand and smiled at the Scot. "I understand. We are done talking of politics and war." The duke sat for a moment, savoring the comradeship the two enjoyed. They were friends, and their friendship transcended the limits of borders and national alliances. This gave Giovanni de Medici a warm feeling inside. No one else in Florence, perhaps in Europe, ever dared to address him the way this Scottish nobleman did. Good and honest men are so often fools, Giovanni thought. But Ambrose Macpherson was a man to listen to. He could almost picture it...Francis, giving Ambrose a title that the Highlander cared little about, then revealing to him his secret intention of attacking Charles. Of course, the French king would know that the Scottish nobleman was on his way to Rome to meet with the Pope. And naturally he would stop in Florence enroute. It was no secret that Giovanni and Ambrose had been friends for years. Perhaps Francis cunningly planned on the Scottish warrior passing such information on to the Medici ruler. But that was what set Ambrose apart from other politicians. He wouldn't allow anyone to manipulate him in any way.

"*Sì*, it is true what you say about my ability to live by my wits. The great sculptor Michelangelo says that, to grace a family tomb, he is planning a series of marble figures that will together be called, 'Victory of the Mind over Brute Strength.' Isn't that wonderful, Ambrose?"

"So long as he doesn't plan on you filling the tomb too quickly."

A chuckle escaped Giovanni as he clapped his friend on the shoulder. "My thoughts exactly. Well, with what's left of this beautiful night, let's speak of more agreeable things. Of art and architecture, of love and women."

"Subjects Your Highness has far greater knowledge of than does his humble servant."

Don Giovanni brightened. "Ah, Ambrose. You are a delightful guest and an excellent storyteller. Such courtesy. But news of you often reaches my ears, my friend. I've heard that the fine collection of paintings you keep in that place of yours in France continues to grow. And from what I hear, the work is second to none."

"Just gross exaggerations and rumor, m'lord." Ambrose smiled. "You should stop by sometime and see the collection for yourself. You'd be a much better judge than those flapping tongues."

"Me! Step on French soil?" He shook his head. "Nay, to do such a thing would be to risk finding my head on the end of Francis's sword."

"There is a good chance of that, I suppose. And not one you would want to risk," Ambrose remarked seriously. "Considering how fond you are of it."

"I am. After all, it is the only one I've got—and a good looking head, at that." Giovanni laughed. "But as I started to say before, I believe you are by far the finest courtier in the world...outside of myself, of course."

"Of course, Giovanni." Ambrose grinned and reached for the golden goblet of amber colored wine. "But since you mentioned the topic of art, a courier came to me this afternoon with a message from the Queen Mother that touches on the subject. Perhaps you can advise me on the best way to proceed."

"Are you asking *my* counsel on the topic of art?" The duke looked sideways at the Highlander. "After all we hear of the things you have, Ambrose?"

"No one in Europe is better qualified to give counsel, m'lord, than you yourself." Ambrose cleared his throat. He would cut out someone's tongue if he could find out who had spilled his guts to the Medici ruler about Ambrose's estate. Friendship wouldn't stop the extremely competitive Don Giovanni when it came to such collections. "I mentioned before that the message is from Queen Margaret. Needless to say, she is looking for the best advice. Must I repeat it, Giovanni? The best!"

"Well, since you put it that way..." He smiled. "It would be a pleasure, my friend. Unburden yourself."

"Actually, I have been asked to unburden you."

"Oh?"

"As you know, Giovanni, even though the king's mother has spent more than twenty-one years in our barren and comfortless castles in Scotland, we have never been able to sway her. Queen Margaret is still bound and determined to bring civilization to us wild and barbaric Scots."

Don Giovanni laughed out loud. "So you'd like me to tell her that she is wasting her time. Is that it?"

Ambrose snarled at the duke. "I can see irony is lost on you. I happen to disagree with her, my effete, epicurean friend. Like you, she wishes to surround herself with—"

"With creations that raise man above the animals. That display the inner workings of the artistic soul. That render man as heroic, as the definitive proof of God's hand on earth. That shape our lives with a timeless aesthetic, a perspective that—"

"She wants pictures." Ambrose drained his goblet and put it down with a resounding clang.

"That's what *you* surround *yourself* with, my friend."

"Nay, there is a difference," Ambrose interjected. "My collection is the work of many fine artists. I don't take a fancy to seeing my own portrait on each wall." As the words left the Highlander's mouth, he spotted a new portrait of the Medici ruler that adorned the nearest wall. "Is that new?"

"I look especially fine in that one, don't I?"

Ambrose smiled. "She wants one of your artists to paint the royal family."

Giovanni paused and slyly scanned the Scot's rugged features. "I should think that France, that devoted ally, could supply Scotland with treasure troves of art—tapestries, lace, the finest cloth of gold and silver. Certainly Francis could send your queen one of his court painters. Perhaps you, with your fabulous collection, could come up with such a painter."

"This is Margaret Tudor we're talking about, Giovanni. She wants only the best, you know that."

"Oh, how I pity you." Margaret Tudor's reputation as a stubborn and coddled queen was well known all across Europe. "And I suppose her letter states *who* exactly she wants?"

"Of course. She wants Michelangelo."

The duke nodded, stifling his desire to laugh openly. "I'm sorry to disappoint your king's mother, Ambrose, but really—"

"I knew you'd never let him go." The Scot put on a menacing glare. "But don't forget, she'll not forgive you. Just imagine me returning to Scotland with no satisfactory response to her request."

"He's a sculptor, my friend. And an aging one at that. For his own good, for the good of Florence, I simply couldn't let him make such an arduous journey."

"Well, you'd better think of something. If she doesn't get what she wants, Giovanni, there will be the devil to pay."

"I know, I know. And it won't be you that has to worry. After all, I understand that she likes you better than the air she breathes." At seeing Ambrose's raised eyebrows, the Medici ruler continued. "Of course, it *is* Scottish air. But never mind. I know if I don't help you, she'll probably send half of Scotland's warriors to join Francis as he attacks Florence."

"Hmm. I wonder if she'll let me lead them."

Seeing the scowl from the duke, Ambrose decided to let his friend think of a plan. Ambrose was a favorite at court with the queen, as he had been years earlier with her husband, James IV. But even at that, he didn't want to risk facing her empty-handed. And unfortunately, what Giovanni had said about Scotland going to war with Italy simply because her request was denied was more than a jest. The queen had attempted in the past to send Scotland into battle for reasons far more trivial than this.

The Medici ruler laid his meaty hand on his guest's arm. "Wait! I have an idea." The duke looked excitedly at his friend. "I know just the man. One of the masters working in Michelangelo's studio. He is perhaps a better painter than the maestro himself. But it would be a great sacrifice for me to part with him, Ambrose. This is a young man with the potential of bringing great honor and prestige to my land. I would only loan him to the *closest* of Florence's friends. Do you understand me? And I would entrust him to no one other than your safekeeping. You must take care of him, Ambrose."

The Scottish nobleman laughed out aloud. "You are too clever for your own good. But I don't buy it, nor do I think Margaret Tudor will."

"I am not making this up just to suit your queen," the duke uttered, his expression serious. "Phillipe de Anjou is the finest painter Florence has to offer. You can see his work for yourself. In fact, as you make me think this through more, the more I realize I might not like to part with such talent."

Ambrose studied Giovanni with a deadpan expression. Though he would never admit it to his friend at this point, the Highlander knew the work of this Phillipe de Anjou. The man was, indeed, an exceptional talent.

"His name—he's French?"

"We try not to hold that against him."

"What should I know about him?" Ambrose asked, feigning ignorance.

"Nothing, other than the fact that I want him back."

"What happens if the queen likes the man too much and tries to keep him?"

"I'll side with her brother, King Henry, and attack Scotland."

Ambrose smiled. "I'm sorry to say, my friend, you and my queen have far too much in common."

"*Sì.*" Giovanni smiled back. "The truth is, I don't think I would like Scottish air, either. Far too damp, from what I've been told. In fact, I'll need to talk to the young Phillipe. He might have objections to your climate as well."

"Too late!" Ambrose huffed. "Your offer has been accepted. Please arrange it with Michelangelo. I will stop and get the young man when I return from my discussions with your good cousin, the Pope."

"He'll be ready...with my regards to your queen, Ambrose!"

Chapter 13

She knew they had to go. It didn't matter where, but they had to leave Florence.

And then the miracle happened. As if the angels themselves had taken her plea to the heavens, Elizabeth was summoned to Michelangelo and told she would be leaving for Scotland in a week.

Scotland, the desolate northland. Cold, damp, devoid of culture, a wasteland with more sheep than people.

Scotland. An absolute heaven. She couldn't wait to get there.

"Where is your sister, child?" An elderly woman charged breathlessly into the attic room. She plunked her heavyset frame on the closest bench, her ample bosom heaving from the exertion. Removing her kerchief from her sleeve, she mopped the beads of sweat from her brow.

"She's gone out to say her last fond farewells to friends." Elizabeth looked up from the packed trunks at her friend. "What are you doing up here, Ernesta? You should not exhaust yourself climbing those stairs."

"Humph! Look who's talking!" Ernesta smiled down at the black-haired child, draped over Elizabeth's back. From beneath the linen shift, the child's arms and legs dangled around the painter. "Come here, little Jaime. Let your auntie finish her work. Lord knows, if she doesn't, no one else will raise a finger."

"Please, Erne—'Uncle'! We can't afford to have Jaime call me anything else in public."

Ernesta removed the cloth from the top of a small basket she'd brought with her. Catching a whiff of the fragrant smell of the cinnamon cakes, the three-year-old girl ran gleefully toward the older woman. "Go ahead, say what you will. Aunt or uncle. She's a lot smarter than any of us. Yesterday, when Pico came to say goodbye, you should have heard her. She chatted away about her uncle and his manly ways as if she were a grownup taught to just say the right things."

Elizabeth smiled at the little girl plunked on Ernesta's lap. Little Jaime. So sweet, so loving, and so bright. Elizabeth would have expected the child to grow up so confused, living the way they did. After all, there had never been any mention of a father, and the mother, though present, had never shown the child even the slightest affection. It seemed as though, from the time Mary had given birth to her daughter, the upset of bearing a daughter rather than a son had been too much for her. Having a girl had ruined the woman's dreams of going back to England in pomp and glory. So the young child had nearly ceased to exist in Mary's mind. But not in Elizabeth's. Since the day Jaime was born, Elizabeth and Ernesta had done everything in their power to look after the child's welfare and to fill the gaping void with love and affection.

Elizabeth continued to cherish the young girl as if she were her own. And the young painter knew Jaime was the bright sunshine, the warmth and the strength that fueled her every decision. That pushed her forward.

Drawing her gaze back to the disorder of the room, Elizabeth let her mind travel back to the past. It had been almost four years since the first day they had stepped into this house.

Leaving the Field of Cloth of Gold, Friar Matthew had accompanied Mary and Elizabeth as they'd made their way southward through France to the port city of Marseilles. There Elizabeth had met the friar's old friends Joseph and Ernesta Bardi for the first time. A deal was struck between the two men and to this day Elizabeth wondered how Joseph Bardi had so obviously gotten the short end of the deal. So, while Friar Matthew had turned around and returned to his flock outside Paris, Mary and Elizabeth and the Bardis continued on to Florence.

Joseph Bardi was an itinerant wool merchant, struggling to find a foothold in the thriving markets of the Italian city-states. Friar Matthew had known the childless and elderly couple for all of his adult life. He knew them to be people into whose care he could entrust the two sisters, and he'd been correct. Upon meeting them, Elizabeth had felt an immediate sense of kinship. They had never once ridiculed her masculine disguise nor her dream of becoming what she had set out to be. In fact, during the sisters' first year in Florence, Joseph Bardi had been the one to find her first commissions in the small, remote churches in the rolling countryside to the north of the city.

Ernesta Bardi was a smart businesswoman who for over forty years had been an indispensable part of Joseph's life and his commerce. But even more than that, Erne was a woman—proud and full of life. Not having children of their own had allowed Erne to travel and be a part of her husband's life in the markets of Europe. As the result, she was the one dismayed at the prospect of having the sisters in her house. The last thing she wanted was to be tied to a wild, pampered, and pregnant Mary...and to the child that was due in the winter. But despite her reservations about the younger, Ernesta had grown to cherish and respect the older sister, as well as the child borne of Mary. As difficult as it was for Ernesta to admit, she loved what chance—and the friar—had brought to her. A life that had once been so quietly focused on her husband's trade, now bustled with the activity of the young family she had taken in as her own.

Elizabeth stood and dragged one of Mary's trunks into the corner of the room. Her sister would certainly not be happy when she found out they wouldn't be taking all her clothes on their journey.

The climate and physicians of Florence had been very good for Mary. The physician in France had prescribed the miraculous *unguentum Saracenicum*, a mercury-based ointment, and the doctors here had continued the treatment. Everyone knew that mercury was poison, and yet the medication reduced dramatically the horrible sores that Mary hated so much. Elizabeth worried incessantly about the irrational behavior her sister occasionally displayed, and about the bouts of stomach pain, but Mary would fight like a wild animal at any suggestion that she give up what she saw as a cure for her illness. She was more than willing to endure both physical suffering and an occasional mental lapse in exchange for the return of her good looks.

"Pain is the price of beauty, Elizabeth," she would say. "But, of course, how would you know that?"

So as the original symptoms of the disease disappeared, Mary had seemed to become as healthy as any other young woman of her age. But for Elizabeth, the most pleasing miracle of all had been that Jaime was born free of the pox.

Soon after the disappointment of finding that it had been a daughter that she'd borne and not a son, Mary had given up her dream of returning to Henry's court in triumph. Faced with few options, she set her mind to make the most of their life in Florence.

Dragging a second chest alongside the first, Elizabeth sighed. She had sorted out Mary's wardrobe, and the one chest they would be taking contained only the finest, but most appropriate dresses.

She thought back over the steadily increasing amount of clothing that had been accumulating over the past few years. It amazed her that they'd been able to keep themselves afloat. She could no longer count the times she'd put her foot down and brought Mary to her senses—for however short a period. Somehow, however, Elizabeth had managed to keep up with the money she required the reluctant Joseph and Erne to take from them. That had been Elizabeth's condition from day one. She would only accept the gracious hospitality of these generous people if, and only if, they would accept some pittance of rent for the space the sisters occupied. But Elizabeth knew that even though the Bardis had accepted her terms, the couple spent ten times the amount she gave them on their young charges.

"How did Mary take the news?"

Elizabeth looked up in surprise. She had been so caught up in her own thoughts that she'd totally forgotten Jaime and Ernesta.

"It's been so quiet up here." Ernesta continued, not waiting for the young woman's answer. "I would have thought that she'd have at least one good crying fit over your decision."

Elizabeth had never thought it safe to tell the truth about the circumstances that had driven them to Florence and to the Bardis. And as if they understood, the subject had never been brought up. Last week, after her discussion with Pico, Elizabeth had confronted Mary about the details of what had taken place. That had been when a teary-eyed Mary had at last confessed to her older sister the news of her encounter with an Englishman from Henry's court. Upon hearing the story, Elizabeth had known that it was time to run. Mary, shortsighted as she was, had spent a great deal of time flaunting the story of her past liaison with king of England. After all, she'd wanted to impress the young nobleman. The man, knowing Sir Thomas Boleyn and hearing of his daughters' disappearance years back, had taken a keen interest, asking the woman more questions. That had been when Mary had recognized her error and had fled.

For the past four years, the two sisters had been faceless, nameless—women lost in a time when war and change threatened to unhinge the entire world. No one, not even their own father, had any knowledge of their whereabouts or even their existence. For four years they had been safe. But on the other side, Joseph had kept Elizabeth apprised of the news of England. She had even overheard a conversation between two English merchants once, about the power that Sir Peter Garnesche had lately acquired in the shifting sands of English court politics. When Mary had told her of being so foolishly discovered, Elizabeth feared it was only a matter of time before Garnesche would hear the news of them. And to protect the power and position he now held, he would come after her—or send some assassin to do his dirty work.

"It must be really bad, child, if you don't even want to talk about it."

Elizabeth shook her head in response. "She wants to go. She really does."

"Oh? Well, I suppose I shouldn't be surprised. I could never understand her, anyway." Ernesta stood up and took the little child by the hand. "We'll go down to the garden and give you time to finish up. Joseph said his men will be over bright and early in the morning to pick up the trunks. I wish we didn't have to go to the farewell party at Condivi's tonight. But we won't stay long. We all need to get our rest tonight. We'll be on the road for over a month."

"I still think you two are going too far to watch over us."

Ernesta clucked her tongue in response. "We wouldn't have it any other way. You should know by now that Joseph and I won't let you three just go off into the wilderness."

"But you have a business to run. You should not just throw everything over just for us."

"Nonsense. You heard Joseph. We're going on this trip not just to see you safely ensconced there, it's good for us, too. The wool that has been coming out of Scotland in the last couple of years has been constantly improving. We *have* to go. With this trip and the one we'll take when we bring you back, we could build enough contacts to begin trading. Who knows, it could mean a fortune."

"I'm sure that's the only thing on your mind," Elizabeth said skeptically. "Erne, do you know if Joseph has gotten any response from Queen Margaret's envoy?"

"You know he wasn't planning on hearing any. But I don't think we need to worry. From what I hear, the Baron of Roxburgh's mission in Rome has nothing to do with us, so I'm certain he'll be glad to know we decided not to wait for him. He would have thought us a nuisance, anyway. You know these nobles—talking, feasting, God knows what else. It'll be fine. We'll be in Scotland before he even leaves Rome."

Chapter 14

The ground shook from the thunder of two massive horses pounding side by side through the gathering dusk.

Ambrose Macpherson, Baron of Roxburgh, stared ahead at the lights of the torches that set the city of Florence aglow even in the midst of the growing darkness. He looked over at his friend, Sir Gavin Kerr. From the giant warrior's expression, as black as the thick mane that ruffled in the wind, Ambrose could tell that the knight was still angry with him for setting them on the road before they'd planned. Gavin, newly arrived from Venice, had been ready to enjoy a brief but leisurely stay in Rome before the two started their long journey back to Scotland. But yesterday, as Ambrose finished his talks with the Pope, the painter's message had arrived.

So, before he could even get enough information to talk his friend out of any hasty decisions, Gavin had found himself on the road to Florence.

Ambrose Macpherson knew he was in no position to divulge to Gavin all that he'd been privy to in these sensitive discussions in Paris, Florence, and Rome. But he had to act. Ambrose knew if they didn't stop the painter from traveling north, then the unsuspecting artist was certain to encounter the advancing armies of Charles as the Holy Roman Emperor moved south. And having such a small number of men in his company on this trip, Ambrose was in no mood to confront any larger forces just to save the stubborn hide of an impulsive artist.

Ambrose turned and shouted to his companion. "I have a shilling says you can't beat me to church at the top of the next rise, you gruesome son of a goatherd."

"Goatherd?" the giant roared. "I'll bury your ugly face in the dust of this horse before that rise."

Ambrose laughed and urged his steed a half length ahead.

The message from Phillipe de Anjou had said that he could wait no longer—he was leaving for Scotland. What's the rush? Ambrose thought with annoyance. Worse, his plan was to go north to the Rhine River, to Cologne, and across to Antwerp for passage to Scotland. Right into the middle of a probable battle between Francis and Charles, Ambrose cursed. In the painter's message, he had mentioned the name of a Florentine merchant—Bardi or something, a man obviously as empty-headed as the artist himself— who was going to escort him to his destination. So there was no need for Ambrose's service. Well, that was true enough. Taking that route, they'd all be dead in few days, the Highlander thought.

They had ridden hard since yesterday, stopping only to change horses, following the old Roman road from the sprawling congestion of the hill city northward. Through the moonlit night and the dusty, sun-drenched day, the two had ridden through a blur of towns and villages. Now the sun was low as Ambrose and Gavin crossed into Florentine lands. Driving themselves to reach the city before its heavy gates were closed for the night, Ambrose peered ahead through the dusky light as they neared the serpentine Arno.

"Do you think we can make it?" Gavin yelled, spurring his breathless steed ahead still faster.

"Just hide your ugly face, my friend," Ambrose returned, peering over at the giant. "I don't want you to scare them into closing the gates before it's time."

"You scurvy Highland blackguard. It's usually just one look at *your* scarred dog's face that makes people pass out."

"That's not passing out, you hideous beast. That's called swooning," Ambrose shouted with a grin as they made the last bend in the road before the straight run toward the gates. "And women like to languish at my feet. After all, I do have a remedy for their affliction."

Gavin shook his head. "One of these days, Ambrose Macpherson. One of these days."

Florence's ancient walls rose before them, and Ambrose and Gavin swept across the wide stone bridge and into the city as the company of armed men prepared to close the heavy gates.

Reining in his horse, Ambrose turned and eyed his dust-covered friend. "You do look like the devil, Gavin."

"Of course I do. It makes me all the more endearing. But you can sit here and talk all night. This handsome devil is going to find food and a bed."

"Very well. I'll go find the painter, and we'll meet at that inn you like—the Vista del Rosa—down by the cathedral."

"Aye, the Rosa." Gavin sighed. "I can see that bonny lass Pia right now, pouring me that bowl of wine. But how will you convince the painter to come with you? That is, if he's still in Florence."

"Well, his message said they were departing tomorrow, so he'd better be here. And as for convincing, the man has no choice. We are here, aren't we?"

Gavin looked around at the town, alive with people who appeared dressed for a feast day. Nightlife in Florence was far different than nightlife anywhere else in Europe. "Aye, we're here. But our men are not. They're still a day's ride behind us. And this Phillipe fellow seems to be in a bit of a rush. How do you plan to convince our impatient artist to wait around for a couple of days?"

"I'll talk to him first. But if that doesn't work, I may just tie and gag him."

"But Ambrose, you always tell me that's my style, not yours."

"True." The nobleman shook his head. "I have to get away from you. You are clearly a bad influence on me."

"Flatter me all you want, Ambrose. You still owe me that shilling."

With only a scowl for an answer, the Baron of Roxburgh turned his steed around and headed across town.

Elizabeth quietly tiptoed away from Jaime's little bed. The child had at last fallen sleep. Elizabeth was hardly surprised. With all the excitement and the tumultuous goings-on surrounding the upcoming journey, the painter was amazed she'd even been able to coax the little girl into closing her eyes.

"Are you quite certain you don't want to go?" Mary called.

Elizabeth placed her fingers to her lips and moved closer to the center of the room. A wooden dividing screen, ornately decorated with birds and flowers, separated the private changing area from the rest of the large room. Mary peered over the top, watching her sister advance. At the last moment Mary stepped around the end of the screen and whirled about in front of her sister.

"So what do you think?"

Elizabeth gazed at the maroon satin dress, the bodice hugging the young woman's figure and the neckline cut low enough for a generous display of Mary's ample bosom. Stepping back to get a better look, Elizabeth couldn't avoid tripping over one of the piles of clothing lying about. "For God's sake, Mary! I already packed all this once!"

"I know, I know. But I couldn't decide what to wear." The young woman grabbed a black silk shawl from a nearby bench and wrapped it around her shoulders. "I was trying to follow your advice. It would have been much easier to just go and have a new dress made for tonight, but you keep complaining about...well, it doesn't matter. Because after all, there wasn't really enough time to have something nice made. And...oh, well. I'm off."

"Don't forget, we are leaving at sunrise."

Mary turned her pouting face on her sister. "How could I forget? Joseph and Ernesta will be there at Condivi's house. I know the way they are—they'll be watching my every move. And Erne already told me right out that I *will* be coming home with them tonight. Really...as if I were a child! Oh, well. Ciao!"

Elizabeth watched in silence as Mary turned on her heel and disappeared through the doorway. Even now, Elizabeth found it difficult to blame her sister. Mary's life had certainly not turned out the way she'd expected.

Gazing about her at the mess, she sank onto the edge of a trunk. Life was nothing like she'd hoped it would be, either. Elizabeth squeezed her eyes shut and lowered her head into her hands. She had never imagined herself so unhappy, so unsatisfied.

This is foolishness, she chided herself, forcing her eyes open. The tub she'd carefully filled with water from the kitchen seemed to beckon to her from its spot by the open window.

Elizabeth stood and crossed the room to it. This was surely to be the last bath before they reached Scotland. Closing the double shutter slightly, she backed away and pulled her work smock over her head. Unlacing the tight leather corset she'd devised that bound her chest tightly, she sighed deeply as the familiar pressure on her breasts eased. Slipping out of the rest of her men's clothes, Elizabeth picked up the silk dressing gown her sister had carelessly discarded and held it to her lips. The smooth, texture of the material felt so good, and yet so foreign to her skin. Even the faint scent of rose water struck her as exotic. Pulling the robe on, she walked to the looking glass behind the screen and gazed at the somber creature standing there. With her short hair and fiery red scar, she looked like a man. But the soft curves that showed beneath the silk told another story.

Elizabeth looked at herself in the mirror. In the reflected light a glint of metal flickered from the dark valley between her breasts. Taking the great emerald ring in her hand, she gazed down at the rich green of the stone, at the gleaming gold. Just like her own identity, her own true self that lay hidden beneath layers of false shields, after all these years, she still carried, hidden close to her heart, the precious gift. Of course, it was not the ring, but the memory that went with it that Elizabeth cherished. She thought of him quite often—the man who had been the first and the last to make her feel as a woman should feel.

How odd that now she should be going to Scotland. Elizabeth wondered if she would see Ambrose Macpherson there. She'd recognize him, but he could never recognize her.

With a sigh Elizabeth slipped off the leather thong that held the emerald ring over her head and hung it on the dividing screen.

The sound of people making their way along the street wafted in the open windows and tugged her attention away. Yes, she had tried to pretend—to fool herself—into believing she was happy. She wandered to the window and peered past one of the shutters. The crowd of revelers was just turning the corner at the end of the street. Above the darkened villa across the small street, a million stars glimmered like diamonds on the black satin fabric of night.

Elizabeth shook off the nonsense that cluttered her mind. She had reason to be proud. It had taken her four long years to achieve the status she enjoyed today—status many men worked their whole lives to achieve...often without success. But she had talent. She'd worked hard to establish herself, to display her gift while keeping secret the lie beneath it all. So in the process, Elizabeth Boleyn had fooled everyone, including herself.

Four years ago she had set her mind to do the impossible, to achieve something no other woman had ever done before. And she had done it. In fact, if it hadn't been for Mary blabbing her true identity and her past connection to King Henry to an English knight a week ago, they would still all be staying in Florence for a good long while. But even with Mary's public admission, tomorrow she would be traveling to the court of Scotland to paint the portraits of the royal family.

But now, standing alone in the dim light of her room—the same familiar ache settling in her chest—Elizabeth looked up into star-studded sky and thought of the price she had paid. She could never bask in the warm glow of her successes. Not as a painter, nor as a woman. Never.

Impulsively, Elizabeth strode quickly to her sister's chest and rooted through it. Pulling out a small bottle, she turned to the tub and uncorked the vial.

With an air that was almost triumphant, Elizabeth poured out the rosewater into the bath. "Tonight, at least, you can be a woman!" she whispered, slipping the robe from her shoulders and lowering herself into the fragrant warmth.

Ambrose tied his horse by the small piazza and walked toward the front door. Peering up at the darkened house, he wondered if his friend Gavin had been right about the artist already being on the road to Scotland. But then, seeing a shadow pass by the partially open window on the top floor, the warrior stepped up and knocked at the door.

Ambrose hadn't run into any difficulty locating the place. Although those he passed had not known of a resident by the name of Phillipe de Anjou, they all had seemed to know where the merchant Bardi lived. Now, standing before the entryway, Ambrose looked back at a boisterous group passing by. One of the men paused long enough to shout in rather bawdy terms a specific offer for some female living within the walls. But then, seeing the Highlander standing on the steps, the man hushed his words and continued on hurriedly. Ambrose knocked at the door once again, but this time less patiently.

The heavy carved door swung slowly open on its noisy hinges. A thickset older man peered out at the giant suspiciously.

"I'm here to see the painter."

The man continued to gawk wide-eyed at the warrior.

"The painter? Phillipe de Anjou?" Ambrose asked curtly. "Does he live here?"

"*Sí*, m'lord."

"I'm here to see him."

"You can't, m'lord."

"Is he not at home?" Ambrose demanded shortly. He was tired and his patience was wearing thin. "Where has he gone? I need to find him tonight."

The porter shook his head, denying the request and trying to push the door shut.

Ambrose placed his heavy boot firmly in the doorjamb and stopped the door from flattening his face. The porter's face reflected his sudden terror.

"I mean no harm to anyone." Ambrose didn't need a hysterical servant on his hand right now. "I'm the Baron of Roxburgh. A friend of Duke Giovanni. I am to take the painter to Scotland with me. Now where is he?"

The man's face brightened with recognition at the Highlander's words. "Baron! We didn't...Signor and Signora Bardi were not expecting you."

Ambrose really had very little interest in the Bardis. "Then the painter Phillipe *is* at home?"

The porter's eyes involuntarily flickered upward, and Ambrose knew he had arrived in time.

"Signor Bardi is dining at Signor Condivi's tonight. We expect them back shortly. But if you will wait here, I'll get the letter that my master wrote for you. It's the letter that I was to give to you if you arrived after they had departed tomorrow."

Without waiting for a reply, the man disappeared inside the house, leaving the door ajar.

There was no time to waste. Ambrose wasn't about to let the merchant make decisions for him. The servant had said nothing about the painter being out with Bardi, and, following the direction of the man's gaze, Ambrose had a good idea where he was. He had not ridden like a madman for the past two days just to be left standing at the door.

Pushing through the entryway, Ambrose stepped in a large, darkened central hall. The embers in the fireplace at the far end were enough to illuminate the room with a dim amber glow. The heavy furniture looked well made, but not ostentatious. This Bardi wasn't a poor man, but he was clearly not one of Florence's merchant princes.

There was no sign of the porter. Quietly Ambrose worked his way across the room, easily finding the stairs. As he got ready to make his way up from the ground floor, his eyes were caught by the large portraits that decorated every wall.

Even in the dim light, they were magnificent. The bright oils gleamed in the flickering glow of the fire, and although the features of the subjects depicted were not discernible in the dark room, the bold colors and dynamic movement captured in the paintings were evidence of a master artist.

Climbing the stone steps to the first-floor landing, Ambrose paused before an open window and gazed at a painting on the wall. The waxing moon was just rising, and the Highlander's eyes lingered on the Madonna and Child. There was something familiar in the face of the Madonna. But it wasn't the customary depiction. The pout on the Virgin's face was subtle, but unmistakable. The Christ child's round face, however, projected the joyful innocence of a child at play, and the tiny hands that reached up for the Madonna's face were so realistic that Ambrose could not resist reaching out and touching the canvas.

He knew this man's work. He looked closer. There was a signature on this painting. There wasn't any on the one that hung in his study.

Suddenly a sound from somewhere at the back of the house roused the warrior, and he continued up the stairs, taking them now three at a time. At the top, Ambrose stood and looked down a short hallway at a partially open door.

Like the first hint of dawn, a beam of golden light spilled into the unlit corridor. The Highlander slowly and carefully worked his way to the door. Noiselessly, he pushed the door open and entered the large room.

The silence that greeted him was complete, and Ambrose let his eyes roam, taking in the total disarray of the room. To his left, a tall, painted dividing screen stood, and on a small table against the wall directly ahead, a small oil lamp cast its warm light on the wall. The warrior's eyes were immediately drawn upward to the painting that hung above the lamp. It was a panoramic scene of noble pageantry, and around the equestrian figures at the center, tents spread out like nuggets of gold amid the rolling green meadows.

Ambrose smiled, recognizing the depicted event. Moving closer, he studied the painting. Calais. Obviously the artist had been there.

Elizabeth Boleyn. That was what Ambrose best remembered of the event. The Field of Cloth of Gold. She had walked out of his life without ever completely entering it. But standing there, lost in the picture, Ambrose felt in his chest that gnawing sense of loss. That same gnawing ache he felt every time he thought of the woman. For the life of him, he couldn't explain why he savored her memory as he did. Still, wherever he went—around the globe, in every court in Christendom, in the midst of street crowds—his eyes continued to search for her. He sometimes wondered if she was happy with the man she'd run away with. Yes, he had pursued her far enough to know that Elizabeth Boleyn had never returned to England with her father. Neither had she returned to her home in France.

This painter has more than just skill, Ambrose thought, shaking off his melancholy. The man has a social conscience and real depth of understanding. Ambrose focused on the masterwork before him. The depiction of the poor, the mockery of the class differences— these things spoke volumes about the artist. And then the joust. Looking closer, Ambrose couldn't help the smile that was creeping across his face. This man had painted Garnesche and him, with the exception that Ambrose was wearing a kilt. No armor, just his tartan and kilt. Ambrose didn't recall meeting any of the court artists during his time at the event.

Ambrose chuckled to himself and then turned. As he did, his eyes were drawn to an object hanging from the wooden screen. Hanging at the end of a leather thong. A ring.

An emerald ring.

Chapter 15

Elizabeth closed her eyes tight as the sting of the soap worked its way through her eyelashes. Finishing the work of lathering her hair, she reached blindly over the side of the tub for the bucket of clean water, but her hand failed to find the handle. Cursing quietly, Elizabeth tried to rub the soap from her eyes with the backs of her hands.

The shock of the water flooding over her head jolted Elizabeth upright. Forcing her eyes open, she stared up in alarm.

Then her heart stopped.

"You are as beautiful as I remember."

Her mouth began to move, but her tongue failed to respond.

Ambrose looked down at the incredible beauty before him. She was rising like some raven-haired Venus from the watery recesses of his mind. The smooth glistening skin of her face, of her shoulders and arms, the curves of her full, round breasts threatening to emerge from the covering bath, the full inviting lips, and the large black eyes, mesmerizing and demanding in their power.

Elizabeth gathered her knees to her chest and, crossing her arms, tried to cover her exposed flesh. Her mouth felt dry, her throat constricted. Ambrose Macpherson stood motionless before the tub in his Highland gear. She blinked uncertainly, somehow expecting that he would disappear at any moment. Her mind was playing tricks on her. The figure looming above her couldn't be real. The dark, handsome face was just a figment of her overly active imagination. But the giant simply continued to stand there, his powerful frame relaxed, his stance wide and confident. This was the way she remembered him. The knee-high leather boots, the kilted hips, and the Macpherson tartan crossing his chest. His dust-covered gear brought back another memory. The memory of a fighter just leaving the tournament grounds. And then the intense blue eyes—yes, he was just as she remembered.

"This *must* be a dream," she finally whispered.

"It must be," Ambrose repeated, as he knelt beside the tub and took her shining face in his hands. Pulling her close to him, his eyes swept over her features and then locked onto her wet, inviting lips.

My God, he's real. The realization hit her as Ambrose's thumbs caressed her cheeks and his eyes roamed her face. Elizabeth's mind told her to panic, to pull away, to tell him to leave. But her heart wouldn't let her. She just couldn't. Since she had last seen him, there had been something growing in Elizabeth that she couldn't deny. Tonight, right now, there was nothing she wanted more than to be kissed by this man. She wanted to be touched, to feel as she'd felt once before.

Closing her eyes, she lost herself in the moment as he tipped her chin up, reaching for her lips. Hovering somewhere in the hazy cloud just above the subconscious, Elizabeth felt her protective shield, her armor peel away, only to be replaced by another garment. Soft, delicate, it was a fabric of sheer magic, it was a moment of release. Feeling his face descending to hers, Elizabeth knew she had no choice but to respond.

As Ambrose touched his lips to hers, he felt her hands reach up and caress his face. Their lips brushed gently in search of remembrance.

As if outside herself, Elizabeth felt her own body shudder as Ambrose's hands reached into the water and encircled her waist. His mouth was covering hers now, and she opened her lips willingly to his.

As his tongue delved into the depths of her mouth, a heat coursed through her body, scorching her with a sudden flame. Elizabeth's startled hands flew up to encircle his neck. Her lips molded to his and her body ached with the need to follow. A boldness took control of her as her hands traced his back, his neck.

Ambrose was oblivious to all that he'd come for. She had awakened in him a desire so fast, so unbridled, that he was in near danger of falling victim to his need. There was only one thing that mattered. He could see the passion in her eyes. She was in his arms, and she was willing. He wanted her. One moment Elizabeth was half submerged in the tub, the next she was standing in his embrace, his arms about her waist. Ambrose's mouth moved insistently against hers as a rush of wild desire directed his action. His hands roamed her back, cupping her buttocks and pressing her against his arousal. He smothered her gasp with his kiss as she pressed her length against his.

He was losing control. Suddenly conscious of it, Ambrose forced himself to consider whether he wanted to take her now or slow down and prolong the pleasure he so enjoyed giving. Decisively, he dragged his mouth away, leaning back unsteadily and savoring the moment. His heart pounding, Ambrose looked down at the incomparable splendor of her naked body. She was more beautiful than Venus. His hands slid over the symmetrical perfection of her breasts, and then moved without hesitation downward. His mouth recaptured hers, again muffling her gasp of pleasure.

The cool breeze from the window enveloped Elizabeth's wet skin, and she started, suddenly aware of the moment. As if emerging from some other world, Elizabeth caught Ambrose's hand with hers and stopped its journey of exploration. Then, pulling her mouth away and looking down at herself, a shock of full realization struck her.

Ambrose, sensing immediately her mood change, sighed deeply. Not again, he thought. He seemed to remember them being here before. He remembered a night long ago, of being fully aroused. He remembered her, on the verge of giving herself to him and then putting a halt to their lovemaking.

"I want you, Elizabeth," Ambrose began, but his words died away, his eyes lingering on her face. She had closed her eyes; she had turned her face away. She almost looked afraid.

Elizabeth tried to force down the lump in her throat.

Ambrose recalled the bruised and bloody face she'd displayed the last time he'd seen her. The warrior could guess the reason for her fear. His voice hardened as he asked the question. "Where is he?"

Elizabeth opened her eyes and looked at him questioningly. The burning sense of shame quickly replaced her desire to understand, though. Turning from him, she stepped away and picked up the robe. Slipping it across her shoulders, she wrapped herself in the clinging silk before looking back at Ambrose.

A cold blanket of anger quickly replaced what had been flames of desire in Ambrose's mood. The Highlander's eyes swept over the room. Seeing her sitting in the tub after discovering the ring, he hadn't taken even a moment to scan the area beyond the screen. He had been so pleasantly shocked that his attention had focused only on her. But now, looking around at the open trunks, at the piles of paintings interspersed with the jumbled masses of women's clothing, Ambrose saw the confirmation of his first suspicion.

"It was he! Wasn't it?"

"Who, Ambrose?" she whispered, all too aware of his eyes searching the room.

"Phillipe...the painter. He was at the Field of Cloth of Gold. He was the man you ran away with, wasn't he?"

Elizabeth stared at him in silence, startled by his questions.

Ambrose watched her expression. Her face, clouded in a frown, was more beautiful now than it had been when they first met. The years had healed the damage of the brutality she had faced in the Golden Vale outside Calais. What had once been a jagged gash along her cheekbone was now only a thin line of a scar. Her bruises had left no mark, and the complexion of her skin glowed in the lamplight. Oddly, she still wore her hair short, and the shiny, black locks were drying in soft waves around the black eyes that looked so intently into his own.

Unable to restrain himself, Ambrose reached up and smoothed the furrows that marred the wide, intelligent brow.

She stepped back from his touch.

Ambrose's expression hardened. He knew he should walk out and let her live the life she'd chosen. But his curiosity held him in place. The way she had softened in his arms, the way she had mirrored his own intense desire. He was certain she had been responding to *him*. Unless, of course, she was all too accustomed to such casual attentions. He cursed himself for the softness he'd shown. Who was it the drunkard passing by had called for, anyway?

"How did you find me?" Elizabeth asked. Her sense of survival now demanded answers to a hundred questions. Had it been Mary's indiscretion that had led him to her? Did this mean that now everyone knew of their whereabouts? When would Garnesche's men arrive?

"You talk as if you think I was looking for you." His words were cold, and they were intended to hurt.

And hurt they did. For the briefest of moments she had assumed his presence had to do with their short liaison years back. Elizabeth had thought he'd valued her and had found her after a long search. But obviously she'd been wrong.

"Let me change the question. May I ask what Your Lordship is doing in my humble quarters?" Elizabeth asked, moving farther back and putting a distance between them. "I don't recall inviting you here."

Ambrose let his eyes travel the length of her. The thin robe did little to cover the beautiful body beneath. He let his gaze linger suggestively on her breasts before moving lower. "If the way you greeted me was no invitation..."

"Don't!"

"Don't what, Elizabeth?" He took a step toward her. "Don't look at you? Don't desire you? Don't touch you? Don't hold you in my arms? Is that what you are asking of me?"

"Aye."

"Then don't look at me as you do. Don't melt in my arms at the first touch. Don't stand so provocatively near—"

"Stop!" she exploded.

Ambrose looked up in surprise. She stood facing him, challenging him with her glare. Her eyes blazed, her face flushed with her obvious anger. She looked ready to attack. This was the kind of physical fury a man might expect from another man, but not from a woman. And she was hardly at the point of hysteria. Ambrose knew from experience that this was where most women broke down, dissolving in tears, running away.

"I asked you a question, m'lord, that required only the simplest of responses." She felt the fire burning in her cheeks. "What happened between us just now was a mistake. I'd forgotten my place and your position. What happened should never have taken place."

He didn't believe her words, and he knew she didn't believe them, either.

"When last we met, I made a proposition." Ambrose studied her every move. "Was this man's offer so much better?"

"I try not to cry over what is past."

"Do you care for him?"

Elizabeth didn't know how much he knew about her life, but he clearly didn't know that Phillipe de Anjou and Elizabeth Boleyn were one and the same.

"Is that so difficult to answer?" he pressed.

Elizabeth peered at him from where she stood. She needed to get answers to her questions, but at the same time she didn't want to push him out prematurely. Was it attraction or need? She didn't know. But she was finding that the reality of having him in the room was a lot more difficult than dreaming of him nostalgically.

"I don't have to answer your questions. You, however, are still standing uninvited in this room, and I don't know why or how you come to be here."

Ambrose had come to convey a painter safely to Scotland. As he stood gazing on this strong-willed woman, the irony that she was the artist's mistress struck him. From what he had ascertained from Duke Giovanni, the warrior's understanding was that Phillipe was a shadow of a man, talented but frail. Here standing before him, however, was Elizabeth Boleyn, a woman of strength and beauty who seemed unable or unwilling to break out of the bondage of what Ambrose knew must be an unfulfilling relationship. Her response in his arms had been too immediate, too strong, too willing.

This was a challenge Ambrose would look forward to. Whatever the bond that held her to the painter, Ambrose set his mind to break it. As difficult as it would be to travel with the artist, Ambrose decided then and there that Elizabeth would accompany them during this journey, and before they reached Scotland, he would make her his own mistress. He had let her go once, but he wouldn't let that happen again. She presented a formidable challenge. One that he looked forward to immensely.

"Apparently you have no intention of answering my questions, either," Elizabeth concluded, taking the ring from the screen.

Ambrose watched the way she hung the leather thong around her neck, unconsciously laying the circle of emerald and gold gently between her breasts. The action, so innocent and yet so seductive, was a ritual that she'd apparently done a thousand times.

"Do you wear the ring against your skin like that when you make love to him?"

Elizabeth's eyes shot up.

"I find it hard to believe he's never asked you who gave it to you. What did you tell him? Have you told him about the passion we shared? Or does he even care how, to this day, you willingly accept my advances?"

Though Elizabeth felt her face burn with his words, she couldn't let him have the upper hand. He unnerved her; that was obvious. But it all had to end there. This was a conversation she dared not continue.

She turned her back and moved toward a pile of Mary's clothing. She needed to cover herself. Standing in the thin robe before him was too uncomfortable. Too vulnerable. She talked with her back to him.

"We haven't even seen one another for four years, and yet you ask so many questions. I don't ask you matters of your personal life. Why not do the same for me?"

"I see I've struck close to the truth. You're running away. Hiding."

She gave him a sidelong glance. "I am doing no such thing." She picked up the first dress that she came across. "Remembering your passionate nature, I need to get into something more proper. That's all."

Elizabeth moved quickly behind the wooden screen. Assured that she was hidden from his view, she tried momentarily to make some sense out of Mary's clothing. It had been four years since she had last worn a dress. But looking at the garment, she realized she'd never in her life worn the style of clothes her sister now wore. With a sigh she removed the robe and stepped into the gown.

When the chemise flew over the top of the screen, Elizabeth bolted upright.

"If you're truly concerned about my unbridled passion, you'd do well to put on an undergarment first. There's no telling what I'll do if you step back over here dressed only in that gown."

Elizabeth looked down at herself. Oh, my God, she thought. The neckline of the crimson colored gown draped below her breasts. She was completely exposed. Hurriedly, she pulled the chemise over her head, working the garment under the dress. "You are certainly quite knowledgeable about women's clothing."

I've certainly had more than enough practice removing it, Ambrose answered silently. His eyes once again took in the room.

The painter had obviously gone out with Bardi. Ambrose knew other men like this Phillipe. It was typical that he would leave his beautiful mistress behind. Men like him were afraid of the competition. Afraid they wouldn't measure up among other men. Well, Phillipe de Anjou was about to face the toughest competition of his life.

Struggling to subdue the willfully revealing lines of the dress, Elizabeth again considered her guest, searching for a clue to explain Ambrose's presence here. Moving from behind the dividing screen, she brightened with an idea. "You must be in the service of the Baron of Roxburgh."

Ambrose scowled at her. "Who?" Grudgingly, he was beginning to understand why the painter wouldn't take her out. She was simply too damned beautiful.

"The Baron of Roxburgh."

"Never heard of him." Ambrose moved to her side. He reached up and pulled at the chemise that covered the skin from her breasts to her collarbone. She slapped his hand away.

"Come, now, Scotland isn't that large a country," she scoffed, letting him turn her around and gasping for breath as he yanked tight the ties on the back of the dress. "The place has only six sheep and a dozen lairds to watch them, from what I hear. You must know him."

"I serve no one but the King of Scotland and the Regency Council that acts in his name. But your perception of Scotland is a bit off the mark." His voice was low and husky.

She turned and faced him. This was the proud and noble Scot speaking. "Is it?"

"Aye," Ambrose said with a drawl. "Scotland is a place like none you've ever seen. How can I describe the look of the storm tumbling across the moor? Or the torrents of a foaming Highland stream rushing through the deep green of the glen. I'm telling you, from the rolling river valleys of the Lowlands to the pine forests of the north to the wild, mountain peaks of the Outer Hebrides, it is a place that catches hold of your heart, your very soul. And once it has you, lass, it never lets go. It is a part of you, as you are a part of it."

Elizabeth paused and looked at him pensively. She hadn't expected this outpouring of emotion over his homeland. "It sounds lovely."

"It is lovely." Ambrose paused, his blue eyes intent upon her. "Like you."

She stepped back. He was charming her. Again. She felt herself melting inside. It was the same feeling. After all this time. When she answered, she could hear the slight tremor in her voice. "I suppose my knowledge of your home *is* a bit incomplete. Obviously Scotland is more than just sheep."

"Aye," he responded, his eyes piercing hers. "There are two cows, as well, wandering somewhere in the Highlands."

He watched as the dance of her smile reached her eyes. Her beautiful black eyes.

"Mama?" The child's voice called out uncertainly from the darkness beyond the dividing screen.

Elizabeth looked quickly into the surprised face of the Scot and held her finger to her lips. Without another word, she disappeared around the screen.

Ambrose, caught off guard by the child's voice, listened uncertainly to the murmuring voices for a moment.

A child. He should have known. She sounded like a small one. Of course! What else could have driven a woman like Elizabeth back to the painter? When she came to his tent at the Field of Cloth of Gold, he wondered, was she already carrying the child?

It took only a few moments for Elizabeth to settle little Jaime down once again. Casting anxious glances over her shoulder, she thought gratefully that it was a blessing Ambrose Macpherson wasn't in the service of this Baron of Roxburgh. It would be far too difficult for her to travel with him and keep up her disguise. He would probably see through it, in fact, and that would ruin everything.

But she could feel her heartbeat race at the very thought of being near him. No, she thought. Put it out of your mind. You must go to

Scotland. You must paint. Phillipe de Anjou is expected, and Phillipe de Anjou must comply.

Hearing the steady breathing of the little girl, Elizabeth pushed her hair back away from her eyes and quietly crossed the large room. Smoothing the fine dress over her slender hips, she stepped past the dividing screen into the light.

"I'm sorry, m'lord. But you'll have to..." She stopped.

Ambrose Macpherson was gone.

The young maid's jaw dropped. She stood stock-still, the stack of dresses that she had been carrying scattered around her feet.

Elizabeth, hearing the footsteps, turned briskly from the window. She had opened the shutters and was looking outside for the Highlander who had been standing in her apartment only moments before.

"I can't see anyone leaving the house," Elizabeth murmured, almost to herself. "Katrina, did you pass anyone coming up the stairs?"

The young woman continued to stare with her mouth open.

"What's wrong?" Elizabeth moved toward the young maid and grabbed hold of her two hands. "Have you seen a ghost? Has something happened?"

Katrina shook her head from side to side.

Elizabeth followed the woman's gaze. She was looking at her. At her dress. "You've never seen me in a dress, have you?"

The woman continued to shake her head. "No, I..."

All of Bardi's servants had been told the truth of Elizabeth's sex. After all, from the very beginning, it was clear that it would be very difficult to live under the same roof and not share the truth. But there had never been any question of their loyalty. "I look foolish, don't I?"

"You look stunning, Signor Phi...signorina. You are like a dream." The young girl's eyes scanned the painter's face. "But your scar...it is gone...your face is beautiful."

Elizabeth smiled. "Can I tell you something?"

Katrina crossed her heart quickly.

"I paint my face. I redden the scar to accent it. I darken under my eyes to look older."

The woman's eyes widened in awe once again.

Elizabeth shook her head in amusement. She had definitely made an impression on the young woman. "Katrina, did you see anyone leaving when you came up?"

"No one, signorina."

"Don't start calling me that. This dress hasn't changed who I am. Have you been downstairs? Did anyone come to the door?"

"No one, signorin—I mean, Signor Phillipe."

"Are you certain of that?" Elizabeth asked, her perplexity showing in her face.

"You know the porter, signor. He guards that door with his life when Signor and Signora Bardi are not here."

Baffled, Elizabeth turned and strode back to the window. The street was empty. Where had he come from? Where had he gone?

Had she conjured this man?

Elizabeth glanced about the room wildly for some trace, some sign, that Ambrose Macpherson had been standing here with her.

Nothing. She saw nothing.

Chapter 16

Joseph Bardi quivered under the blazing words being directed at him. The nobleman had not stopped his tirade since entering the room. *Offending, dishonoring* Don Giovanni, the Queen of Scotland, and, even more, the Baron of Roxburgh Joseph decided fearfully that he should consider himself as good as hung right now. He only hoped his end wouldn't be terribly painful.

"Please, m'lord," Bardi put in quickly, breaking into the other man's harangue. "We only meant to relieve Your Lordship of all unnecessary burdens. The last thing we intended to do was bring you rushing to Florence in the manner you've described."

"Taking a painter safely to Scotland is not a toilsome burden, so long as you know the safe route to travel." Ambrose looked at the nervous twitch in the merchant's face. He'd scared the man half to death. "I have given my word to the Duke of Nemours to see to the task myself. The regions to the north of us are rough and dangerous lands. My anger comes from you taking on the task so blindly, without any advice."

Bardi heard the giant's voice lose some of its edge. Perhaps the worst was over. But the Scottish lord still needed to be told of the rest. "M'lord, I am not certain if the duke made mention of the painter's companions. You see, he won't travel without them. And we were concerned that you might have objections to taking so many, and—"

"And you thought if he arrived in Scotland with his entourage, then the Queen wouldn't send him back and they could all stay?"

The merchant wrung his hands, nodding disconsolately. "The truth is, m'lord, he doesn't have many that accompany him. Just a young woman and a child. And perhaps a couple of servants. He is very attached to them."

"He is married?"

"Oh, no! No, it isn't that. You see—"

"I have no problem with that." Ambrose tried to suppress his smile. He had been correct in assuming that Elizabeth was only a mistress to the painter.

"And then there is the two of us," Bardi put in hopefully. "My wife and I. We hoped to be able to see them to safety and—"

"You don't trust them in my hands?"

"Oh, no! No, m'lord! That's not it at all. You see, I am a merchant, and I was hoping that perhaps I might meet and come to some bartering arrangement with wool merchants in Scotland. And as for my wife...well, she is very fond of the little child. M'lord, she could be...no, she *will* be a great help on the journey." The merchant watched a scowl darken the man's intimidating scar. "I know it all seems like so much we are asking. But I can assure Your Lordship, we are all well-seasoned travelers. We will cause you and your men no trouble. No inconvenience, I swear, m'lord."

He would take them; Ambrose knew he would. Elizabeth was definitely going, so he supposed he had to take them all. But so many people!

The warrior turned to the study's small open hearth and kicked at the embers. A small burst of sparks exploded as the fire flared up. What Ambrose really wanted to think about was how to break Elizabeth away from her lover. Well, first he had to size up his foe.

"Get the painter."

The merchant looked at him wide-eyed. It was way past midnight. The household had settled in their beds long ago. In fact, Joseph himself had been awakened by a terrified servant with the news that the Baron of Roxburgh was about to break down the front door.

"Didn't you hear me?"

"Now, m'lord? You want to speak to him now?"

"Now!" Ambrose repeated.

Seeing the man's hesitation, Ambrose took a step toward the door. "If you don't get him, I will." Was Elizabeth lying in the painter's arms? Ambrose found himself getting angry at the thought.

"No, no, that won't be necessary. I'll go after him myself." Bardi jumped quickly toward the closed door. This Scotsman certainly has a way of unnerving a person, he thought. He just hoped Elizabeth would be able to deal with him. She was often a lot better in difficult situations than he was. "Please make yourself comfortable. I'll awaken him and bring him to you, m'lord."

Ambrose watched the man's hasty retreat, then turned his attention toward the darkened inner room. The furnishings were well made here, too, but as he'd seen in the great hall and in the corridors, they were rendered practically invisible by the large number of portraits that dominated the walls and that drew the eyes upward in an impressive display. He strode to the closest one.

It was portrait of a child. A young child, still soft and round with ebony-colored hair. Against a harmonious background of light blues and grays, the face of the child stood out like a flower or a patch of sunlight in the dark room. Ambrose grabbed a candle from the desk and, lighting it in the fire, brought it closer to the painting. The eyes...the eyes of the child. He knew them. The large black eyes that stared back at him were Elizabeth's. Then he lowered the light and saw the brushes. The paintbrushes clutched in the tiny plump hand.

Elizabeth tripped over the tub and fell with a thud.

"Are you hurt?" Joseph whispered from behind the panel.

"Why, in God's name, must he come now?" Elizabeth hissed under her breath, standing up once again. She pulled the stockings up her legs. "Why couldn't he wait until morning?"

"Trust me, I tried. But he's a bear, Elizabeth. I'm sure the Baron of Roxburgh is one powerful and difficult man. When he wants something, he wants it *now*."

"I'm trying to sleep, if you don't mind," Mary called out, her complaint answered by a hush from the two standing in the dark.

"How am I going to paint my face?" Elizabeth asked softly. "I don't want to light a candle and awaken Jaime."

"You don't have to," Joseph whispered. "It's fairly dark in the study. Let's just go down and agree to whatever he says. Then we can send him on his way. I think I've talked him into taking all of us with him."

"Why do we have to go with him, anyway?" Elizabeth pulled the loose shirt over her head. "We could travel on our own."

"No, no, Elizabeth! Please don't talk that way. I thought he was going to hand me over to the Medici's executioners for suggesting that. That is out of question. We'll have to go with him. There is no other way."

Elizabeth cursed under her breath as she stepped around the wooden screen. "Do I look convincing?"

"Absolutely. Let's go and get it done with."

The Baron of Roxburgh was sitting in a straight-backed wooden chair in a dark corner of Joseph's study. His face was hidden in shadow, but Elizabeth could see from the man's long, muscular legs and broad chest that he must be an imposing figure. His high boots shone in the fading firelight, one leg crossed over the other. The doublet that covered his white shirt and hosiery was made of well-tailored black satin, and richly appointed with strips of black velvet. The glint of the jeweled broach clasping the man's dark tartan caught Elizabeth's attention. The size of the diamonds and rubies, even from a distance, was impressive. As he turned slightly in his chair, the light picked up the raised metalwork of the broach. A rampant cat sitting above a shield that had a ship depicted on it. Elizabeth felt a sudden stir at the sight. She didn't know how, but she knew the design.

This was a side of Scotland that Elizabeth had not experienced before. The image of wealth and power that was being displayed here was far different from the power that Ambrose exhibited. While Ambrose was rough-hewn, strong, and true, he always wore the gear of the Highland warrior he was. With the exception of the tartan, this man was dressed in fashion of the day. He had the look of the perfect European courtier.

"M'lord, I'd like to intro—"

"Go!" the baron commanded abruptly, cutting Joseph off. "And shut the door."

Elizabeth and Joseph exchanged a quick look, and then the merchant bowed and backed out the door.

Elizabeth couldn't see the man's face, but his voice carried the weight of authority. This was clearly a man who meant to be obeyed, but the painter felt her temper flaring at the rough treatment of her friend in his own study. If this was a sampling of what they would have to put up with on their journey, then she would have to put this nobleman in his place now.

"M'lord, I am not certain if anyone has brought this to your attention, but this is Joseph Bardi's villa. As the rules of etiquette provide, it is discourteous to throw a man out of his own study."

The baron's boot slammed to the floor. "Into the light, you."

"I believe you came here to speak with me." Elizabeth tried to deepen her voice. "Not to order me and my friend about."

"I asked to see the painter."

Elizabeth clenched her hands into fists. Again. So many times during the past four years, people had only seen the frail build in their first encounter with her, and nothing else. And so many times, she had to give her sermon, as Pico called it, and lose her temper before they were convinced.

"I am the painter."

He disregarded what she said. "Do as you are told. Get the painter."

Angrily, she took a step closer to the man, her clenched jaw grinding. "Before we get started on this journey to your homeland, I have to make one thing clear. If you have any desire to arrive in one piece, then you'd better change that disdainful tone of yours. Now, *you* demanded to see me at this god awful hour of the night. So here I am. What is it you want?"

"In one piece?" Ambrose studied her anger. Elizabeth's face was now shining in the light of the candle. "That sounds like a threat."

"Take it as you wish."

"You are too puny for such swaggering."

"I have been known to split a man's head with my words and twist his body into a crawling, earthbound snake with my brush."

"And you think this strikes fear?"

Her hands were tight fists at her sides.

"Push all you want. But be aware the next time you walk inside some chapel or cathedral. As you stand looking up, admiring the scene as so many others do, don't be surprised when you see your own face looking back at you. In fact, everyone will see your features gracing the face of a devil." Elizabeth showed no sign of mirth. "And you can be assured, it will be a very lowly and very ugly devil."

Elizabeth waited for a response. But there was silence. An eerie, awkward silence.

"You *are* the painter."

Elizabeth watched him straighten in the chair. She wished she could see his face. "I am Phillipe de Anjou." As often as she'd said it before, the words still felt odd leaving her mouth. She saw him stand up, and her blood ran cold. Though his face was still shadowed in the darkness of the room, she knew. From his full height, from the way he stood. And then she glimpsed the colors of his tartan.

Not being able to control the gasp that escaped her lips, Elizabeth turned and ran for the door. But he was there before her, blocking her exit. She turned again and tried to run to one of the shuttered windows, but he grabbed her roughly from behind and swung her around to face him.

Elizabeth felt the pressure of his strong fingers crushing her arms. She wouldn't scream or complain. She had no choice but to make him understand. She looked up into his eyes. They were cold, angry. Nothing like what she had seen in the past.

"Talk."

Elizabeth tried to shrug off his hands, but he wouldn't let go. Suddenly the icy coldness of panic coursed through her. This wasn't the gentle and caring nobleman she had met before. This man was more judge and executioner, demanding to hear her final testimony. For all these years she had tried never to be overly concerned about the possible consequences of her life—of her work—in the studio. But now the truth, the ugly truth, was about to catch up to her. The Baron of Roxburgh, Ambrose Macpherson, was a close friend to Giovanni de Medici. If he spoke out, if he revealed her secret, she would be hung and then burned by the leaders of the Florentine guild. For, as a woman, she had lied and betrayed all the artists in the profession. She would be found guilty. She was a woman working as a man. This was a crime far worse than any they could ever pardon.

"What are you planning to do?" she asked quietly. She was working hard to hide the shiver that raced through her body.

Ambrose had to fight the urge to pull her into his arms and comfort her. That would have been so easy to do. She was afraid. Afraid of him, he could tell.

But he was angry. He had been taken for a fool by a mere woman. He'd never suspected it. She had not given even the smallest hint that Phillipe and she were one and the same. And then he'd seen the child's portrait. The softness, the love shown in the picture—this had disturbed him. For the few moments before she'd come down, he'd been confused. And then the painter had walked into the study. Not the man he'd been ready to challenge, but Elizabeth.

And now he didn't know what his next step should be.

Elizabeth lowered her eyes from his intense blue gaze and stared at his broach. She couldn't take this long silence. He hadn't answered her. He would surely hand her over. She would never say good-bye to Jaime.

"Start explaining."

"Isn't it all too obvious?" she whispered. "And does it really matter? Is there anything I could say that would change your mind?"

"You think my mind is made up."

She looked down at the rough hold of his fingers on her arms.

"Isn't it?" she asked. "If I were to pour out my soul and speak the truth, would you give me a chance? Or are you just going to hand me over to be hung?"

He eased the pressure of his grip. "I am giving you a few moments to present your case. But for a change, I need to hear the truth. And only the truth," Ambrose backed her to a chair and pushed her into it. "Start from beginning, from the Field of Cloth of Gold."

Elizabeth looked up from where she sat. He towered over her. Once again his face was a dark silhouette of shadows and dying firelight. She wondered for a moment what "truth" he wanted to hear. Sitting there in the darkened room, she dared not even hope that this meant he intended to give her a chance.

"Silence won't work to reprieve your present situation," Ambrose growled ominously. "Do I have to remind you what your punishment would be for lying, for pretending to be what you are not, for delving into the secrets that your guild brothers protect so religiously? Do you know what these Florentines would do to you? To start, they would proclaim you evil—an abomination. Do you want me to just give you over to them?"

She looked down and shook her head.

"Then speak. I need to know when and for what reason you came up with this perverse idea."

"But...it is not perverse." She could no longer hold back her tongue. "I am not evil. I have never acted in any way that might bring indignity to anyone. If, as I have pretended, I really were a man, I would continue to be praised...rewarded...for my talent and my hard work. But now, being discovered, I am suddenly a demon. I am some unnatural denizen of hell simply because I have a God-given talent that I have chosen to employ. Simply because I needed to work to feed my family."

Ambrose watched her blazing face, her power. It was obvious that she believed every word she spoke. "But you had a family. You had a place in society, a home. Why did you leave it?"

Elizabeth paused. She couldn't tell him everything. There was nothing that told her she should trust him. No, Elizabeth thought, there was no reason to trust him. After all, even if she had not been totally forthright, she was certainly not alone. Look at him. When he'd arrived in her bedchamber earlier, he had not been completely candid. The Baron of Roxburgh, indeed.

"I'm having a hard time believing you, Elizabeth, because you are saying so little." Ambrose watched as her face reflected some inner struggle. Finally she peered through the darkness and shrugged her shoulders.

"I had to run away from my father."

"Sir Thomas Boleyn?"

Elizabeth nodded slowly. "I don't believe he's ever considered me a true daughter. Not that it matters. But I had to get away."

Ambrose watched her shoulders drop in resignation.

"Why did you have to get away? I'm certain that your father's feelings for you were not an overnight revelation."

Elizabeth watched as he moved away and sat in a chair by the desk. He was keeping a distance between them.

"It's true," she whispered, shuddering at the memory of all that had taken place that day. "But he'd never in the past tried to...dispose of me the way he was planning to the night before I ran."

"Dispose of you?"

"He was sending me to his master's bed," Elizabeth said, trying to keep the bitterness out of her voice. She watched as his eyes shot up to hers. "The King of England happened to take a fancy to me the last day of the tournament, so the disgusting, blackguard summoned my father. Henry wanted me for his bed."

Ambrose thought back to the day. To how beautiful she looked in the grandstands. To the attention he'd paid to her after accepting from Francis the English king's lost wager. His face darkened.

"Aye, I was ordered to go. By my own kin."

"The bastard!" Ambrose cursed under his breath. The joust. He hadn't known who Elizabeth was when he spoke to her after the joust. But it was so typical of King Henry's viciousness. No Scot would make public advances to the daughter of one his men without someone paying the price. Henry couldn't punish Ambrose for his attentions to Elizabeth. And Boleyn had his uses. But the daughter, beautiful as she was, would make a pretty plaything. And she would be made to suffer for Ambrose's advances—before he discarded her.

"Did you go?" He asked the question through clenched teeth. Elizabeth was not the one to blame—he was.

"No. I would have died before going to him." Elizabeth gazed at the single candle sitting on the worktable. A moth fluttered about the light. "I told my father that."

"Was he the one who beat you?"

"Aye. Both times." She turned her gaze back to him. "As you can imagine, he wasn't at all pleased with my answer. That was when I knew I had to leave his house. He provided for me in Paris. As long as I stayed in his household, I belonged to him. Like a dog or a sword or a piece of furniture. He could trade me, barter my body." Her eyes flashed with anger. "I would have preferred death to such a life. I value myself more than to allow anyone to use me as he planned."

Mixed feelings for this woman pounded at Ambrose's brain. He couldn't tell what was worse, the guilt that was nagging his conscience that something he had done may have set all this in motion or the simple concern that was tugging at his insides. He shook his head. "Tell me, lass. How did I fit into your plans? Why did you come to me that night?"

Elizabeth looked down at her hands. She wasn't willing to admit to him the truth about her plan to lose her virtue. "You are a hero. Handsome, chivalrous, sensual. And you showed interest in me. Would you believe if I told you that...well, curiosity was the primary reason?"

"Nay." Ambrose suppressed his smile. "But if I did believe you, then I suppose I have to assume it was disappointment that drove you out." He watched a slow smile tugging at her lips.

"Quite to the contrary, m'lord." She could feel the heat of his gaze on her face. "Truthfully...I got scared. Scared of myself and my reaction to you. It was all so much at once. I knew I had to leave France, my family, everything I ever held dear. I couldn't accept any more complications in my life."

"You didn't have to run. I remember offering you protection."

You offered me your bed, she thought.

"It would have been wrong to impose myself on you or on anyone. I knew that I could take care of myself. I knew I had a talent," Elizabeth continued. "I had already sold some of my paintings, so I knew I could do it. It was my fate, my destiny to live by my own means, by my talent. I could feel it. That was my moment to try. If I didn't try it then, my chance would be gone forever."

Ambrose watched her entwined fingers on her lap. She was good. In fact, she was more than good. She was an exceptionally talented artist. From what he'd seen of her paintings at Giovanni de Medici's palace, from what he'd seen in this villa tonight, and from the one piece that he had himself, Ambrose knew without question that Elizabeth Boleyn was indeed a gifted artist.

He knew he couldn't expose the truth. After all, he himself was more responsible for the situation she was in today than anyone else. Henry had just wanted to use her and even a score—Ambrose understood the politics of court life. But could he take her to Scotland and present her to the queen? No, of course he couldn't. The men in Florence might be completely blind to a beautiful woman, but Ambrose knew that her ruse would never work in Scotland. She would be discovered before she stepped ten paces on Scottish soil. Perhaps even before—Gavin Kerr would probably spot her as a fake. Perhaps the best thing for him to do was simply to walk away and ask Giovanni for a different artist. He could tell the duke that he'd never seen this Phillipe fellow. She had hidden her identity for this long, she could continue indefinitely. Perhaps that was the best answer.

"Please take me with you."

Ambrose started at the request. He wondered, briefly, what she was asking. The possibility of her taking his offer, even after four years, still raised a stirring in him. And that was damn startling, considering.

"Please take me to Scotland. I won't disappoint you. I give you my word." The hesitation Elizabeth had seen in the nobleman in the past few moments had nearly unnerved her. She feared the silent argument that the man was having with himself. She couldn't let Ambrose Macpherson leave them behind. She *had* to talk him into taking them to his queen. There wasn't much time left. "I will agree to whatever conditions you set."

Ambrose watched her in silence. This was fear speaking. He had been involved with enough negotiations to know when desperation and fear had taken over. Elizabeth wasn't even trying to cover her fear. She was willing to throw herself into his bed in order to save her pretty neck. As much as the idea of having this woman for a short while appealed to him, this wasn't the way he wanted it to happen.

"I know your queen has been waiting for a long time for a painter of some quality. Michelangelo told me that she had asked him to go to Scotland ten years ago to paint the royal portrait. But he'd been in the middle of a massive sculpting project for Pope Julius's memorial and used that as an excuse not to go. With the terrible troubles that Scotland had in that time, he said no painter he knew was willing to travel there." Elizabeth continued to talk fast. She needed to win him over. "The stories of the war between England and Scotland were dreadful—I remember when Flodden happened and you lost your king. Michelangelo said he even heard your queen blaming him for the death of her husband. It was rumored that she said if he had gone to paint them in the summer of 1513, the king might not have gone to war. The maestro says he heard she's become obsessed with the idea. I can remedy that."

Ambrose listened quietly to her words. He was certainly glad that he'd not spoken earlier. He would have had to swallow his words. She wasn't giving herself to him. She wanted him to help her with her masquerade. And everybody knew of Queen Margaret's superstitious ideas. They were no secret. She was more superstitious than the Florentines, and they were the most credulous people in Europe.

But more importantly, Ambrose didn't believe a word Elizabeth said about why she wanted to go. There was something else.

"Please, no one needs to know the truth. I can do the job to your queen's satisfaction." Elizabeth wished he would say something. "It will only be for a short while. I promise not to be a nuisance, and I will stay out of your way. Please, give me the chance and let me try."

Ambrose had to admit this was much more to his liking. If she were throwing herself at him, he'd pass on the opportunity. But this had promise. It presented the possibility of challenge, of the charms of seduction.

"Nay, lass. She'll have my head on a pike over Stirling Castle if she finds out I've brought a woman to paint the royal family."

"She doesn't need to find out! She *won't* find out!"

Ambrose continued as if he hadn't heard her. "Did I hear you mention something about being agreeable to my conditions?" He stood and walked to the fireplace. Leaning his broad back against it, he watched her confused expression.

"It all depends on what they are, m'lord." Elizabeth said, suddenly fearful of what was hidden in his words.

"The first condition of taking you with me is that you accept these terms."

"Are they many?"

"Possibly only a few." He crossed his arms. "It all depends on my mood during the journey."

"How could you expect me to accept them when I don't know what they are?" Elizabeth protested weakly.

"I am certain if I approached Don Giovanni with—"

"Agreed," Elizabeth broke in. "I'll accept your conditions so long as you accept one of mine."

Ambrose frowned at her. "You are in no position to bargain."

"I am in the position to ask."

"What is it?" he ordered. "What is your request?"

Elizabeth stood as well and pushed the chair aside. "My family goes with me. To Scotland."

"Your family is in England. I'll not go there to get them."

"You don't have to." She leaned against the desk and stretched her legs.

Ambrose watched her shapely legs showing attractively through the thin hose. These Florentines are blind, he thought.

"Mary and Jaime are with me here. I am responsible for them, so they have to go with us."

"Mary is your sister," Ambrose remembered. "She disappeared when you did."

"You searched me out!" Elizabeth stated with surprise in her voice. The idea that this nobleman might have tried to find out about her whereabouts after they separated four years ago had never occurred to her.

Ambrose ignored her comment. "Your sister, as I recall, was trouble in the making. This is a long journey to Scotland. She'll be disturbing my men. I know already I don't like it. And this Jaime, who is she?"

Elizabeth paused. She couldn't go without them. How could she leave Mary and little Jaime behind? That was no option. And the way the Highlander spoke, he seemed somehow willing to take her and only her. Ambrose Macpherson wouldn't understand the bond that connected the three of them. Unless...

"The child..."

"Your daughter."

Elizabeth stared.

"I won't leave her behind. I have to take her."

Ambrose watched her face. "How old is she?"

"Merely three."

Ambrose pointed at the painting on the wall. "Is that her?"

Elizabeth nodded in silence.

"She looks like you." His eyes traveled from the portrait of the child to the face of the woman standing in the study. "Who is the father?"

Her eyes shot up to meet his. She had not expected him to ask. "He is not around."

"Who is the father?" he repeated the question.

"Why do you ask?" she protested. She had not expected to have to lie like this. Now, already, she was afraid. Afraid of getting caught in her own web of lies.

"One of the conditions," Ambrose said shortly, "is that you answer my questions."

"If I answer, does that mean that you'll take us with you?"

"I'll tell you once I have the answer."

It was impossible to reason with the man. Joseph was right—Ambrose Macpherson was used to having things his way and only his way. "He is dead. It doesn't matter who he was. He's dead."

Ambrose could hear that there was no regret in her voice. Had this man simply been another "curiosity" for Elizabeth Boleyn? As Ambrose himself had been? But there was a difference. She had been interested enough in this other man to stay and share her passion. After all, she had borne his child. The man was dead, but Ambrose still felt a gnawing pang of envy. It didn't make sense, but he did nonetheless.

"What was his name?"

Elizabeth panicked. What happened if she picked a name that he knew? She wished he would stop his questioning. "His name..."

"What was it? And how did you two meet?" Ambrose was becoming less patient with his string of unanswered questions. "How did he die?"

She took a deep breath and resigned herself to going through with it. "Phillipe de Anjou." Seeing the surprised look on Ambrose's face, she felt encouraged and continued. "He was an artist. A French artist I knew in Paris. When I ran from Calais, we met in Paris, and he brought me here. He died when we stopped in Milan, so I took over his name and his work." Elizabeth breathed a sigh of relief. "That's it. All of it."

"How did he die?"

"How?" she repeated. How the devil would I know, she cursed inwardly.

"Was he poisoned? Did someone stab him? Did he fall off a wagon? There are usually reasons for a young man dying."

"Oh!" she acknowledged. "But...but he wasn't young. He was old. He died of old age...and a fever."

"You slept with a rickety old man and gave him a child?" Ambrose nearly smiled openly. Now he understood her willingness in his arms.

"You have no right to talk about him so flippantly." Elizabeth looked away. "Phillipe was a good man, and he cared a great deal for us. I remember him fondly, and I cherish his memory. I would appreciate it if you would stop your mockery of something you don't understand."

Ambrose studied her downturned face. He couldn't see her expression. But from the small shudder of her shoulders, he guessed she was upset, perhaps even crying. Hell, he might as well take her and the whole herd of them. So what if she was discovered? If she was unmasked in Scotland, she'd have a better chance of surviving it there than she would in Florence.

"You are going with me."

"You mean we're all going, m'lord." She turned her gaze back at him, wiping her eyes with the backs of her hands.

Ambrose could tell that she looked flushed. "Your daughter and you."

"My sister, my daughter, and I."

"Nay. Your sister is trouble."

Elizabeth faced him head-on. "I need her for my façade. Everyone thinks Jaime is hers. It's important."

"Where we are going, it won't matter. Be ready, we'll be leaving Florence in a week."

She shook her head in argument. "I cannot come up with new charade in such a short time. Please, m'lord, I'll...I'll offer you a deal."

"You have nothing to offer," Ambrose reminded her.

"Conditions?" She watched his expression.

"Go on."

"I'll abide by your conditions—any and all that you state—until we reach Scotland. And in return you'll take my family and the Bardis."

He looked at her incredulously. "A moment ago it was your daughter and your sister. Now you've added your friends. I am starting to feel that with every passing moment, I'm losing a larger share of this bargain."

"Then accept." She said matter-of-factly.

Ambrose appraised his opponent.

"Aye. With conditions."

Chapter 17

"We missed the damn boat!"

"I know! We all heard you!" Elizabeth wasn't about to be publicly humiliated by this man. She returned Ambrose's glare without so much as a blink. "Everyone in Pisa heard you!"

Standing on the dock beside the empty slip, Elizabeth looked back and saw her fearful traveling companions were keeping a safe distance away from the angry nobleman. It had been Mary once again, disappearing at the last moment for no apparent reason. She had no sense of the value of time or of schedules. But Elizabeth wasn't going to make excuses for her or anyone else. She saw no need to explain. Certainly not to the arrogant Lord Macpherson.

She had not seen him since they'd met in Joseph's study in Florence. His directions, as he'd departed that night, had been to be ready in a week and meet him in Pisa. But he had been courteous and offered to send his men to assist the group in bringing their belongings to the port city near the mouth of the Arno.

And she'd been daft and accepted his offer.

His men had indeed arrived this morning. But they were not there to help. They had arrived with specific orders from their master. Mary couldn't take her three chests full of clothes. Joseph couldn't bring his merchandise. Elizabeth couldn't bring in her paintings. They were to travel light, with only enough to be carried on horseback. Those had been Ambrose Macpherson's directions.

And Elizabeth had disobeyed his orders. Every one of them. But he didn't know. Not yet.

It still amazed her, even hurt a bit, to realize how wrong she could have been about him. She had been so fooled by the façade of concern, by the sensual and passionate approach this man so easily used to overwhelm her. But that was before she'd seen the real man. She felt the tips of her ears burning at the very thought of the weakness he perceived within her—at the thought that she'd been so blind to the truth beneath his practiced technique. Ambrose

Macpherson, the Baron of Roxburgh, was a pigheaded, aggravating man who demanded things be done his way. Joseph had been right about him from the beginning.

"We missed the damn boat!"

Elizabeth turned at the sound of the roar from the far end of the dock and watched as a second Scot came storming toward them. The wind was whipping the man's black hair about his face, so she couldn't see his expression, but his size, she had to admit, was more than intimidating. Ambrose was a giant, but this one looked half a head taller.

"I can see you Highlanders are very limited in your use of words," she whispered loudly enough for Ambrose to hear.

"Say that when he's closer, and he'll break you in half." Ambrose responded shortly. "Gavin Kerr's from the Borders—a Lowlander—and he thinks Highlanders are barbarians—"

"And he'd be correct, of course!" she broke in.

"This is a long journey and you can be certain that I'll do my best to live up to that reputation."

She cringed at his words.

Ambrose gazed down and studied Elizabeth's face as his bearlike friend paused to look at the group of tardy travelers cowering near their baggage. She was extremely good at darkening her fair young skin under the masking pigments. But she still looked good. Damn good.

"Does he know the truth?" she whispered, not taking her eyes from the angry black-haired warrior. "The truth about me?"

"What truth?" Ambrose snapped. "Does anyone know the truth about you? I don't know what the truth is."

Elizabeth's temper flared. "I have answered every question you've asked. I understand neither your harsh words nor your sour mood." Her voice softened. "Why can't you just leave the past behind? Why can't we just be on our way?"

Ambrose looked straight out across the diverse collection of ships, galleys, and barges crowding the wide, muddy river that would carry them out to the Ligurian Sea and into the Mediterranean. He was still upset, and he was having difficulty controlling his temper. This was a first for him.

"Gavin Kerr has no reason to think you're anything other than what you say."

Elizabeth had chosen not to reveal her past liaison with Ambrose Macpherson to the Bardis, and she had not told them that the nobleman knew she was a woman, either. This was a complication she didn't want them to worry about. But she had to tell Mary the truth. After all, her sister was still under the assumption that Elizabeth had surrendered her maidenhood to this Highlander.

"Gavin is a trusting man. I haven't told him of your inventtiveness."

"Thank you," she whispered.

Ambrose turned to her with wonder. He had not expected those simple words. Quickly regaining his frown, he growled at the small painter. "Which means he'd as soon kill you as look at you."

"Oh!"

"Is this the goddamn painter that has left us sitting on our arses for the past two days?"

"Aye, Gavin. This is Phillipe de Anjou."

"What are you, a dwarf?" he rumbled, glowering down at Elizabeth.

Elizabeth drew in a deep breath and glared back. "There's nothing wrong with my size. But the baron tells me you got to be the size you are by eating stolen English cattle."

Gavin's eyebrows shot up, and he glanced quickly at Ambrose. "Oh, he did?"

"Aye," she continued quickly. "He says you've even been known to stop and roast the carcasses before devouring them...occasionally."

Elizabeth watched as the corner of the Border dweller's mouth started to turn up. He was a huge man, as broad and as tall as Michelangelo's statues of Hercules. His face, as fierce as his expression was, had the handsome, chiseled features of the marble gods. What he lacked was the hint of humor that danced just behind the blue eyes of his Highland friend Ambrose Macpherson. Nor had he the easy smile. He hadn't the fluid confidence of his stance, either.

Nor, she decided, could she imagine him holding any woman the way Ambrose had held her.

"Tell me," she asked, pressing her advantage. "Is it worth your while sitting on your arses waiting for good meat?"

"Aye, lad," the Lowlander conceded thoughtfully. "Particularly when it's stolen meat."

"Then, Gavin Kerr, remember this. You've just stolen me and my friends from the Medicis, and when your queen rewards you for what you've brought her, you'll see that the wait was worth your while."

A broad grin broke across the warrior's face, and with an abrupt movement, Gavin clapped Elizabeth hard on the back of her shoulder, launching her a half step forward.

"Well, Ambrose. This lad will be all right, I'm wagering. Though you are a scrawny thing, Phillipe."

Ambrose gave her a once over look. But his face showed nothing of what he was thinking. He knew what was beneath.

"Perhaps we can fatten you up a bit during this journey. Make you strong. Like a man," Gavin boomed.

"He is a painter," Ambrose said under his breath. "He is fine as he is."

Gavin ignored his friend's remark. "I haven't seen any of your paintings. Though Ambrose tells me you've quite a talent."

"Has he?" Elizabeth remarked with surprise, casting an eye on the nobleman.

"Aye, though—nothing against you—I doubt he knows much about it," Gavin rumbled conspiratorially. "He is only a Highlander, after all."

Elizabeth watched as the two exchanged a glare. She had a strong suspicion that this bantering was constant between these two men.

"Well, Gavin," Ambrose broke in. "Did you find us another ship? Or are we just going to sit around here for a week or so longer?"

"As a matter of fact, you see the bow of that galley about eight quays in that direction?" Gavin pointed at the ship. "They sail for Marseilles with the morning tide, and I was able to secure us a berth. Though it wasn't easy. The captain wasn't very excited about having two dozen Scottish warriors along."

"That's no surprise," Ambrose said under his breath.

Gavin looked at his friend. "And I didn't mention your name."

"Good."

Elizabeth looked from one man to the other. "Is there something that you two would like to tell me before we get any farther along on this journey?"

"Nay," the two men answered in unison.

Without another word, the Scots turned their backs on her and walked away, and Elizabeth stood, her hands at her side, looking after them as they moved together down the dock.

Elizabeth cringed as the two sailors dropped Mary's trunk into the hold of the galley. The sun was low over the western waters that extended beyond the wide mouth of the Arno, and though the troop of Scots warriors were drinking noisily on the dock, she was determined to keep a close watch on things as their luggage was loaded aboard the merchant vessel.

She looked at her friend standing beside her. "Joseph, do you have any idea why the baron would want to hide his true identity from the captain of this ship?"

Joseph turned his back to the high gunwale and smiled at the painter. "Aye, I do."

Elizabeth waited patiently as the merchant looked up into the rigging at the two masts of the galley. She knew it was the kind of ship Joseph had traveled on many times in his search for markets. From what Joseph had just finished telling her, she now knew that the two-masted galley was the workhorse of Mediterranean sea trading, and its design had not changed for as long as anyone remembered. This ship had forty-eight oarsmen who would propel the shallow-hulled vessel forward regardless of the wind's direction.

"This is one of the first of its kind," Joseph said enthusiastically, pointing toward the stern of the vessel. "From what I hear, beneath the high deck back there, they have expanded the cabin space."

"My friend, the cabin size of this galley is not my worry right now," she said quietly. "I am more concerned about putting all of you in jeopardy. Joseph, I need to know what information you have about the Baron of Roxburgh."

Joseph peered at the animated group of sailors gathering not far from where Mary stood pouting in the sun. An uneasy feeling crept through him.

"Well, Joseph?" Elizabeth prodded, still waiting for the details but not hearing any. "Would you care to tell me what you know?"

"No."

"Please, Joseph," she said shortly. "If you are planning to act like those two pig-headed Scots, then I'll be taking my complaints to Erne."

Joseph breathed more easily as he spotted his wife moving purposefully toward Mary through the throng of people milling about among the stalls of fishermen and farmers that crowded the stone quays. He watched as she sent the seafarers on their way with a mere frown. Then her face brightened as she glanced up at the ship and saw him, and he answered her nod with a smile and a wave.

"Well, in that case, I'll tell you what I know. But you must keep it to yourself. I just cannot afford having hysterical women on my hands during this journey."

"Is it that bad?"

"Nay! Not at all. But you never know how some people will react to something they've assumed for a long while was only just gossipy word of mouth."

She hung on his every word. As Joseph looked over the crowds moving about the pier, she nearly snapped. "Please, Joseph! The suspense of this is getting the best of me. Tell me what you know."

Joseph looked away from her once again, but this time his eyes searched for Ambrose Macpherson. He had no desire to be caught speaking about the baron by the man himself.

"The first night when he came to us in Florence, I had no idea that the baron of Roxburgh and Ambrose Macpherson were one and the same man."

And that makes two of us, Elizabeth thought.

"But seeing his broach and colors of his tartan, I knew soon enough," Joseph continued. "I think that was when I became really frightened." The last words were spoken quietly, as if to no one but himself.

"At any rate, the stories go back some time and have to do with pirates in the seas west of England. Years back, as I remember, anyone who traveled the Irish Sea knew the names Macpherson and

Campbell and feared them. They were the fiercest pirates ever to navigate those waters."

"He's a pirate?" Elizabeth asked with great deal of hesitation. She quickly lowered her voice to a hush as she looked around. "We're traveling with a pirate?"

"Not Ambrose. His father," Joseph went on. "He even had license for it. King James of Scotland gave exclusive rights to his most courageous noblemen. Their job was to defend the Scottish waters and to bring in whatever revenue they could by raiding passing ships."

"They were thieves!"

"No, my dear. Even today this is considered a legitimate—even noble—profession, and the practice is continued by every king in Europe. English, Spaniards, French—they all do it. It is part of the shipping business. To trade in these dangerous waters, you have to protect your vessels and your merchandise. And the best way to do this is to be a pirate yourself. If you are not, then you'd better be prepared to pay large sums of gold and hope they will work on your side."

Elizabeth's eyes found Ambrose where he stood talking with the ship's captain on the stone quay. "Then he's one, too?"

"A pirate?" Joseph followed the direction of Elizabeth's gaze. "No one knows for sure. Alexander Macpherson eldest son, Alec, now leads the Macpherson clan and, the word is, being married to the Scottish king's sister, he finds little time to sail the high seas. That leaves Ambrose and the youngest brother, John. Both these men have lived on the sea from the time they were children. They both could take up the father's trade. But now, I find that Ambrose is now the Baron of Roxburgh, as well. And from what I hear, the baron is known to have more castles—and more gold in them— than any king in Europe. So for him to continue in the family piracy business is a bit unlikely, although there are a few of us that hope he would."

"You hope he would?" she asked, turning to him in surprise. "Why?"

"The mystery. The adventure." Joseph smiled. "Macphersons have long been heroes. They are part of history. They're a tradition. No one wants to see the legends disappear. What man wouldn't want to tell his children of sailing with the Macphersons across the open seas? And, like everyone else, sailors are intrigued with legends. Particularly living ones."

Elizabeth shuddered involuntarily as she gazed at Ambrose across the dock. Once again he wore his kilt and his tartan, but now a black cloak was fastened around his shoulders. A long sword hung from the leather belt. His blond hair fluttered loosely about his face in the gentle breeze. He was tall, powerful, free. He was the very image of what she would have thought a pirate might be.

Even more.

Chapter 18

The body lying in the bunk shook with silent tears.

Elizabeth stepped inside one of the darkened cabins and looked about her in alarm. She had just left the stern deck and her companions, going in search of her sister Mary. No one had even seen the young woman since they had stepped aboard the vessel hours earlier. The oily taper that lay propped up in a tin box gave off a smoky light and filled one side of the room with a dim haze. Elizabeth peered into the darkness and then spotted her.

Mary lay face down, wrapped in a rough, wool blanket. Even from where she stood, Elizabeth could see the young woman's small shoulders trembling with barely perceptible sobs that occasionally escaped her.

Elizabeth moved to the bunk and sat quietly on the edge. Her hands moved gently on her sister's shoulders, caressing her, trying to ease the pain the younger woman was feeling. Mary turned immediately and threw herself into the Elizabeth's arms.

Now, once again safe in Elizabeth's familiar embrace, she wept openly. Elizabeth listened, unable to console her with anything more than the soft touch and the gentle rocking motion that had been part of them since childhood.

"I've never hated myself as I do now," Mary whispered bitterly, clutching her sister as tight as she could. "My name is a demon that precedes me. I am not a human being, but a disease. One to be avoided. To be cast off and shunned."

Elizabeth pulled her sister's face away from her shoulder and gazed into her tearful eyes.

"Did someone say something to you?" The painter's voice shook with emotion. "I'll not allow anyone offend you in this way."

Mary just simply shook her head. "It is not what someone else does to me, Elizabeth. It is what I do to myself."

The tears fell down her pale skin as she continued. "And it is not up to you to right what I continue to bring on myself."

Elizabeth stared at her sister in disbelief. She had never heard Mary speak words such as these. Something must have happened. "Tell me what has happened, Mary. Talk to me."

"Oh, how I wish I could just be a simple little girl again. Pure, untainted. Living again at a stage in my life when worldly possessions mean little. Then I would be free to choose...for love." She paused, staring at the shadows that flickered across the walls.

Mary's face became nearly trancelike as her eyes locked on the far wall. Elizabeth reached over gently and touched her brow. But there was no fevered heat on the skin, only cold. She was ice-cold. Elizabeth picked a blanket lying on the bunk and wrapped it around her sister, wondering if Mary was about to have another of her attacks. She had been so good for so long that they'd thought she had beaten the pox. Elizabeth wondered if her hasty decision to go to Scotland was the reason Mary was going through this right now. She winced at the thought that she may have put the young woman's life in jeopardy by dragging her along. Elizabeth ran her hands over her sister's arms, trying to bring back some of the warmth in her chilled body.

"You should have seen me. I was so foolish. I was standing at the pier with my heart in my hand."

Elizabeth listened in silence.

"He approached me. He was coming toward me. I saw his eyes, as large as life, were on me. His tartan whipped about in the wind, but he charged on. My heart stopped beating. I knew what he was about to say. He was about to..." Mary looked down at her hands.

Elizabeth felt a knot form in her own heart. It was pain. Dull and heavy.

"He stopped. He stopped just a breath away. I looked up, and I was lost in what I saw. Once again, here I was—a young girl, blushing madly, my breath caught in my chest and my temples pounding with the excitement. It was like...first love. Though I'm sure now that I've never loved any man, still I knew."

Elizabeth looked down at her own fingers as they clutched the blanket in her palms. She felt a burning ache in the back of her throat.

"He just stood there, looking at me with a half smile tugging at his full lips. I felt whole, cared for, sought after. It's been a long time since I've felt that when a man looked at me. He was like a dream creature that God had at last sent down to me. To awaken something in my soul. Something that has been sleeping. Or dead. Then..."

Elizabeth couldn't look up. She sat where she was, silent, waiting.

"Then his friend called him. Lord Macpherson called him away."

Elizabeth clutched her hands as she took a small breath. "Gavin Kerr!"

Mary looked up dreamily. "It was he. The man never spoke a word. But I..." The tears once again took control. She wept silently.

As Elizabeth pulled her into her arms, she thought back over all the time Mary had spent in the company of so many courtiers in France and in Florence. But she had never seen her so broken, not even when she'd discovered that her newborn child had been a baby girl and not a male as she'd hoped.

"This is the first time we've met, but I know him. He is the man of my dreams, Elizabeth. He is the one that I have waited..." Mary paused and looked questioningly at her sister. "But I haven't waited, have I, sister? I gave myself away in the first bed that I fell into. I was impatient. Selfish. I didn't wait, did I? And now. Now I have found him, but now...I'm being punished."

Mary's eyes were glazed and unseeing. Elizabeth took hold of hands that reached out and clutched at the air. That scratched at invisible enemies. She didn't know how to calm her sister's fears, how to undo the torment she was bringing on herself. Mary's breaths were coming in short, quick pants. Her voice was thickening, as if someone had her by the throat.

"His friend called him. Took him away. Probably to tell him to stay away from the pox-ridden wench. They all know me. They know my reputation. And what they say is not even a lie. I know it. It is the god-awful truth that I am nothing more than a diseased wench. A used-up old whore."

"Stop it, Mary," Elizabeth ordered, as she tried to hold on to her sister's hands. The young woman jerked them away and hid them behind her.

"You know it's true. And Gavin...he went by me again, later, while we were boarding the ship. But he never looked. Not once. Aye, he has been told, warned, reprimanded. For looking. Just for looking." Mary rocked back and forth on the bunk, her words coming out in moans now. "I want to wash myself. I want to get rid of this grime that I've accumulated over the years. I want to be wanted. By him. Is that so much? But I can't. I was no innocent, Elizabeth. I know. I knew. Standing there, I lost it. My dream! I searched for him, and then, after finding him, I lost him. I was dirty. I am dirty! Oh, God...so dirty!"

Mary began to rub her hands hard on the blanket, but Elizabeth caught her wrists and held them tight.

"Then I saw me. I saw my life. God helped me see. I never knew, for all this time. It was I. All this time. I sought out this fate, this destiny. After the first time, after Henry got me with child, I could have stopped. You told me it wasn't my fault. You said that. The blame was Father's. But he tried it on you, and you didn't let him. No. You were strong. I was weak. And then, after that, I still didn't stop. Always I knew someday I'd find him, but I was impatient. I still didn't..." Mary folded over and cried. She cried into the blanket. "I don't deserve him."

Elizabeth leaned over and held her. That's all she could do. Just hold her.

There was darkness and nothing else. Elizabeth clutched the side of the bunk and swung her legs over the edge, but the floor seemed to open under her. There was a lurching motion, and she was thrown into the air, rolling as she fell. And then she landed. She felt her skull crack hard against the rough wooden floor. From the above her, Elizabeth heard a sliding, screeching sound of metal against wood, and then the weight of the chest was on her. She flinched with a sharp pain that shot through her shoulder as she tried to push it away. But the ship lurched again, and the chest dropped onto her wrist.

She could hear the muffled, heavy, rattling sound of boxes being thrown about around her. The ship's cabin continued to rock, and Elizabeth, completely disoriented, began to crawl helplessly forward. Around her the darkness was deathly.

"Mary!" she called. "Mary! Are you here?"

Elizabeth had fallen sleep holding her sister. The troubled young woman at last had settled quietly to rest, and Elizabeth had stayed beside her.

Suddenly the cabin floor seemed to drop away below her, and Elizabeth heard the crash of another box a foot from her head. Her hands flew up instinctively, and she rolled away from the spot. She dragged herself to her hands and knees, and scrambled in the direction she thought she'd come. But the wild motion of the ship fought to thwart her attempts.

"Mary!" she called loudly. But the hollow sound against the walls was answered only by the roar of the wind beating against the ship's sides.

So dark. There was no glimmer of light, no hint of which direction the door could be. And the storm. Panic began to crawl up from the small of her back. She had to open the door. Where was Mary? Where were Jaime and the others? She had to get out.

Elizabeth moved, pushed hard as she struggled to her feet. Her hand reached a wall. Good. The cabin wasn't that large. But then the boat shuddered and dipped and rolled her once more, downward and into the wall.

She heard the noise from above and behind her. The sound of more trunks and boxes ready to crush her.

As they reached the crest of another mountainous wave, Gavin scanned the rolling seascape for some sign of land, but there was nothing to be seen beyond the wind-whipped foam of a gray-green sea and the blackness of the low-hanging clouds.

"Damn the sky," the Scot cursed into the stinging salt spray. "It was blue not two hours ago."

As the galley slid uncontrollably into the trough between the waves, Gavin gripped the railing of the high stern deck. This is a lunatic's life, he thought. Give me a good battle and firm ground to stand on. He looked forward at the troop of Scottish warriors huddled in the bow and guessed more than a few of those men were thinking the same thing. Around the place where he stood, groups of travelers were sitting on the wooden deck, and the prayers of a number of them were as audible as the weeping of the old couple sitting directly at his feet.

Ambrose had just gone below again, having herded most of his own charges out of the tiny cabins. Gavin couldn't help but smile at the thought of the seamen's expression when the baron had so emphatically made his intention clear. Crowded deck or not, those in Ambrose's care were not going to be below decks if the ship went down.

Gavin glanced downward over the short rail in front of him at the painter's sister. She had been standing there looking out over the wild sea for some time now.

The Scot's gaze lingered on her as she clung to the railing on the far side of the ship and began slowly making her way forward. She was a bonny lass, and Gavin had heard her name was Mary.

Always uncomfortable in the company of women anyway, Gavin could only wonder now what could possibly be going through the young woman's mind. So unlike others, who needed a group of people to keep their company, this one was such a loner. So much like him.

Gavin had first seen her on the pier. From a distance, it had looked as if she were standing there waiting...waiting just for him. Her eyes, her smiles had seemingly been directed solely at him. He had turned around—actually looked about—to make certain there was no one else she was looking at. But there wasn't. And then Gavin had strode toward her.

A step away, he had stopped. Before he could even speak, it occurred to him that she seemed to need something—something from him. But she was so beautiful, and his tongue had knotted up in his head. He thought for a moment that she was about to speak. And whatever she had to say, Gavin was willing to hear.

Then Ambrose had called. They needed to finalize their agreement with the captain of the ship before they departed.

He had not seen her again before the galley sailed in the gray predawn light.

The ship heeled over slightly as it began its ascent up the side of the next watery mountain, and suddenly a crossing wave crashed over the gunwales, hammering free the great wood casks of olive oil that had been lined up and secured with such orderly precision. The galley's crew scrambled about, attempting to secure the huge barrels that now floated as free as twigs upon the flood. The shouts and curses came back to Gavin in snatches as the howling wind and the roaring sea overwhelmed all other sounds that struggled so feebly before them.

One of the wooden casks tumbled through the midsection of the ship, now awash with the deluge. All eyes in the stern were upon the barrel, but from the corner of his eye, the Scot saw another smaller wave break over the starboard bow, and the water swept aft, engulfing the black-haired lass.

As he watched in horror, the wave knocked the woman flat, submerging her momentarily before she reappeared, floating with terrifying speed across the deck toward an opening where the water was draining overboard.

Without a second thought, Gavin vaulted the short railing before him as the flood carried the woman ever nearer her certain doom.

The warrior waded against the surging current, driving his legs against the thigh-high water. Gavin's hair whipped across his face, blinding him for an instant with brine as Mary neared the gaping hole.

The giant was still a half dozen steps away, lunging wildly ahead, when the woman's body reached the side of the ship. The vessel tipped again, and the seawater rushed with even more force through the opening.

As the young woman's head disappeared, Gavin dived into the swirling foam. For a moment the giant thought the lass was gone, but then his fingers closed over one of her trailing ankles.

Driving his knees under him, Gavin Kerr struggled to his feet, dragging with all his strength the unconscious woman back into the ship. With a heave, the giant hauled the young woman up into his arms and tossed her over his shoulder. Then, working his way back through the receding water to the short ladder to the stern deck, the Scot climbed quickly and lay the sputtering lass in the waiting arms of the huddled travelers.

Below, Ambrose kicked open the first door. There was no sign of her. After bringing the others up to the stern deck, he had realized she was the only one missing. Why doesn't this surprise me? he thought to himself. Holding the wick lamp in one hand, the baron held the door open with one foot and peered in. The room lit up slightly, but even in this light, he could see she wasn't there. He stepped backward into the narrow corridor and moved deeper into the bowels of the ship.

Ambrose's shoulders nearly scraped the sides of the passageway and he needed to keep his head low as he moved toward next cabin—the cabin he'd seen Elizabeth's sister Mary come lurching out of when he'd come below earlier.

Before he could reach it, though, the ship shuddered with the impact of a wave, and the hatch door behind him slammed open. A gust of wind and spray swept into the passage, killing the flickering light, and Ambrose was left cursing in the darkness.

Feeling his way toward the cabin door, the baron found himself thrown into one bulwark as the galley lurched again, seemingly dropping a yard as it did. Steadying himself, Ambrose found the wooden latch and shoved the cabin door open.

"Uh...Phillipe!" he called into the pitch-blackness of the room. "Are you in here?"

Straining to listen through the sound of the gale and the waves, Ambrose pushed farther into the cabin.

"Here." The reply was weak and small.

Ambrose stepped in, clear of the door, only to slam his hip squarely into the corner of a large chest directly before him.

"Damn," he cursed. But before he even had the word out, another abrupt shift of the galley threw the warrior backward against the closing door, leaving him staggered against the bulwark with the offending chest tipped onto his outstretched legs. "The devil!"

"Stop complaining and get me out of here." Elizabeth pushed the clothing that was inhibiting her breathing away from her face. She wondered vaguely whose chest had been opened by the movements of the ship.

"Where are you?" Ambrose called, as he took a step in the direction of her voice. His knees rammed the side of another chest. "What the devil is all this? I thought I said you were not to bring anything that cannot be carried on horseback."

"I don't recall discussing anything of the sort," she lied. Gripping the side of a chest, Elizabeth pulled herself to her feet. She stretched her legs and flexed her hands. Amazingly, nothing appeared to be broken.

Another sharp dip of the vessel once again sent her flying, this time in the direction of the baron's voice.

"Ambrose!" Elizabeth called as she landed with a thud on the hard wood floor.

"Aye?" His voice now came from the proximity of the floor, as well.

"Please help me. I believe I've bruised every bone in my body." The cabin floor tipped once more and Elizabeth felt herself sliding across the floor, with the sound of luggage sliding after her. "Help me!"

Her hands fluttered about her wildly with the hope of grabbing hold of something. Anything. But to no avail. With another crash, the young painter hit the far bulwark a moment before a collection of trunks, furniture, and loose clothing came tumbling after her.

His hand found her ankle, and Ambrose pulled the limb toward him.

"You are turning me upside down," she called. "I don't need that kind of help, m'lord. My stomach is about to empty itself as it is, and it doesn't need any encouragement."

His other hand took hold of her leg as he searched for a better grip.

"Ambrose Macpherson, you keep your hands off of me. This is no time to behave in this manner." While one of her hands tried to fight off his hand as it moved up her thigh, the other reached out in search of the rest of him. Elizabeth was buried under a landslide of baggage, and she needed him to get her out from under it. She struggled against the onslaught. "Where are you?"

"Make up your mind, my bonny one." His hand slid over her round backside. She tried to squirm away. "Do you want me, lass, or don't you?"

"Oh, Ambrose. I'm so glad you came for me." She now clutched him hard around the neck.

The vessel heaved and dropped again. Elizabeth leaped up and wrapped her legs around his waist, burying her face in his neck. "Please get me out of here."

"This is no way to behave, m'lady, if you want out of this cabin." His voice was hoarse.

"I can't help..." Another sudden drop made Ambrose lose his balance and fall backward. Elizabeth dropped like a sack on top of him. "...it."

"Really?" She whispered sheepishly as she struggled to pull one of her legs out from where it was pinned beneath his buttocks.

"I thought I'd never get out of here, Ambrose. And then you came." She snuggled quickly beside him as she heard the sliding chest. "Though I'm beginning to think we'll never get out. Is the ship about to go down?"

"It might." He rolled to his side and pushed her from him as another chest crashed into his back.

Elizabeth heard the groan that escaped his lips as they were pushed across the floor into a pile of clothing.

"We could die! Drown! Where is Jaime?" she asked in panic.

"Right now, everyone is huddled safely on the stern deck. I saw her in the arms of the merchant and his wife."

"My sister?"

"She came up, as well." Ambrose reached behind her and found the solid wood of the bulwark behind the clothing. And right at the point where it met the floor, he found the rope. Running his fingers around it, he gripped it tightly.

"Are we the only ones left below decks?"

"The last ones."

The ship heeled over, but Ambrose held on to the rope and kept them where they were.

Elizabeth felt her body crush against his as the cabin deck sloped sharply toward him. She found her hands planted on his chest. She could feel his heartbeat. Her chest, her hips, the length of her entire body were molded against him. Her head gave in to the powerful pull and nestled against his neck.

It was almost as if the fear she was feeling had wrought some incredible change in the universe. She'd never felt her senses so alive. The smell of wind and salt water on his skin, the warmth of the cocoon that he'd made for her in his arms, the power of his build—they were all so intoxicating. Seemingly unable to control herself, Elizabeth let her lips brush against the skin of his neck. She found herself wanting to touch him. Her fingers traveled over the smooth linen of his shirt and then, finding the opening, moved inside.

"I like your timing, lass," he growled, lowering his head and capturing her mouth. The kiss was hot and carnal, his tongue thrusting hungrily into her velvety recesses.

She took him in, with a desperate longing. She'd not known how much she needed him. Not until today, when she'd thought that the object of Mary's attraction had been Ambrose Macpherson.

Now the roar of the storm outside, the darkness that engulfed them, everything seemed to add to her overpowering need to have him, to experience him, to wrap herself around him. he world she knew, the solid world of precision, color, and light, was no longer the real world. It was another world, more dreary and unattractive than the undulating blackness she was a part of now. That other world was like some far-off dream, falling away farther and farther with every billowing wave of the sea.

She wanted him, and she would have him.

Elizabeth's hands tore at the fasteners of his shirt. Her fingers greedily devoured his skin, exploring and kneading every sinewy muscle.

"Is this it, lass?" the Highlander asked hoarsely. "Is this the way it's to be?"

"I want you, Ambrose."

"No stopping. No running off. No sudden fit of insanity." Ambrose paused. "These are my conditions, Elizabeth. If you want me, you will have all of me."

"I accept your conditions," she whispered, her mouth tasting his skin.

Ambrose released the rope with one hand and pulled at her doublet. He, too, had crossed into a world of desire. Of course, it was a realm that he was far more familiar with than she. But vaguely, hovering somewhere about the level of consciousness, the idea took shape that he was feeling these sensations as if for the first time. They had come so close before, the two of them. But not like this. The change, the urgency of their need was perhaps due to the place, to the time. Perhaps even to the storm that roared outside and within.

He wanted her now, and she would have him.

Ambrose wanted to feel her skin against his, as he pulled down at the shirt she wore beneath the doublet. Instinctively, one of his legs crossed over her hip, trapping her writhing body under its weight. Yanking the shirt open in front, he found yet another tight, thick layer of cloth frustrating his attempts. Pulling at the laces that held it in place, he pushed the material away. All at once his hand was filled with the full round orb of one of her breasts springing free. Hauling her toward him, he crushed her body against his—skin against skin, flesh against flesh.

Elizabeth pulled her hand from his chest and took hold of his bare knee. Clutching his thigh, her fingers delved uncontrollably beneath the folds of his kilt.

Ambrose slid his leg lower, making room for his own hand as he slid his fingers into the juncture of her thighs. The thick breeches inhibited his search, but all the same he kneaded with the touch that he knew she sought. The moan that sounded somewhere deep within her triggered an even wilder desire in him, and as he stroked her rising pleasure, he slanted his mouth roughly over hers.

Elizabeth encircled his member with her fingers. Running her hand over its length, she trembled with anticipation.

His head fell with a thud against the floor. "How did I ever let you get away from me before?" he gasped. "I need you now, Elizabeth. I won't wait. You are driving me out of my mind."

She tightened her grip on him, hearing his groan of pleasure. "I want you, too. Once, before we die. Take me, Ambrose Macpherson. Make me yours."

Everything around them—the storm, the turbulent action of the boat, even the constantly shifting baggage around them—was forgotten, and he let go of the wall. Rolling toward her, Ambrose moved on top of her.

"You are not going to die, my sweet." His hand reached to pull open her breeches. "I'm not letting you die. There is far too much passion left for us to enjoy. And we just can't let all that go to waste."

Ambrose pushed aside the ring that hung between her breasts. His tongue flicked momentarily at a hardened nipple before moving to the other, where he settled, finally, suckling her tender flesh.

Elizabeth arched her back, gripping his hair and pulling his face tighter against her breast as his other hand made contact with the moist folds of her womanhood. She heard her own breath coming in gasps as his fingers began to stroke rhythmically, while the colors of heaven danced like fire before her eyes.

The sound of running footsteps and the door slamming open froze the two at once where they lay. Elizabeth held her breath as Ambrose's mouth lifted from her breast.

"Damn."

Gavin peered inside the darkened room. His dim wick lamp only shed the dimmest light in the area by the doorway. All he could see was a room in utter shambles, the jumbled collection of clothes, trunks, and boxes scattered everywhere that the lamp illuminated.

"Ambrose? Are you here?"

The voice that reached him was muffled by the sound of the wind and waves hammering on the hull of the vessel. "Give me a moment, Gavin...to find my way."

"Have you seen Phillipe?" Gavin asked, raising his light. "No one has seen him come on deck. His family is concerned. Ah, there you are."

Another lurch of the boat caused Gavin to brace himself against the doorframe. The young painter was standing with his back to him, and from what Gavin could see, Ambrose was holding the man and trying to steady him on his feet. But the movement of the boat wasn't helping the two. "You were gone so long, Ambrose, I thought you might have fallen and cracked that thick head of yours."

"I came after...Phillipe, but the damn door slammed shut on us." Ambrose put his great hand squarely on Gavin's chest and backed him out of the cabin. Elizabeth followed behind. "But why the hell am I explaining all this to you?"

"Because I have more sense than you." Gavin watched as Ambrose and Phillipe came fully into the light. His eyes widened. They were a mess. Ambrose's shirt was torn open in the front, while the painter's doublet was stuffed into his breeches rather than hanging over them, the customary way of wearing it. "You two must have had quite a rough time down here."

Ambrose glowered at him. But then he caught the painter by the shoulder as a dip in the ship nearly sent them all flying.

"I mean with all those boxes and loose things flying around." Gavin grinned. "You are just the right size to make a good battering ram, Ambrose. But Phillipe, I'd say, is not really strong enough."

"There is nothing wrong with him," Ambrose growled. "What are you waiting for? Are you going to stand there all night flapping your jaws or are you going to lead us out of here?"

Gavin straightened himself to his full height and snapped at him. "You foul-tempered Highland horse thief. I came down here to save your neck, and this is what I get in return."

"Just go," Ambrose rumbled more gently, slapping his friend in apology and turning him down the passageway. "You got me at a bad time, Gavin. Just go."

Gavin turned grudgingly away. "You might want to bring a blanket for your sister, painter," he said, directing his words over his shoulder at Elizabeth. "She is soaked through and needs a bit of comforting."

"Mary? Why, is she hurt?"

"Just wet. A wee bit of water down her gullet, that's all."

Elizabeth turned to go back into the room, but Ambrose blocked her way. "Go on up. I'll fetch it." He grabbed a cloak off the wall and placed it around her shoulder. The caressing touch that brushed her face went unnoticed by the other man, but Elizabeth felt it throughout her body. In the dim light of the passageway, she glanced up into his mischievous eyes, then turned and followed the giant warrior out into the raging storm.

The force of the wind nearly knocked Elizabeth back into the passageway, but she shielded her face against the biting salt spray that drove hard against her. Squinting her eyes, she could see the galley's crew working to secure the huge casks at the forward end of the deck, and it looked like they must have lost a number over the side. As she watched, a small wave crashed over the side of the gunwale and washed across the deck, but did no further damage.

"It appears the storm's easing up a bit," Gavin shouted at her. He jerked his head up toward the stern deck above them. "Your sister's up here."

As Elizabeth started up the ladder, the ship crested a wave, and she held tight to the rungs as the vessel dove into the next trough. When the motion of the ship allowed it, she scurried up to the top and grasped the low railing as soon as she could get her feet planted solidly on the deck.

Groups of travelers crowded the deck, but before she could search out her own party, a loud crack sounded above her, and she turned in time to see the very top of the closest mast break off. The sailors working forward stood frozen for a moment, gazing upward at the damaged gear. Then, springing into action, the men leaped into the sagging rigging of the aft mainmast and swarmed up the ropes, securing the dangling masthead and tightening the remaining lines. Though the two large triangular sails of the galley had been trimmed when the fierce storm winds had first blown up, those masts would be essential if the merchant vessel was going to complete the voyage to Marseilles. Without the use of the canvas, the sailors would be rowing the remainder of the distance—not a welcome thought for the experienced seamen.

Turning her back on the action above, Elizabeth searched the huddled groups for her family and friends. Finding them sitting out of the wind in the protective shelter of the high railing, she worked her way over to them.

Jaime was asleep in the arms of Ernesta, and Joseph sat beside Mary, his cloak rolled up beneath her head. The young woman's eyes were half closed as if she were about to fall asleep. The ragged looks of concern on her two friends' faces startled Elizabeth, and she put her hand on Mary's forehead.

"What happened, Erne?" she asked quickly. Mary's skin was cold and clammy. "Did she have another attack?"

"We don't know," Joseph answered, glancing at his wife. "She didn't come up with us right away when the baron sent us up from the cabins. Your sister—"

"She was on the lower deck," Ernesta broke in. "She was at the railing and a wave nearly washed her overboard. She swallowed quite a bit of water. She hasn't said a word since Sir Gavin carried her up here. I am not sure if she is even conscious."

Elizabeth looked anxiously at her sister. Mary's black hair was plastered to her head, and her skin had a deathlike pallor.

"Mary," she called softly. Removing her cloak and spreading it over her sister's wet clothes, Elizabeth rubbed Mary's hand between hers and tried to stir some warmth into her cold body. "Mary, can you hear me? Come on, my sweet. Open your eyes. Look at me, my love."

There was no answer but the occasional gusts of wind and spray. Elizabeth watched for some flicker of life on her sister's wan and vacant features. She ran her hands through the young woman's hair. Grabbing a corner of the cloak, she tried to wipe the water from her face. "Look, Mary. The storm is passing. It is going to be a lovely day. You'll see. Come on, my beautiful one, talk to me."

Gavin stood a step away, watching the careful ministrations and listening to the gentle words that the painter spoke. There was so much affection apparent in the young man's words. But he didn't like the pale look of the young woman. From where he stood, she looked ill. Terribly ill.

"Go to her."

Gavin turned at the sound of the Highlander's voice over his shoulder. "Go and help Phillipe, if you want. He could use the extra hand."

Gavin frowned at Ambrose. Was his interest in the young woman so apparent? "Why don't you go yourself?"

Ambrose handed the blanket over to the black-haired warrior. "I'll be of more use helping with the mainmast."

He watched his friend pause and then nod in agreement. But even as the Lowlander walked away, the baron couldn't move. Standing there as Gavin carried the blanket over to the travelers, Ambrose found he couldn't tear his eyes from Elizabeth. He ached for her. They once again had come so close to making love. But this time it hadn't been Elizabeth who had halted the onslaught of desire. Her passion had been as unbridled as his own. He had felt her spirit soar.

Ambrose wanted her. All of her. Body and soul.

Forcing himself to turn away, Ambrose gazed up at the brightening sky above the sailors working so far aloft. The sickly green of the heavens was giving way to shades of gray, and he knew that the back of the storm was broken.

Elizabeth. He wanted to call her name. Shout it so that all might hear. And know.

He knew there was more than just thwarted lovemaking behind his growing obsession with this woman. More than just the beauty that she kept hidden from the world. There was something even more mysterious about her. And its allure was driving him wild.

True, he had lied about helping the galley's crew with the damaged sail. The crew had everything under the control; he could see that. But Ambrose knew he needed to keep his distance from her right now. He had to keep a tight rein on his own desires. He wanted her. No, he needed her. In his entire life, he'd never become so fiercely attracted to any woman without having her.

And Ambrose knew Elizabeth wanted him, too.

Cursing under his breath, the baron cast a quick glance over his shoulder and then strode abruptly to the ladder. Dropping to the main deck, Ambrose moved swiftly through the tangle of fallen lines toward the bow of the ship, where his soldiers were beginning to stretch and shake out their wet belongings. As he neared them, he could hear their friendly taunting of one another. The sea was becoming calmer by the moment, and Ambrose knew the soldiers could hardly be sad about that.

A few moments later, the blond-haired giant stood gazing toward the stern deck. Patches of blue could be seen in the sky beyond the end of the vessel.

"Damn!" Ambrose banged his fist on the railing. It was under his skin, and he couldn't shake it.

He glanced around. He had to hide his feelings. She was pretending to be a man. He simply couldn't show his feelings or his interest. As much as he'd like to, he couldn't drag her away to his cabin, or risk a stolen kiss.

They had to act...indifferently toward one another.

Try as he might, he simply could not understand Elizabeth's motivation for carrying on this masquerade. No matter how impossible her father's demands had been, that was four years ago. But even then, he found it difficult to believe that Elizabeth Boleyn had had no other options available to her.

As he stared out at the groups of travelers, Ambrose became more and more convinced there were things the young woman was hiding. There were too many unanswered questions. And the sight of the sister, Mary Boleyn—once a court favorite but now living alone with her sister—had also added to his suspicions. Why in God's name where these two living as they were?

Ambrose smiled grimly. Well, here was a challenge. Finding the truth. Finding answers to his questions—to all of his questions—before they reached Scotland.

But more than that. Ambrose also planned to have Elizabeth Boleyn in his bed before they reached Scotland.

Though the orange sun broke through the clouds low in the western sky, the seas remained high as the galley made its way westward toward Marseilles. The sailors unfurled what canvas the vessel's masts could handle in the still gusting wind.

On the stern deck, Elizabeth continued to sit beside her sister, while Gavin Kerr hovered over them by the railing. Mary, still lying motionless, seemed to drift in and out of a haze, oblivious to everything around her. Elizabeth tucked the blankets around her sister, talking continuously, her voice soft but insistent as she tried to keep her sister's body warm and her mind in the realm of the present. But Mary seemed unable to respond. Gavin just watched from where he stood, not knowing what to do or how to help.

During the short periods when Mary would fall into a kind of restless half sleep, they could see her face contorting in expressions Elizabeth had never before seen, even during Mary's worst bouts with the illness. It seemed as if she were dreaming. Dreams of intense fear alternating with dreams of intense sadness. Even when Mary was indeed sleeping, there were tears. Elizabeth watched the drops roll down her sister's face and disappear into the black folds of her hair. Elizabeth wiped the shimmering tracks away tenderly.

"Do you want your sister to get a chill?" Ambrose looked back as Elizabeth and Gavin turned their scowling faces on him. They were concerned, but neither was seasoned in sea traveling. "It's bad enough that the movement of the boat has made her sick to her stomach. Look at her. She is green."

Seeing the startled face of Elizabeth, the Highlander knew he needed to take some responsibility. "Gavin, take Mary down to the cabin. Phillipe, you'd better arrange for someone to get her out of those wet clothes. Sitting around and letting the dampness settle around her bones will not help her."

"How about the waves?" Elizabeth asked. "Is it safe to go back below?"

Ambrose's look spoke volumes.

"I suppose it depends on who's going," he said in a low voice.

Elizabeth couldn't help the blush that spread quickly across her face. She glanced around quickly at the others, but no one even dared to question the baron's words.

"It should be safe enough now," Gavin said as he gently scooped Mary up and stood. She remained limp and immobile in his arms.

"Take her into the first cabin," Ambrose ordered. "Phillipe and I need to finish an earlier discussion in the other."

"You did say we are going to survive this storm, m'lord," the painter growled. "Perhaps another time."

Elizabeth glared at him before taking the sleeping Jaime out of Erne's arms and helping the older woman to her feet.

"Another time, then," Ambrose returned softly.

Chapter 19

Feminine wiles, she thought, scoffing. What good are they to me? It is difficult to bewitch a man, while you're among men, when everyone thinks you're a man.

And Ambrose Macpherson was an obstinate man. But she already knew that. Over Elizabeth's objections, the baron had refused to allow them to stay in Marseilles, insisting that they travel the two hours to a nearby monastery that served as a hostelry for travelers. In spite of her disapproval, Ambrose had hired a closed oxcart and herded Ernesta and Jaime into the conveyance. Laying the weak but conscious Mary carefully among the baggage, Gavin Kerr shared a look of concern with the painter while explaining the baron's plan for the younger woman. Mary was obviously still quite weak, and Ambrose had no intention of worsening her condition by forcing her to travel at their pace. The Highlander knew the monk in charge of the infirmary where they were headed, and based on past experience he knew that there was no better physician anywhere. The monks would look after the young woman and care for her until the time came when she would be strong enough to travel again. At such time she would be welcome to come and join the painter in Scotland.

Though Elizabeth couldn't believe what she was hearing, Gavin clearly agreed with everything Ambrose had proposed. She had begun to think, because of the attentions Gavin Kerr had shown Mary, that perhaps he was growing fond of her younger sister. But obviously she was mistaken. The black-haired warrior might be concerned about Mary's health, but his allegiance to Ambrose remained unchallenged.

Riding out of Marseilles, Elizabeth had wracked her brain for a way to convince Ambrose that leaving Mary behind was simply out of the question. Neither of the men knew the source of Mary's illness, but Elizabeth had lived with it for the past four years. Nearly every time, as quickly as the symptoms would manifest themselves, they would disappear. And Elizabeth knew the only lasting remedy lay in love and care and in being surrounded by those the afflicted one trusted. In Mary's case, that will always be me, Elizabeth vowed.

Mary's sickness was changing, and Elizabeth knew that better than anyone. No longer just the cause of hideous physical disfigurement and intense bodily discomfort, the pox was now affecting her sister's mind. In her moments of mad anguish, Mary expressed a desire to die. These were not the childish and dramatic displays of her adolescence, but the momentarily insane desires of one whose mind had become unhinged.

But Elizabeth had learned how to deal with these trying moments. And at a time when Mary was vulnerable to these attacks, Elizabeth would never leave her sister alone.

Elizabeth knew she had a formidable challenge on her hands. She had to convince Ambrose Macpherson that taking the younger sister with them on the rest of the journey was the best course of action. But she also knew that trying to bully him wouldn't work.

Feminine wiles. That had to be the answer. Elizabeth wasn't blind to the heated attention the man directed at her. He wanted her. If she could only use that to her advantage, perhaps he would agree to her conditions.

Conditions, she thought with a smile.

Elizabeth nodded to the old monk who would watch over Mary through the night. Her sister was resting in the monastery's infirmary. Gently, she pulled the door partially closed and stepped into the darkened hallway.

Since their arrival the day before, Elizabeth had not been able to leave Mary's side. Mary had been extremely nervous about Elizabeth leaving her alone, even for a moment, but her fears were beginning to subside.

Elizabeth headed down the stairs. She had to change his mind. The baron's message had said they were leaving tomorrow. With Mary, Elizabeth thought. That was the only way she would be leaving tomorrow.

The noise of the people crowding the refectory reached her ears before she even stepped into the room. She looked about her. The travelers crowded the long tables laden with an evening meal.

Elizabeth looked down at the hands that clutched at her legs. Jaime. She picked up the little girl and hugged her tightly.

Ambrose watched the simple show of affection from where he sat.

Jaime jumped out of Elizabeth's arms and scampered off to play with a half dozen kittens that were rolling in the rushes in the corner of the room.

Looking back at the long tables, Elizabeth saw Ambrose motioning her to a seat beside him, and in spite of her dilemma she found herself blushing at the prospect of sitting beside the golden-haired warrior.

Moving toward the seat, Elizabeth paused briefly and gave Joseph and Erne the latest news of Mary's condition. Even they were under the impression that they would all be leaving the next day without the younger sister. Elizabeth assured them that such a rumor was false.

Turning toward the baron, Elizabeth realized Ambrose was watching her carefully.

"So at last she's given you permission to leave."

Elizabeth looked down at him and remained standing where she was behind the bench. He patted the seat next to him. She kept staring.

"You're angry," Ambrose said, amused.

"Nay, Ambrose. He is just tired. That's all." The hard slap on the back from Gavin forced Elizabeth to take her seat at the table. She had not realized that the Lowlander had been standing right behind her.

"I have to admit, Phillipe. After Ambrose, you are the most loyal man I've ever met in my life. The way you care for your sister. It is a wondrous thing." Gavin seated himself on the other side of the painter. "Even though you and the baron here have very different styles, I'd have to say that you both have compassionate natures and great hearts."

Elizabeth snorted at his comment.

"You disagree?" Ambrose asked, grabbing her by the back of the neck and turning her face toward him.

"Am I to be allowed to answer the question, or perhaps you'd care to do that, as well?"

"By all means. I'm all ears."

She watched the young kitchen boy as he placed another platter of food in front of them. "I happen to take offense at the thought of anyone connecting your bullying approach and mindless decisions to my peaceful and reasonable ways."

Ambrose snorted. "Reasonable?"

"Actually," Gavin chirped in from where he sat, "what I said was meant to be an insult to Ambrose. Everyone knows he hasn't a great heart—it's about the size of a berry. But I never expected you to be offended, Phillipe, my friend."

"You be quiet," Ambrose snapped at his friend before turning to Elizabeth. "Would you care to dwell on why you take offense at my actions and decisions? This should be interesting, considering the fact that you've hardly had an opportunity to witness *any* decision that I have made."

"I have been around, m'lord. And I can hear." Elizabeth stared straight ahead, toying with the food in front of her. "And I can see."

"Nay, you haven't been around," he responded curtly. "You have been locked away with your sister ever since we arrived."

She turned sharply in his direction. This was no place to discuss what she had in mind. "Do you care to take this argument outside?"

"Nothing would please me more." He stood at once.

"Don't, Phillipe," Gavin advised seriously from where he sat. "He could beat you into bloody mash. And I think he is in no mood to argue."

"I can take care of myself," she stated under her breath, patting the surprised warrior on the arm before following Ambrose out of the hall.

Elizabeth had wanted to be alone with him. She knew she needed to get him away from the rest of his men so she could work on him, use whatever interest he had in her to take him in hand. It was the only leverage she had right now.

But now her eyes riveted to his broad shoulders as Ambrose led her through the winding stairwells to his room—no doubt the finest in the hostelry—Elizabeth felt the prickly heat of panic surging through her, draining her of the strength to climb even the next step. She knew what he was after. But Elizabeth couldn't let him make love to her. She began to fall behind.

The man thought she was experienced—that she had lain with other men and had even born a child. And he thought that she was as hungry for him as he was for her.

Of course, Elizabeth reasoned, why would he think otherwise? Elizabeth had given up the lie of telling herself that she could do without him. Her mind and body cried out for him. But she knew that this yearning for him must be controlled. She had to hold him off.

If Ambrose were to find out that Elizabeth had lied, then all hope of getting her family to safety would be dashed.

Elizabeth had seen the way men had treated Mary after they had taken what they wanted. Kings or commoners, men were quick to lose interest once their appetites were satisfied.

No, once Ambrose knew the whole truth about Elizabeth—once he had found out what a total fraud she was—he wouldn't just leave Mary behind. He would go on without Jaime, without the Bardis, and without Elizabeth herself. How disappointed he would be, once he had her.

Somehow, Elizabeth knew, she had to put him off. Enchanting a man is easier said than done, she thought, her mind racing.

Ambrose pushed open a heavy oak door on its loud hinges and turned toward her. "After you."

She remained where she was, but tried to peek past him into the semidarkness of the room. Not much was visible from where she stood.

"M'lord, I don't think—"

"After you." His voice was commanding, and Elizabeth stepped reluctantly into the bedchamber.

The room was larger than the cell that Elizabeth was supposed to share with Joseph and a half dozen of Ambrose's men. Not that she had spent any time there, considering the hours that she'd remained at Mary's bedside. Though she would have preferred to be closer to

Ernesta and Jaime, they were closeted in a separate section of the hostelry, a section that Elizabeth doubted had any rooms quite like this one. For it was clear from her first glance that Ambrose was being treated like royalty.

The room, situated in the corner of the stone building, had been paneled below and plastered above, and the bright blue color of the woodwork shone attractively even in the fading light of day. A number of small wooden chairs were clustered around a well-made wood table, and a mat of woven rushes covered the floor. Against the far wall, a huge bed brooded ominously, its stuffed mattress high and frighteningly full. Elizabeth quickly looked away.

The shutters of the four small windows had been thrown open, and the young painter crossed the room to one of them. She gazed down at the walled garden, and at the orchards and vineyards that stretched in an orderly fashion into the distance. This was a prosperous monastery, of that she had no doubt.

"Long way to jump."

She turned around and saw him standing casually at the end of the bed. She could see the door to the room was already barred from the inside. "I came willingly, didn't I?"

He smiled. "If you call dragging ten steps behind and shuddering at every corner, willing, then I can't wait for what's to come."

Elizabeth fumed. "No one is forcing you to lie with me, m'lord. You were the one who came after me first, if you recall."

"You came to my tent."

"You came to my room," she retorted.

"I didn't know you were there." Ambrose shrugged. She was getting riled up, and he had to admit, he was enjoying every moment of it. He had been away from her too long. In fact, he had been somewhat startled earlier in the day when, after seeing that she was absent again at the noon meal, he'd realized that he was actually angry at the sister. Envious of a sick woman. That was bad.

"When I came to Bardi's villa in Florence, I came after a painter. Instead, I saw you."

"Such disappointment you must have experienced!" she said, her voice dripping with ironic concern. Bewitching and feminine wiles be damned, she thought. "Has anyone told you, m'lord, that you are the most empty-headed, insensitive, self-centered man ever to walk this earth?"

"Nay. No one...other than you."

Ambrose gazed at Elizabeth. At her arms crossed defensively over her chest, at her angry face, at the short hair that shone beneath the puffy hat and lay in waves against her face. His eyes traveled lower and took in the shape of her beautiful legs, showing so provocatively through the hose.

"Stop appraising me like that! I'm not some prize heifer."

"I thought that was the idea," he responded, as his eyes continued their journey. "I thought men were supposed to be able to look at you without any fear of detection."

"If, m'lord, all the men in Scotland are going to look at me the way you do, then certain questions arise."

Ambrose let his eyes slowly, ever so slowly, return to hers. "To answer your questions, all of your questions..." He took a step toward her. Elizabeth stepped back against the window frame. The Highlander swung a chair around and sat, straddling it and facing her.

She waited for him to speak, but he sat silently. For the first time in years, Elizabeth felt the vulnerability of men's clothing. Her painter's clothing, as comfortable as it had been, now felt strangely insufficient. She longed for the layers and layers of dresses that Mary wore.

A blush crept into her face as she looked away from the handsome nobleman. There were no barriers of modesty between them. But then, perhaps there never had been.

"You fascinate me, Elizabeth. You always have. No woman has ever called me empty-headed, insensitive, or self-centered. And certainly no man would dare to say such things to me. In fact, contrary to your opinion, most women think me intelligent, gallant, and considerably perceptive of the needs of others. But then again, I am not with most women. I am with you. So, I suppose, that explains that."

She bit her tongue in her effort to stay silent.

"And as far as my disappointment at finding you in Florence, you are once again wrong, of course." He paused, waiting for her to jump in, but she didn't rise to his bait. "From the moment I first laid eyes on you, I have been anything but displeased. From that day at the Field of Cloth of Gold, you have had a way of drawing me toward you. And I have advanced with pleasure—and anticipation. I have thought about you quite a bit. To be honest, I have spent four years thinking about this moment. You have surprised me, excited me, and enchanted me. Elizabeth Boleyn, you have driven me to a madness that no other woman ever has. It is time for you to supply the cure."

Elizabeth looked down at the weave of the mat under her feet. She could not trust herself to meet his eyes. "What would you like me to do?"

He stood up and walked to a bowl of water that sat on the trestle table. She watched as he soaked a towel and wrung out the water. Elizabeth held her breath as he walked toward her.

Halting a step away, he handed her the wet cloth.

"What I would like you to do is to be yourself. At least while you are with me. I want you to wash away the disguise that covers the truth about you. I want to see you for who you really are, as I've seen you in the past. I want to see the passionate woman who exists beneath these clothes." He took her chin gently in his hand and lifted it until her eyes met his. "You want me, Elizabeth. As much as I want you. And don't try to deny it. Your eyes have betrayed you from the first moment we met."

He spoke the truth. She couldn't deny his words.

"I want to make love to you, Elizabeth. I mean with no interruptions, no one running away, no life-threatening storms or anything else to stop us. Those were my conditions, you recall."

She nodded. "That's the way I want it, as well," she whispered, still holding the cloth in her hand.

"Then—" he gestured toward the locked door with a slight smile—"don't you think we are safe at last?"

Elizabeth raised herself on her toes and pressed a fleeting kiss on his chin before skipping around him. Then, throwing the towel across the room and into the bowl, she turned to face him.

"You are right about me and about the way I feel about you. I won't deny that." She whispered the words. "But not here. We can't make love here. When at last we do make love, I would like us to be in a place separate from all these others. I would like to dress as a woman and come to you as myself. I would also like to have the peace of mind that we have more than a few moments that we could share. I am not being greedy. Perhaps a night. That's not so much to ask, is it?"

Ambrose moved closer to her again. "We could have that. All of what you ask for. But wouldn't it be worth our while to remind ourselves of the delights we have in store? Perhaps just as a token to hold us over for the far greater night to come? For the bliss that awaits us?"

Elizabeth circled behind a chair as he slowly, ever so slowly, stalked her. "Nay, m'lord. I don't think that is such a good idea."

"But I think it is," he continued. "And I think it won't take much for me to convince you, as well."

Elizabeth pulled a chair back and blocked his advance. "As I think more about this, I'm becoming more and more convinced that it's a terrible idea. After all, you're leaving tomorrow without me, and—"

Ambrose came to a halt. "You are not being left here, Elizabeth. We are all leaving tomorrow."

She stared at him momentarily, her eyes widening.

"Oh, thank you, thank you!" Elizabeth tossed the chair aside and threw her hands around his neck at last. "Thank you!"

Ambrose stepped back as she attacked him. "What are you thanking me for? This is no different than what we planned to do before we left Florence."

"Of course it is!" she whispered happily, kissing him squarely on the lips. "You just said we are *all* leaving tomorrow. That means Mary is coming with us. That means I won't need to stay behind and finish the journey to Scotland without your assistance. That means you and I will have our moments together. Moments to share—" Ambrose grabbed her by the chin and forced her to listen to him. "You are going with me, my sweet. And your sister is staying here where she can be cared for properly. These people shall give her the best care there is. And when she is better, I will even send my men back to accompany her to Scotland. Now, is all that clear?"

Elizabeth slapped his hand away. "Let me make something clear to you! I am not going to leave my sister all alone in a strange place with anyone—and I don't care if Avicenna himself is going to doctor her! If she stays, then I stay. Is *that* clear?"

Ambrose stared at the young woman momentarily. "Is your skull so thick? Have the beatings you've taken in your life so damaged your wits that you can no longer think rationally? You are endangering your sister's life by taking her on so difficult a journey."

"I know my sister better than anyone—and that includes you, these monks, and any other physician you might find between here and Paris." She took a step back. "Mary's illness is not of a physical nature that can be cured by medicine, or by sleep. She needs love, care. She needs the knowledge that she is well cared for by people that she knows. The death of Mary will not be taking her with us across France. The death of her will be leaving her alone here among strangers."

Ambrose pushed her down in a chair. "You listen to me, young woman..."

Elizabeth sprang back up. He pushed her down again, keeping his hands securely on her shoulders. She struggled for a moment, then sat, glaring up at him.

"Your sister is not a bairn. I might be able to understand your feelings if they were directed at your daughter, but Mary is a grown woman. And based on what I've witnessed in the short time that I've spent with you two, I can see that she is nothing more than a pampered, selfish woman who demands to be at the center of *your* attention. Elizabeth, she is using you."

She'd heard all this so many times before. She simply didn't need someone else preaching to her what she already knew was—at least in part—the truth. But it wasn't the whole truth. Her voice softened. "But she is sick, Ambrose. She truly is."

"But you just said it yourself. She is sick in mind and not in body." He looked down into her troubled eyes. "Elizabeth, she is robbing you of your life. Of a time that you could be spending with your daughter, or with others if you choose to. Tell me one thing: Why is she with you? Why is she not fluttering about, enjoying English court life? It is where she belongs. Your father is very much in favor there."

Elizabeth shook her head. She couldn't tell him.

"She is unhappy, lass," he pressed. "That's obvious even to strangers. Must you pay for her unhappiness? Is she punishing you for the life she is leading? Why can't you send her back?"

"Please stop!" she pleaded, pushing him back. Standing, she took both of his hands in hers. She held them tight. She needed his strength. "I know, I've heard all these things before. And I agree with much of what you say. Mary needs her own life, separate from mine. But leaving her here is not the way. I cannot cut her loose and leave her to drift here. Not here, where she knows no one. I promise you. I give you my word that I will find a place where she can live her own life. But let me take her to where she has friends. Where she won't be left alone."

Ambrose gathered her hands in his. The desperate pleading note in her voice was one he'd never heard before. This was a far different side of the strong and willful Elizabeth Boleyn. She was speaking from her heart. He couldn't let her down.

"Paris," he said firmly. "We'll take her as far as Paris. You have friends, family there. She can get the help and support you say she needs. But no further. That is my condition."

"Thank you!" she whispered, throwing herself into his arms.

Chapter 20

He knows peace who has forgotten desire.

Ambrose wanted to place his fingers around her delicate neck. She stood leaning peacefully against the low railing. A gentle breeze riffled through her black tresses. Her beautiful face—no longer hidden behind the concealing pigments—was now adorned with only the gentle color left by the early summer sun and the softly caressing wind. How could she be so content, he thought, while his own body burned so? Her constant nearness, the daily sight of her over the past fortnight was maddening. Ambrose Macpherson was on fire.

"The last time I traveled along this river, Mary and I were on foot."

Elizabeth gazed out at the rolling farms and vineyards that came right to the edge of the smooth-running Seine River. The midday sun was sparkling off the water, and the long, wide barge was gliding lazily through the countryside of Champagne northward toward the merchant town of Troyes.

Ambrose had been true to his word. And to make the journey easier for the still weak Mary, the baron had hired a series of boats and barges to take them north along the broad, brown Rhone River to Lyons, and then onward along the Saône River, to Dijon, and finally to the Seine. Elizabeth and Mary had followed the same route, but southward, during their trek from the Field of Cloth of Gold to their new life in Florence. But it had been a long and arduous walk with a pregnant Mary.

Elizabeth knew that the Highlander's decision to travel the waterways had made for a slower journey, but it had been far more comfortable.

"Do you think your soldiers are already in Paris?"

"Nay, lass," Ambrose said, glancing over his shoulder to make sure Gavin was nowhere within earshot. He was below with Mary, the Highlander decided. "If my men have already reached Paris, we'd see a glow in the sky at night from the sections of the city they've set ablaze."

Elizabeth cast a look past the body of the baron, toward the stern of the boat, where Joseph and Ernesta were sitting with the tillerman and a number of the boatmen. Jaime was playing on the deck with one of the kittens she'd received from the monks outside Marseilles. The little girl had a piece of line that, to the giggling delight of the child, the kitten was playfully stalking and pouncing on.

"Tell me." Ambrose spoke softly as he moved to her side, leaning against the same rail. "Tell me about the time you traveled this route."

Elizabeth could feel the brush of his shoulders against hers. It was an intimate act, but one that was noticed only by the two of them. She shivered in spite of the warm sunlight. She wanted his arms around her.

"There isn't much to tell. We set a pace Mary could handle, and we walked."

Ambrose studied her long fingers, the delicate hands of the artist that created depictions of life truer than the subjects themselves. He wanted to lift those fingers to his lips. He found himself wanting to trace a line with his lips from her fingertips to her wrist. Up her arm, along her shoulder, down to the round fullness of the breasts he knew lay so tightly bound.

He still remembered the feel of her beneath him, the taste of her on his lips. Damn that Gavin. If he hadn't come down to the galley's cabin after them, they would had made love. Right there among the rolling trunks, in the midst of the storm. She had been ready then. They had come so close, but to no avail.

And then, at the monastery, he'd wanted her. But she'd asked him to wait, and Ambrose found it difficult to deny her anything.

So he found himself still waiting. And waiting.

"I remember swimming at that bow in the river," Elizabeth said, pointing to an eddy in the bend just ahead. "It felt so wonderful, the water so clear and clean."

Ambrose followed her gaze. "Did you swim with any clothes on?" His voice was huskier than usual.

Her head turned sharply toward him. She saw the clouds of passion lurking in his eyes. She smiled.

"No clothes. Nothing on. I was quite naked." She took a quick step to the side and gave herself some distance. "It was sunset. I rose out of water and walked to the stony beach. There was nothing to dry my body with, so I let the summer breeze lick my skin dry."

She took another step back and stood facing him, somewhat amazed and amused by his reactions to her words. She looked at the clenched jaw, the way his eyes roamed her body as if she wore nothing now.

"Even then, I wished you there with me," she whispered.

"I want you, Elizabeth."

"We can't. Not yet. You promised, Baron."

Turning back toward the railing, she could feel his eyes still burning into her. Without looking at him, she reached up and slowly undid the top tie of her shirt, spreading the material with her fingers to let the soft breeze caress her skin.

"It's quite warm today. Don't you think so?" She threw a coy glance at him.

"I'll kill you, Elizabeth Boleyn. I'll kill you with my own two hands."

Below, Mary sat on the bunk, mesmerized by the tale, her back against the curved hull of the barge. The trencher of food lay untouched on her lap.

Gavin paused to take a sip from the bowl of wine that sat between them. His face was grim with the remembrance of so much destruction.

"Go on. Please go on," Mary prodded impatiently.

"I lay there, looking up at the sky. Well, at what passed for a sky that day. It was more like night than day. The rain was pouring from a sky, thick and gray. Nay! It wasn't gray—it was black with fog and with smoke from the German guns the damned English had brought up. They had been firing since morning—round after round. After a while, you don't know if the pounding of the explosions are coming from your head or from the next hill."

The young woman tried to imagine the fear Gavin must have felt.

"As I told you, it had been raining for two days, and the hills were slippery—they were thick with muck and with blood. Scottish blood. The treachery of that filthy Englishman Surrey and his vile henchman Danvers, Satan's own brother—that was what defeated us. They'd agreed to a truce until the rain stopped. And then the bastards circled around, put their bloody guns in place, and lay waiting for us.

"It was a terrible thing that battle. Flodden field. We, the men of the Borders, fought like wild men. We were faithful to the king and to our oaths to serve him. Each man of us fought like he possessed the heart of the Bruce and the soul of the Wallace. But some, I'm ashamed to say, hung back when they were called upon. Many of the Highland clans—not the Macphersons, but many others—showed how long they can remember a slight. Those sheep in men's clothing watched as the Lowlanders and the men loyal to the king were mowed down like corn before a gale. It was a shameful thing.

"But a Scotsman fears nothing when his blood is up, and when the king took up the lance himself, we followed him down that muddy hill into the ranks of the English.

"For three hours, we fought with the valor of the auld heroes down there—knee deep in bodies and in blood. But when King Jaime went down, fighting like the true warrior he was, our hearts were broken.

"They drove us across the hill. I saw my two brothers die like the gallants they were, and somewhere—not far from the king—some swine bashed my head from behind as I fought with another. I went down with the dying and the dead, and lay there unconscious for I don't know how long.

"I awoke, hearing a moaning sound and the noise of battle beyond. I tried to sit up and realized it was I who was moaning. All I could see was the dead and filthy sky. All I could feel was the rain pelting my face and the crack in the back of my head where my brains were trying to seep out. I pushed myself up and felt the ground spinning about me.

"The dead lay thick on that hillside. Thousands on thousands. It was a sight that defies telling

"And then it struck me. The English guns had stopped. I knew what would come next. They'd be scouring the dead for rings and for gold. The camp followers and the shirkers. They'd be cutting the throats of those still living, and stripping all of their weapons and their armor. I tried to look down the hill through the smoke. I could see them at the bottom. Like vultures. But I couldn't stand. My legs wouldn't move. I knew I was finished."

Gavin stopped.

Mary was suddenly aware of the tears coursing down her face. The warrior was silent, his eyes closed. She moved the tray from her lap. "Please tell me."

He opened his eyes and returned her gaze.

"I lay back down to wait for the end. At any rate, I would die fighting, I decided, and readied a short sword that lay in the mud by my hand.

"And then I saw him. He was wandering in a daze among the dead, his broad sword dragging beside him. He appeared half blinded by the blood that was still running like a river from the great gash across his forehead. He was a Highlander, a man nearly my size. He was searching among the dead. I called to him, and he came to me.

"'Where is the king?' he asked. 'Dead,' I told him. I saw his eyes flash with anger, with a silent, unutterable rage. Then he looked off down the hill before looking back at me. 'Go,' I said. 'Save yourself. It is finished here.' He just kept looking at me, but I knew he was thinking of the king.

"Then I saw his eyes clear, and he took hold of my arm. Ambrose Macpherson lifted me up and threw me over his shoulder like I was no more than a bairn. He carried me. For all that night and for two days more, he carried me. Back into Scotland."

Mary Boleyn stared at Gavin as the raven-haired warrior drank down the remainder of the wine.

"He saved your life," she whispered.

"It was more than that. Much more." He looked up toward the narrow sliver of light that was squeezing its way through an opening in the plank ceiling. "He gave me hope, a chance for a future. He showed me what courage is. The strength that comes with compassion. He taught me that brotherhood goes far beyond the ties of kinship.

"And what took place on that bloody journey was only part of what Ambrose Macpherson has done for me. The greater part lay thereafter. I had lost my only family, my two elder brothers, the ones I loved and looked up to. I was a defeated warrior, and as my body healed, my mind's desires dwelled on hate and loathing. Hate for others like the treasonous Highlanders and the bloody English. Loathing for myself.

"But Ambrose changed all of that. He stayed by me as my legs began to work again. As I began to heal, he showed me that we must live out our lives, whatever our fate." Gavin turned to Mary and smiled. "I know you wouldn't think it, since I haven't stopped talking since I met you, but I am an extremely reserved man. I shy away from people. If left to myself, I would just crawl under a rock and remain there. When I was a child, my father contemplated sending me to a cloister to become a monk."

Mary smiled, the tears still glistening on her cheeks.

"I just can't see that," she replied quietly, watching him drifting off into a world long gone. She looked down at her hands. "Thank you, Gavin."

"For what? For boring you to death?"

"Nay, for making me see." Her eyes returned to his face. "So many times we only recognize the gallantry that occurs in the heat of battle. So often we are completely blind to the valor that takes place under our noses."

"You mean your brother?" he asked.

She nodded slowly.

"He is a fine man, Mary. Many might judge him hastily, based solely on his appearance. But I know they would be wrong. He might not be strong on the surface, but he has the spirit of ten warriors." Gavin remembered how Phillipe had so fearlessly faced Ambrose, time and time again. "But the most important thing for you to know is that he loves you. That is apparent in everything that he does."

Gavin looked into the pale woman's expression before continuing. "You probably know that Ambrose had planned for you to be left behind at the monastery outside Marseilles until you became well enough to travel." He saw her nod. "Well, you should have seen your brother. He raised hell. He was prepared to fight the baron if he didn't agree to take you with us. He has spirit, Mary. Phillipe stands up for what he believes in."

Mary leaned her head against the wooden hull. This was only a trifle compared to the things Elizabeth had done for her in her life. Gavin knew only the tiniest fraction of it. And Mary was beginning to see it all so clearly now. As if she were awakening from a deep and dreamless slumber, her eyes began to focus. Suddenly she could remember so many things. Recollect so clearly. Holy Mother, she prayed, forgive me for being so blind.

Mary considered for a moment what life with her must be for Elizabeth. She was very sick, perhaps more so now than ever before. This time was different. Mary knew that there could be no getting better this time. The physician at the monastery at Marseilles had confirmed her fears. She was dying. She knew it, though no one else did. She couldn't let Elizabeth know. Not yet.

She never slept. For two weeks now, every night as she had lain awake in her bed thinking, seeing her past relived before her eyes, she had felt the sickness taking over her brain. And then during the days, she'd listened, watched Elizabeth sitting so supportively, so lovingly beside her. Her sister, the one who accepted her as she was, in spite of her flaws, her ailments, her complaining tongue. Elizabeth had remained at her side for years—constant, true. Elizabeth had always been there. Been there for her. But what had Mary ever done, ever given her in return? Nothing.

Even sending Gavin—that had been Elizabeth's doing. Mary knew she was far beyond hope. Her time for first love was far behind her now, and the past weeks had brought that message home clearly to her. But she wasn't devastated by the realization. And when Elizabeth had sent Gavin down to her, she had found a companionship such as she had never known before. A camaraderie that she had never even thought of seeking.

But they had found that special relationship. They were friends. Other than Elizabeth, Mary had never even had a friend. But here they were. A man and a woman. Two people so different from one another. Two people who had gravitated toward each other's company. That had been Elizabeth's doing. Once again her sister had done that for her.

Mary's thoughts went back to the morning, when her sister had been beside her. She had not made any attempt to mask her complexion today. Even though Elizabeth still was dressed as a man, she had the undeniable freshness of a woman. And Mary knew the cause. Even from where she lay below decks, Mary could see the love that her sister carried for the Highlander. Elizabeth might not be ready to admit it to herself, but she was in love. In love with Ambrose Macpherson.

And Mary also knew her sister would never do anything about that. As long as Mary herself lived, she knew her sister would sacrifice every chance of love and of happiness to take care of her. She knew nothing would stop Elizabeth from continuing to provide her with the care and the companionship as she had always had.

Well, now it was Mary's job to cut the ties. She had to think of something. Elizabeth deserved some happiness of her own.

But first Mary wanted to see Jaime.

"I'm not going, Mary!"

"You *are* going," the younger woman ordered. "How many times do you think you'll have the opportunity to meet with the King of France?"

"But I have been presented at court before. You know that, and—"

"But never as an artist." Mary's voice shook with emotion. "Never as the painter all Europe is talking about. You have joined the top tier, Elizabeth. Your talent, your gift is finally being recognized. You deserve this attention. It is the moment artists work for their entire lives with only the slimmest hope of achieving. It's what you want, isn't it?"

Elizabeth let her head drop into her hands. "Nay. I don't know!" The news that King Francis wanted to meet Phillipe de Anjou at the Constable of Champagne's hunting lodge in the forest to the east of Troyes had caught her off guard. "I don't know anymore. I don't know what to do."

Ambrose's soldier had hailed the barge from the riverside that morning. Word had gotten to the king of the Florentine painter's commission with the Scottish royal family, and Francis wanted to greet this native son as he journeyed on to the north.

"Please! For me, you should go," Mary cajoled as Elizabeth raised an eyebrow at her. "This is an opportunity for me to live just a bit of it once more, through your eyes, through your experience. When you get back, you can tell me of the people who were there, the way everyone dressed, the latest talk of court. Please, Elizabeth. Go!"

Elizabeth stood and moved to the side of Mary's bed. The younger sister opened her arms and Elizabeth fell into the embrace. The two hugged fiercely as they rocked gently in each other's arms.

Mary was changing. Elizabeth could see it, feel it in her heart. It had been three weeks. Three weeks on the barges, traveling the rivers. With each passing day, Elizabeth had seen her sister strengthen in her affection toward those around her...while her body visibly withered. So many times Elizabeth had questioned her own judgment in making this journey. But it was too late.

"I can't see how I could—"

"Elizabeth—" Mary pulled back to look into her sister's eyes—"I heard you and Erne whispering about my health last night." At seeing her older sister's protest, Mary hushed her gently. "Please understand, my love. For once, I am living my life the way I should have lived it all along. I am happy." She paused. "I know I am dying, and I know that all of you can see it, as well. But it's strange, Elizabeth, because I really don't mind the thought of it." She held her sister's soft face in her hands. "And I want no sorrow or tears from anyone. I've had a full life, and I was given a chance to...well, to correct it by coming on this journey."

Mary gathered Elizabeth in her arms once again. "But, God forbid, most of all I want no deathwatch around me. I want to live to the last day—to the last breath. And I'll be here, I promise you. I'll be waiting for you when you get back. Go on this trip, Elizabeth. It will be good for me. Please."

Elizabeth lay her head against her sister's shoulder.

"And perhaps," Mary whispered smilingly in her sister's ear—she knew she needed to press her advantage now—"It would be good for you and Ambrose to be away from the rest of us for a few days. You two deserve some time alone. Just the two of you."

Elizabeth, color spreading like fire through her face, drew back momentarily from the sick woman's embrace and stared at her. She hadn't expected this.

"Do you think I don't see the way you feel about him? Come, now, my love. It's branded on your face anytime he comes anywhere near. Even anytime his name comes up. It is right there in your eyes."

Elizabeth looked away. Truly, she hardly knew how to hide—or deny—her feelings for him. Feelings that were growing more and more obvious with each passing day. How could she stop the way her blood pounded in her veins when he'd look at her in a certain way? Or the way her skin burned when he chanced to brush against her? Indeed, she knew she could hardly ignore the way her throat knotted when she'd seen him crouching so attentively beside Jaime while the little child showed the baron how her kitten's claws worked. It was difficult for Elizabeth to explain, even to herself, why tears had welled up in her eyes watching the Highlander unpin the broach on his tartan to show the little girl his family's coat of arms—a cat with outstretched claws sitting atop a decorated shield.

Elizabeth's heart and mind struggled as the desire to follow the path of love, if for only just this time, pulled against the sense of responsibility she felt for her sister.

"Such foolishness, Mary," she scolded, hugging her sister to her once again. But even to herself, the words of denial sounded feeble, at best.

The two women pulled apart and turned as the door of the cabin open lightly on its hinges. D'Or, the yellow kitten Jaime had named for its golden fur, was the first thing they saw as it leaped into the middle of the room. Then, behind her, the shadow of the little girl followed the animal in.

"D'Or wanted to visit," Jaime whispered shyly from the entryway.

Mary opened her arms as the young girl ran in and threw herself into the mother's embrace. Elizabeth choked back her tears. She loved them so much. Both of them. So many years she had hoped, she had prayed for this to happen. At last. Thank you, Virgin Mother. At last.

Elizabeth stood up from the bunk and started for the door. They needed as much time as they could have together, to make up for those years.

"Elizabeth!"

She turned at the sound of her sister's voice.

"Take that satchel with you."

"What is it?"

"Something for you," Mary whispered, her face aglow. "Something for your little trip. And Elizabeth..." She waited until her sister's attention was fixed on her. "You are going. Today."

"I don't think leaving you—"

Mary interrupted her, nestling her chin in Jaime's hair. Her eyes glowed with affection as she gazed into Elizabeth's face. "Believe it or not, we can do without you for a couple of days." The younger sister smiled happily and turned playfully to her daughter as she spoke. "Besides, Gavin has already told me he won't be going with you. He'll be staying with us. So you see, you don't have anything to worry about. We'll see you in Troyes. Gavin said we'll dock there and enjoy the market fair while we wait for you. I've always wanted to see the market fair at Troyes."

Elizabeth hesitated another moment, but her sister's gaze was direct.

"I need this, my love," Mary said quietly. "We both need to live every moment we have left. Give us this time."

Chapter 21

Frenchmen are as blind as Florentines, Ambrose thought, still somewhat stunned and hardly amused as he and Elizabeth rode along. If the armies of these two powers meet on the battlefield, he surmised, they'd better do so on a very sunny day...or they'll march right by one another.

The sojourn to the encampment of King Francis had involved an unexpected change in plans. Originally they were to travel to a hunting lodge in the forest to the east of the town, but that was not to be. Disembarking from the ferry on the east side of the river at Bar-sur-Seine, Ambrose and Elizabeth had been met by an emissary of the king, and they'd been escorted to the well-traveled highway that led eastward toward the Marne River and, eventually, to Geneva and Italy.

There, in a pavilion of cloth of gold that shimmered in the bright morning sun, the two travelers found King Francis trying on hats made by the craftsmen of Troyes, while twenty thousand armed men eagerly awaited his royal word to get on with their invasion of Italy.

And, to Ambrose's utter amazement, no one even guessed that Elizabeth was anyone—anything—but Phillipe de Anjou.

The painters that the king had brought with him to record his anticipated triumphs over the Emperor Charles's forces were uncommunicative, but grudgingly compliant when Elizabeth reluctantly agreed to the king's request to do a portrait of him as he sat in armor at a camp table, the maps of conquest spread before him, chatting with Ambrose about his route. Working quickly—a skill the artist had honed through her experience painting on rapidly drying plaster—Elizabeth created a treasure that won the praises of even the most reserved critic with its elegant structure, masterly brushwork, and astonishing display of color.

The entire visit was extraordinary, in Ambrose's view, but dining with the king would have been an ordeal for both painter and baron. Ambrose knew that, once ensconced in the dinner conversation with the French king, he would have been expected to elaborate in detail on the results of his visit with the Pope in Rome, and with Don Giovanni in Florence. And, Ambrose knew all too well, any involvement with Francis meant certain entanglement in more political intrigue. So the Highlander had been delighted when Elizabeth, professing sudden illness, had requested to be excused of His Majesty's gracious presence. Receiving a bag of gold as a reward for his "wonderful work, and the honor he was bringing on France," Phillipe de Anjou had bowed his way out of the pavilion of the king, and the Highlander had joined in the escape.

They had not needed an escort back. Ambrose had assured all parties of that. So they rode in the golden light of the late afternoon sun, winding their way along the edge of the great forest east of Troyes.

Elizabeth grabbed her hat and yanked it off her head. She shook her hair loose in the light, early summer breeze. Her horse cantered easily behind the massive charger and its silent rider.

Before they had left the camp of the king, the Highlander had changed back into his Scottish gear, and Elizabeth gazed on him admiringly. His broadsword hung across his back, and his tartan's colors shone brightly in the evening light.

Ambrose Macpherson would cut a dashing figure in any company, she thought proudly. And every word he spoke, often so charged with his own wit, had been heeded very carefully by King Francis and his advisers.

Elizabeth wondered whether anyone had caught her gazing at him during their visit at the camp.

The painter tore her eyes away from him and looked around at the serene countryside. So beautiful, she thought. She glanced back at the baron and then out again at the rolling fields of flax. All the years she had lived in France, she had never seen nor traveled in this land east of the Seine.

"You know these parts well," she called out, watching his back. He had hardly said a word since leaving the French king's camp. "Thank you for taking me back a different way. I don't know when I would have had an opportunity to see these parts again."

Elizabeth waited for him to turn around, to slow his horse, to acknowledge her words—but he never did.

She kicked her heels into the side of her horse, urging him on. Reining in at the side of the nobleman, she looked at his grave expression. "What have I done now?"

Ambrose paused, then turned and returned her gaze. "Guilty conscience?"

"Nay," she said matter-of-factly, rising to the challenge in his tone. "This is just my advance movement prior to an attack on your cranky disposition."

Ambrose realized once again that her ability to pass as a man wasn't just due to the way she dressed. Elizabeth even had the aggressiveness. "I am not cranky."

"That's the truth. You are foul-tempered, disagreeable, and irritating. Does that cover it?"

"Couldn't have done it better myself."

Elizabeth shook her head as he once again fell into a brooding silence. Everything had gone beautifully at the king's camp. It had been a short visit, but all the same, she couldn't remember doing anything that would have annoyed the baron, nor recall anything happening that might be the cause of his present sullenness.

Once again Elizabeth nudged her horse ahead, this time cutting in front of the baron and leaning over in an attempt to catch his steed's bridle.

"What are you up to?" He drew in the reins of his horse, bringing the animal to a halt. Elizabeth's horse followed suit. "Are you trying to break your neck?"

"Nay," she responded, reaching in again and making a grab at his reins. Ambrose yanked the charger's head around, but she persisted. "I'm trying to make you talk."

"I have nothing to say."

"Don't patronize me with such nonsense! You're a chattering magpie. A flap jawed diplomat. Nothing to say!" she scoffed.

Ambrose scowled at her. "If you were a man, I would consider breaking your neck for saying what you just said."

"Well, I am not a man. So I suppose you'll simply have to live with it."

"If I had ever had the misfortune of becoming involved with you, I would have locked you away a long time ago. For good, I mean."

"Well, that never happened, either, by the grace of the Holy Mother. So you be damned. I am free to say what I want."

Ambrose glared at her smug face. "Let me give you some advice, lass. It is very dangerous business, trifling with an angry man. And I *am* an angry man. Or are you too blind to see that?"

"Blind? Ha! Why in God's name do you think I am taking all this abuse, you thick-skulled Scot? Of course I can see you are angry! I just need to know why. Did I cause it? Did I do anything that was improper? Speak to me, why don't you?"

"Just let it be, Elizabeth."

"I won't!"

"I'm in no mood for this."

"Well, I am!"

Ambrose glared at her. She glared back.

"You are not going to give this up, are you?"

Elizabeth shook her head defiantly.

Ambrose took a deep breath and looked away, gazing into the deepening shadows of the nearby forest. She was the most stubborn woman he'd ever known. No, that wasn't it. This woman cared for him enough to demand an answer. "You aren't the one that's the problem, Elizabeth!"

"Not acceptable, Ambrose Macpherson. I am *not* accepting such an evasion for an answer."

"It's *me*, damn it!"

Elizabeth continued to glare at him. "If it's your own doing, then why must *I* take the brunt of your vile conduct?"

"If you would let me be, then you wouldn't need to even witness my 'vile' conduct."

She tried to speak more calmly. "My good baron, I think I've been around you enough in the course of this journey to know when I am the cause of your distress. And that certainly seems to be the case—"

"I lied," Ambrose broke in.

"What?"

"I lied."

"To whom?"

"To Francis. To the King of France. Our host. I lied."

"Politicians always lie." She glanced away under the withering heat of his glare. "Never mind. Tell me, what did you say that was such a crime?"

"I lied to Francis about you. About you being a man. And some other grave political matter. And they believed everything I said." Ambrose had indeed lied to Francis about Duke Giovanni's power. He'd decided to buy his friend some time. Florence didn't have a chance against the troops of Francis. This was the best help Ambrose could give Giovanni right now. "I made fools of all of them."

"You didn't make them fools, Ambrose. They are fools." She struggled to suppress a smile. "But m'lord, if this is the way you feel here in France, how will you feel once we reach Scotland? Are you going to take me to the closest tree and hang me once we get there, so you won't have to lie to your queen?"

"That's not a bad idea." He paused and considered. "I wouldn't need to put up with this kind of quarreling, and my conscience would definitely rest easier."

"Wonderful!" she responded, throwing her hands up dramatically. "But let's not stop there. After all, we still have a long journey ahead of us. Perhaps it is too great a distance to carry such a heavily weighted soul as yours must be. Aye, far too long a time to wrestle with such troubles. But what can we do? Alas, no priest in sight to lighten your burden. Are you certain there is nothing I could do right now to ease your suffering soul? To put your conscience to rest? Ah! I have it. Perhaps a sacrifice is in order, an offering to cleanse the soul..."

Ambrose watched her extravagant act with growing amusement as she carried on her animated talk. Then his eyes began to see her again. Elizabeth. He studied her bright face; her intelligent, shining eyes; the very sensual woman who hid behind it all. Without even trying she had a way of clearing everything else from his mind. "I like the last one."

Elizabeth stopped midsentence. "Which was the last one?"

"The offering part."

She smiled brilliantly. "I'm glad that's the one. I was just moving on to maiming and immolation after that." Elizabeth reached into her saddlebag and removed the pouch of gold that she'd received from the French king. She tossed it to Ambrose. "The next church we pass by, drop this bag in as an offering."

The Highlander looked blankly at the woman.

"Offering?" she continued. "An offering for your soul?"

"There is nothing wrong with my soul." He tossed the bag back into her lap. "It is my body that suffers."

Elizabeth reddened and paused for a long moment before responding. "That's a dilemma. I believe I'll need some time to think of a remedy for that one."

Ambrose nudged his charger up close to hers and, without warning, slapped her horse hard on the flank. As Elizabeth's steed bolted, the Highlander spurred his own animal in pursuit.

"But wait!" Elizabeth yelled, holding her position firmly on the horse. "I need more time. I don't have an answer yet."

"Have no fear!" the baron shouted. "I know the remedy!"

The Marquis of Troyes certainly likes to hunt in comfort, Elizabeth thought, trying to look appreciatively at the things around her as she wandered somewhat apprehensively about the spacious bedchamber. And if this is how he accommodates his guests, how must he pamper himself?

"Honestly, I don't want to know," she said aloud, running her fingers over the fine lace-covered comforter that lay upon the huge damask-canopied bed.

This grand country manor—a hunting lodge, they had called it—was truly a palace by anyone's standards. Turning off the highway and plunging into the darkness of a forest road, Ambrose had led her, without any more words being said, to this place.

Now, seating herself on the edge of the bed, a recurring thought kept plucking at the strings of her anxiety.

His body! she thought. His suffering body! Sacrifice for his body? Elizabeth shook her head. No, he didn't mean it. This was just his way of tormenting her.

Elizabeth laid back on the comforter, a weariness suddenly overtaking her. Then, as if stung by something unseen, the young woman leaped from the bed.

Elizabeth moved to the middle of the floor, helpless, as fears that lingered in her soul flared up like the flurries of stars that shoot westward in the summer night sky. She felt them all, coursing through her in waves of heat and cold. All the anxiety of being a woman and yet not a woman. Complete and yet not complete. Experienced in the ways of the world and yet lacking all knowledge of courtship by men.

A woman still untouched. Wanting him and yet still not knowing if Ambrose's attentions focused only on the physical. She wondered if he'd missed her as she had missed him. If he even saw her as a being worthy of his interest. Had he brought her here to satisfy their bodies' desire? Well, what of their souls? she asked herself.

Elizabeth wrapped her arms around her. You're making more of this than there is, she told herself, finding cold consolation in the thought.

Crossing the room, she tried to organize everything in her mind. This was the place where they were first supposed to meet Francis, so it was natural for them to stop. And it was getting late, so of course they would stay the night. Then tomorrow they would go on to Troyes. It was all explainable, logical.

Listen to yourself rationalize, she thought guiltily.

Relax, Elizabeth reminded to herself. This is a house full of servants. A house large enough to hide in and never be found by Ambrose. There was absolutely nothing to worry about. If she didn't want him to make love to her, then...

"What a lie!" she whispered with a sigh.

She couldn't deny it. She missed him. Pacing back and forth, Elizabeth realized she was fighting two battles at once. Battles she could not hope to win—at least not here. At least not now.

She shrugged again, pushing all thoughts of love from her mind. Moving to the spacious window, she looked outside. From the moment she and Ambrose had ridden up the winding path to the main house, Elizabeth had found herself admiring the lodge's design—the perfect balance of practicality and aesthetics. Modest-sized fields and pastures, carved out of the forest to produce enough food for the table of the marquis, eventually gave way to stables, kennels, and the most extraordinary gardens the young painter had seen anywhere.

And at the center of it all stood the lodge itself.

It was a magnificent building. Tall stone towers and turrets topped with conical slate-covered roofs adorned the multitude of peripheral wings that branched off with symmetrical grace from the main wing of the lodge. Though the towers were of stone, the walls of the lodge itself were of wattle and wood, and the X-designs of the supporting timbers created a strikingly picturesque look.

Elizabeth couldn't wait to see the rest of this architectural gem. Even the windows, luxuriously abundant and glazed with innumerable panes, had promised an interior that would be bright and airy.

And she hadn't been disappointed. The splendor of the place was truly inspiring.

Paintings, carvings, and tapestries filled the walls of the great rooms and the corridors leading to the bedchambers. Elizabeth turned around and faced the chamber she was occupying. This room on its own was a feast for the eyes in the glow of late afternoon light that spilled with reckless extravagance through the four open windows. Tables, chairs, a chest, and even a small fireplace—all part of the Marquis of Troyes's design to furnish each and every visitor with more comfort and hospitality than even a royal guest might expect elsewhere.

Very thoughtful, Elizabeth decided, smiling as she headed for the cheese, bread, and wine that sat so invitingly on the table.

The knock on the door stopped Elizabeth dead in her tracks. She stood in the center of the room, looking uncertainly at the great oak door. Ambrose had his own bedchamber. It was clear he was a regular guest here, for it appeared it was his customary room. It was just past the wide and gracefully carved staircase.

The sound of another gentle tap urged the young woman forward. Elizabeth moved quietly across the chamber and then stood listening, her hand steady on the decorative wooden latch.

"Who is it?"

The timid voice of the woman on the other side of the door could hardly be heard through the thick wood. Elizabeth opened the door slightly and peered out at the young maid standing patiently in the hallway.

"Mademoiselle, I was asked to come and help you dress and also to bring you this."

Elizabeth looked down at the satchel the servant held in her outstretched arms. She recognized it as the one Mary had sent along. Then her eyes shot up to the young woman's face. "What was it that you called me?"

"Pardon me, m—madame," she stuttered apologetically. "I—I didn't know...no one told me if 'mademoiselle' is appropriate or 'madame.' I am so sorry. I—"

"No! No! That's not it!" Elizabeth swung the door open and gestured for the young maid to step in. "I was just surprised by..." She shook her head. Had Ambrose notified the household of her true identity? She turned and watched as the girl moved through the room, opening chests and selecting fine chemises, hosiery, puffy-sleeved blouses of the whitest silk, and an elegant dress the color of a narcissus flower. "To whom does all this belong?"

"The marquis's mother, m'lady. The master's parents visit here quiet often." The young woman held the dress up and cast a quick glance at Elizabeth, smiling happily at the evident match. She spread the garment on the bed. "But she would insist upon you wearing them—considering that you have arrived without your trunks and servants."

The maid continued to bustle about the room as Elizabeth's hand caressed the rich texture of the yellow brocade cloth of the dress.

"We do this quite often. Though the seamstress will be disappointed that your size and Lady Elizabeth's are so close." The servant looked up before continuing, and Elizabeth smiled, thinking how quickly the young woman had lost her shyness. The maid chattered on. "Oh, how interesting! You have the same names. It is not always so. The sizes, I mean. Why, the last time Sir Ambrose brought—I meant to say, the last time—I'm so sorry, madame. I talk too much."

Elizabeth watched the young girl's reddened face.

"Does he travel here often?" she asked gently.

"I—I shouldn't..." she shook her head. "It is not proper to tell a lady about the one before."

"Does he come here with many ladies?"

"No, madame." The young maid shook her head. "I heard from the older servants that he used to. He and the duc. He is Sir Ambrose's close friend. But now, since the duc has married, Sir Ambrose has been coming alone. With the exception of this visit, madame."

Elizabeth listened quietly. She didn't care much about the duc or his pastimes, but there was one thing that the young woman had made clear—the purpose of this sojourn was to satisfy his desires, after all. Conditions. It all came down to this. The conditions that he'd spoken of in Florence. They were here to share her bed.

Of course! What could she have been expecting? She would be a fool to think otherwise. Elizabeth walked to the satchel that the young woman had placed on top of the bed. The one she'd picked up in Mary's room. Something for her, Mary had said.

Pulling open the thongs that held it closed, Elizabeth dumped the contents on the bed and gazed down at a linen-wrapped package and a note addressed to her.

A note from her sister.

Elizabeth, my dearest! What pleasure this brings me, knowing you are—for at least one moment in your life—away from the cares you shoulder so unfailingly. For so long, my sweet, you thoughts and your actions have tended to everyone but you, yourself. How different we are, my sister. For how many years now, you have lived so serious a life—while I have lived so frivolously. Well, for once, follow your heart's lead. For once be a woman as God intended you to be. And know that we are secure and lovingly yours, Mary.

Elizabeth placed the note gently beside the package and untied the ribbon that held the linen wrapping tight. Picking up the diaphanous silk nightgown that Mary had packed for her, the young painter gazed silently at the garment until her eyes clouded over.

Then, reaching up, she found the ring that lay close to her heart. Gently, she removed the leather thong from around her neck and laid the emerald ring on the side table.

For so many years she had kept and cherished this token as a symbol, as a reminder of Ambrose. So many times, she held the emerald ring in her hand and dreamed. But now, tonight, reality was pressing.

Tonight, this memento would serve no purpose.

For tonight, at least, there was no need for pretense. Tonight, Elizabeth Boleyn would live as a woman. Would have her chance to love. She would have Ambrose Macpherson body and soul.

For tonight, at least, Elizabeth would have no need for this ring.

Chapter 22

Ambrose patted the gray, shaggy hound that lay by his feet and then stood up to go after her.

Too long. Far too long.

Stretching his frame, the baron turned toward the door. He was growing old waiting for Elizabeth to come down to dinner. He was tired, hungry, and though he almost hated to admit it, anxious to spend time with her. The last servant he had sent up had returned with the news that she had finished with her bath and was dressing. But that had been an hour ago. He should have followed his instincts and gone after her himself.

Ambrose found himself once again becoming quite cranky. And justifiably so, he thought. She was doing it to rile him. He was certain of it. He could just see her sitting in that room, waiting—just waiting to see how long it would take him to reach the end of all patience.

Well, the vixen was going to find out.

By the time he reached the door of the sitting room, the Highlander was in a full rage. Yanking the door open, he took one step into the corridor and stopped.

There she stood.

The words he was forming to greet her with upstairs withered, forgotten on his tongue as he gawked helplessly at the vision before him. His eyes drank in the sight of her as if trying to quench some inexorable thirst. But somewhere deep inside him, Ambrose knew that there was no relief.

Though her raven hair was short and her expression challenging, she was all woman beneath. She was clad in a soft yellow dress that draped off both her shoulders, leaving them exquisitely bare. He was certain his mother had worn the same dress, but somehow Elizabeth looked quite different in it. And wonderfully so.

Ambrose's eyes traveled the surface of the exposed shoulders to the full curves of her breasts and then up again to the ivory splendor of her throat. And as he returned again to that beautiful face, so full of challenge, so full of life, he felt that familiar stirring in his loins.

Elizabeth smiled. Ambrose was wearing black. His blond hair was tied back, but the strands that spilled onto the ebony velvet of his doublet gleamed in the light of the room. The fine hose that displayed the contoured muscles of his legs was also black, so only the gold chain that hung about his neck and the puffy white sleeves that pushed through slits in the arms of the doublet offered any contrast to the image of power that emanated from his richly dark attire. Just standing in his presence, Elizabeth felt her pulse quicken.

Ambrose had to control an overpowering urge to pull her into his arms at once and devour her whole.

Elizabeth pushed past him and stepped into the room. She didn't have to look to know that he followed close behind. The sound of the door closing behind them made her shiver as emotion and anticipation mingled in a volatile mix.

Like some huge and fragrant oak with branches that spread around her, Ambrose Macpherson had, even in his absence, dominated her world for a long time—indeed, he affected her very senses. Now she couldn't stop herself from melting inside at the thought of how it would feel to hold him, to kiss him, to feel the very weight of him.

Elizabeth was obsessed with him.

Wrapping her arms around her middle, she gathered herself and stood waiting in the middle of the spacious chamber. The room was warm, and the small wood fire crackling noisily in the hearth was comforting and homelike. The shaggy gray hound trotted over to inspect her and, satisfied with the gentle pat he received, settled himself once again by the fire.

Four years ago, she had been ready to give herself to this man. She'd even thought, momentarily, that the mere physical attraction that she had felt for him could carry her through the act. But now she felt a longing that far exceeded what she felt then.

Tonight, walking to this room, stepping within his arms' reach, was a dream. She had waited long enough. She knew that. But she also knew that she had waited for *him*.

There were many things she had for-gone in her life. But this was one thing she wouldn't turn her back on. For now he wanted her, and she had made up her mind that he would have what he desired.

Ambrose bit back his smile as he leaned against the door and watched her turn and face him. She was struggling, he could tell. His silent scrutiny was unnerving her.

He let his eyes once again peruse every aspect of her dress, her body, her face. She avoided his gaze. There was a pink blush that had spread across her beautiful face. She looked exquisite and...so innocent.

"Do you approve?" Her voice trembled slightly as she glanced briefly at him.

He nodded silently.

"This dress..." She looked down and caught sight of her partially exposed breast. She looked away quickly and crossed her arms in front of her. "It's so beautiful. My wearing it simply doesn't do the garment justice."

Upon hearing no response, she turned her gaze to him. He remained where he was, leaning against the door, his arms crossed over his chest. She looked down at her own pose. Mirror images. They were standing the same way. She dropped her hands to her sides at once.

"You look beautiful."

She waited for more. But he said no more. Uncertain of what to do next, Elizabeth glanced anxiously at the baron again. Truthfully, she had come downstairs fully prepared to be ravished on the nearest table. And she had decided that would perhaps have been the easiest solution for both of them. That way, she would never have time to dawdle over the rights and wrongs of the act.

And there would be no time to reveal to him the truth.

The truth that she wasn't the woman he thought her to be. The truth that Jaime wasn't her daughter. The truth that she was a virgin. And the most troublesome truth of all—that she simply hadn't a clue about how to make love to him.

She was afraid.

And now she found that his flattering expression, his bold blue eyes, his smiling compliments were beginning to irk her. She wished he would do something.

"Hungry?"

"For food?" she questioned hesitantly.

"Aye, I'm starved."

Starved? For food? She nearly snapped. What's wrong with this man? she wondered. Let's get on with it! Elizabeth turned away from him, disgusted with herself for not having more knowledge of the game of love, more experience in dealing with men on this level. "I have no appetite."

She glanced around again as Ambrose moved toward her. He was smiling confidently. "For food, I assume."

She held her breath. At last.

He took hold of her hand and placed it in the crook of his arm. "Too bad." He started toward a door on the other end of the room.

Unable to stop herself in time, Elizabeth held back, resisting gently. "Where are you taking me?"

"To a room beside the great hall. To watch me eat." He paused, taking a firmer grip on her hand. "Unless you would prefer to have dinner served here in this room."

Elizabeth scanned the room quickly. There were chairs, a table by the fireplace, a reed mat on the floor. Her eyes lingered on the mat. It looked comfortable enough. And they were alone. "Here. I prefer it here."

She allowed him to escort her to the table. He sat her in a chair and moved away.

Elizabeth watched him as he strode to a door and spoke briefly with someone just outside.

No longer having his intense blue eyes on her, Elizabeth felt she could breathe once again. She had to get control of herself and her emotions. She looked about the room, noticing for the first time the marvelous paintings that adorned each wall. Rising to her feet, she crossed over to them and studied each canvas one by one. They were mostly the works of Europe's most renowned painters.

Ambrose gestured for the servant who had spread the food on the trestle table to leave them. With a cordial bow, the man departed.

As he moved behind her, the baron could tell that she once again was feeling at ease. Lost in the artwork of the lodge, she was in her element. He smiled. Fate had played a trick on him.

He studied her profile, the faint line of the scar that barely showed on her skin. She smelled of wildflowers in an open field. His eyes caressed her slender neck. The soft curls that came short of hiding the exquisite splendor of her ivory skin. He could almost taste that skin under his lips. He wanted her so much that it hurt.

Elizabeth heard him come near. Then she felt the gentle touch of his lips on the skin of her neck. She looked down and saw his hands encircle her waist. She leaned back against his body.

"It's time," he said huskily.

She turned slowly in his embrace. Facing him. Holding her heart in her hand.

"Aye. The food is here, Elizabeth. It's time to eat."

Elizabeth reached up, placing her fingers around his neck. She wanted to strangle him. "Why are you doing this to me?" The sound of his laugh soothed her heart.

"Doing what?" he protested coyly, as he pushed her hands behind his neck and crushed her to his chest. His lips came down and brushed fleetingly across hers.

"Making me wait like this. Why are you doing this? I thought you wanted to make love to me." She concentrated on the cleft of his chin. "What are you waiting for? When are we going to...do it?"

Ambrose looked at her with raised eyebrows. "A wee bit impatient, wouldn't you say, lass?"

"If you're going to pretend that you did not bring me here to make love to me, then you are a liar, Ambrose Macpherson."

"Nay. But our lovemaking can wait, wouldn't you say? Perhaps until we've eaten some of this food. Then drunk some wine. Then we'll go for a walk outside. There is full moon out there. Then I might be able to persuade the gardener to cut you some fresh flowers—"

"Stop it!" She yanked her hands from behind his neck and struck him solidly in his chest. "Why must you go on like this? And don't tell me this is some Scottish courting ritual. I know it's probably the same thing you've used on all the women you bring to this place."

Ambrose paused and looked teasingly into her face. "Nay, Elizabeth. I'm not courting you. And for your information, I don't play games like that with women. I have no need for it. In fact, by the time I've closed the door to this room behind them, we've already made love twice in the bedchambers and once on the stairway."

She pushed at his chest and tried to get away. He wouldn't let her. She punched at his chest once again. She was hurt. He ensnared her hands with his own. She gave up her struggle.

"Then why?" Elizabeth whispered. "Why are you doing this to me? If you are so disappointed—if you don't want me—then why don't you just let me go. Why did you bring me here, anyway?"

"To make love to you. To ravish you. To make you forget everything and everyone. To hear you cry out my name with more feeling than a she-wolf howls in the light of the full moon."

Elizabeth shuddered in his arms as she hung on his every word.

"But first—" Ambrose smiled mischievously— "I have to give you a taste of what you've given me. That's all. Waiting, Elizabeth. Waiting. The agony of wanting someone. The physical pain of languishing ever so patiently without really knowing for sure if she intends to go through with it. I've waited for you for quite some time now, my sweet. Shall we turn the tables? You see, two can play that game, lass. And now, shall I make you wait as I have?"

"This is quite different, m'lord. I'm here tonight at my own free will. I want to be here in your arms. This is no fate or accident that has thrown us together. I'm here because I want to be here."

"You have never been in my arms any other way, but still—"

"I want you, Ambrose." Elizabeth placed a hand gently on his lips, silencing him. "I want you now. Please take me."

He stood still, looking at her.

She moved her hand away from his lips and caressed his cheek. Her fingers traced the line of his jaw, the line of his cheekbone, and then she touched the scar that crossed his forehead. "I will not put a stop to this lovemaking. I'll not make you wait again. Ever. That I promise."

Elizabeth stood on toe and kissed the point of his chin.

Ambrose tightened his grip. He couldn't wait any more than she could. He watched her eyes close as she brushed his lips, his face with light kisses. His body, coming alive at her nearness, pressed against hers. His hand moved up and cupped her breast through the soft fabric.

Elizabeth shuddered at the feel of his hand and opened her eyes. Like the sky in spring, the blue of his eyes glistened as he gazed into her face. Reaching behind his neck and removing the leather that bound his hair, Elizabeth ran her hands through the thick flaxen locks.

Ambrose found himself lost in her eyes. He wanted her more than the air he breathed. What he'd said earlier of waiting all faded quickly into oblivion. What was it about this woman's touch?

But Elizabeth lowered her eyes, feeling her skin burn at her own awkwardness. "I, too, have waited," she whispered, laying her face against the soft dark velvet of the doublet. "I, too, have suffered."

Ambrose placed his lips in her ebony hair. My God, he wanted her. He couldn't wait.

"We have such little time together," she continued. She turned her gaze upward again, her eyes searching his face for a sign. "Tomorrow we will be back with others, and this dream will all come to an end."

"Is this a dream, lass?" he asked quietly.

"I don't know what it is!" she whispered. "I'm living the life of a man, but the feelings that threaten to burst out of my every pore tell me I am a woman. I don't know what is dream or what is real. But I do know one thing, Ambrose. I want you."

"Waiting—" he began.

"Nay!" she broke in, her voice quiet but clear. "Let's not waste this moment with bad feelings and grudges."

As Elizabeth lifted her lips, his mouth descended on hers.

Ambrose slid his fingers into her hair as he crushed her mouth to his. He'd begun to say that waiting was a fool's game. But that thought was gone—dispersed in the moment like smoke in the wind. Now he had one purpose in mind. He wanted to make love to her. He wanted to show her the reality of what she should believe. She was a woman. A very desirable woman. Certainly she was a talented painter—she had that to be proud of. But now he wanted her to know how much they needed to be only themselves. A man and a woman. No pretense, no façade, just themselves.

They had so much time to make up for.

Ambrose lifted her in his arms as he headed for the door. She wrapped her hands around his neck, her mouth resting on the skin of his neck.

"Not here?" she murmured, a small smile playing on her lips.

"Nay, lass." The Highlander smiled back at her and pushed through the door. "Nor on the stairway, either."

Chapter 23

The massive oak door swung easily on its hinges as the two swept into the room. Ambrose kicked the door shut with his foot as he carried her to the bed.

All the way up the wide stairway and through the long corridor, Elizabeth's mouth had never left his. Kissing him, she had been coaxing him on until they had burst into the bedchamber.

He was mad with desire.

There was no thought of gentle caresses, soft touches, beautiful words. Elizabeth tore at his velvet doublet, searching for the feel of his skin. She urged him on, and he followed her passionate demands with wild abandon.

Ambrose whipped the comforter from her bed and dropped her into the billows of down as he detached his mouth from her lips. A momentary flash of conscious thought told him that he should step away, slow this reckless pace. If he could only pause for a breath, regain control of his discipline, of his desire. Then, gazing down at her, he could see the clouds of passion in her eyes. Her hair spread in disarray on the smooth white linen, and her flesh showed above the top of her pulled-down dress.

He knew there was no hope. Lowering himself onto her, he was ready to take all that she wanted to give.

Elizabeth couldn't lie still. Her mind raced into a thousand new worlds, worlds she'd seen only in her most vivid and wondrous dreams. Her heart pounded wildly, her blood roared in her head. She pushed at his clothes and grasped him by the neck, wanting him closer against her body.

"Take me, Ambrose. Please! Take me now."

There was no thought beyond the actions of their hands. Mindless to anything else but the fulfillment they each sought, they tore at one another's clothes. Elizabeth felt Ambrose rise from her and then saw him above her, stripping the doublet and shirt from his upper body in a single motion. She tried to reach for the tie that belted his hose, but instead fell back as she felt herself dragged by the ankle to the edge of the bed. There he stood, and Elizabeth looked up to his handsome face, his eyes burning with desire.

Ambrose pushed her dress up to her waist as he freed himself. The soft silk of her undergarment tore in his hands. He was lost in his abandon. All discipline crumbled like spent tinder before the flames of carnal need.

"Elizabeth," he whispered, his voice raw with emotion. His fingers dug into her hips as he pulled her closer, spreading her legs apart and moving between them. "Only this once, we'll not take our time."

Clinging to the sheet, she raised her hips to him as he pressed into her soft, moist folds. "Take me, Ambrose."

In a single motion, he plunged deep within her.

Elizabeth let out a sharp cry as she reached up and grabbed him around the neck. She was seized with a momentary shock of pain. She gasped for breath and held him.

My God, he thought, she was a virgin. The thought cut like the cold, keen blade of a knife into a brain dulled and confused by the fires of desire. Ambrose took a deep breath and tried not to move. He was fully rooted within her. The tightness of her threatened to kill him. But still he remained motionless. His heart hammered against his chest, and his breath was coming in short, quick pants.

Then, gently, the Highlander lowered her to the bed. "You were a virgin," he growled.

"Don't hold it against me," she whispered, trying to lighten his scowl. The pain was beginning to subside. She ran her fingers caressingly over his chest.

"Why didn't you tell me?" he asked, pushing himself up onto his elbows. Looking down at her passion-filled eyes, he saw a tear break away from the corner of her eye and disappear into her dark hairline. "Jaime. Whose daughter is Jaime?"

"Please don't be angry," Elizabeth pleaded in a ragged voice. "I'll tell you all you want to know. I'm sorry." She covered her eyes with the back of her hand. "I'm sorry I've disappointed you."

He looked down at the woman stretched in his arms. He was the first man to lay with her. Without being able to explain it, he felt a deep sense of pride.

"How could I be disappointed?" Ambrose protested, as he took her face softly in his hands. "Shocked. Pleased. Surprised. Curious even. But not disappointed, my sweet." He leaned down and his lips over hers. Her hand once again encircled his neck, and he drew her up tightly to him.

Elizabeth arched her hips as he gathered her in his arms.

Ambrose shifted his weight, and Elizabeth gasped as a new sensation replaced the discomfort. As he partially withdrew, a feeling of intense heat, of torrid pleasure emanated from the very core of her. Ambrose slid into her again, and somewhere in her head Elizabeth felt as if a rod were being drawn across the taut string of a lyre. A single note resonated throughout her entire body.

Again, ever so slowly, he withdrew, and again the love tone played within her. A rhythm began to envelop her, coming from within, and yet tied to the motion of her lover. Higher and higher the pitch of the sound went, and Elizabeth found her body rising and falling to the pulsating beat.

Over and over, Elizabeth's hips rose to accept Ambrose with every stroke. He wanted to make certain that Elizabeth found pleasure before he did.

Her fingers dug into his shoulders. She kept pushing, arching against him rhythmically, urgently.

Then she called his name. As if the earth shook, as if her existence depended on the hold of the arms around her, Elizabeth coiled around him. Within her brain a million notes exploded in a chorus of light and sound, color and music. Every singing fiber of her being on fire, her body lifted into his as lightning bolts of reds and yellows thrilled through her—elevating her into a crystalline dimension she had only dreamed could exist.

As her body went taut as a wire, Ambrose plunged one last time. Then, momentarily spent, he fell into her welcoming embrace.

Elizabeth caressed his damp skin, gathering him tightly in her arms. For her, the earth had stopped turning as they'd made love. But now, lying there with him, her breath shortened as a knot formed in her chest. Then, without warning, Elizabeth felt tears well up and wash down her face. In the span of a few precious moments, he had been able to release in her a world that had been hidden deep within. A wondrous world.

Because of him. Lying there, she knew it was because of this man, Ambrose Macpherson, that she felt as she did. From the first moment that he'd turned his attention to her in the grandstands at the Field of Cloth of Gold, he had changed her life. She needed him. She loved him.

Elizabeth brushed her lips against his hair as he rested on top of her. She could feel the pounding of his heartbeat beginning to slow. She cherished the feel of his weight. The strength that flowed from him.

Ambrose lifted himself and rolled off of her. Moving to the middle of the bed, he pulled Elizabeth to his side. She was a tangled jumble of dress and sheets. He looked down into her beautiful face and felt his heart tighten. She looked like a dream, curled up beside him. The burst of passion, the powerful explosion he'd felt only moments ago, had subsided now. But it had been a first even for him. Never in the act of lovemaking had he felt a commingling of spirits as he had felt with her. A sense of completeness swept through him. A sense of oneness that pacified the body, soothed the soul.

But it wasn't only the strength of their passion that brought such peace, it was the way she felt now, lying in his arms. It was the feel of her body against him, as though she had been made to fit there and only there, where she lay at this moment. In his arms, beside him. She belonged to him.

His voice was gentle when he asked the question. "Why didn't you tell me the truth, lass?"

The young woman looked up and saw the softness in his expression. "I suppose I was afraid."

"Not of me!" he exclaimed, as his thumb wiped away the traces of tears that were drying on her face.

Elizabeth found herself leaning into the warm touch of his hand. "A bit afraid of you, and a bit afraid of myself."

He looked up into the dark canopy above. "You were an innocent when you came to me that night at the Field of Cloth of Gold. What a fool I was for not seeing it." He turned to her. "But why did you come? Why did you lead me on so with your pretense of experience?"

She coiled the sheets between her fingers. There was no reason to continue to evade telling him the truth. "I've already told you of my father. Of his plan to send me to King Henry's bed."

He nodded silently.

"In part, that's why I came to you that night." She searched for the right words. "That afternoon, after the joust, my father told me that Henry wanted my virginity. His foolish physicians had told the king a virgin's innocence could cure his pox. Unfortunately, I was there, at the wrong place. At the wrong time."

Ambrose cursed the stupidity of such backwardness. "You didn't believe them, did you?" he asked, already knowing the answer. "The arrogant bastard. Using his power over those too innocent to resist."

"I never gave my father a chance to go through with his threat." She moved closer to his side. "I came to your tent hoping that you would make love to me. It's true I was determined to teach my father a lesson. But my coming to you went beyond that alone. If I were to step into womanhood, I was bound that I would make that transition with the person of my own choosing."

"But you could have told me the truth. I could have taken you out of there without the hell you have put yourself through. It didn't have to be the way it was."

"How could I have done that to you?" she protested, raising herself on her elbow. "Here you were, the most handsome man in the entire Golden Vale. The most charming courtier, a champion among warriors, perhaps the most eligible bachelor in the Europe—"

"Perhaps?" he broke in with a smile.

"You had your choice of women," she continued. "And I should presume so much? Simple, plain Elizabeth Boleyn."

"The bright and the beautiful Elizabeth Boleyn."

She clapped him gently on the chest. "There is no need to flatter me, m'lord," she continued. "There I was. Wishing my innocence away, but deathly nervous about going through with it. I was just so afraid to reveal the truth and find myself thrown out of your tent."

"I never threw a woman out of my tent."

She dropped her head on his chest. "Please, don't depress me."

Ambrose smiled as he ran his fingers in her hair. "Of course, that was before I met you. I've turned so many of them away since."

"Liar!"

Ambrose laughed as he drew her face up to his for a kiss. "I was the real disappointment, wasn't I? It was I who didn't come through as you had wished."

"But you did!" She rolled on her stomach, propping herself on her elbows and looking at him with a twinkle in her eye. "As far as everyone else was concerned, we did sleep together that night. They all believed me. Even my sister Mary."

"And that ruse served your purpose?"

"I ran away," she whispered quietly, growing serious again. "And here I am. So I suppose it did."

Ambrose turned onto his side and laid his hand gently on her back. "There never were any husbands or lovers."

She shook her head. "Nay, and there was never anyone by the name of Phillipe de Anjou."

Silent for a moment, the Highlander ran his hand over the curve of her buttocks, smoothing the dress beneath his palm. He stopped.

"But what about Jaime? She looks so much like you that it was only natural for me to assume she was yours." Ambrose gazed into her face. "She's Mary's daughter, isn't she?"

Elizabeth turned her head and looked him straight in the eye. She trusted him. There was no danger for the child in Ambrose knowing the truth. "Aye. Jaime is Mary's daughter."

"And the father?"

"Henry of England," she said quietly. "This has been a secret between Mary and me. Only we know. And now you. But we must keep it that way."

Perplexed, Ambrose stared at her. "Even someone as heartless as Henry would care for his offspring. The child would be treated nobly."

"We know that. It's not Henry who worries us most." Elizabeth paused, searching for the right words. "It's our father. He bartered away two daughters. He'll treat Jaime no differently. She's happy with us. We have been able to provide for her. We are giving her everything she needs. She's better with Mary and me than she would ever be in the English court." Her voice took on an imploring note. "I just can't risk endangering her life. Please understand."

How could he not understand? Ambrose knew how illegitimate children were perceived in the royal families. They were the pawns of those in search of power.

And Ambrose had enjoyed playing and talking with Jaime many times during this long journey. She was the spitting image of her aunt—in looks and in character. Jaime had spirit.

"You would do best to keep her as far away from that court as you can."

Elizabeth gazed into his blue eyes, confident in her decision to confide all in this man.

"Thank you," she whispered quietly.

He traced her lips gently with his fingers. Moving closer, he kissed her tenderly.

"Jaime is a lucky child." His fingers trailed over the silky skin of her chin to the hollow of her throat and along the line of her collarbone. "She's lucky to have you."

Elizabeth shook her head slightly, denying the compliment.

"Ambrose," she said quietly, after a moment's pause. "I have a question to ask you. Well, actually a permission, of sorts."

He laughed. "Permission? Elizabeth Boleyn asking permission?"

"Forget what I said," she scowled. "Consider it a question."

"Aye. That's more like my Elizabeth."

"The ring." She turned and reached over to the table and picked up the ring and leather thong.

"Henry's ring."

Elizabeth paused and gazed at it.

"Ambrose, I wore this for years as a keepsake. As a token of your attentions to me. Of what I carried in my heart." She lifted her eyes to his. "But now I'd like to put it aside...for Jaime."

The Highlander looked into her misty eyes.

"She doesn't know her father's true identity. In fact, she might never know...but I thought it might be a good thing for her to have this someday." She caressed his chest. "So what do you think?"

Ambrose's face was serious as he placed his hand over hers, holding hers still.

"That is fine with me, Elizabeth. But I have one condition."

"Another condition?"

"Aye. Perhaps a final one."

"Very well. What is it?"

"You can't give me away."

Elizabeth smiled. "Never."

The gentle breeze kissed the two entangled bodies with its soft dawn touch. Elizabeth paused for a moment, listening to the song of a lark outside, and then lifted her lips from Ambrose's naked chest. She brushed her black hair away from her face and smiled down at his tortured expression.

"What about now? Will you take me yet?"

"You're the devil's lass, Elizabeth Boleyn," Ambrose muttered through gritted teeth. With a growl that rumbled from a place deep in his chest, the baron threw Elizabeth onto her back and moved on top of her. Securely pinning her hands under his, he grunted contentedly before letting his mouth travel leisurely along the soft skin of her neck, her shoulders, the firm white flesh of her breasts.

He cursed himself for the hundredth time for acting like an unprincipled knave, taking her the night before as he had. And what was worse, he'd silently promised to take his time thereafter. But the next time had been only a few short moments after the first time. And once again they had been too crazed to take and to give what they each had waited so long to share. Again there had been no gentleness, no taking their time.

So once again Ambrose had renewed his promise to go slower the next time.

It had been a wondrous night. How many times he had broken his promise, he couldn't remember.

Ambrose had to admit it was very difficult—nearly impossible—to go slowly with a woman like Elizabeth. In bed, the woman was a she-devil. A raging moor fire, one that incinerated everything in its path. Even now she continued to writhe restlessly beneath him. As he moved from one breast to the other, eliciting a low moan from her, he considered how the morning light would show nearly every inch of his skin gloriously scorched.

Indeed, he had awakened her out of her half-sleep only moments ago with a gentle touch, a seductive whisper. He wanted to show her the ways—the many different ways—that he could give her pleasure. But he also wanted to show her there could be more to their lovemaking than simply lust. He wanted to show her the dreamlike moments that could precede it. He wanted to show her the tender side of romance.

But she had immediately taken charge. Her sense of curiosity, her need to discover had hours earlier laid waste to any remaining vestige of constraint. In the graying light, Elizabeth's lips had roamed freely and extensively the length and breadth of his body—exploring and delighting in the sweet torment she knew she was inflicting. Ambrose sighed deeply and took her taut nipple firmly in his mouth. She had given him incredible pleasure, but now it was his turn.

Feeling like a goddess, Elizabeth wallowed in the billows of the soft mattress as Ambrose paid homage to her body. Several times she tried to move, to follow his lead in these acts of love, but each time his hands nudged her gently back onto the pillows.

Ambrose slid his fingers over the soft triangle of her womanhood. Uttering a gasp, she worked herself up once again onto her elbows.

"Just lie back, love," he ordered, bringing his face close to hers. "This is my turn."

She gazed at him as his lips gently skimmed her cheeks, her lips.

"This is just not fair," she whispered with a smile. "I want to please you, as well."

His mouth covered hers, his kiss delicious and thorough. When Ambrose was finished, there were no arguments left in her. Indeed, sighing contentedly, Elizabeth felt her body and her spirit growing ever more soft and warm in his arms.

"Aye, lass," he growled huskily. "But you are pleasing me by staying as you are."

She closed her eyes as he lay her back on the bed. Ambrose paused for a moment to note the look of trust in her face. His eyes surveyed the smooth skin and the womanly curves of her beautiful and giving body. Only he himself truly knew the tenderness—and the fire—that coexisted in that body.

They had only a short time remaining there at the hunting lodge. Soon they would rejoin the others. Continue their journey to Scotland. Once beyond these walls, Elizabeth would again become

Phillipe de Anjou. And then what? Ambrose thought. Perhaps she really could continue pulling off the deception. Pretending to be what she was not.

And he himself? Ambrose ran his fingers lightly over the sensitive skin at the top of her thighs, smiling faintly at the shiver his action provoked. What of him? He would go back to longing for her, and waiting for her.

Ambrose sighed, his face growing serious in the light of the approaching dawn. A sense of urgency crept into his soul. Suddenly it became overwhelmingly important that she remember what they shared here tonight. Crucial that she recall the night with longing. Essential that Elizabeth think of it often—and want it back again. More than that, she must want him. Again and again.

Yes, Elizabeth must give up this farce and be his. As a woman. She must belong to him. Only him. He would protect her, cherish her. But he couldn't require her to give it all up.

Ambrose knew that art, for him, merely filled some void in his life. To Elizabeth, it was a love, an addiction far greater than any profession. To him a hobby and a pastime, no matter how great its value. But to her, painting was a passion. Ambrose knew he would have to compete with that.

The Highlander had a challenge before him. He had to show her a better way, a better future. He had to teach her love. His love. Then, perhaps, she would stop her pretense of being a man. Then, perhaps, she would be his.

She could paint. No matter if others frowned at her for being a woman—she could paint for him. She would always have a place beside him.

This was his chance.

As Ambrose lowered his mouth to her belly, Elizabeth's hands drifted to his shoulders. But her lips parted and her breath caught in her chest as he moved his lips even lower.

He left nothing untouched. His lips tasted the sweetness of her, lingering over every inch of her skin. Elizabeth's senses tingled and inside, a bubbling mass of molten heat began to erupt and pour into every corner of her body, flooding her consciousness with a glowing white heat.

"Ambrose!" she called out weakly, as his lips stoked the blaze of erotic passion already raging within her.

She cried out his name again. This time in desperate need. The flames of desire threatened to consume her. Elizabeth's body arched, her breath shortened. Her eyes could no longer see the objects in her chamber. Her insides were coiling, melting, reforming.

"Ambrose!"

The Highlander raised his face slowly and moved with excruciating care up onto her body, trailing kisses that scorched her skin from her navel to her chin.

Then, once again taking possession of her mouth with his, he slid into her. Slowly. Ever so slowly.

As he did, Elizabeth's mind went white, a pulsating inferno exploding in the deepest recesses of her body and her soul.

Pressing her knees together to deal with the passing twinge of discomfort, Elizabeth put her hand out and leaned against the corridor wall.

Ambrose had warned her that she could be uncomfortable in the morning. He'd even suggested that perhaps they should take it easy.

Too caught up in the delirious heights of passion they'd soared to, Elizabeth had been nothing if not definite in her unwillingness to put a stop to—or even slow for a moment—their hours of love. As far as she could see, this would have to be a memory she would savor for a lifetime.

So the longer she could extend this night of bliss, the better the remembrance, she thought.

And Ambrose Macpherson had gladly obliged.

But eventually, as the rising sun gently nudged the full moon over the western hills, the private realm of night love gave way to the reality of the day.

Responsibility called to them. They had to leave.

"Could I get something for you, madame?"

Elizabeth nearly leaped out of her skin as the voice of the elderly man croaked quietly behind her. But the voice quickly registered. She'd met old Jacques, the estate's diminutive steward, yesterday on their arrival. Once again she wondered that none of the servants of the lodge so much as raised an eyebrow at her men's clothing. Elizabeth turned to face him slowly.

"Nay, but thank you." Her mind raced. "I was just admiring the collection of paintings on my way down."

"They are beautiful, aren't they?" He gestured toward the canvases that adorned every wall. "This is the work of some of the finest and best-known artists in Europe."

"Quite impressive," she murmured. "They are brilliant. I am a...I've a fondness for work of all painters. I just wanted to take a better look before we depart."

Jacques's face creased into a thousand wrinkles as he beamed at her interest. It was obvious to Elizabeth that the man took great pride in those things for which he was responsible.

"M'lady, what's displayed here in the main corridor and on the stairways represents only a small portion of the collection. The valuable pieces hang in the rooms downstairs."

The old man winked conspiratorially and nodded his head toward the stairs. The young woman smiled as the little man took hold of Elizabeth's arm, limping along beside her.

"If you would allow me—" he nearly cackled in a hushed voice— "I could show you my most favorite works."

"What are they? Raphael's original sketches?" she teased. Glancing back at the work hanging from the walls, she wondered how they could be any finer than what she'd been looking at. "You don't have Leonardo's notebooks, do you? There is talk in Florence that Leonardo kept secret journ—"

"You can see for yourself." Jacques pointed to a door as they reached the bottom of the great stairs. It was a room Elizabeth hadn't yet been through.

"These are what my master calls his 'hidden gems.'" The steward pulled a ring of keys from his shirt and opened the door with a flourish. As Elizabeth stepped inside of the giant room, her mouth opened in amazement. "They are all the early work of the world's greatest artists. The masterpieces of the—as yet—undiscovered. I believe this is the reason the master loves to spend so much time here."

The man continued to talk as Elizabeth stood in awe, her eyes taking in the hundreds of canvases that adorned the room. They were beautiful. All of different styles, some primitive, some using the new boldness of the Italian colorists. She walked toward one of the walls and began her survey of the works. Some were signed, but the signatures of the artists were clear from the styles and the composition and the brushwork of the paintings themselves. Elizabeth could identify the creator of nearly every one. "He must have sent people around the world to have all of these brought here."

Jacques shook his head. "The master is very proud to say that he chose and purchased every piece in this room himself. Finding the work of genius, he says, is not something one delegates to others."

Elizabeth moved farther down the room. She paused before the startlingly realistic, and unflattering, portrait by someone she didn't know, a painter named Hans Holbein. His work hung beside the work of Durer.

"And the master believes there is real value hidden within *these* pieces," the steward continued. "In spite of the fact that most of these paintings were done to feed an empty stomach, they are not—as you see in the use of colors and in the subject's depictions—traditional in any way. These painters' talents, these men's minds, were not limited by the restraints of set boundaries."

"Not these *men's* minds, Jacques. These *artist's* minds."

Elizabeth and the steward turned at once. Neither had heard Ambrose follow them in.

The elderly man bowed a greeting to the baron before heading for the door. Elizabeth watched with curiosity a silent exchange between the two of them. There was nothing said, but it seemed Jacques understood.

Ambrose glanced back as the door closed behind him. Then his gaze returned to Elizabeth. She stood once again in her men's clothing, her femininity disguised. In spite of the masculinity of her look and her attitude, his blood ignited. He knew what lay beneath.

Elizabeth blushed openly as she looked at his handsome face. Again Ambrose had donned his Highland gear for their ride into Troyes, and her pulse quickened at the memory of their bodies lying so closely together. She could remember every sensual touch, every bold act, every moment of joyous ecstasy. She cast a quick glance at the closed door.

"Do you think anyone in the lodge guesses what we were up to last night?"

Ambrose answered her with silence.

She turned her gaze back to him. He looked suddenly dangerous. He took a step. She backed away. He followed. Elizabeth moved around the table.

"Ambrose..." she warned in a low voice.

"They don't guess, love. They know what we were up to until dawn." He reached with the quickness of a cat and captured her wrist. "After all, I'm quite certain everyone heard you."

Elizabeth looked nervously at the door and then at Ambrose. He was smiling.

"What are you doing?" she asked, reluctantly allowing him to pull her from behind the table.

"I am about to make love to you."

"Here?" she whispered, her eyes widening at the prospect.

"Here, on this table."

Her heart hammered in her chest. She felt her face burn with heat. "You are not. Someone might walk in!"

Ambrose silenced her opposition. He crushed his mouth to hers.

"Ambrose," she protested, trying to catch her breath. Her hands halfheartedly pushed at his chest. "You said we have to be on the road. We can't do this here." She shivered with excitement as his lips fastened on the skin of her neck. She could feel his hardening manhood rising beneath the soft wool of his kilt. "I—I have the wrong clothing. It won't work."

Holding her tightly, Ambrose pulled first at her doublet, then pushed at her breeches and her hose. Her gasp of surprise turned quickly to a moan of pleasure.

"Don't forget where we are, my love," he said, nodding smilingly at the paintings around them. He lifted her gently onto the desk. "No boundaries."

Their love was fast and powerful, his strokes smooth, their release pure and complete. Spent, she gazed up to the ceiling, her limbs tingling from their frantic lovemaking.

Ambrose placed a kiss on her lips as he straightened, offering her a hand up.

"We can't just do this anytime or anyplace you feel like it," she scolded, a smile tugging at her lips.

"Aye, we can." He tried to help her with her hose, but she slapped his hand away. "As long as we both want it and we both enjoy it."

She couldn't deny his words. She had enjoyed it. Fiercely so.

Elizabeth watched him from the corner of her eye as she tidied her attire. He wasn't tired of her. He still wanted her. Lying in the bath, she'd had her fears of how he would feel now that their night was through.

"We'll have breakfast before we get on our way." His words were so calm and self-assured. "Gavin will probably reach Troyes about midday today. If we ride hard, my sweet, we could get there this afternoon."

Ride hard. She cringed at the thought of it. Elizabeth wasn't sure she was ready to ride at all.

"Ready?" He stood, fresh as summer breeze, holding out his hand for her to take. "Let's eat."

She took his arm and allowed him to lead her toward the door. She imagined the faces of twenty servants plastered to the outer door listening. Uncontrollably, a flush of embarrassment colored her cheeks. Discreet. They needed to be more discreet. Approaching the door, she once again let her eyes roam the wonderful treasures that adorned every wall in sight.

Suddenly she came to a halt. There, to her left, between the two bright windows. Her eyes riveted on her own work.

Ambrose followed her gaze. He'd wanted her to find the piece herself. In fact, to make it possible he'd asked the steward, Jacques, to be sure Elizabeth was shown into the study this morning. And he'd followed, unable to pass up the opportunity of seeing her expression when she found out.

He stood, beaming expectantly. Elizabeth whirled on him.

"You worm!" she burst out.

Chapter 24

She was thoroughly prepared to skin him alive.

Ambrose took a step back as Elizabeth advanced on him, an old broadsword in hand. She'd pulled the weapon from the display of armor before the Highlander could gather his wits. Her vehement exclamation was the last thing he'd been expecting. Nor, Elizabeth arming herself was the least expected response.

"Put that thing down before you hurt yourself," he ordered. She didn't even pause in her advance.

"There is only one person who is about to be hurt!" The long, heavy blade flashed in the sunlight. "And that's you."

Ambrose ducked as the weapon cut through the air only a hand-span from his head.

"Well, why not use my sword, then? It will make for a quick death." He moved nimbly around the table. "At least it's sharp, lass."

Her eyes locked on the table.

The table! Elizabeth's rage flared to new heights.

"Nay," she seethed. She swung the blade again, as Ambrose pulled back. "That will be too kindly an end for you. I'd like to see you die a slow and painful death!"

Totally perplexed, Ambrose gazed wonderingly at the fury etched in her face. There was no question, she had to be rabid. "Can't we talk about this first?"

Elizabeth ignored his entreaty. "So," she hissed. "Is he late?"

He looked at her with raised eyebrows.

"Don't look so innocently at me! Was your plan for him to walk in while you had me spread on the table?" She leaned on the table and shook a fist at him. "Or was it last night? You must have had them put me in *his* room. That way he could walk in on us there, I suppose!"

Ambrose put both his hands on the table and looked questioningly into her eyes. "Who are you talking ab—"

The sword arced straight overhead, the edge of the blade cutting deeply into the wood at the spot where the Highlander's hands had rested.

As lithe as a cat, the warrior grabbed her by the wrist and wrenched the sword out of her grip. As he looked up with a wry smile, Elizabeth punched him squarely in the face.

He hardly blinked as she held her hand in pain.

Ambrose reached over the table in an attempt to grab her by the shoulder, but she jumped back, tripping and falling clumsily on her buttocks.

"Let me ask this again. Who is this that you talking about?" Ambrose moved around the desk.

She shrank from his approach. "Don't you come near me!"

"Who do you think was supposed to walk in while we were making love?" He reached down, trying to help her to her feet.

"Don't touch me!" She tried to fight off his hands, but he had the advantage.

"Elizabeth!" He gathered her in his arms, restricting her movement. But she fought in his grasp, snarling like a caged she-wolf. "What have I done? Who do you think was supposed to walk in?"

She tried to knee him between the legs. As he held her at arm's length, the legs of the two combatants tangled and they fell with a thud.

"The Marquis of Troyes, you fool!" She tried to bite him, but he pulled back. "Or whatever else you want to call him. The Constable of Champagne! The Duc de Bourbon!"

"Who?" he asked, dumbfounded. The baron grunted as she landed a kick to his groin area.

Elizabeth quickly rolled away from him and sprang to her feet. She pointed an accusing finger at the wall.

"He is the man that bought that painting from me!" She glared down at where he crouched in pain on his hands and knees, his head tucked into his chest. She reached out and touched him on the shoulder. "My God! What did I do? Ambrose!"

The warrior moved like lightning and struck decisively.

Elizabeth blinked up into his face. He had her flat on her back, his weight checking any movement on her part. "I can't breathe," she gasped.

"Fine! That makes two of us."

Elizabeth tried to free her hands, but there was no hope. He had her. "I hate you!"

"Nay, lass. You don't," he returned. "But let's start from beginning. What was it you said about Bourbon walking in here?"

"You heard me!"

"What the devil could have given you that idea?"

"Let me go first, you bully. Then I'll talk."

"Not a chance, my sweet. I value my...my life too much." He placed more of his weight on her body, and she gulped for air. "Ready to talk?"

Elizabeth grudgingly nodded, and Ambrose eased himself somewhat to the side.

She took in a deep breath and looked up into his serious expression. "My painting, you boor! The one on the wall. I sold that to Bourbon four years ago at the Field of Cloth of Gold. He is a collector of paintings."

"So?"

"Isn't this his place?" she asked through clenched teeth. "The title, the estate, the lodge. All these paintings—aren't they all his?"

"What difference does it make who all these things belong to?"

"Not a damn bit of difference!" Elizabeth snapped back.

"Well, then?"

She sighed deeply. "If you think I am simple enough to fall for this pretense of innocence now, you are mistaken." She waited for an answer. A protest. Something! But the baron said nothing. He simply continued to stare at her blankly. Finally she couldn't hold back any longer. "Wasn't it your plan to bring me here, to take advantage of me, then to allow Bourbon to walk in and catch us in the middle of something? And don't give me that shocked look, Ambrose Macpherson. I know how men's minds work. I have lived as one of you for the past four years."

She took a breath to control her anger and disappointment. "You wanted to fling me in his face, to flaunt me like some rare animal that you'd hunted down and caught. I know your way! After all, the last time you two met, didn't you fight over me? Admit it, you just wanted to rub his nose in it. You wanted to show off your catch...before you discarded it!"

He stared at her in disbelief before a smile crept across his face. Suddenly his body began to shake with laughter.

She watched him in silence as he rolled off of her and wiped a tear from the corner of his eye. The knot that had grown in her throat now threatened to choke her as her eyes misted over. "What I've said is true, isn't it?"

Ambrose heard the heartbreak in her voice. It was hardly more than a whisper. She tried to sit, but he pulled her roughly to his side. Once again she tried to fight him, but he gathered her in his embrace so tightly that she couldn't move.

"Aye, I brought you here. But there was no taking advantage of you, my sweet. If you recall, you attacked me first. And secondly, I don't show off what's mine. In fact, I tend to be quite private with what I have. I think it comes from being a second son. So what's mine, stays mine. And I don't flaunt those things in front of others. Finally, I'm sorry to disappoint you, but there will be no 'discarding.' Nay, lass, don't look so surprised. I'm keeping you. The question is, love, what am I going to do with you?"

"Don't try to fool me with cheap, endearing words, you fake. I know you don't mean them." Elizabeth turned her face away as a tear escaped, leaving a glistening track down her cheek.

"I can call you anything I like, Elizabeth." Ambrose took her chin in his hand and gently drew her face back toward his. "Because I do mean what I've said. But that *was* an impressive story you just told."

"It was the truth!" she muttered, trying to look away.

But he wouldn't let her. "Nay, lass. It wasn't."

"Then it must have been close enough to the truth," she responded, pulling an arm free and gesturing toward the room and its contents.

"None of it was!"

She shrugged her shoulders. "Go ahead, continue to lie, if you like."

He started to reply, but she cut him off immediately. "But don't forget, Ambrose Macpherson, I am not believing a word of anything you tell me."

"Aye, Elizabeth," he said seriously. "I'll try to remember that. Your—"

"Let me up first," she demanded. "I am quite uncomfortable like this."

"Too bad. I don't trust you." He glared at her. "Now let me start—"

"Did I tell you that I don't trust you, either?"

"You did."

"And that I hate you?"

"I believe you said that, too."

"That—"

Ambrose's hand closed tightly over her mouth. "If you refuse to be silent and hear me out, I'll have to gag you."

She mumbled something into the flesh of his hand.

"Very well," he responded, not understanding a word she'd just said, but reading the flashing look in her eyes quite clearly. "We can do it like this if you prefer. At least this way you will listen to what I have to say."

Ambrose knew he had to make it short before she had time to decide on the next weapon she'd use to fight him off with. "Elizabeth, don't be misled by a bunch of titles that are truly meaningless. Others might be misled into believing they mean something, but you shouldn't be. To you, I am and always will be Ambrose Macpherson. But, in the eyes of the world, anyway, I am also Baron of Roxburgh, Lord Protector of the Borderlands. Francis I of this land has also seen fit to bestow on me the title Marquis of Troyes, Constable of Champagne—more honorary a title than anything. But in any case, my sweet, the titles and this hunting lodge and everything else inside these walls—including these paintings—belong to me."

He gazed for a moment as the shock registered in her eyes, then let go of her mouth. "Well?"

"You are a liar!"

"Jacques!" he shouted, releasing her.

Elizabeth quickly scampered to her feet as soon as she realized he wasn't restraining her any longer. He was already on foot and striding away from her. Reaching the oak door, he jerked it open, and the elderly steward scurried in.

"Tell her who is master here, Jacques. Tell her."

The older man looked questioningly from Ambrose's face to Elizabeth's. Then his eyes lit on the sword lying on the marred table.

"You don't have to lie for him," Elizabeth consoled, approaching the little man. "I'll protect you."

"Lie, m'lady?" The man looked wide-eyed at Elizabeth. "I never lie."

"Tell her about what we've done here, Jacques," Ambrose prodded. "Tell her everything."

Elizabeth stood still as the steward began to talk. He confirmed everything Ambrose had spoken of earlier. Of how the nobleman had owned this estate for quite a few years. He spoke with obvious pride of the construction of the new lodge. And of how the baron was a generous benefactor of artists and a true connoisseur of fine artwork. He spoke of Ambrose's parents, the good Lord Alexander and Lady Elizabeth Macpherson, and how they occasionally came to stay at the lodge, in spite of the laird's advancing age. He also talked about other lodges and town houses that the baron had built around the continent. Being a diplomat and traveling often, Ambrose was well known for the quality of his holdings and his ability to offer hospitality to kings and cardinals in places all over Europe.

The man continued to talk, but Elizabeth wasn't listening. Ambrose was leaning against his desk, his arms crossed at his chest. His piercing eyes were on her, admonishing her. She looked down.

"That's enough, Jacques," he said commandingly. "You may leave us now."

The older steward turned with a quick bow to the two of them and crossed to the door, closing it behind him.

She studied the pattern of the wide oak flooring for a long moment, then turned her attention to the glistening sweat on her palms. She couldn't recall a time in her life when she'd felt quite so foolish.

"Well?"

Elizabeth glanced hesitantly at his face. She nodded toward the table. "You can use that dull sword if you'd like."

"What good would that do?"

"Well, you must be about ready to cut out my tongue," she whispered.

"Knowing you, it would most certainly grow back!" Ambrose smiled at her. How could she go from so a fiery devil to so serene an angel in such a short span of time? "Come here!"

She looked up. He wasn't angry.

He motioned to her.

She walked toward his open arms and nestled inside. She laid her face against his chest. "I—"

"Next time we have a disagreement," he said, cutting off her apology, "would you please give me a chance to explain before attacking me with a weapon of war?" He rubbed his chin against her soft hair. He loved the feel of her in his arms. He loved the serenity of this embrace. Perhaps almost as much as he loved the heat of their battles.

Then there will be a next time, she thought with pleasure. My God, she loved this man.

"I'll try to remember."

"Are there any more questions that you might like to ask?" He pulled her away from him and looked into her sparkling eyes. His thumb brushed away a tear from her soft cheek. "Do you want to know about your painting? How I came to have it?"

She nodded slowly.

"I bought it. From Bourbon, that is."

"Did he charge you a lot?"

"A fortune, the bastard."

Elizabeth didn't know what to say.

He smiled. "We are friends. Bourbon and I have become friends since that day at the Field of Cloth of Gold. It is humorous to think about, but the fight over you did bring us together. But I think you should know that the duc's affection for you didn't last too long."

"I am not surprised," she smiled. "He had little regard for women and the long-term relationships they sought."

"Aye, that was truly the way he was," Ambrose smiled wryly. "But he has changed. He just had to find his soul mate. And that he has."

"Well, I'm glad for him." Elizabeth kissed him on the chin and lowered her eyes again, not wanting him to know that thoughts of that nature were right now coursing through her own brain. "How was it that he sold you my work?"

"He is in trouble with Francis, these days. Political nonsense. I've been working on getting him a pardon. But the king doesn't forgive very quickly those who oppose him. So, for a short while anyway, Bourbon and his wife have gone to Burgundy. Since he needed all the gold he could get his hand on—and wouldn't take what I tried to give him—I offered to buy some of the paintings he's been collecting."

"And mine was among them?"

"Aye, but the knave never told me it was your painting. He didn't even give me a clue, other than saying that he'd bought it at the Field of Cloth of Gold."

"He didn't know." Elizabeth smiled. "I sold the work to him, but I never said it was mine."

"Ah. Well, I suppose I can't hold that over his head, then."

Ambrose wondered, though, whether Bourbon actually did have suspicions about the identity of the artist. There had been no secret between the two of them that the feelings Ambrose harbored for Elizabeth far exceeded any affection the Frenchman had for her. And when the two had discussed the sale of the artwork, Bourbon had seemed quite coy about parting with this particular painting.

She pushed her body closer against his, sighing contentedly.

"What do you think you're doing, Elizabeth Boleyn?" he asked huskily. Her soft, touch, so completely innocent, made his body hard and his blood roar.

"Apologizing." Her hands roamed his chest. "I want to make sure that you won't hold what I did earlier against me."

"Hmmm. Perhaps, then, we should also consider what you did to me four years ago, as well." He pulled her doublet over her head in a single motion, smiling as he gathered her to him again. "And then you can talk me into staying here an extra night. I believe Gavin can use another day to show your sister and your friends the market fair at Troyes. Jacques tells me a great fire burned half the town last month, but that the fair has come back as strong as ever. It's really quite something."

"Then perhaps I can show you the nightgown Mary sent along." Elizabeth giggled, blushing in spite of herself. "It, too, is quite something."

"A bargain, then."

"A bargain," she whispered happily, lifting her lips to his.

Chapter 25

Gavin Kerr looked about at the market fair of Troyes in admiration. It did appear that there was almost nothing in this world that a body couldn't buy there.

"Come, Gavin." Mary pulled at his arm, smiling weakly. She drained the last of her cup of wine and handed it to him. "You should see your face. It can't be as bad as all that."

The nobleman glanced at the young woman's frail body. She seemed to be growing thinner every day. She wasn't well enough to go through all this excitement. And he'd told her so before they left the barge. But Mary hadn't heard a word he'd said.

"I'd be contended just to watch, Mary. The people, that is." He pulled her to a low stone wall and forced her to sit. She hardly ate anything anymore. For days she'd only nibbled at the food that he himself had brought to her. Only an occasional sip of something to drink. It was amazing she had enough energy even to walk.

Stretching his legs before him, Gavin cursed inwardly for letting himself be talked into bringing Mary to the market fair for the second day in a row.

When the barge had arrived the previous midday, Mary and the Bardis had pressed him excitedly to take them to the fields on the outskirts of town which, for three months of every year, served as a major center of commerce for all of Europe. Now, gazing at the people walking by, Gavin was amazed at the sight of beggars and peasants roaming with nobles and merchant princes. For these summer months, at least, the fields of Troyes belonged to all and had something for everyone.

So far, the travelers had seen only part of the huge fair, but the Bardis had already seen a half dozen fellow merchants whom they seemed to know quite well, all working their trade. For the place was alive with the sound and smells of commerce. And the fair not only offered such exotic goods as spices and carpets from the Far East, but also novel entertainments and unfamiliar foods at every turn. There were even three silent and mysterious men from the New World, on display inside the tent of a Spanish trader of precious gems.

Yesterday, Jaime had come to the fair with them. Gavin smiled, recalling how delightful the young girl's excitement had been to behold. But keeping track of the child on the day's excursion had visibly drained a considerable amount of energy from her ailing mother. Today, when Mary had begged to go again, Ernesta Bardi had stepped forward, volunteering to watch the child if Mary insisted on going to the fair once more.

But it wasn't just Ernesta who was worried. They were all quite concerned now about Mary. Bodily, she was frail and becoming weaker with each passing day. But her spirits remained high. Though everyone, including Mary, knew that there was no getting better, they were amazed at her placid exterior. She showed no trace of fear.

But Gavin knew. For on the long voyage from Marseilles, Mary had told him of the disease and the mercury treatment she had been undergoing for the past four years. How strange, he thought, and how special—this relationship between them. Never, with any other woman, had he shared such trust, such confidence, as he shared with Mary.

And from the first, it had been special. The first time he had knocked at her cabin door, she had asked him in and professed how much she loved him. Mary Boleyn had acted as though she'd known him all of her life. She had known him from her dreams. She'd confessed that she'd waited all her life to catch up to him and that now she had somehow done it. But in the same breath Mary had told him that she couldn't have him. Her sins and her past would not allow it.

He'd stood beside her bunk, speechless in the face of such openness.

And when she'd continued, asking for his companionship, his friendship, for the few days or weeks that she had left, how could he deny her?

Gavin Kerr couldn't deny her. And he hadn't. And now he was more than glad that he hadn't.

As private a man as he was, Gavin Kerr had poured out his life story to her when she'd asked about it. Every triumph, every disaster. Every strength, every weakness. His tales had welled up inside him and spilled out.

A few times, when he asked questions about *her* past, about *her* family, she'd just shaken her head. "Nay, my friend. This is my turn to listen."

So Gavin had not pressured her. She told him enough. And if this was what she wanted, then he would abide by her wishes. He knew—they all knew—that the time she had left would not be long.

Mary leaned against Gavin's shoulder as a shudder coursed through her body.

"Cold?" he asked, placing his arm around her, rubbing her emaciated upper arm.

"Just the ghosts of the past, my friend." Mary cast a weak smile at Gavin and then peered once again into the crowd. Though she had said nothing to anyone, lately her imagination had been playing tricks on her. The moments were not like the attacks she'd had in the past. These just involved seeing things. Trivial things from her past as well as things that had been incredibly important in her life. Things good and bad. Sometimes on the boat Mary had found herself dreaming, hallucinating in broad daylight. She had found herself experiencing events all over again. Moments from her early childhood—a wounded bird in a sunny garden; a long, wet ride in the growing gloom of a winter evening, wrapped inside the warm smell of a man's lined cloak. She sometimes became confused as people from the present and situations of the past would commingle in a whirling mix of time and place. And there were times when she couldn't tell what was real and what was not.

She stared at a group of men not ten yards from where she and Gavin sat. They looked at her; she peered back. Do I know them? she asked herself. She squinted as the sunlight flashed brilliantly off the silver buckle of one. Past and present. Keep them apart.

She looked up to Gavin. At least he was real—of that she was certain.

"How can you enjoy this, Mary? Being in the midst of this chaos." His eyes were locked on a pair of arguing merchants.

"It's just for a short while longer, you gruff old bear," she teased, following his gaze. Her throat was strangely dry and an odd numbness was spreading through her back. She felt weaker than usual. Taking her cup back from Gavin, Mary looked into the empty vessel.

"I'm going to hold you to that, lass," he grumbled. One of the merchants appeared to be complaining about the location of the other's cloth booth, but Gavin could not get the details, since the two were speaking some language he was unfamiliar with. A crowd had gathered quickly. The Scotsman glanced past a group of armed mercenaries at the booth in dispute. It looked like the young assistants of both combatants were hurriedly setting out trinkets atop makeshift tables. Gavin smiled wryly, nudging Mary. "If I'm not mistaken, these two noisy enemies are going to become fast friends as soon as this crowd of onlookers grows just a bit larger."

Mary looked vaguely at the warrior. The numbness had begun to spread into her shoulders and neck. Her eyes were drawn past his dark face to the sky above. The heavens were beginning to flash a number of different shades of gray and blue and green and red in a rapid succession of moments. Sounds of the crowd were fading in and out, and the young woman stared in calm wonder when she saw Gavin's lips move without any accompanying utterance. In fact, she was hardly even surprised to hear her friend's words tumbling unintelligibly through the air after a moment's delay. She was losing her mind. But her throat still felt dry.

"Are you all right, Mary?" Gavin asked in alarm. The young woman's eyes were glassy and unfocused. He took her by the shoulders and shook her gently. "Mary!"

"Aye, Gavin," she replied. "I'm here."

"Lass, we need to get back."

"Gavin, would you be kind enough to get me a cup of something to drink? Some more wine, perhaps."

The giant stared at her, uncertain for a moment what to do. He could hear the slight slurring of her words.

"Please, my friend. Just a cup of something." She handed back the cup to him. "I'll be fine here until you come back."

Gavin looked around him. They had bought Mary a cup of wine at a merchant's tent just before sitting. It couldn't have been more than two or three tents away.

"Aye." He nodded. "I'll be back before you know it. But Mary, promise me you won't move!"

She smiled at him as he stood. As his words of concern for her registered in her brain, a warm feeling swept through her. "How solemn would you like that promise to be, Gavin?"

He gently took her hand and brought it to his lips. "Just a simple one will do. I'll return in a moment."

Mary watched him disappear into the milling blur of the crowd. She tried to focus but soon realized wearily that she simply couldn't manage it. Her head began to spin with the exertion, so she closed her eyes. Turning her body, she let her face take the full warmth of the afternoon sun.

Mary felt herself drifting. Suddenly she stood in her father's tent. He stormed back and forth, his hands cutting the air in his rage. "But it *is* his child, Father. Please. Believe me."

The shadow fell across her face and with it came the coldness. She opened her eyes and saw through the haze a number of men around her. Some stood behind the low wall, casting their shadow over her, while the others seemed to be blocking the crowds. She squinted her eyes. One stood in front of her, his shining buckle hurting her eyes. She gazed up, but could see no face. The radiant light dazzled her, but the shadowy darkness pushed through her like a rod of cold steel.

"Where is your sister?" The words echoed in her brain.

She didn't return to the tent.

"Where is—"

Nay. Father, I—

"*Where?*"

A rough hand gripped her arm. He was hurting her.

She saw him. He wasn't her father. *What do you want from me?* Mary tried to scream. Her mouth opened, but she could hear no scream. There was no sound.

Where is Gavin? she thought with a panic. Where is Elizabeth?

She tried to look about, but everywhere colors streamed out of the blackness, crashing into her, and then swirling around her.

Brittle glass rainbows exploded into glittering shards of whites and yellows and scarlets before melting into luminous pools around her feet.

Mary heard a man's voice. More than one was talking, but the noise of the fair crowded out all discernible meaning. And then one word penetrated her brain.

Poison.

"Where is...*Tell us*!"

Poisoned. She listened. She'd been poisoned by the wine.

Mary waited for bright space of unconsciousness to envelop her. Nothing. She waited for the heaviness that would dull her senses, but still nothing.

They were no longer talking to her. She tried to focus, to understand what they said among themselves. Elizabeth. These men were looking for Elizabeth.

I know you bastards, she thought bitterly. Killers. The same ones who came to the tent four years ago. They were English, too. Yes, she remembered. They were after Elizabeth. *But you can't kill her*, she screamed inwardly. *Not my sweet Elizabeth.*

And then there was silence. And sunlight.

Mary pried her eyes open. Once again she could see. There was no one around her. Peering through the bright mist, she could make out the shapes of people in the distance. No sounds, no one blocking her. No men around her. She felt the place on her arm where she thought the man's hand had been, but there was no pain. Only the numbness that was growing more profound with every breath. She gazed to the right, where Gavin had gone. She wracked her brain, trying to remember how long ago he'd left. She stared at the dirt before her.

Weakly, Mary turned her glance once again up the pathway. She squinted at the shape coming toward her.

Elizabeth was walking toward her. The younger sister stared hopelessly at the approaching figure. At her wave, her smile.

From the corner of her eye, a movement drew her attention. Mary turned in time to see the buckle flash again in the sunshine. As the man walked past her, she could see the dagger hidden beneath his cloak. His hand was on the weapon, holding it to the side, away from her sister's view. But Mary could see it.

Elizabeth waved at Mary excitedly. Her sister was out among people once again. Even from a distance, she could tell there was color in her face. "Thank you, Virgin Mother. And thank you, Gavin," she murmured. Mary was getting better. She would improve. She had to. Elizabeth knew that there was so much that mattered now. So much for Mary to live for.

Elizabeth turned to look for Ambrose. He wasn't far behind, his hand clapped on Gavin's shoulder as they walked. She gazed at his face as he listened to the black-haired giant's words. She turned back toward Mary, but the heavy cloak of a tall warrior blocked her way.

"Nice to find you at last, Elizabeth Boleyn." The clothing was French, but the voice undeniably English. His hand grabbed at the shoulder of her doublet.

Elizabeth knocked his grip loose and jumped back, only to see the dagger coming right at her heart. She knew immediately that she had not jumped far enough.

As the dagger flashed in the sun, Mary stepped between them, shielding her sister from the blow.

The blade of the dagger slid through the thin young woman, and the killer's thrust deposited her in Elizabeth's arms.

As the two sisters fell to the ground, Elizabeth, stunned by the attack, held Mary instinctively.

The momentary calm that ensued was abruptly broken by the sound of shouts, and then the outbreak of total chaos around them.

"Mary!" Elizabeth cried, pulling her sister's cloak away from the wound. The cut in her dress was jagged and wide, and the dark stain of her blood was spreading rapidly through the material.

"Mary! Oh, God!" She pressed at the wound, trying to stop the flow. But as she did, she felt Mary's warm lifeblood draining out the wound at the back, covering her hand. "*Mary!*"

The young woman was gazing up into her face. She was conscious, and Elizabeth could see peace in her face.

"You are not dying on me, Mary!" The tears rolled down Elizabeth's face, mixing with her sister's innocent blood. "You can't die, Mary! You saved my life. You can't leave me."

Elizabeth watched her sister's small, trembling hands reach up to her face. "Death had to face me before he got to you. Hold me, my love. Just hold me."

Weeping, Elizabeth gathered her sister in her arms and they rocked. Just as they always had.

"I am ready, Elizabeth." Mary's voice was weak. "It's time."

"Don't!" Elizabeth sobbed as they held one another. "Please, don't go."

"All will be well," Mary whispered. "I am ready. But Jaime..."

"Quiet, Mary," Elizabeth cried. "We need to get you back to the—"

"There is no time for that, Elizabeth," Mary murmured. "My sweet. Protect Jaime. Keep her away from Father. Keep her from Henry. Please, promise me."

A spasm of pain shook the young woman's frail body.

"I promise. By the Holy Virgin, I promise. Don't go. You just can't. Please."

"My love..."

Mary's eyes lifted to the sky beyond her sister's grief-stricken face, and Elizabeth saw them widen, as if in surprise, before another look transformed her face. A look of joy, lighting her from within.

And then she was gone.

Chapter 26

The shock of Mary's death stayed with them all.

The barge moved quickly down the Seine toward Paris, while the French countryside, still wet from the passing downpour, shimmered in the late afternoon sun.

Ambrose walked on the deck, solemn and silent. Leaving Elizabeth alone in the cabin below, sorting through Mary's belongings, had been difficult for him to do. But she had been clear in her request. She wanted to be left alone for a while. And he respected that. Elizabeth needed time to grieve the sister she'd lost.

They had buried Mary under a threatening sky among the wildflowers in the small plot beside the Church of St. Madeleine. The funeral mass inside had been a somber affair, and the grim, stony image of some saint—Ambrose wondered if it was St. Madeleine herself—had overseen the ritual with an immutable countenance of gloom. But for all, it had been a moving ceremony, and the clear and vibrant tones of the Offices of the Dead and the Te Deum still echoed in Ambrose's memory.

But as Elizabeth had tossed dirt into her sister's grave, Ambrose had been filled once again with anger about the unresolved crime. True, the man who had pierced Mary's heart with a dagger lay dead, cut down by Gavin's sword. But there had been more to it. Things that Ambrose could not yet understand. Low as he knew many to be, English knights were not famed for drawing swords on an ill and defenseless woman. Ambrose could only guess what connection may have existed between the two. But even that made no sense. Had the dead warrior been Mary's lover, it was still unclear to Ambrose why the Englishman would travel so far to murder the young woman in so public a display of barbarity.

Ambrose was truly at a loss. The killing could also be related to Mary's short-lived position as King Henry's mistress. But Ambrose knew that there was no talk of Mary bearing a child by Henry. But if unseen powers were plotting to keep her away from the English court, why should they murder her when they knew she was enroute to Scotland?

Ambrose was very aware of other rumors, though. Reports were spreading far and wide of the new infatuation of the restless English king. Everyone knew that Henry had recently been eyeing Thomas Boleyn's youngest daughter, Anne Boleyn. But even if this was true, the Highlander could comprehend no reason to kill the older sister.

Ambrose stared out at the road that ran alongside the river. That road, too, led to Paris. The baron had an idea that Elizabeth knew the answer to some of his questions. But the time wasn't right for him to ask. Not yet.

This morning, standing by the grave of the younger sister, all he had been able to think about was Elizabeth and her well-being. Mary, as pampered as she'd been all her short existence, had been the center of the older sister's life. Now Elizabeth's desolation was etched across her face.

Publicly, Ambrose had to keep his distance. She'd asked him to. As much as he wanted to, as much as his heart ached to reach out for her, he could not console her in her grief.

He'd watched her face as she struggled to conceal the pain of her loss. It hurt him that Elizabeth couldn't show her grief in a way that would have been natural for her. His own heart tightened as he watched the young woman actually will herself to be a man. Against all odds, he watched her successfully hammer back the tide of emotions, burying the sorrow within her with only an expression of sadness on her face.

The Highlander ran his palm along the wet railing of the barge. He was sick of this pretense. He couldn't go along with it anymore. Not after all that they'd shared on this journey. Not with all that they felt for each other.

Yes, he would wait. He would even help her, if he could, as she worked through her grief. But then it would be time.

Ambrose turned his face resolutely toward the bow of the boat and moved forward. They would find another way.

As the baron strode along, a movement on the forward deck caught his attention. A sad smile crossed his face when he saw it was Jaime, playing on a coil of thick line with her kitten.

"Good day, lass," he greeted her gravely. She glanced up at him with a shy smile but quickly turned her eyes away. Ernesta and Joseph Bardi had been keeping a close watch over her, but as far as he knew, no one had really spent any time talking to the child about the loss of her mother.

"And how is D'Or this afternoon?"

The little girl just shrugged her shoulders.

Ambrose studied the quiet child. He wondered if Elizabeth had given much thought to where Jaime's future would be spent. The court of King Henry appeared out of the question, and hearing what he had about Thomas Boleyn, Ambrose could only assume that Elizabeth would be drawn and quartered before allowing the child to spend so much as a moment under her father's care.

"She's turned out to be a fine sailor, hasn't she, now?" Ambrose prompted, sitting himself on the deck beside the heavy ropes. The kitten scrambled up from the inside of the low coil and eyed the baron curiously.

"My mama is in heaven."

Ambrose gazed at the little one's bowed head. Her words were matter-of-fact and carried a lot of conviction. He watched her small hands prying the kitten's claws free in a half-hearted effort to pick the little animal up.

"She won't be coming back to visit, either," Jaime continued. "Erne said Mama is never coming back. But she also said that Mama loved me very much and that she'll always be watching over me."

"What Ernesta told you is true, Jaime." Ambrose gathered the animal up in his hands and placed her on the child's skirt.

Jaime gently stroke the fur of the restless cat, quieting D'Or into a comfortable purr. "It's really quite pretty in heaven, you know. Ladies wear nice, bright dresses, and they laugh a lot."

"Did Signora Baldi tell you that, too?" Ambrose asked with a smile.

"Nay. That I figured out myself." She paused and cocked an eyebrow at the sky. "I remember the days before she got really sick. Whenever mama wore a pretty dress, she was happy. And in Uncle Phillipe's paintings, the angels and the saints always wear nice, bright dresses. So I know that's what heaven is like."

"This is all very reasonable, Jaime," he conceded, reaching over and scratching behind the kitten's ears.

She looked up into Ambrose's face. "Have you been there?"

"To heaven?"

She nodded.

Ambrose shook his head. "Nay, lass."

"Nor I." She looked back down at her kitten. "Maybe someday I'll go and visit her there."

Ambrose gazed steadily at the child. "There is no hurry, Jaime."

"Is Uncle Phillipe going to heaven?"

"Perhaps someday!"

Jaime grabbed the baron's hand at once. "Please, tell her not to go!" The tears splashed onto her cheeks immediately. "She can't go. Not without me."

Ambrose lifted the child and hugged her tightly to his chest. The way she took an immediate comfort in his embrace, hugging him tightly in return, brought a smile to his face. "Don't you fear, lass. She is not going anywhere. Your Aunt Elizabeth is not about to go anywhere without you."

"Oh!" The child's tiny hand flew to her mouth. "I—"

"Don't worry," he whispered in confidence. "You didn't give her secret away."

"Then who did?" she whispered back.

"She did it herself. Your uncle...your aunt told me herself."

Jaime threw her arms around his neck, hugging him fiercely. "You know our secret. That makes you family."

Ambrose felt his heart melt at the show of affection.

"Aye, my bonny one. That makes me family."

The fist rapped gently at the cabin door once again. This time he heard the soft footfalls as she moved to open the door. Finally, he thought. Hanging the lantern on the hook on the wall, he waited patiently, but when he glimpsed her tear-stained face, Ambrose's heart nearly broke. But before he could even say a word, the door started shutting on him again. Instinctively, he shoved his boot into the doorjamb and shouldered his way in.

"Please don't." She took a step back. "I—I can't see you now. I can't see anyone. I simply need to be alone. Please."

Ambrose fought his first impulse—to pull her into his arms, to comfort her in her pain. He fought his desire to take hold of her, to promise her that he would take care of her. He fought all of that, for he feared actions such as those would be misinterpreted. He feared words about the future would sound hollow while she struggled to let go of the past. He watched her continue to back away in the murky light of the cabin.

"You've been alone down here long enough, lass." The baron looked about him for candles. For two days she had remained locked away in this cabin. For two days he'd been trying to get her to open the door. Only Ernesta Bardi had gained access, but the meals she'd brought down remained untouched. "Elizabeth, it's time you joined the world once again. We need you."

She sat heavily on the bunk where Mary had spent so much of her last days on the journey. "Nay, you don't," she muttered glumly. "And I need more time to pull myself together."

Ambrose reached back into the narrow passageway for the lantern and used the flickering flame to light a number of candles, beating the cabin's gloomy darkness back. "I know of no reason that you should be in any better shape than the others. And, as I told you before, we need you. Jaime, the Baldis. My God, even Gavin Kerr does!"

"No one needs me!" Elizabeth gathered her knees to her chest. She was cold and empty inside. "And please don't lie to make me feel better. I know I will work through this myself. I guess it is simply a matter of time. Isn't that what they say? Time is the great healer, I've heard."

Ambrose nudged open the small window of the cabin with the heel of his hand and stepped back as the fresh night air rushed in. He filled his lungs with the cool breeze, leaning his back against the closed door.

"Elizabeth, tell me what you smell when you breath in this air." The Highlander watched as the young woman lifted her chin a fraction. "Tell me."

The painter paused for a moment. "I smell the night scents of the river. I smell the clean cold of the water, and the faint odor of fish that mixes with the smell of earth."

"And the scent of grapes."

He paused as she nodded vaguely.

"Those are the smell of living things, Elizabeth. Growing things." He moved to the bunk and sat beside her. "You are alive. But she is gone. It is time now for you to accept this and let her go. We never know when our time here is finished, but I've seen many people in my life who walked around more dead than alive. I won't be letting you become one of them."

She leaned her head against her knees to hide the tears that rolled uncontrollably down her face.

"You don't understand." Elizabeth squeezed her eyelids shut. She wanted to tell him that the dagger that robbed her sister of her one chance to regain the happiness in her life was meant for her own fraudulent heart. Indeed, she struggled to tell him how she had put their lives in danger. All of their lives—including his. Those killers knew of her identity. They had tracked her down and found her. And they would find her again. Who would be the victim next time? She shuddered at the thought.

Ambrose placed his arm around her shoulder and pulled her to his side. "I might not have known your sister as well as I should have, but I know that she was a woman who was, perhaps for the first time in her life, beginning to appreciate the things that life had brought her, instead of mourning forever the things she had lost. Elizabeth, she could only have learned that from you. Right now I see you hiding yourself away, and I know this is not the Elizabeth that your sister finally learned to appreciate so much."

"I'm not hiding."

"Aye, you are. And you know you are." He gently caressed her back. "You are hiding because you don't want the world to know that you have a right to grieve. You are hiding because you are afraid of admitting who you are."

She looked up at him, her anguish showing in her eyes. "Please, Ambrose. This is not the time."

"But it is, lass," he continued. "You need to face the truth now, not sometime in the distant future. Out there, at this very moment, messengers are taking the news of your sister's death to the English court. And to your father."

She looked up at him in alarm. Her voice was low and guarded. "Did you send them?"

"To the *English* court? Nay, Elizabeth. Not I." He held her ice-cold hand in his. "But the man who killed your sister was an English knight. And he was killed by a Scot. Now, think. That market is filled with merchants from all over Europe. If the word is not being conveyed by English merchants, then the Flemish merchants are doing it. They all know how much money there is to be made conveying information. In fact, I heard your sister's name going through the crowd, though how that happened, I don't know. But the fact that she was an Englishwoman, the daughter of a member of the king's council, is no small matter. All Europe knows the power and influence Thomas Boleyn wields in Henry's court."

Elizabeth had heard all this about her father before. But she'd always assumed he would just count her long dead. Now a thought that had been nagging at the corners of her consciousness pushed to the forefront. "You think he had something to do with this, don't you?"

Ambrose said nothing, considering how far to take this.

"Tell me," she persisted, her voice flat and emotionless. "What interest would he have in me now?"

"His interest would be to destroy you, Elizabeth." The Highlander decided to go all the way with this. To scare her. To bring her to her senses. "To make you suffer for your rebellion years back. He could feel he owes that to his king."

"We'll never cross paths. I am going to the Scottish court."

"Which is ruled by Henry's sister, Margaret Tudor!"

She paled. "Your queen..."

"Would she consider handing you over to your father?" he asked. "Aye, she would. You mean nothing to her, Elizabeth. But what's worse, you have lied to her. And betrayed her, as well."

"I have done no such thing. I've never even met her."

"By then you will have." He pressed. "By the time your father arrives at her court, you will have been presented to her as a man, even though you're very much a woman. You've pretended to be what you are not. But to make matters much worse—Margaret Tudor's a wildly superstitious woman. And you know how superstitious minds work as well as I. She'll think you've done all of this out of sheer witchcraft. To cast an evil spell on her, to bring her bad luck. Now that I think more on it, she might not hand you over."

"She won't?"

"Nay, she won't. She would want to keep the pleasure of burning you at the stake herself."

"You are cruel!"

"Nay, lass," Ambrose said sadly. "I just know my queen all too well."

Elizabeth felt a knot tighten in her gut as the thought of Jaime rushed into her mind.

"Perhaps he won't know," she whispered. "Perhaps my father won't find our trail. Perhaps he won't recognize me."

He shook his head. "What are the chances of that? As soon as he gets the news of Mary's death, he'll also learn that you are traveling with me. Pretending to be Mary's brother for years is all the clue he'll ever need." He took hold of her chin and brought her eyes to his. "I recognized you, Elizabeth, as soon as we met. Your father will, too."

"What will happen to Jaime?"

"She'll go to King Henry's court in the custody of her grandfather, Thomas Boleyn. And that will mean one more earldom for your father."

During those years in Florence, Elizabeth had always considered Garnesche to be the one they should fear the most. Peter Garnesche had been the villain to hide from. But now she knew—it had been her father that she had been running from all along. Indeed, perhaps this cowardly attack at Troyes had been set up by her father. By her own kin.

It was from her father's tent that she had been running, that night at the Field of Cloth of Gold. That night when she had witnessed a murder. But perhaps after all these years, Peter Garnesche had pushed the entire event from his memory. Perhaps he no longer cared.

One thing was certain, though. Ambrose was correct—her father would never forget.

For a moment, Elizabeth considered telling Ambrose about Garnesche's treachery. She had never seen any reason to tell him before. She had never seen any purpose in involving Ambrose in a long-buried secret about a crime that had happened so many years ago. After all, even Friar Matthew had counseled her to let the matter rest.

She stared at the burning candle. Jaime was all that really mattered now. Elizabeth had to make the decision that was right for the child.

"Tell me what you advise, Ambrose," she said simply. She knew she could trust him. She valued his judgment. With the exception of her encounter with the Englishman in the Golden Vale, the Highlander knew everything about her. And she knew he understood her.

Ambrose looked into Elizabeth's alert eyes.

"To start with," he said calmly, "you can't go on sitting in the dark of a boat, mourning a sister who is gone and who entrusted you with her wee one."

"Aye. I know that, too." Elizabeth stood up and walked to the small open window. The night sky was clear, and she could see the moon rising through a grove of trees that ran right to the river's edge. The barge would soon be getting under way again, as soon as the moon rose high enough to cast sufficient light.

With the cold moonlight bathing her face, she thought about the life that she had been living. It had never been easy. But now she would need to carry on the deception when the price of being unmasked was so high. It was no longer just herself now that she needed to fear for if she should be caught. Perhaps—for Jaime—it would be best to try to forget the past four years. Perhaps it would be best to become, once again, faceless and nameless, a woman hiding this time in some remote corner of the country.

"Do you advise that I become a woman again? Become Elizabeth Boleyn once more?" She turned from the window and faced him.

"I am saying you should leave this cabin." He stood and crossed the floor to her. "Jaime needs you. Your being hidden away has bothered her deeply. She saw her mother spending a great deal of time in this cabin before her death. I think she is afraid. She thinks she might lose you, as well. I don't think I have to tell you how she feels about you, but she told me that she wants her Uncle Phillipe to be her mama now."

Ambrose gently wiped away the tears that were rolling unchecked down her face. "Ernesta told me that the wee one depends on you more than she ever depended on her mother. She loves you, lass. And if all this means you should turn back to being who you truly are, then perhaps you should."

Jaime must be cared for, Elizabeth thought.

"And there's something else. It means less to you than it does to me, but there's Gavin."

"What?"

"Aye, Elizabeth. I'm deadly serious. Right now, the man is as broken in spirit as he was after Flodden. He blames himself for the death of your sister, and he sees your withdrawal as proof of it."

"Ambrose, I could never blame him. It was I who should have—"

Ambrose took her face in his hands. "Just tell him. Talk to him."

"Aye," she said. "I'll do that."

Change. She could already taste the sweetness and the bitterness that goes with all change. But she'd had her moments in the sun. She'd had her opportunity to paint. She'd felt the glow of success in doing the thing she wanted most to do. And now it was time to change. There were new pages that needed to be turned.

"I need to find Friar Matthew."

Ambrose raised an eyebrow. "Who?"

"The priest that sold you Henry's ring at—"

"I remember him. The one who helped you get to Florence."

"Ambrose, I'll give up the pretense. But I need a way to support Jaime and myself."

"Elizabeth, I—"

Placing her hand over his lips, she hushed his words. "I can't ask any more of you than what I have already asked, Ambrose. Friar Matthew helped me once before to sell my paintings, under different name. He could do it again. Jaime and I could remain in Paris. We'll change our names. No one will know our whereabouts or who we are. Perhaps it would be better if we moved to one of the villages outside the city. That way I could raise her in safety."

He pulled her hand from his mouth and held it. "I won't let you do that, Elizabeth."

She could see he was angry. "You've just said yourself that we can't go to the Scottish court after what has happened."

"Elizabeth, do the things that we've shared mean nothing to you?" He took hold of her shoulders. "Do you honestly think I could just walk away? Just leave you somewhere in France and forget about you?"

"Ambrose, I don't want you to do anything dishonorable. I don't want to see you shamed before your queen for protecting us. And I also don't want you to do something for us simply because it is the honorable thing to do."

She looked into his cobalt-blue eyes. They burned her soul with their intensity. She knew she loved him. She hated the thought of parting from him. She could feel the ache of longing in her chest even now. But she wasn't about to let him hold on to them for the wrong reasons. "I won't accept your charity, Ambrose. We can look after ourselves."

"Damn honor and damn you, Elizabeth Boleyn! Can't you see what I feel for you?" No longer could he hold back the emotions hidden just beneath the surface, feelings straining to surge into the open. "Don't you know what you've done to me? How my life has changed since we first met at the Field of Cloth of Gold?"

His fingers were digging into the flesh of her arms. But she prized this mild pain. "Aye. I've ruined you."

"Don't jest with me, damn it," he growled, shaking her once firmly. Ambrose quickly let his hands drop to his sides as he realized what he was doing. "Look at me. I've become a raving madman. I used to be cool, controlled, even-tempered."

She reached out and brought his hand to her face, gently placing a kiss on his palm. "I like you better this way."

His hands framed her face. His gaze locked with hers. "Is that all you will admit feeling for me? Elizabeth, I think from the day we first met, your eyes have betrayed you. You care for me as I do for you. Are *you* willing to walk away, to forget?"

She shook her head as tears once again coursed down her face. "I am simply trying to do the best thing, Ambrose. That's all."

"The best thing for whom, lass?" he asked gently. "The best thing for Jaime? What you think is best for me? Forget the last, for what you've just suggested is as wrong as it could be. Elizabeth, in this room you are the one who is bound up by your sense of honor and duty to those who depend upon you. You place everyone above you. You think of everyone but yourself."

Elizabeth stood shaking her head. "Nay, I—"

"And also, don't try to talk as though 'honor' belongs in some male dominion. Nay woman, you are living proof that it is not."

She couldn't stay away from him any longer. She slipped her arms about him, placing her face against his chest, holding him tightly. She needed his strength. She needed his love.

Ambrose held her trembling body against his.

"Elizabeth, it has taken me a lifetime to find you and another lifetime to get you back." He kissed her soft ebony hair. "I don't know if you perceive this to be right or wrong. But know this, lass. I am not letting you go. The past two days have been worse than a thousand years in hell for me. I never want to go through that again. I never want to be away from you again. Never. Do you understand?"

He lifted her chin and looked into the shimmering blackness of her eyes.

"I love you, Elizabeth. Tell me that you won't leave me. That you—"

She reached up and silenced his words with a kiss.

"I never thought I would ever hear you say those words," she whispered, kissing him again and again. Her lips could not get enough of him.

Ambrose grabbed a fistful of her hair and drew her face back, forcing her to look into his eyes. His lips lingered a breath away from hers.

"And what about you, Elizabeth? I've waited as long as you have."

Elizabeth gazed longingly into the depths of his eyes.

"I love you, Ambrose. I need you."

Her simple declaration was all he needed to hear. The grip of his arms tightened, his mouth descended. Their eyes, blazing with intent, never left one another as he drew her onto the bunk.

She needed him. Physically. Spiritually.

He needed her as he needed every part of himself. Deep within, he knew they were to be one, now and forever. Deep within, he knew the change had already occurred.

As the boat rocked in the restless current, Elizabeth moved past her grief, turning to life, to love. Like shipwreck survivors, starved for days, they clung to each other in a gathering storm of love.

Ambrose drew her to him, and her heart grew stronger with each passing moment. Caught up in the act of living, of loving, Elizabeth hardly felt herself shedding the weight of her grief. But she was, and the flames of her passion grew to a raging inferno, supplanting the darkness of death with the brilliance of being.

Together, they loved. The impatient hands, the roaming mouths—feeling, tasting—they were two paramours exulting in the quickening expression of their love. The radiance of their love soon dispelled all lingering shadow of loss.

In the lovers' frenzied desire, garments flew to the floor. Their clothing removed, Ambrose moved on top of her.

"Marry me, Elizabeth." His hands moved over the full curves of her breasts, the soft lines of her belly. "Tell me you will marry me."

She lay back on the bunk, her body quivering to his touch. While his lips teased and suckled the rosy nipples, his fingers gently slipped into her moist folds, finding within the nub of desire, stoking the flames.

Elizabeth groaned. "I think I...I think I'd be in heaven."

"A lovely place, no doubt, my love." Ambrose nipped at her jaw, kissing her neck, tracing a line with the tip of his tongue into the soft contours of the valley between her breasts. "Don't make me wait any longer, Elizabeth."

She pulled at his hair, pushing him onto his back. With a smile, the Highlander helped pull her on top.

"I am stubborn," she growled. "Opinionated, too. And head-strong."

She shifted her weight on him, moving her legs until she straddled him.

"I love that about you."

"I am emotional and short-tempered. I'll probably drive you out of your mind."

"I can live with that." His fingers played over the lines of her tender flesh. Her body was so perfect. He wanted her now. He wanted to feel himself buried deep within her. "And it will be an improvement over my present condition."

She gasped as he lifted her onto him.

"Tell me, Elizabeth," he rumbled, his voice ragged with desire. "Tell me."

"Aye, my love." She lowered herself gently as he entered her. She whispered her response. "Aye, Ambrose. I'll marry you."

Joined in the love embrace, the perfect fit, they locked out any specter of fear and loss. At this moment all that mattered was the two of them. All that existed was the affinity of two hearts and minds. Two bodies and souls. They would have time—a lifetime together—to face the enemies and intruders that awaited them. But for now, for tonight, each lived only for the other—together basking in the glow of fulfillment.

Chapter 27

Gavin remained behind when they left Paris.

Once Elizabeth surfaced from her mournful isolation, the warrior soon recovered from his sorrow over Mary's death. But he couldn't quite grasp the truth about his friend Phillipe de Anjou.

With Ambrose standing behind her, glaring at the black-haired giant, Elizabeth told Gavin the truth—that she was a woman. Dumbfounded, the Lowlander had been unable to utter a word. But when he finally stammered out that he didn't believe it and required proof, Ambrose had been at his throat, at once.

And Gavin had believed her.

They sailed out of King Francis's new port at La Havre, going west around the tip of Cornwall and north through the Irish Sea to the Scotland. The seas of the Solway Firth tossed their little ship, but soon the travelers found themselves making their way past the red stone walls of Sweetheart Abbey and the round towers of Caerlaverock Castle and into the calmer waters off the village of Gretna. There Elizabeth and Ambrose, together with Jaime, the Baldis, and the baron's company of soldiers, secured horses and began their trek into the hills east of Gretna and on into the green, rolling valleys of the Borders.

On the second day's ride, they dropped down into the river valley of the Teviot, and followed its sparkling waters east, toward the ancient border stronghold of Roxburgh Castle. As they rode along, Elizabeth's eyes continued to survey the lush and fertile farm land, the broad expanses of forest, the rocky upland moors. The place struck her with its beauty, its wildness, its strength. She didn't know if she had ever seen a sky as blue as the one that covered the open spaces that they crossed.

To Elizabeth, the Borderlands between Scotland and England presented a study in pastoral beauty. Small, neatly thatched cottages stood side by side with rugged stone and sod huts. Flocks of sheep grazed on craggy hills, while cattle roamed the river's grassy edge. As they rode along, farmers and fishermen doffed their hats to the passing baron, and children and maidens ran alongside the warriors, dispensing fresh bannock cakes and wildflowers.

Once, after riding between two high rocky outcroppings as they continued to follow the river, Elizabeth spotted a large group of buildings as she gazed south into the distance. That was Jedburgh Abbey, she was told, one of four powerful abbeys in the Borders. It was the good monks there, Ambrose told her, who centuries ago had begun to develop the land for agricultural use, raising their sheep and their crops, educating the local farmers, and bringing civilization to a vagrant people long beleaguered by marauders from the north as well as the south.

It had always been a hard place to live and prosper, and Ambrose had been sent there to bring about justice for the industrious and protection for the oppressed. And he had done just that. That was four years earlier, not long after his successes at the Field of Cloth of Gold. It was then that the queen and the Regency council had given the Highlander the title Baron of Roxburgh, Lord Protector of the Borders.

Finally, with the summer sun setting behind them and their own shadows stretching out before them, Ambrose leaned over and pointed at the four square towers rising on a tall hill above the river valley. Roxburgh Castle.

They were to be married in Benmore Castle, the Macpherson clan's stronghold in the Highlands. That was the tradition. Benmore was the place where Ambrose's parents had wed. It was the place where his brothers and he had been born. Where his older brother Alec and his wife Fiona wed and now lived with their children...when they were not in the Western Isles or at Fiona's own ancestral home, Drummond Castle.

Ambrose had sent a messenger to his family from Paris with the news.

Elizabeth had never been to the Highlands. She'd never been surrounded with a lot of family, but the thought of it all appealed to her. It appealed to her, and it made her a bit nervous. But if that was what Ambrose wanted, then she wanted it, as well.

However, Ambrose insisted that they stop in the Borders before going anywhere. They had business to attend to first.

So as the travelers neared Roxburgh Castle, the warrior thought over their plans and the best course of action. They had so much to do, and Ambrose wanted Elizabeth and Jaime safe while he took care of the immediate problems that only he could look after.

First, he needed to send a message to Giovanni de' Medici about the artist he would never get back. But he knew he couldn't tell the truth, not yet. Perhaps sometime, years from now, Elizabeth and he would make a visit to the Florentine duke.

And then, Ambrose needed to consider the Queen Mother. She represented the most pressing of concerns. Though the Highlander had deliberately overstated to his beloved what Queen Margaret's response might be upon learning about Elizabeth's sex, he honestly had no real assurance that the queen might *not* turn Elizabeth—and Jaime—over to her brother's ever faithful counselor, Thomas Boleyn.

Margaret Tudor could be quite spiteful and completely capricious, especially if she felt she had been slighted in the least. She was a woman who Ambrose knew it was a mistake to cross. When she decided she wanted something, she would stop at nothing to get it. And she wanted a painter. A Florentine painter.

The Highlander knew he would need to see her in person. He knew it was the only way.

"You don't know how sorry I am to have to leave you alone here, my love." He caressed the short waves of her satin-soft hair as they coiled around his fingers. Her hair was getting longer.

"I won't be alone," she whispered, smiling as she lay on her stomach beside him. "Aside from the five hundred and twelve sheep I've counted from our little window, you are leaving me with several hundred soldiers. I'm certain at least of dozen of them talk, and—"

"The last time I counted, there were only five hundred sheep!"

"Ah, well. You know how it is. Springtime in Scotland, love and...bairns is the word, isn't it? Well, there isn't much else to do, is there, my sweet?"

"Hmmm. I like the sound of that." Ambrose drew the covers off her back, exposing her smooth skin. He smiled as she moved right into his arms. "But this doesn't make it any easier for me to be going."

"It isn't supposed to," she whispered, snuggling closer.

Ambrose gathered her tightly to his chest. He still couldn't get used to the thrill he felt holding her close. The way she had taken possession of his heart, as if it had always belonged to her, filling it up until he felt that it might burst.

It felt so right. He watched her as she moved in, taking possession of his house and all who lived there. Yes, they, too, took her in, accepted her as their own, as if she'd always been there. One of them.

As Ambrose held her, he thought about the journey ahead. Amid all the uncertainties that lay before them, he knew one thing for sure. He would be the one at a loss when he left her tomorrow to go to Stirling to meet with the queen. He would be the one so utterly heartsick about being away. It was an odd, new knowledge for him, for he had always been one who lived on the road. Smoothing her ebony hair, he hugged her fiercely.

Five weeks earlier, when they had arrived at the grim and menacing Roxburgh Castle, Ambrose had sensed that Elizabeth was startled by the hulking mass of rough gray stone. The giant military fortification certainly had nothing in common with Florence, that lively city of art and culture where she'd been living the past few years. Indeed, the dark halls, the nearly empty rooms, and the pervading attitude of constant vigilance were a far cry from his own hunting lodge on the edge of the forest to the east of Troyes. This was the place that had never held any future for him. On the frontier border with England, Roxburgh was simply a fortress designed and fortified to keep the border skirmishes to a minimum, and it was a place from which the Scots might offer a first wave of defense should the English decide to invade.

It was a place of war, a place of men. Aside from the laundresses, no women worked in the castle at all. But Roxburgh offered distance from the court that Ambrose wanted for Elizabeth and Jaime, so here they would stay for a short time. So, rather than departing for the court at once, the baron decided to stay around awhile and help her get acclimated.

She hadn't needed much help from him, however.

Ambrose already knew. His men adored her. His servants respected and obeyed her wishes. Needless to say, he and Jaime loved her, and he couldn't imagine life without her.

"Ambrose."

He looked down at her sober face. Her black eyes glistened, glowing in the light of the candles that illuminated the room.

"Tomorrow, when you leave..." Her fingers drummed lightly on his chest. "Erne and I talked earlier today. She'll be going on with you and Joseph to Edinburgh."

"I thought you enjoyed her company," he said with surprise. With Ernesta Bardi gone, Elizabeth would be alone here with Jaime. "I thought she was a help to you."

"I do, Ambrose! She is! But...well, I can't have her wasting her life playing nursemaid to us."

"Is this Elizabeth Boleyn, the woman who knows what is best for everyone else but herself, speaking now?"

"Nay! It isn't!" She slapped him on the chest. "Don't make fun of me, beast. I am telling you this because I'm certain this is truly the best course for her and for me."

"How so?" he pressed.

She paused to gather her thoughts. "Ernesta Bardi is a merchant's wife; she is a smart businesswoman in her own right. A person who has played large part in her husband's successes. And she had a life—a full life—with Joseph, their business, their travels long before Mary and Jaime and I walked into it."

"She seems to have enjoyed filling it a bit more with the three of you."

"To some degree that might be the truth. But now I want her to feel that she can go back once again to the life she chose for herself, without having to tag along after us. She should feel comfortable walking away from Jaime and me, with no fears or worries over our wellbeing. I'd like to see her traveling with Joseph and enjoying the time they have left together. And I want her to be able to come back and visit whenever she wishes."

"So the two of you talked this out?"

"Aye."

"And she agrees that it is time to move on without you?"

Elizabeth nodded. "It took some persuasion. But I convinced her." She placed a kiss on his chest. "Erne is quite happy for us, you know. And she and Joseph will travel to Benmore Castle for our wedding."

"Oh, they will?"

"Aye, in spite of all the stories we've been hearing about those Highland rogues."

"So you've been hearing stories?" he responded, a wry grin tugging at the corner of his mouth.

"Aye, we have. So we'll all be seeing one another again in no time."

He combed his fingers through her hair. The silky black tresses tumbled over the back of his hand.

"Why are you doing this? Why so soon? You hardly know anyone in this pile of rock. Why send her off now?"

She gazed into his eyes. "Because I need to toughen up. And I need to prove something to myself. That can't be done with Erne here."

"Tell me, love. What do you need to prove?"

Elizabeth glanced away for a moment before turning her eyes back to his face. "I need to know if I can adjust to this new life. Without anyone pampering me or taking care of me. Since we arrived here, Erne has done everything for me. In a way, she is treating me the way Mary liked to be treated. It doesn't matter what it is—small or large, minor or significant. She is always there for me, helping me. Running my bath, helping me dress, seeing to my meals."

"Perhaps this is the first chance she's had an opportunity to show you how much she loves you."

"That's what we talked about today." Elizabeth felt tears welling up in her eyes. "You are right. That was exactly what she was trying to do, and more. She's always thought I've been somehow deprived of even little luxuries, of simple comforts that I should have been enjoying for the last few years. So now she wants to make up for those times."

Ambrose gently wiped away a tear from her cheek. "Well, she's too late. It's my job to give you things, my love. Only mine."

"I don't need to be spoiled, Ambrose." Elizabeth smiled. "Ernesta loves me, and I love her. That came across today stronger than ever before. We were like a mother and daughter, sitting next to each other, holding hands, pouring out our insides, and retelling stories from the past. Sharing hopes for the future. After we were done, she was certain of my happiness. To her, that seemed to be all that mattered. So she agreed to go."

He watched as her face clouded with a frown. "You are unhappy, though."

"Not true." She took hold of his fingers and brought them to her lips. "I have never been happier than now—with you. But something *is* gnawing away at me."

"What is it?"

She rolled onto her back and stared up at the dark, rough-hewn timbers of the ceiling.

"I don't know if I still can function in the role of a woman."

The Highlander started to laugh.

She turned onto her side, propping herself up on one elbow. "I'm serious."

"Nay, lass. You can't be." He smiled and reached out, his finger tracing her full lips. "Elizabeth, you are a woman. All woman."

His fingers brushed over her cheek.

"I was a man. All man. For four years."

"Nay. You weren't."

Running along the smooth lines of her shoulders, his fingers grazed the skin of her upper arms and lightly moved onto the soft orb of her breast.

"I was, too," she whispered, her eyes clouding over at his touch.

"You are obstinate, Elizabeth Boleyn."

Her voice was low. "You've known about this quality for quite a while, Lord Macpherson."

"Aye, I have." His mouth descended on her lips and he kissed her. "I am not complaining. I love your flaws, my sweet. You can keep every one."

"I have no flaws, only an abundance of talent." She watched the smile that pulled at his mouth. "But if you laugh at me one more time, I'll..."

"Aye, lass. You'll what?" he teased.

"I don't know." She sighed happily, snuggling back against his side. "But give me forty years or so. I'll think of something."

Elizabeth considered for a moment how much she loved the way it was between them. They teased, they argued, they laughed for hours on end. Together, they rode out into the neighboring valleys, enjoying the late summer weather—more often than not, taking Jaime with them. Ambrose showed her the countryside, told her about the people of the Scottish Lowlands. About their history. About their heroes.

But as he talked, his stories always returned to the Highlands When he spoke of home—of the wild, craggy peaks, of the rushing mountain streams and the storms so fierce and sudden, of the people so free and so alive—Elizabeth could see the faraway look come into his eyes. And she loved it.

In the daylight hours, before the other inhabitants of the castle, they acted so properly. Intelligent, reserved—two refined people who would soon marry.

But at night, their lives took on a different dimension. Enamored, reckless—two lovers who desperately, physically needed one another.

"Do you think I am making a mistake? In sending Erne away?" she whispered. "Do you think once she goes, your people will catch on to my façade and dislike me?"

"Hardly!" Ambrose hugged her hard against his chest. "Do you really think *anyone* could dislike you, Elizabeth? Don't you see how they all love you?"

Elizabeth rubbed her cheek against the warm skin of his chest. "Aye. It's true that your men treat me well. But when I think about the future...I want to say the right things, Ambrose. Do the right things. Be proper. I don't want to be a disappointment to you in front of your family, in front of your friends."

"You'll never be anything less than my greatest treasure, my love. Trust me."

"There is so much I don't know, so much I need to learn." She looked up and gazed in his eyes. "I want to fit. So desperately, I want to belong. I've never truly had a home. Not one that mattered, before this. But it matters now, Ambrose."

"You belong, Elizabeth. You belong to me, and I to you. And you've always had a home. You made that out of yourself...for your sister, for Jaime. Stone walls do not make a home. The warmth, the love you carry in your heart, that's what it makes it." He kissed the bridge of her nose; his lips brushed across her damp cheek. "I, on the other hand, have always had houses. Too many of them. Scattered across the continent. My friends laugh at me because of them. But I never felt tied to any of them. I couldn't make any of them a home." He kissed her lips. "Because I hadn't found my home. But now I have. I've found you, Elizabeth."

She missed him desperately, and for two weeks her mind and her blood had been racing. Almost frantic, at times she felt as if she only had moments left to get her life, and everything around her, in order.

Ambrose had gone two weeks ago. The Bardis had gone with him.

From the moment they'd left, Elizabeth had felt the rush of emotions surge through her. Things had to get done. Inside. Outside.

Robert, the tall, young warrior who commanded the battalion while Ambrose traveled, stood behind her, nodding his approval while she ordered servants here, soldiers there. He and Jaime followed her everywhere she went. She sent for masons, for carpenters. Roxburgh Castle would be a changed place by the time Ambrose returned. Elizabeth hadn't worked out all the details, but the creativity in her soul took flight. Her imagination soared.

And she moved as if there were no tomorrow. Frequently, thoughts of her sister Mary pushed into her consciousness, and she would think, wondering if her actions now were the result of some lingering guilt she carried concerning Mary's death. The true murderer who sent the assassins, the real reason behind the attack, these things were still unknown. But the truth at the bottom of it all still haunted her—the dagger had been meant for Elizabeth's heart, not her sister's.

Garnesche remained in her memory as much as her father. Even simple things like the training of the men in the courtyard or the movements of torch-carrying soldiers along the paths in the evening would bring back memories of the crime she'd seen committed on a dark night in the north of France. And she wondered what tomorrow would bring. She wondered if there would be a tomorrow.

Mary was never given the chance to experience what the future would bring. But as violent as her sister's death was—Elizabeth knew—Mary Boleyn had died at peace with the world. She had been given a chance, perhaps a second chance, to bring a sense of harmony, of goodness back into her life. And she had taken hold of that chance with both hands.

As Elizabeth stood in the center of the chaos of renovation going on around her, she wondered if perhaps that same goodness was what she, too, sought after. For Jaime, for herself, and for Ambrose. Perhaps she, too, was looking for that sense of peace, of serenity.

"M'lady!" The warrior's voice was commanding and sharp. "You simply cannot go up there."

"I can, Robert. And I will," Elizabeth asserted as she pushed her way around the agitated Highlander. She turned to Robert as she climbed the first step. "Did the baron not specifically order you to see to it that my wishes were followed? *Didn't* you hear him say that?"

"I did, m'lady."

"Very well!" Elizabeth turned and started up the steps two at a time toward the top tower room.

"But wait," the man called out after a moment's delay.

She stopped and took a deep breath. She had to save her full fury for when he reached her. This was the last tower to be looked into. With dozens of workers busily working in the other sections, it was only natural for her to want to extend the effort to this final area of the castle. It was clear to her now, though, how cleverly Robert had contrived to keep her away from this corner of the castle.

The young warrior had been one of the first loyal friends she'd found at Roxburgh. Having trained years back as the squire for Ambrose's elder brother, Robert had been with Macpherson family since boyhood. From what Ambrose had told her of the young man, Elizabeth knew Robert to be a prime example of the devotion and the courage that every Highlander aspired to.

"M'lady. I do need to talk to you about..."

Elizabeth turned slowly and faced him. Though he stood two steps lower, they were at eye level. "Robert. You haven't stopped talking since the baron left."

"Aye, m'lady. But this is important." The young man racked his brain for some ideas. "This concerns the time when the baron was on the Isle of Skye with his brother, Lord Alec."

"In Skye?"

"Aye, m'lady. When Lord Ambrose was staying at Dunvegan Castle. It's a place that the MacLeod clan keep, a wonderful fortress, with—"

She rolled her eyes and then broke in unceremoniously. "It is amazing to me, Robert, that every time I have tried to come to this tower, you have managed to entertain and distract me with more stories about Ambrose's past. It's worked before, young man. But it won't work now. I am up to your tricks." She turned on her heel and quickly started running up the steps.

The young man cursed under his breath. Macpherson women! What was it about them? They were all the same. Headstrong and opinionated. The elder Lady Elizabeth, Lady Fiona, and now this one. Perfectly matched, they were.

Elizabeth quickened her pace as she heard the warrior once again chasing after her. She reached the landing, but he caught up to her at the last moment, moving in front of her and blocking the door.

"What is it now?" she asked impatiently. "Let me guess. You just remembered I failed to stop for the noon meal, and if I don't eat, then Lord Ambrose will have your hide for that transgression, as well."

The young man brightened at once. "How did you know, m'lady? You've read my mind."

"Get out of my way, Robert. Or else."

"It's for your own good, Lady Elizabeth. Please listen to me. You don't want to be exposed to what is in there."

She matched the man's troubled expression with a sardonic look of her own. "Are there dead bodies lying about? Is it a torture chamber?"

"Much worse," Robert replied, shaking his head slowly. "You had just better stay away."

She glared at him menacingly. "You know, of course, that by trying—with these ridiculous ploys—to keep me out of there, you've only succeeded in thoroughly piquing my curiosity. Robert, it is no longer possible for me to leave that door closed."

He nodded. "I know I've made it difficult for you, m'lady. But you see, I'm not seasoned in the ways of ladies of such quality as you."

"Don't flatter me. It won't work."

The young warrior dropped his head to his chest. He wasn't certain to what degree he should go to stop her from seeing what lay beyond the door. True, the baron had instructed him to keep her away until he arrived. But he had a pretty good idea that physical restraint was the only thing left now that might keep her out of the tower room. And Robert wasn't about to risk laying a hand on Lord Ambrose's lady.

"And don't try to make me feel sorry for you. That won't work, either." She crossed her arms over her chest. "Now step aside."

He took one last look at her. She meant business. There would be no distracting her. He stepped to the side, allowing her approach the door.

Elizabeth let her gaze wander from the forlorn expression of the warrior to the metal key lock on the door. It was one of only two in the castle. She took a step closer. Her hand reached out and grabbed the door handle. Then she took a deep breath. Robert had done a good job. She paused, her outstretched arms still, her heart pounding. She listened for a noise. For any sign of life. What was it that was hidden inside the chamber? she wondered. Then she pulled hard.

The door wouldn't budge. Locked. She set herself and pulled again. To no avail.

She turned slowly, ever so slowly, in the direction of the young man. "Get me the key, Robert. Go and get it now."

He nodded at once and headed down the stairs quickly.

"Thank you, thank you, thank you Lord," he whispered. He couldn't imagine what had gotten into Evan Kerr, his second in command, to make him lock the door to the tower room. Lord Ambrose never locked that door, nor the door to his bedchamber, but Robert was glad it had been done this time. Robert took three steps at a time and disappeared down the circular stairwell. With any luck, he thought happily, Lady Elizabeth wouldn't be able to find him until Lord Ambrose returned.

Elizabeth watched him speedily depart, and then she turned once again to the door. The large keyhole might offer some view, she thought. Looking through the hole, she could hardly see. Dust and a spider web blocked the opening. It occurred to her that it didn't look like anyone had used a key in there in quite some time. She straightened up and grabbed the handle with two hands this time. The cold of the metal made her shudder. She pulled hard.

There was a give. A slight give of the door. She yanked harder. The scratch of the heavy door against the frame made a screeching noise.

She pulled again with all her strength. The loud scraping sound eased as the dark oaken door swung heavily on its hinges toward her. She stepped back, waiting for the door to come fully to a stop.

Her heart slammed in her chest. She looked straight ahead into the brightness. Light from the room flooded the dark landing where she stood. Hesitantly, she took a step in. And then she stopped.

It was a workroom. The most beautiful workroom she'd ever seen. Through windows larger than the thin arrow slits found in the lower rooms, sunlight poured over the freshly whitewashed stone walls. In the corner, three long and heavy rolls of canvas sat. There were benches and easels standing at the ready beside a brazier. A thick clean mat of freshly woven rushes scented the room. A dozen small casks of what she knew would be oil and water and pigments lined one wall.

Elizabeth turned around, taking in everything at once. She moved to the rolls of canvas. As she ran her fingers over the texture of the cloth, she knew immediately the canvas was of the finest quality.

Growing increasingly dazed, the young woman worked her way past the casks of paint to a wall where a heavy sheet covered bundles of artwork. She laid her hand gently on the material and pulled the sheet off the rows of paintings stacked so carefully against the wall. Emotion clouded her eyes.

The sight of the first one unleashed her tears. The Field of Cloth of Gold. The second version of the one she'd lost in the tent fire at Calais. The one that she'd painted from memory in Florence. The only record that remained of where it had all begun.

Her fingers played over the depiction of Ambrose in the work.

"I love you," she whispered to him.

Then, carefully, she looked at the other works lying behind the first one.

They were hers. The paintings she'd thought had been left behind in Florence. They were all here, sitting in this room. He had them brought here for her.

She heard the sound of footsteps and turned at once. It was Robert. His body filled the door.

"M'lady, I need to speak with you."

"This room," she whispered. "You tried to keep me out."

"I'm sorry, m'lady. This is your room," he said quietly. "A present from Lord Ambrose to you. Your paintings from Florence had not yet come when he left for court. That's why he didn't bring you here himself. The casks of materials he sent for just arrived from Edinburgh yesterday."

She moved about, tears rolling freely down her cheeks.

"It's a lovely room."

"Aye, m'lady. This is the castle's warmest room in winter, with a beautiful view of the valley. He wanted you to feel at home. He wanted you to have a place to work. But m'lady—"

"I love this place," she broke in, standing in the middle of the room and looking at the young warrior. "I love him."

Robert watched the happiness that glowed in the young woman's face. He didn't want to disturb this moment for her, but he had to tell her she was needed downstairs.

"You can leave me, Robert," she said gently. "I need some time to pull myself together. No one can handle this much happiness all at once."

"I'm sorry, m'lady. But there are people who need to speak with you."

"Can't they wait?"

He shook his head. "Our men have just escorted them in."

"What people?" she asked. "The masons from Edinburgh, the ones Ambrose was sending?"

"Nay, m'lady. Your father."

Chapter 28

Elizabeth was out of breath when she burst into the hall. At once, her eyes scanned the great room in search of the child. Robert had said that her father, Thomas Boleyn, had been left talking with Jaime when the warrior came after her. The rest of her father's men had remained in the outer yard of the keep, under the watchful eyes of Ambrose's soldiers.

Panic began to sweep through her as she looked about the vacant hall. The room had been alive with artisans and workers an hour ago when she and Robert had left for the south tower. The dust of their efforts still lingered in the air of the hall, diffusing the light of the high windows. But only silence and emptiness greeted her now.

Then, at last, she saw him at the far end of the great room.

There he sat, on the baron's high-backed chair by the side of the vast, open fireplace. A goblet of wine sat on the floor beside him. He was speaking in a low voice with the child. Jaime sat on the hearth at his feet, playing with her kitten D'Or and obviously keeping her eyes averted from the visitor.

Thomas Boleyn's head swung around, and he came instantly to his feet.

With her heart pounding, Elizabeth took a step toward him and the child. She clenched her fists in an attempt to keep her hands from trembling at her sides. She watched as Jaime ran past the old man and skipped happily into her open arms. The sound of the little girl's footsteps echoed off the high walls.

Elizabeth crouched before the young girl and hugged her fiercely. "Go to my bedchamber and stay there until I come for you," she whispered in the child's ear.

Jaime nodded but continued to hold on to her neck.

Elizabeth peered into the dark eyes that mirrored her own. They were filled with fear, uncertainty. "I'm frightened," the little girl whispered. Her voice was as soft as the drop of a leaf on a cool fall day. "He says he is my grandfather."

"That he is," Elizabeth returned softly.

"He told me that he's planning to take us away. To England. Just you and me. But we can't go, can we?"

"Nay, Jaime. We can't."

The young child nodded and leaned closer, whispering in her ear. "I didn't answer any of his questions."

"You did the right thing, love." Elizabeth ran her hands down the soft black tresses that fell to the child's shoulders. "Now, you go."

Jaime withdrew her hands from around her neck. "When is the baron coming back? I want him here with us."

"I miss him, too, Jaime."

"He wouldn't let anyone take us away." She cast a quick glance over her shoulder at the man waiting behind her. "I know he wouldn't."

Elizabeth brought the child's hands together and kissed them both. "That is true, love. And nobody is going to take us away while he's visiting the queen. We won't let them. Now be on your way."

The young girl raised herself on tiptoe and placed a kiss on Elizabeth's cheek before running out of the hall with her kitten at her heels.

Elizabeth didn't turn, but remained crouched where she was until Jaime's footsteps faded on the steps outside of the door of the great hall. Then she raised herself to her feet.

Sir Thomas looked frail and bent with age. Elizabeth let her eyes take in the man whom she had feared and had run away from just four years earlier. The years—and the pressures of his life—had taken a visible toll on the man. He was much thinner than she remembered him. His body seemed to be wasting away, and his shoulders stooped as if he were carrying some enormous weight. Even in this fine summer weather, her father had wrapped himself in fine, thick wool and a fur-lined doublet of cloth of gold, with a heavy cloak that lay draped over the arm of the chair. His black eyes were set in a face etched with deep lines of worry.

Elizabeth's eyes widened as he opened his arms. He took a step toward her, his hands still outstretched. She felt a pang in her chest. A deep, ancient sorrow sprang from within her, as sharp as the green blade of the narcissus cutting upward through the frozen ground of spring.

So many times as a child she had wished for this, dreamed of her father's affection, of his open embrace. But they had been only a dream.

He took another step toward her. She fought the urge to run to him, to seek that shelter. But shelter from whom? she thought. From whom has she ever needed shelter? From this man. Her eyes narrowed. It was this man—her own father—who had pushed her away, pushed her to the edge, to the place from which there had been no turning back.

He moved closer.

As much as she wanted to backtrack, turn and run from him, she forced herself to remain where she was.

Elizabeth looked into his eyes. She searched for the truth there, for some reminder of the reason for her anger. But there was nothing. No flash of power, no hint of temper, no fire of life. They were just the eyes of a very tired old man.

Suddenly she didn't know how to respond.

Sir Thomas reached her.

Elizabeth stood in silence as her father placed two hands on her shoulders and lightly placed a kiss on each of her cheeks. She fought her impulse to flinch, to pull back. She also fought the conflicting impulse to return the simple display of affection. She bowed her head, unsure of what it was that she wanted.

"It does my heart good to see you, Elizabeth," he said, touching her hair and gauging its length. But his face was impassive, and he made no further comment, at last letting his hands drop from her shoulders. He took her limp and unresponsive hands in his.

"I cannot say the same," she whispered. Though her hands and her tone were like ice, she could feel her cheeks burning. Though she put on a face of stone, her insides were quivering. For the first time in a very long while, Elizabeth felt weak and vulnerable.

He tightened his grip on her hand and drew her gently toward the chair where he'd been sitting when she came into the hall. She went.

"I didn't come all the way to Scotland to quarrel with you," Sir Thomas said.

"Then why did you come?"

"I have come seeking peace, daughter."

"Peace?" she asked shortly. "Peace between whom?"

"Between you and me, Elizabeth. Perhaps peace for the sake of Jaime."

She watched him pull a chair for her next to his. Then he gestured for her to sit. In a show of continuing defiance, she stood beside the chair.

"Jaime and I were living in peace. Before you came."

Sir Thomas gazed at her for a moment and then sat heavily in the large, high-backed chair. His eyes surveyed the empty hall, taking in the chaotic conditions. "He has left you already."

She felt her stomach go taut at his words. "We are to be married."

"Aye, your mother and I were to be married, too." His voice wavered unsteadily. "But I left her."

"You can make no comparison here," she replied icily. "You were after power, not her."

He looked vaguely into the embers of the small fire smoldering in the hearth.

"She had nothing to give. No dowry, no position."

"She gave you everything she had. Her heart, her love."

"Aye, that she did. But those things were not enough for me," he whispered. He turned his gaze upward to her face. "And they won't be enough for the Scot."

"You have a heart of stone," Elizabeth returned. "Ambrose has a human heart—flesh and blood, good and true."

"I am a man. So is he."

"You are a monster!" she replied, her voice on fire. She waved her hand at his garments. "You simply cover yourself with cloth of gold."

"Cloth of Gold," he said after a long pause, speaking almost to himself. "Where this all started."

Hundreds of words rushed into her brain all at once. There was so much she could say. These two men were light and darkness, joy and sorrow, heaven and hell. Words alone couldn't do justice in differentiating these men. But Sir Thomas sat there, hollow, expressionless.

"I thought you came in peace," she continued, her voice now calm once again. She wasn't about to expose her soul to him. "I haven't sought your counsel for years. I don't need it now."

"Elizabeth," he said, gazing at her profile until her eyes turned back to him. "I don't blame you for feeling as you do."

She moved to the fireplace. She shivered slightly at a coldness that was seeping into her bones. Placing a log on the embers, she watched the sparks and the small flames that licked the dry wood. Suddenly she winced as the pain she'd first felt so many years ago once again pierced her scarred cheek. With her back to him, she traced with her finger the mark he'd given her. She knew the scar was faded, hardly noticeable. But she wondered about the scar on her heart.

"Why are you here?" she asked, still with her back to him.

"I told you before, to seek peace."

She stood and turned, facing him. "Why? Why now, after all these years?"

He paused and looked at the palms of his open hands. "I looked for you before this. But after your tent burned at the Field of Cloth of Gold, you disappeared completely."

She stood silently.

"I wanted to bring you back," he continued. "But I wanted you back for the wrong reasons. I sent people after you. I had them search everywhere. I sent men to Paris, to the households of every friend and acquaintance you ever had. I even went as far as to set a bounty."

She stared at her father. This was more the man she had known.

"Aye, I wanted to get you back. To teach you a lesson. Nothing would have made me happier than to drag you to Henry and show the king how he mattered more to me than my own child."

The silence in the hall was deadly.

"But you couldn't find me," she stated.

"Nay, daughter. I couldn't find you." Sir Thomas took a deep breath before continuing. "But I know now that this was the Lord's will. He wanted me to wait and to learn. Some of life's lessons are long and hard in coming."

"And you think you have learned some lesson?"

He smiled bitterly. "Aye, I have, Elizabeth. I've learned from my children."

"You mean from the only one left to you. From Anne."

"Nay. From all of three of you. Daughters that I looked down upon for most of my life. Daughters that I simply considered to be trifles, at best merchandise to barter with. To trade away for my own prosperity, to improve my own position. Nay, Elizabeth. It isn't just Anne whom I've learned from. I've learned my lessons from all of you."

She sat down before the fire, watching his faraway gaze.

"You were the first, Elizabeth. You, my strong and high spirited girl. You, who combined your mother Catherine's goodness and her beauty with my stubbornness and drive. You were clearly the best of your mother and me, joined in one person. And I hated you for it. From the time you were a small child, I could see your mother in you...and I could see myself. Aye, the better part of me. The good and gentle Thomas Boleyn who existed once, long ago. The man who wouldn't leave his true love for all the gold in the world. But you were even stronger than I. You were smarter. You had a belief in something greater, as well. Something that I never had."

"And you still hate me. The person that I was. The person that I am."

"Nay, nay, nay. A thousand times I've cried out in my sleep for forgiveness. It's true. You see, each night, your mother is with me. She haunts me, Elizabeth. In my sleep. And in my waking hours, as well. Oh, I know I can never be absolved of the sins I have committed. Sins against her. Sins against you, our only child. But still I beg her to let you forgive me."

She looked down. The burning coals of sorrow showed in his eyes. She didn't want to see that look. She couldn't afford to pity him. Not now.

"What could you have learned from me?" she asked.

"You have an undeniable strength in you. Conviction. You are like fire itself—pure and uncompromising. I tried to compromise...nay, make you throw off your principles. But you stood against me. You stood against your king. I believe you have never feared any man, no matter what power or position they hold." He shook his head in admiration. "You are the strongest woman I have ever known. You were willing to surrender your innocence to a Scot rather than give an inch. Aye, you taught me a valuable lesson, Elizabeth, about the power of the human spirit.

After you left me that night with your face marked and bloody, I knew that not even a sword to your throat or a dagger to your heart could sway you to do wrong against your will."

Elizabeth remembered that horrible night as if it were yesterday.

"You showed strength like none I'd ever seen. In man or woman." The old man's voice was barely a whisper. "Strength that I have never had."

Sir Thomas leaned down and rested his head in his hands.

"And then there was Mary. My pitifully young and inexperienced Mary. She was merely a child, always a child, pampered and cared for. She was forever what I couldn't force you to become. Young, naive, malleable. If you are like fire, Elizabeth, then she was like the clay of the earth. So easy to mold to my own greedy ambitions. I never loved Mary's and Anne's mother. She was nothing more to me than a stepping stone into a better class of society. I admit that with only disgust for myself. And true to my character, I manipulated Mary for my own purposes. Just a pretty face to use and send to Henry's bed. And she went willingly. To some extent for the excitement of it, I suppose. But also because her father commanded her to go. She never questioned me."

"You rejected her, Father. You didn't believe her when she came back to you with the news that she was carrying Henry's child."

"I knew she was telling the truth. But once again I allowed myself to be swayed by your cousin, Sarah Exton. Her and her conniving ways. Like a fool, I let her convince me that I would have more power over the king if I were to send Mary back to Kent, to keep her tucked away until the baby came. I always knew that was Henry's child. We just couldn't let her throw away a chance for real wealth. One thing I never expected, though, was that she would run away."

"You didn't know she was with me?"

"Aye, we did figure as much. After we found no trace of her in the tent. Nor any sign of her, alive or dead. Then we figured that was the way of it. We knew Mary was not strong enough to do anything, or go anywhere, on her own. And later, when I received her letter months afterward, we knew for sure."

"A letter?"

"Aye, the letter she sent me after losing the king's son in childbirth."

Elizabeth kept her gaze steady, fighting down the surge of feelings that coursed through her. She still remembered the days after Mary gave birth to Jaime. How Mary rejected the child since she wasn't a boy. It certainly fit. Sending a letter to their father would have been Mary's way of punishing him for making her run the way he did.

"I have had moments, Elizabeth. Dark and awful moments. When I would think of the terrible dangers, the misery that you two must have faced. Alone. With no kin to help you through the childbearing. To think that she bore a son of royal blood, the son that Henry so much desired. And then to lose the child."

The anguish in his voice was but a reflection of the ghastly despair that Elizabeth could see in his eyes.

"She taught me a lesson," he continued. "Her dealing with her fate the way she did. I saw Mary as easy and weak, but I see now I was wrong." He looked at Elizabeth with softness in his expression. "She grew strong, I suppose, by watching you. No longer the clay of the earth, but the earth herself."

"Mary learned from her own sorrows, Father."

"Aye. I reckon we all learn in just that way." The stone face turned again to the smoldering fire. "I mourned her son. And no longer for what the child could bring me. I mourned losing my only grandchild. And all the while I never knew about your Jaime."

"Jaime." The words withered on her lips, and she dared utter no others.

"Until today, I didn't know of Jaime. I never suspected that you and Mary each left the Field of Cloth of Gold carrying a child."

Elizabeth returned her father's gaze.

"The Scot's child."

Elizabeth nodded slowly.

"How typical of my life, daughter. What a mess I have made of it all. Because of my own selfish greed and ambition. All the while I mourned the death of one, I missed celebrating the birth of another."

Elizabeth remained silent. Mary had chosen this course of action. Up to the final moments of her life, the young woman had wanted her daughter to be kept safely away from their father and his scheming ambition. Now, hearing of the letter Mary had sent earlier, Elizabeth was even more certain of the appropriateness of the decision. This was the way Mary wanted it.

"Aye, Mary taught me a lesson." The older man shook his head. "Her letter was full of hate, full of anger. She blamed me only for the loss of her child. I know she was right. I knew it then. I know it now. This was the same daughter who had respected me, followed my orders, and...perhaps even loved me in her childlike way. I brought it all on myself. I drove Mary to hate me. She had every reason. You have every reason."

Elizabeth watched his body shrivel even further as he leaned back in the deep cushions of the chair. The young woman had never dreamed that this moment would ever come to pass. It was certainly not something she would ever have asked of her father. But yet, here he was. Of his own free will. Seeking her out.

"You two were gone, and I felt the tearing in my heart that I knew I might never repair, a rending ache that I knew I deserve to suffer. But I'm only human, Elizabeth. So I turned to Anne. She was my only chance, the only one left for me after Sarah Exton's death."

"Madame Exton is dead?" Elizabeth repeated. The news of the woman's death, a woman she'd feared and hated for so long, didn't bring her any joy. It all seemed so long ago, as if Madame Exton and Elizabeth's childhood belonged to some other life, to some distant past, somehow disconnected from the present.

"Aye. She died a horrible death. A crippling pain that ate away at her. She died curled up in a corner of her room, fighting us off like a crazy woman."

Elizabeth shivered in spite of herself.

"And then, after she died," Sir Thomas continued, "I went to Anne. She was still a child. I thought perhaps I could undo what harm I had already done. I thought I had learned enough from the two of you, from the mistakes I'd made. I thought I had the answer."

"She must have wept to see you changed."

Her father stood and walked stiffly to the hearth. He shook his head without turning.

"Nay, daughter. I was too late."

"Too late for what? Is she ill?"

His laugh was short, devoid of any mirth. "Anne's ailment is not of the body, Elizabeth. It is her mind. Her very soul."

Elizabeth stared at her father as he turned and looked at her. Anne was only a child. It couldn't be that she, too, had contracted the pox. It couldn't be.

"You look horrified, daughter."

"Does she have the same sickness as Mary?" she asked at last.

"The pox?" Sir Thomas shook his head. "Nay. Well, not yet, anyway. Her ailment is that she is too much like me. Her mind is infected, poisoned with dreams of power and how she will wield it. Even at such a tender age, Anne has already planned her route carefully. She knows what she wants, and she has laid the groundwork to get it. Anne long ago planted the foul seeds of her desires. She is tending her weeds even now."

"I find it odd to hear you, of all people, speak so harshly of your daughter's desire for a place in society, Father. Who are you to find fault in anything she does?"

Their gazes locked, and Sir Thomas looked at his daughter. And then he nodded.

"Aye, you are right. I am no one. And true, daughter, I've made mistakes. Many mistakes." He sighed deeply and shuffled back to the chair. Sitting down heavily, the old diplomat clutched the carved arms of the chair and stared into the fire. "Here I am, an old man. While others my age bask in the warm love of their families, contented in the happiness of their children and their grandchildren, here I sit, Thomas Boleyn, Viscount Rochfort, Earl of Ormonde, and member of the king's council, in another man's chair, in a savage and hostile land, begging my daughter for forgiveness."

Elizabeth could see plainly the anguish of this man's soul, etched in every line of his face.

"I must live the life that I have carved out for myself, I know. I am lonely and unwanted, and that is perhaps only just. But I see Anne asking for the same, and I must act. I turned my back on one woman I loved, married for power, and then turned again on the children who might have cared for me. Anne's future promises the same sad fate. She has watched me and her soul is corrupt,

Elizabeth. God help me, I have helped her create the beginnings of her own ruin."

Elizabeth turned her face toward the small windows of the hall. She didn't want to know these things. Anne's life was her own business. The youngest sister had never been one to ask for help, even as a child. Elizabeth knew her little sister was smart. She always had shown a cleverness that far exceeded Mary's. But even if it were true that Anne had grown in the image of their father, perhaps that was a good thing. Perhaps a bit of that hardness was necessary to survive in the world of the English court.

"Elizabeth," Sir Thomas said, drawing her attention back to himself. "Anne has set her mind to marry King Henry."

"Marry? But she is only a child."

"She is nearly seventeen," he replied.

Elizabeth's thoughts turned back to the events four years earlier. Mary had been seventeen when the English king first bedded her. Even though she was a child, Anne could see the pain that Mary had gone through. And what of marriage? she wondered. What of the future? Elizabeth shook her head slowly in disbelief.

"But the king has a wife already," she argued.

"Anne has set her mind to change that."

"Why?" she cried. "Doesn't she know what he did to Mary? Doesn't she know of his sickness and just how little he values the women he beds?"

"The king's physicians say his pox is cured."

A lie. That's all Elizabeth could bring herself to think. A lie. "Why is Anne doing this? Is she taken so with a man more than twice her age? Does she love him?"

"Love?" Sir Thomas laughed. "I once was fortunate enough to love. Aye, to be loved, as well. But I threw it away. Anne hasn't even had that. She cares for no one but herself. Anne doesn't love Henry. She wants to be queen and nothing else. It is power, Elizabeth, that your sister longs for."

Elizabeth stared at her father. "But you don't seriously think she could become queen, do you? M'lord, you are close enough to the king to know. Is there even the remotest possibility that Anne could succeed?"

There wasn't so much as a hint of triumph or even happiness in the man's words as he answered. "She will. Anne succeeds in anything she sets her mind to. The drones at court are already buzzing with talk of annulment. But I want no part of it."

Elizabeth looked at him doubtfully. "You don't approve of her ambition."

"I don't." He paused and then shook his head. "Oh, I won't try to impress you with any newfound scruples I might have regarding Anne's plan. She is older than her years, Elizabeth, and she knows what she wants. But what she won't see is that she, and all of us, will pay a price. She thinks this is all just a lovely game of chance. She can spin the wheel...and ride only to the top. She will not consider the consequences, the potential for failure. Consequences that will be heavy for all of us when the wheel turns again."

Elizabeth tore her eyes away from her father's face and walked to the bench beside the open hearth. A coating of fine dust covered the surface. Absently, she pressed an open hand in the dust and lifted it, examining the distinct print her palm and fingers had left.

She couldn't care less about English politics and couldn't really see what effect Anne's actions could have on her own future. Elizabeth never planned to step on English soil for the rest of her life. But still, she knew that something in her heart longed for the youngest sister that she and Mary had left behind at the Field of Cloth of Gold. Right or wrong, Anne was still her sister, and Elizabeth cared deeply about her well-being.

"What kind of trouble do you think awaits her? You don't think the king would harm her?"

"Nay. Not the king. Henry is captivated by her wit and charm...for now." Sir Thomas picked up the goblet of wine from the floor beside the chair and drank deeply. "From what I see, the king has already allowed himself to be convinced that his marriage to Catherine of Aragon offended the laws of God. After all, she was wed to his older brother, Prince Arthur, before him. The special dispensation he received from the Pope? Merely the result of political maneuvering. He now believes that the miscarriages that the queen has had over the years have been a sign. He has no sons, Elizabeth, and he no longer believes Catherine is capable of delivering one. I believe Henry intends to make Anne his wife."

"Then what is it that bothers you? That will surely bring the family far more prestige. Far more power. The very things you yourself have worked your whole life to attain."

"The marriage cannot last. And if it doesn't, Anne will assuredly pay for it... somehow."

"How so?"

"Those who dwell in the corridors of power do not give up their place so easily. All the old, noble families in England will align themselves against such a match. The Poles, the Courtenays, these are Queen Catherine's supporters. They will not soon forget if she is packed off to some convent. And they will not forget the woman who was the cause of the queen's banishment. The king needs the support of these influential families; they wield great power in England. A time will come when Anne will be a great liability to Henry, and then..."

Elizabeth stood stock still beside the table, watching as her father shrugged his shoulders and averted his eyes.

"Cardinal Wolsey, The Lord Chancellor," Sir Thomas continued, moving back to the open hearth. "He has let it be known that if the king's marriage is annulled, then the king must marry one of the French king's sisters. That's the only way to put an end to the conflict there. Wolsey and the nobles don't see eye to eye on much, Elizabeth, but they will stand together on this. I have friends in every corner of the court, daughter, and I hear a great deal. They will fight the queen's annulment from every angle. From what I hear, the Pole family has even sunk so low as to seek the aid of one of the king's favored henchmen, a ruffian named Peter Garnesche. They will do anything to dissuade the king from proceeding the way he appears intent on going."

Elizabeth stared blankly, and Sir Thomas looked sharply at his daughter.

"You know of him, don't you?" Sir Boleyn said, gazing at Elizabeth's paling expression. "He cut quite a figure at the Field of Cloth of Gold—until your Scot knocked him down a peg."

"I remember him."

"Well, the somewhat hot-blooded Sir Peter has made himself quite indispensable of late to the king. In fact, I don't believe the king has made a decision in the past few years without talking it out first with Garnesche. I know the man employs spies that feed him information."

"The man is a brute."

"It is interesting that you should say that, Elizabeth. Because since his rise to power at court, Peter Garnesche has never been too excited about our family. And now, with the king's attraction to Anne becoming stronger every day, I have no doubt he will side with the old noble families. No one tells King Henry what to do, but Garnesche will surely try to steer the king away from Anne."

"Is that all?" Elizabeth's voice was tight. "Is that the extent of what he would do?"

The elder man shrugged his shoulders and sat down. "I just don't know anymore. I've written Anne off. She doesn't listen to me, and I don't want any part of her schemes. I don't."

Elizabeth watched Sir Thomas close his eyes and lean his head heavily against the back of the chair. He looked old and fragile. Four short years had wrought an incredible change in this man. Her mind raced back over all that had been said. Despite all the bad blood that had existed between them over the years, Elizabeth somehow couldn't help but believe the things that her father had told her. She tried to think back, to remember everything that had taken place on the sad day when Mary had taken the blow from the dagger that had been meant for her. Sir Thomas couldn't have been responsible. He no longer had any motive for such an act.

It had to be Garnesche. Perhaps, seeing Anne growing closer to the king, Garnesche was becoming wary of what information might be passed to the king through Anne. Information that might incriminate him.

Elizabeth shuddered at the thought. She had not been in contact with her sister Anne in the past four years. But now, with Anne's growing influence, perhaps the English knight feared a reunion between the two sisters.

That's it, Elizabeth thought. The sleeping dog is awake, and he's after me.

She had to keep her distance at all costs. That was clearly Elizabeth's best option.

"Are you happy, Elizabeth?"

"What?" she asked, roused from her thoughts.

"Are you happy, daughter?"

"Why do you ask now? You have never concerned yourself with such things, Father."

"You are the only one left."

"Anne is not dead."

"To my mind, she is," he murmured under his breath. "You and Jaime are all that I have left."

Elizabeth saw Sir Thomas's eyes glisten in the failing light. She felt differently now than she had when the old man arrived, but Elizabeth wasn't about to let her father fool himself into thinking the impossible.

"Father, neither I nor my daughter will go back to England with you."

"It doesn't have to be there," he said quietly. "You could go to Calais, or to France. I'll look after your expenses."

"I won't go," she said, her voice taking on an edge of determination. "I am staying. This is our home now. We are not leaving it."

Sir Thomas straightened his tired body in the chair. "I didn't come here to uproot you for no reason. I came in peace. I want to see you happy, child. Everything I have is yours. I don't want you to stay in this wild and desolate edge of the world just because you have no place else to go."

"You don't understand, Father," she returned. "I am here because I want to be here. No one has forced me to it."

"But look at yourself, Elizabeth. Abandoned in this pile of stone."

She looked into Sir Thomas's face questioningly. Into his eyes, dimmed with age; his expression, saddened with remorse.

"I haven't been abandoned here, father. The baron and I are to be married." She tried to stay calm, to ease the tension in her voice as she answered his charge. "I know it is hard for you to believe, but Ambrose Macpherson loves me—and I love him. And our love is not bound by the endless quest for worldly wealth, nor by the corrupted politics of ambition."

He looked at her. "You have nothing to give him, Elizabeth. No dowry, no title. Though, if you would let me, I could—"

"M'lord, he wants me. Only me. For who I am. Not for anything I have."

"Then he is a better man than I."

"Aye, Father," she whispered. "Far better."

Elizabeth watched as the old man's eyes reddened, welling up with tears. Sir Thomas made no effort to hold them back, nor to hide them as the glistening droplets rolled down his wizened face. She stared at the old man for a moment, struggling with her own feelings as her father's emotions spilled freely in the fading light. Thomas Boleyn, the same man who walked away so easily and so coldly from her mother, leaving her to a life so wretched that only suicide could relieve her pain. Thomas Boleyn, the same man who shamelessly sent his own flesh and blood to lives of disease and disrepute. Thomas Boleyn sat before her now. But life had shown him the vileness of his ways. And he had changed.

Elizabeth looked deeply into her heart. She knew she could never be the doting daughter. She knew she didn't feel the care and concern, the respect and trust, that one friend should feel for another. She even wondered how she could honor him as a man in the twilight of his years.

But gazing at the broken man, Elizabeth knew that she could not deny the sorrow she felt for him. Pity pressed at her heart, stirring in her an aching sorrow for a man who had wasted his life in the pursuit of the wrong things. And who knew what happiness he had thrown away.

Elizabeth walked to him and drew him to his feet. Placing her arms around him, she felt the ache in her own heart disappear as he laid his head upon her shoulder.

He was punishing himself enough. She wouldn't add to his suffering.

Chapter 29

Benmore Castle was a heaven plucked from the sky.

With only three days until their wedding ceremony, Elizabeth gazed somewhat anxiously out the leaded glass windows of her bedchamber, her eyes searching the distance at the purple heather-covered hills that surrounded the broad Spey River valley. The rugged autumn Highlands in which the Macpherson stronghold was located offered breathtaking beauty, but even in the sunny, noonday light, they presented no sign to the bride of any approaching bridegroom.

"He'll get back in time," Elizabeth asserted firmly to no one, adding wistfully, "but the messenger said he would arrive today."

With a last look down the valley, the young woman turned toward the mirror, tucked a loose strand of hair into her lengthening braid, and started for the door. Lady Elizabeth, Ambrose's mother, had assured her at breakfast that, although the trip from Stirling, where the queen was holding court, could be slow in bad weather, she was certain that her son would appear anytime, now. Elizabeth smiled as she pulled open the heavy oaken door. Never had she ever felt more welcome—more a part of a family—than she had been feeling since arriving at Benmore to the open arms of Ambrose's parents, Lady Elizabeth and Lord Alexander. The laird and his wife had taken her and Jaime in as if they were their own long-lost bairns. Indeed, from the first moment they had ridden across the wooden bridge that led into the castle courtyard, little Jaime, clutching her kitten, had been treated like a precious princess presenting herself to her kingdom.

After all, Benmore Castle was the domain of men. Elizabeth had watched in amusement as Jaime looked wide-eyed on the trio of young boys that scurried around the travelers' horses.

Ambrose Macpherson was the second of three sons. The eldest brother, Alec, was married to Fiona, a warm and wonderful woman who had immediately befriended Elizabeth. It wasn't until a week had passed that Elizabeth learned from the local priest that Fiona was also the half-sister to the king. The couple had three sons, as well as a handsome sixteen-year-old ward, Malcolm MacLeod, who had just arrived from the Isle of Skye for the wedding.

So, needless to say, with all the boys in the family, the attention and the treatment that young Jaime had been getting was exceptional. Elizabeth wasn't sure the little girl would be fit to live with after all this pampering.

The young bride also looked forward to the arrival of Ernesta and Joseph Baldi, who were due anytime now. Elizabeth couldn't wait to share with Erne some of the stories of Jaime's experiences en route to the Highlands. She knew that the older woman would be delighted to see how happily the little girl was adjusting to her new surroundings—and her new family.

Tripping lightly down the hall, Elizabeth considered how quickly the weeks had flown since she and her father had stood holding one another in the partially renovated hall at Roxburgh Castle.

A few days later, as Elizabeth's father prepared to depart for London, a stern-faced Ambrose had returned from the Scottish court, storming into the Border stronghold like a lion protecting his pride from a rogue intruder.

With little time to explain all that had passed between her and Sir Thomas, Elizabeth had been pleased, and a little relieved, to see Ambrose perceive quickly the change in the relationship between the two. Watching him proudly, the young woman was certain that her fiancé was calling into play all of his diplomatic skills as he assumed the role of cordial host, welcoming the aging Englishman. Elizabeth was convinced that her father had carried from Scotland great respect and even perhaps a glimmer of fondness for his future son-in-law.

As she moved down the corridor toward the circle of stairs, Elizabeth paused and looked out a small window onto the courtyard. Not an hour earlier, on the stone cobbles below, she had seen Jaime being entertained by the MacLeod boy, who together with Fiona's lads had brought a number of falcons up from the mews.

Letting her gaze travel upward to the great Macpherson coat of arms, carved into the stone wall across the courtyard, Elizabeth felt her eyes well up with tears again as she remembered how, after her father's departure, she had relayed to Ambrose her father's news of Mary's letter. And when she told the Highlander the tale she had told her father about Jaime's parentage, Ambrose had hugged her to him, telling her that he would swear by that story until the sun fell from the sky.

"I love you, Elizabeth," he had growled. "Jaime's our own now. And by God, that's how it will stay."

And she loved him. By the Holy Mother, she loved him more than life itself.

Dashing a tear from her cheek, Elizabeth hurried to the stairwell and went downstairs to the corridor below. She was running late. Fiona probably had the children all ready and waiting.

Elizabeth, on arriving, had taken it upon herself to do a portrait of the Macpherson grandchildren as a gift for Lady Elizabeth and Lord Alexander. Fiona had been her accomplice from the onset, gathering all the children together for a number of sessions in the sitting room by Ambrose's bedchamber.

Collecting the children, Fiona had included Malcolm and Jaime, though at first Elizabeth had been uncertain as to whether it was proper to have Jaime there. But Fiona wouldn't have it any other way. She knew the Macphersons well, and she'd told Elizabeth in no uncertain terms that Jaime was their granddaughter, and they, too, wouldn't have it any other way.

Stepping into the dark hallway, Elizabeth picked up her skirts and ran down the hall. Passing by Ambrose's bedchamber, she paused, seeing the heavy oak door standing partially open.

Accompanied by his brother Alec, Ambrose had left for court at once after bringing them to Benmore two weeks ago. From what he told her, Elizabeth knew that he still had unfinished business to tend to. Ambrose's first trip to court had been cut short by the news of Thomas Boleyn's arrival at Roxburgh Castle. After his brief stop at Edinburgh, Ambrose had barely reached the court at Stirling when word reached him, and he had ridden out without a moment's delay to get back to her.

And as much as Elizabeth's hours since arriving had been filled with activities and with preparations for the wedding, she missed him terribly.

Elizabeth glanced at the doorway. Knowing his quarters would be theirs after the wedding, she took a step toward the room. And then, unable to stop herself, she pushed open the door. The bright sunshine, pouring through the open windows, bathed the room and drew her in at once. Her eyes traveled over the fine furnishings and then came to rest on the large canopy bed that sat empty at one end of the roomy chamber.

She felt a flush of excitement wash over her at the thought of being able to share his bed once again. Their bed. She couldn't wait for him to get back. Crossing the room, she touched the fine cloth of the damask curtains.

Elizabeth turned with a start, hearing the door swing fully open on its hinges. The smiling figure swept into the room. He was back.

"Ambrose!"

He opened his arms as she ran and threw herself into them. He lifted her into the air, and they hugged fiercely in the open doorway. They had only been apart for a fortnight, but it seemed to Elizabeth as if months had passed since he had last held her like this. He kissed her hungrily, and she kissed him back.

"You are here." She pulled him by the hand into the room. He paused only long enough to push the door closed and to drop the heavy bar in place.

"At last." He held her tight. "I never want to leave you behind. Not ever again. From now on, wherever I go, you go."

She smiled. "I like that."

His hands framed her face. His blue eyes gazed into hers. "Everywhere I went, wherever I turned, I was looking at you. Your beautiful face, your brilliant, black eyes were always there before me."

"I've watched every traveler that has trod the path to Benmore. I've studied every line of this valley through my window." She raised herself on her toes and kissed him. "These days have been the longest I have ever known, Ambrose."

"And the nights?" Scooping her up in his arms, Ambrose carried his fiancé to the bed. "Have they, too, been long?"

She nodded with a smile. Running her fingers through his hair, she looked dreamily into his eyes. The jolt of excitement, the knowledge of what was to come, made her quiver with joy. But she had to bank her fire. They had time. From his slow steps, his graceful movement, she knew he was savoring the moment. She had to control her desire and do the same.

"When did you get back?" she asked. She could hear the tremor in her own voice.

"Just a few moments ago." Laying her gently on the bed, he stretched his long body beside hers and gazed longingly into her eyes. "I missed you more than I would have thought possible."

"I missed you, as well," she murmured. "Every day has been harder and harder to bear."

"I hope my family's been behaving," he growled. He couldn't keep himself away from her inviting lips. His mouth descended on hers, devouring her attempt to answer. Her lips opened to receive him. Ambrose's hand found its way to her breasts, and he cupped one gently as his knee moved against the junction of her legs. Her moan of pleasure went to the very core of him.

Suddenly he couldn't get enough of her. He could take her that instant. But, as always, he wanted to enjoy this, to bring her to that exquisite moment of pleasure. He drew back to look at her. Under the round neckline of her mauve colored lamb's-wool dress, the ties at the neck of a white linen blouse attracted his attention, and Ambrose gently reached up and tugged at them.

"Your family..." Elizabeth whispered. His hand made contact with her bare skin. "They've been angels."

Gazing up at him, she felt a longing to recapture his mouth. But those thoughts were quickly forgotten as Ambrose trailed his lips downward over her chin and over the skin of her now exposed throat.

"Keep talking," he whispered. "Tell me."

A gasp escaped her as he softly buried his face in her neck. Elizabeth grasped the tartan that crossed his back as Ambrose took her earlobe between his lips. His warm breath in her ear brought renewed shudders from her frame, and involuntarily her body arched more tightly against his. Her fingers worked themselves lower until she reached his kilt. She began to pull it upward.

"Aye, they're perfect," she purred. "Just perfect."

"You drive me mad, woman. I want you."

Hearing the footsteps of someone passing in the hallway, Elizabeth cried out softly, suddenly alarmed. "Ambrose, we can't. We'll have your entire family banging on the door in a few moments. Everyone will want to see you, now that you've arrived."

He held her down.

"Nay, lass," the Highlander responded, brushing his lips over the soft ivory skin of her newly exposed breast. "My father is out hunting and my mother has ridden out with Cook to choose exactly what we will be serving at an upcoming wedding feast."

He drew his face back and smiled at her.

"No one saw us arrive, other than Fiona."

"But Fiona saw you."

"Aye, and knowing the way my brother Alec feels about his wee angel—and she about him—they're probably already locked away in their chamber, heedless to the goings on of this world."

"I like her very much," Elizabeth whispered as she snuggled back into his embrace. "I know now why they call her the Angel of Skye. I don't think I ever met a person as kind, as gentle, and as beautiful as she is."

"I have."

She stared at him.

"You, my bonny lass," he responded gazing into her eyes. "You are every bit as kind, as gentle, and as beautiful. Far more so, I would say."

"I love you, Ambrose." Elizabeth hugged him tightly. "How did I ever live without you?"

He whispered his response softly in her ear. "I don't care to think of the past, my love. Only our wonderful future—and the next hour or two."

With the tip of his tongue, the Highlander traced a line along the skin of her velvety jaw to her waiting lips, finally reclaiming her mouth. His hands reached down and pushed her skirts up over her hips.

"I was thinking of this all the way back from Stirling."

"Then it must have been a hard ride," she whispered smilingly. "Very hard."

Elizabeth felt once again the surge of the raw desire that was swelling within her. Her lips responded to his, to the heat that was coursing through her veins. Whatever discretion remained within her dissipated like a morning mist. Indeed, the full sun of desire burst recklessly through. She opened her legs as he moved between them.

Elizabeth's senses were filled with him. The scent of him, the taste of him, the warm and throbbing pressure of his body against hers. God, how she missed him. How she loved him. How she wanted him.

"An hour or two..." She moaned as he entered her. "But Ambrose, that's the whole afternoon."

"Hmmm." He pushed himself up on his hands as he drove to the very center of her. "Just what are we going to do with all that time?"

Elizabeth smiled dreamily as she held him tight and gave in to the oncoming waves of pleasure.

The late afternoon sun bathed the two lovers in a golden light, and Elizabeth lounged on top of Ambrose. Her chin was propped up on his chest, and he ran his hands gently through the soft waves of her unbound hair. The silky tresses reached her shoulders now. His fingers traced a frown that was lining her forehead. He smiled.

"Don't mock me, Ambrose."

"Never would I mock you, lass," he assured her, but the glint in his eyes undermined his words.

"You are mocking me." She lay her head down on his chest, averting her eyes.

He rolled her onto her back at once and propped himself up on his elbow beside her.

"Elizabeth," he said seriously, "I just don't understand what frightens you. That's all."

"I am not frightened," she snapped at him.

"Ah, now, that's more like my Elizabeth."

"Just...well, a bit nervous," she continued in a softer tone. "And perhaps a little apprehensive, worried, and maybe..." She rolled her eyes toward the window. "Very well, I'm scared." A tear escaped from the corner of her eye and dropped onto the down-filled mattress.

"But why, lass?" he asked, perplexed. "Elizabeth, think now. You've painted in the studio of the master, Michelangelo. You've received the accolades of Giovanni de' Medici, perhaps the greatest patron of the arts the world has ever known. You've painted the king of France, for God's sake. The leaders of Europe recognize your talent. Why should you fear such...mundane work?"

"Ambrose, it isn't the work itself that bothers me."

"Then what?"

"The queen," she blurted out, turning her gaze back to him. "Queen Margaret."

He paused and looked at her gently. As he considered, his fingers traced the line of her jaw.

"Isn't this what you've wanted? To paint for her? To be recognized by the world as a woman, as well as the artist that you are?"

She felt her eyes well up with tears. "You know that is what I want. But what I fear is what I don't know—what I might have to give up in return." She took hold of his hand as he brushed away a tear, and held his palm against her face. "I am happy now, Ambrose. Having you and Jaime. You two are everything to me. I won't give up this happiness for any dreams that I might have harbored in the past. I love you too much to throw away what I have for some fleeting moment of fame."

"And I love you, too, Elizabeth." The Highlander leaned down and placed a kiss on her lips. "What I told you before, when we were traveling in France, about Margaret thinking you could be a witch—"

"I know. I know. You were just trying to scare me. That part of it doesn't frighten me."

Ambrose gazed into her beautiful eyes.

"If you don't want to go through with traveling to Stirling Castle and painting the king and the rest of the royal family, that is fine with me. But just remember this. The queen will exact no price from you. You are being presented to the Queen of Scotland as Elizabeth Boleyn Macpherson, a talented artist and the wife of her valued servant. I have brought her your work. She has seen it, and she loves it. She wants you at Stirling. You bring an added element of style to the Scottish court. An elegance, a bit of continental refinement. To her, the fact that you are a woman—albeit one with an enormous God-given talent—only makes it better. It adds a wee bit of notoriety to her reputation. Now Margaret can laugh at the other rulers of Europe and say, 'You are all fools. I have the most talented painter of all here beside me and she is a woman.' Elizabeth, if ever there was a chance for you to demonstrate your artistic talents openly, it is in her court."

Elizabeth gazed up at Ambrose, but her face was still clouded.

"But Ambrose, she is sister to Henry, the King of England."

"Aye, she is. What's in that?"

"He is a brute."

"In many ways Margaret is a brute, too. But you were raised with your siblings—a condition, by the way, that Henry and Margaret didn't share. Even though you three were all exposed to the same conditions growing up, each of you, as adults, took her own path. Are you three the same person?"

She shook her head. "But what I fear is that she will turn me over to the English. That she will send me back to England, separating me from you and Jaime, for what I did four years ago."

Ambrose caressed her hair. "She is Scotland's queen, my love. Her ties to her brother are few. Sending you back would be treachery of the vilest kind. She would never treat an invited guest so inhospitably." He paused before continuing. "I don't think I'd be speaking beyond myself to say that she would never risk the wrath of the loyal Highland clans by sending one of their own to the south." His gaze was warm. "And you are one of us, now."

Elizabeth took his hand, and Ambrose brought her fingers to his lips.

"Then...then you think I should go."

"Not you, lass," he responded energetically. "*We'll* go. That is, if you want to do it."

Elizabeth could feel the excitement building within her. Her paintings had always presented her with a path to a new and different life. In doing what she loved, in practicing her craft, she had been forced to lose her identity. She had been required to live the life of another. That was why, when Ambrose had told her that she might still paint the Scottish royal family, she had recoiled in fear.

Elizabeth didn't want to go back to being someone else. She was a woman. She wanted to remain a woman.

Phillipe de Anjou was dead. Elizabeth Boleyn was alive.

"I do want to go, Ambrose. I do."

Chapter 30

For the tenth time today, Elizabeth folded the letter at its seams and placed it on the table.

Looking into the silvered glass, she gazed at the beautiful woman looking back at her. Never had there been such days of happiness, of joy.

Outside her open window, she could hear the crowds in the street below, the bells ringing in the distance. The autumn afternoon air was crisp and filled with the smell of mutton roasting over an open fire. Her mouth was beginning to water from the aroma.

She sat silently, her eyes taking in the flat stomach that would soon display the treasure it carried inside. She laughed quietly. Their child. Hers and Ambrose's. A sister or brother to Jaime.

And now, to top all this joy, she was to meet her sister Anne at last. Here, in this working room, within these walls, today.

"Keep working," she prodded herself aloud. "The time won't go any faster if you just sit and wait."

She roused herself from the three-legged stool and went back to the canvas.

A week after Elizabeth and Ambrose had married, the letter had arrived. Anne's letter. She had read it again and again.

Anne, the young girl she and Mary had left behind so many years back, had written with a heart full of love. Her words were not the words of the person their father had spoken of. No, this was a young woman who understood the pain of separation, the empty ache of loneliness. Anne wrote about how much she longed to see her only remaining sister, her beloved Elizabeth. She wrote of the trials of life at the English court. She wrote of Mary. Each time Elizabeth had moved through the text of the letter, she'd felt her heart swell with emotion at the sad lyric of her sister's words.

The letter had ended with Anne's heartfelt disappointment at not being able to attend Elizabeth's wedding, but she had asked for some chance to meet—to reunite—if only for a few moments.

Anne had said she was sure she would be granted permission to come to visit the court of King Henry's sister.

If only, dearest sister, you could travel to Stirling...

Elizabeth had written back at once. Of course they could meet at Stirling. At the Macphersons' new town house there. Beneath the walled ramparts of the castle of Queen Margaret, where Elizabeth was to be presented at court.

Elizabeth's brushes flew over the canvas before her. The black, mischievous eyes, the pale, reaching hand, the last moments that she recalled of the time she spent with the energetic little sister. Elizabeth hoped Anne would like the portrait. It had been difficult to do a painting of such detail just from memory. But Elizabeth knew it was important for her sister to see the vivid image, and perhaps to know of the thoughts that the older sister, even through the passage of time and distance, had retained of the young woman.

Ambrose had brought Elizabeth and little Jaime to Stirling over a month ago. Elizabeth had been presented at court and, to her surprise and dismay, had found herself, after spending some time in the queen's company, accepting and even respecting Margaret as the strong survivor that the woman was. Sent away at age thirteen to marry King James IV of Scotland, Margaret—by her own admission no more than a pampered child—had been unhappy and lost for a long time. A stranger in a foreign land.

But the turning wheel of Fortune would soon teach the young woman the hard lessons of life. Widowed at the age twenty-four, left in a wild and often barbarous country in the midst of social and political pandemonium after her husband's death at Flodden field, Margaret Tudor had quickly learned the skills needed for survival.

Elizabeth placed the brush with the others in the cup and wiped her hand with the rag on the side table. All the fears she had harbored before arriving at court had soon washed away after her first meetings with the queen. Ambrose had been right in everything he'd said. Elizabeth could clearly see that Margaret perceived herself as a patroness, a great and generous benefactor of the arts and of artists. But the one thing about the queen that most surprised Elizabeth only occurred to her in her observation of the people who surrounded Margaret. The queen was the benefactor of intelligent women. Women of learning and accomplishment. The ones who took their lives and their destinies into their own hands. Women like Margaret herself. The survivors, the strong.

Then, yesterday evening, the man sent ahead by Anne had arrived with the news of her arrival by next noon.

Even though she'd done it herself, Elizabeth now wished she had not sent Ambrose and Jaime away this morning. She'd told Ambrose that she wanted to greet her sister alone, to have a chance to renew their bond of sisterly love before presenting Anne to her husband and her daughter. But there was something else, as well. The damp chill of anxiety had begun to creep into Elizabeth's bones. Even though their father had readily believed Jaime to be his eldest daughter's child, Elizabeth couldn't be certain that Anne would believe the same thing.

Even as a child, Anne had been intelligent beyond her years, and now Elizabeth was conscious of a nagging fear that her sister might discover the truth. After all, Jaime was Henry's child, and with the dreams that Anne had of becoming queen, Elizabeth worried now what discovering Jaime's true identity might mean to the ambitious young woman.

It had been difficult to persuade Ambrose to go. He'd not wanted to leave her side. Finally, after a great deal of cajoling on her part, he'd reluctantly agreed to take Jaime for half a day's ride and return at supper. But that was it. Elizabeth had known she wouldn't be able to wheedle even a moment more out of him, and she cheerfully settled for their compromise. Indeed, since they'd wed, the Highlander had been true to his word—he had not left her alone for more than a day.

Elizabeth smiled and gave a small sigh, thinking of the love that they shared. Life was bliss in Ambrose Macpherson's arms.

The painting was finished. Elizabeth stepped back and scanned the portrait with a critical eye. It was good work. And the young girl's depiction successfully captured the very essence of what she remembered of Anne. But the setting in which she placed the girl was purely the product of her own imagination.

Elizabeth depicted Anne standing before the high platform of an ornate altar. She was dressed in a crimson velvet gown, decorated with ermine, and a rich robe of purple velvet, also trimmed with strips of ermine. A golden coronet with a cap of pearls and stones covered her jet-black hair. Anne's face contained all the vibrancy of a young girl, but her vestments conjured the image of a queen. Indeed, on the high royal seat before her sat Henry. Elizabeth smiled at her representation of the English king. The man looked aged and heavyset, and Anne's arms were reaching out toward the king in a manner of confident entreaty.

The likeness of Henry was probably enough for a beheading, Elizabeth thought, if she ever dared step foot again on English soil.

The gentle knock at the door froze Elizabeth where she stood. She wiped her palms on her skirt and called quietly for her porter to step in.

She watched in anticipation as the heavy door swung partially open. Instead of the serious expression of the old manservant, the bright face of one of the younger servants peeked inside.

"They are here, m'lady."

Before Elizabeth could say a word, the door pushed open fully, and a tall, elegantly dressed young woman stepped in. Elizabeth recognized her at once.

Taking the few short steps to meet her, Elizabeth embraced her sister, gathering into her arms the beautiful creature. "Oh, my Anne. You are here. Here at last."

The painter felt her sister's arms move around her, but she felt something else, as well.

Elizabeth felt ice. A coldness as solid and palpable as ice. She felt it the moment that she touched her. Surprised and confused, Elizabeth pulled back, struggling to hide her disappointment. She had been expecting Anne to have some similarity to Mary. Their sister had been affectionate, tender. Mary returned affection the way she breathed air. It was always natural, part of her.

Elizabeth realized instantly that she had been mistaken. That she had been wrong in expecting so much. She couldn't bring Mary back in Anne. Each one of them had her own individual traits that made her distinct.

Elizabeth watched as her sister stiffly extricated herself from her arms. Then the younger woman turned to Elizabeth's gaw-king servant. "Leave us."

The serving girl nodded hurriedly and backed away at once, closing the door as she retreated.

Elizabeth gazed as the hard smile that seemed to be carved on Anne's face faded quickly. Too quickly. She wondered why the young woman had felt obliged to put on such a false show of joy. She stood silently, somewhat amazed at the hardness of the sparkling black eyes that were riveted to her own.

Anne's look wasn't one of sisterly affection.

Finally the younger woman turned from Elizabeth and unclasped the traveling cloak that she wore. Now Elizabeth could fully appreciate the bright scarlet dress that Anne wore beneath. Sleeves of silk interwoven with fine gold thread puffed fashionably from long slits in the arms of the garment, catching Elizabeth's eye.

The elder sister watched in silence as Anne straightened and fluffed the sleeves.

"You look beautiful in this dress, Anne. You've grown so much. So refined, so perfect." Elizabeth smiled unconsciously. Hardly the child she'd seen last. "And you wear the cloth of gold. The English king's—"

"It is about the least expensive thing that Henry gives me, Elizabeth." She nearly sneered at her sister. "How could I refuse him?"

Elizabeth bit her tongue. This was hardly the greeting—this was hardly the woman—she had expected. She again simply watched as the younger woman made her way around the room, studying every furnishing, every trinket in sight.

"Not bad, for marrying a Scot." She turned to Elizabeth and gave a half smile. "I can see you've done well for yourself. He's certainly the best that this savage place has to offer, for what that's worth. But tell me, dear sister, what did you have to do to get him to marry you?"

Elizabeth stared at her sister, her anger gathering.

"*Not* what you are doing to get Henry to *marry you*." Glancing away, Elizabeth moved toward the painting she'd been working on. The canvas faced away from Anne. She'd be damned if she would show the brat what she'd done for her. Grabbing a white tarp from the table, Elizabeth tossed it over the painting.

"Temper, temper. I can see not much has changed after all these years." She walked casually toward Elizabeth in mincing steps. "I see I'm still not worthy of seeing your work. Still think you can hide things from me, don't you?"

Elizabeth paused. She had begun this meeting all wrong. Anne had no sooner walked in her door than Elizabeth had begun to judge her.

"I'm sorry, Anne," she said quietly. "I didn't mean to be so inhospitable. Perhaps we could begin again."

"You and I? Begin again?" The young woman stood facing her in the center of the room, her laugh short and joyless. "I wouldn't even bother."

"Why are you here, Anne?" Elizabeth asked shortly. "It must have been a long journey for you."

She smiled. "To pay you back, sister dear, for all your kindnesses of the past."

"You don't owe me anything."

"Ha!" Anne laughed again, loudly and without mirth. "Well, we do agree on something."

"Then?" Elizabeth could feel herself getting edgy as the young woman approached. Her sister's black eyes were locked on her.

"As I told you before, I came here to repay you." She stopped on the opposite side of the covered canvas that separated them. "But you are correct, Elizabeth. I don't owe you anything. It is you who owes me. So I am here to collect." Anne suddenly reached out and yanked at the sheet, unveiling the canvas as she moved beside her sister. Her eyes scanned the painting.

The young woman's laugh made Elizabeth cringe. It was a cold and hollow laugh. She could hear no ring of emotion, just an emptiness that reverberated throughout the room.

"I've heard people speak of your talent." Anne reached into the cup that sat on the small table and grabbed one of Elizabeth's brushes. Without hesitation, she dipped it into the paint of her sister's palette. "It's true, you do indeed have a talent for your art."

Anne jabbed at the painting with the brush and, hearing Elizabeth's gasp, turned and gave her sister another malevolent smile as she continued. "But you are blind, dear sister. And simple."

Elizabeth watched in horror as Anne used one stroke after another to cover with broad, black marks the portrait of Henry sitting on the chair.

"You see, if you had any wit at all, you would have depicted *me* sitting in the chair, and that pathetic old man standing with *his* hands outstretched in supplication."

"You cannot control the world with a stroke of a brush, Anne." Elizabeth reached and grabbed the brush from her sister's hands. Anne released it without any struggle and turned her attention again toward the room.

"Aye, I can." She smiled with a backward glance. "I, unlike you, Elizabeth, live in the real world. It's true, I am not like you and Mary at all. I am smart. I use my brain. I observe, I plan, and then I execute. And sometimes, just for the sport of it, I look for weaknesses in people, then I crush them. Just look at what I did to you. A soft, heart wrenching letter. I knew that's all it would take to get you to meet with me. It worked."

Elizabeth scanned her sister's face for some recognizable feature. For some hint of familial feeling that might connect them.

We are sisters, she thought. You don't have to lie, to pretend, in order to see me. But after hearing Anne, Elizabeth felt herself withdrawing. She did not want to deal with this young woman at a personal level. At any level.

"This English king is a great fool," Elizabeth whispered. "How could he—or anyone—be so blind as to fall for you?"

"You are so right, sister!" Anne swung around. "He is a great fool. The greatest kind, a royal one. Oh, I have watched him for years. From the time I moved into his court circle, I've seen how he treats us. The new faces. The new mistresses. Each new woman tumbling into bed with the arrogant lecher. One after another they go. He relieves his lust in them, and then they are gone. Out of sight, and permanently out of mind. Henry is disgusting, Elizabeth, like all the rest of them. The man's brain is in his codpiece."

As she sat herself on the tall, three-legged stool in front of the mirror, Anne Boleyn pulled her skirts up above her ankles. Taking in the reflection, she raised her eyes and smiled at her sister in the glass. "I'll share a little secret, sister dear. I never, ever, let him touch me. No sweet fondling, no tender caresses. Nothing. And after six months of this slow torture, he is mad about me. He is going crazy with desire."

"Why doesn't he just take someone else?"

"Oh, he does. I know he does. But, my dear sweet Elizabeth, those girls are simply substitutes for me." She cast a glance at her sister. "It's true!"

Elizabeth threw the tarp over the painting again and moved to the window. The streets were bustling with activity as laborers wending their way home now mingled with the street vendors.

Elizabeth wished now that her sister had never come. Her eyes scanned the thoroughfare. She was glad Ambrose and Jaime had not yet returned. She was embarrassed. Embarrassed to present Anne to her husband the 'loving' sister she had presumed her to be.

"I know he had a fondness for Mary," Anne droned on. "He used her body and then threw her out. And then he wanted you, but you ran. You *are* simple, Elizabeth. You could have had the most powerful man in the world at your beck and call, if you'd handled it correctly, but you ran away."

Elizabeth turned to face her sister.

"But me," Anne continued. "I went after him. I used my charm, my wit. After the two of you, I knew he liked our looks. Henry is very particular in such matters, you know. So as I got older, I learned to become a predator, and he the prey."

Looking back in the mirror, she pushed back a loose lock of black hair behind her ears. "I used seduction. I pretended to want him. And...I gave him a glimpse of what's to come."

She laughed. "There are so many advantages to living at court. So many opportunities to give him just a quick glimpse of my maidenly charms. Aye, show him the curve of a breast, the shape of an uncovered leg...then hide it. What pleasure to simply stand there, to let him see, to let him drool. To watch the fool go hard. And then to blush, to back away. What matchless enjoyment to say, as he gets near, 'After our wedding, my great bear. We must save something for our wedding night, love.' Then I retreat—my 'honor' preserved, his lecherous desires provoked still further."

"This is a dangerous game you play, Anne. What's going to stop him from taking you against your will?"

"Ah, Elizabeth, you think I'm a fool? He won't," she said with conviction. "I have convinced him that there is something mystical about the feelings between us. He believes there is something 'holy' about me. And he is quite superstitious. I've convinced him that

Queen Catherine cannot bear him a son because heaven has frowned upon their marriage. I once even hinted that I have heard voices. Angelic voices that told me his marriage to Catherine is a reviled and incestuous union between a man and his brother's widow, and that the Tudor reign will end with Henry because of it. I've spend many an hour preaching to him the value of virtue and the utmost importance of my innocence on the marriage night. And he believes me, Elizabeth. He believes me!"

"Anne, think a moment of what you are doing. Whatever do you think will happen if you cannot give him the heir he is after?"

"There is no question," she said dismissively. "When I am queen, I will."

Elizabeth watched Anne as she gazed at herself in the mirror. In that fleeting, unguarded moment, she looked like the innocent child Elizabeth remembered.

"Did your 'voices' tell you that, as well, Anne? That you shall bear him a son?"

"I'm weary of this discussion," she responded. Then, pushing herself back from the mirror, Anne stood and whirled, her face hard and sneering.

"And this brings me back to the reason for my visit today."

"I thought it was sisterly love that brought you here. The 'loneliness,' as you so artfully put it in your letter."

The young woman's expression went cold, her face paling at Elizabeth's words. "Nay, I got over that years ago—not long, in fact, after being deserted by my own sisters."

Then, for the first time since Anne walked through the door, Elizabeth saw a hint of pain in her sister's eyes.

"We *had* to leave you, Anne."

"You...you abandoned me! You left me behind!" She whispered the words, her eyes taking on a faraway look, as if she was reminding herself of what had happened. "One moment I had a family, older sisters whom I looked up to. Sisters whom I loved. Sisters whom I thought loved me. And then, the next moment, I found myself rejected, thrown aside, forgotten."

Elizabeth took a step toward her. "My God, Anne. That's not the way—"

"Stop," she ordered. "Save your lies and your breath. You'll need them in a few moments."

"But you have to hear me. The reason Mary and I ran—"

"Mary and you," she repeated. Listen to yourself. Mary and you. It always was just Mary and you." She took a breath and turned toward the window. "You two cared only for each other and no one else. You shared your affection, your time, your secrets with her. But I was your sister, too. What did you ever do for me?"

"You had my love. Whatever I felt for Mary, I felt for you. Whatever I did for Mary, I did for you. As far as my paintings, you were too young to be shown my work." Elizabeth felt sorrow creeping into her heart. She had been the reason. She was responsible for Anne becoming the woman she'd become. "You were strong, Anne. You were a smart child. At times it might have seemed that I gave more attention to Mary, but it was because she needed it. She was weak in so many ways."

"Standing in the Field of Cloth of Gold with an inferno of tents burning around me, I needed someone, too." Anne stabbed at a tear that got away, dashing it from her pale cheek. "You ran to the fiery tent. I saw you. Wearing the friar's clothing. I ran toward you. Excited. Relieved. But you called for Mary. Only for Mary. Then I stood back and watched. You fought the flames, fought the people for the only sister you cared for. I stood there, scared...alone." Anne turned abruptly toward Elizabeth, facing her head on. "Then you just disappeared. You and Mary both. You left me for good. No word, no message, no farewell."

Elizabeth moved quickly across the floor to Anne and took hold of her limp, ice cold hands.

"I had to run, Anne. I was being followed. I had no other choice. But leaving that place, the Golden Vale, as we did—we hardly knew what was to become of us. Everything before us was so uncertain."

Elizabeth gazed into the downturned face of her sister. How could she explain fears that now seemed so distant?

"Meeting with you, telling you of all that had happened, all that was happening, would have meant putting your life in jeopardy. I loved you too much. I couldn't do that to you. And in taking Mary..." Elizabeth paused. "Mary had contracted the pox and, more than that, she was with child. King Henry's child. She had gone to

Father, but she felt that he had turned his back on her, that he wouldn't help her."

Anne drew her hands out of Elizabeth's and stepped back. "Sir Thomas explained it all. I was a child, but still he explained it all."

"What did he tell you?"

"That you ran away in direct defiance of the king. That to spite the family you wouldn't become Henry's mistress. He said you took Mary, since you loved her best. And I was left behind because I was nothing to you. He told me what I already knew, that I wasn't wanted."

"That was a lie!" Elizabeth blurted out. "It is true that I didn't want to go to Henry's bed. I didn't want my body to be sold by my own father. But I didn't leave you because I loved you less."

"It's too late for this." Anne cried in anguish, starting to back toward the door. "I had to learn, Elizabeth. I had to learn early on that I had no one. No one who would care for me."

"I cared for you. Believe me, Anne. You said you saw me by the fires. Well, did you see my face? The bloody face that our father had given me?"

Elizabeth pushed her hair back and showed her sister the still visible scar on her cheek. She knew from the look in Anne's eyes that she remembered.

"That night," Elizabeth continued, "in that field, my world toppled. I went from being beaten by my own father to witnessing a vicious act of treachery and then murder. I was chased and nearly raped by the same brute who committed the murder. The same one who had my tent burned down. Aye, the same man who then tracked me like I was some animal."

"It's too late, Elizabeth," Anne whispered as she reached the door. Her hand rested on the latch. "It's too late for explanations. The die is cast. It's time for you to pay."

Elizabeth stood, one hand stretched out to her sister. She didn't know what Anne meant, but a cold void in the pit of her stomach told her that something lay beyond the heavy oak door. Nonetheless, she had to try to make her sister listen, to make her understand.

"I fled from the Field of Cloth of Gold without any word because of one man, Anne." She took a step toward her younger sister.

"The same man who hunted me down years later in Troyes. The same man who is responsible for Mary's death. I was the one who was supposed to die there, Anne, but Mary stepped into the knife's path."

Anne stood at the door, silent, taking in every word.

"I want you to know the truth. It's time for you to hear what I couldn't tell you on that field." Elizabeth took another step toward her sister. "He had betrayed his king. Then he murdered the French Lord Constable, the one man who could reveal his treachery. But there was a witness. I was the witness. He has been after me ever since. Killing Mary...that wasn't enough. It is I he wants. And now I hear he stands in your way."

"Garnesche," Anne murmured.

"Aye, Sir Peter Garnesche," Elizabeth repeated. "Anne, you must use everything I have told you to threaten him with ruin. I cannot undo what has been done, but if marrying Henry is the thing that you most desire, if that is the goal you seek, then by all means use the truth to keep Garnesche at bay. But you must be careful; he is a devil—as ruthless a killer as ever walked on the earth."

Anne looked down at her hands, then her eyes ever so slowly moved up until they met Elizabeth's. "But you see, I have already found a way to deal with the man. He no longer presents any problem for me."

"He doesn't?"

Anne shook her head. "I told you before, I had to learn early, Elizabeth."

Elizabeth's eyes riveted on Anne's knuckles, white from her grip on the door latch.

"I've made a pact with him." Anne opened the door slowly on its hinges. "I want Henry. He'll stay out of my way, so that I can have him. Garnesche wants you, Elizabeth. So in return, I stay out of his way, so that he can have you. You owe me at least that much."

The door stood fully open now, and Elizabeth watched in horror as the Englishman stepped into the room.

"It was...very enlightening...seeing you, sister." Anne's eyes were troubled, but her voice was clear. "This time, however, I am the one who must be leaving."

Chapter 31

Peter Garnesche gloated, his eyes full of malice, as the heavy oak door swung shut behind the departing Anne.

Elizabeth backed unconsciously away from the door, her eyes scanning the room for something to use for protection. She could see nothing that might be effective in fighting off the giant. Elizabeth had been betrayed, and she was now at the villain's mercy. She looked into the knight's swarthy face, at the eyes that always hinted of madness.

Elizabeth's face hardened. Though her insides were quivering with fear, she was determined not to show it. No matter what happened to her, she would never give this animal the satisfaction of seeing the terror within her.

"Get out!" she commanded, her voice husky and forceful. "Get out of my house."

"Always the fighter," Garnesche sneered. "Well, I didn't come all this way just to leave."

"One step closer and a house full of men will come crashing through that door."

With an air that was almost leisurely, Garnesche pulled a dagger from his belt and held it out before him. The sharp point was aimed directly at her throat. "Your porter was the only man I could find. And I'm fairly certain he won't come crashing in."

Gazing at the evil smirk on his face, Elizabeth struggled to hide the shudder that wracked her body. She had been a trusting fool, and Garnesche's words struck terror into her heart. Here, in the midst of the bustling town, the house contained no soldiers—no one to protect her. And after all, she had not expected treachery of this magnitude.

"What do you want from me?" she demanded harshly.

"Not much." He took a step closer. "Only your silence."

She backed around the standing easel that held the canvas, cutting a wide radius to keep as much distance between them as she could.

"But that won't be enough, will it?"

"Nay, it won't. But there's no silence like that of the dead, you know."

"You are a greater fool than I thought." Placing one hand behind her, Elizabeth surreptitiously picked up a small palette knife from the cluttered table. She knew it was dull, but she held it tightly, hiding it in the folds of her skirt. "You think you can just kill me and then walk off."

"That is exactly what I intend to do." He continued to move closer to her.

"Then you might as well drive that dagger into your own heart right now, because you are as good as dead. Ambrose will kill you. He'll avenge my death with a fury, the likes of which the world has never seen. And your name will go down in infamy, for he will carve on your heart the names of Mary and the Lord Constable and all the others that you've slain in cold blood."

The fear that flickered across the back of his eyes was momentary, but Elizabeth saw it. The giant's hesitation was short-lived, however. A twisted smile crept back across his depraved features.

"Ah, you frighten me so." Moving toward her, he threw aside the easel and the canvas. Now nothing stood between them. "But right now, this exquisite moment is what I came to Scotland for."

Elizabeth looked about her in terror. She had nowhere to go. She backed away until she hit the wall.

"As we rode north, I envisioned this to be a quick death. A sharp twist of the neck or perhaps a quick slash at your pretty throat." He moved closer. "But being here with you now brings back certain...longings."

Elizabeth watched in amazement as the man quickly unfastened the belt about his doublet. Still holding his dagger, he dropped his sheathed sword to the floor.

"I've looked forward to this moment for quite a long time, Elizabeth. I know now that it is really the reason I came to this godforsaken country myself, instead of sending one of my men. It was meant to be this way. I didn't come to Troyes myself. That was why you didn't die there as I'd planned. Aye, I've dwelled on this many times before. Seeing, in my mind's eye, the moment when I will force you down. Listen to your screams. Feel your strong, tight legs fighting my entry. The moment when I drive my shaft deep inside you."

"It was never the murder that I witnessed that brought you after me. It was this sickness of yours. This insane lust for one you could never have."

Garnesche laughed. "You are so perceptive, m'lady." She moved quickly to the side as his hands reached for her. She backed up again as he steadily approached. "But it's not insanity. It's a dream. Call it a vision."

Elizabeth picked up the three-legged stool with one hand and flung it at his head. He ducked, avoiding it easily.

"I have seen it many times. I can see it now. Again and again driving my body into you, until your cries become moans, and I pour my seed into you. And then you lie in my arms and beg me for more."

"I will die first."

"You are nearly correct in that, Elizabeth. For as you beg, I *will* give you more. And that will be your death wish. Trapped in my arms, my shaft deep within you, I will wrap my fingers around your neck. Your tender, ivory neck. And shortly, when I hear you screaming for release, I will squeeze your windpipe. Tighter and tighter, squeezing and plunging until you won't know whether to scream for release or for breath. But you will get neither."

His hand shot out like lightning, and he grabbed hold of her wrist. Bringing her resisting body toward him, he smirked once again.

"You are sick." With her other hand, Elizabeth stabbed him hard in the wrist. The dull knife broke off at the hilt, the blade clattering to the floor, but the blow was enough to cause the knight to release her, bellowing in pain as he did. Elizabeth ran to the window. It was high above the street, but it was a chance.

Garnesche followed slowly after her, his eyes ablaze with madness.

"I will rest my full weight on your dying body, and you will sink into darkness, looking into my face, feeling me inside of you. You will die seeing my face! Aye, only mine!"

Elizabeth pulled open the leaded glass window so hard that it smashed against the wall of the room, shards of glass shattering around her. The violence of the crash stopped him for an instant, long enough for her to pick up a small strip of lead with a jagged piece of glass protruding from it. Garnesche paused and looked at the makeshift weapon.

"Ambrose will hunt you down," she whispered. "He'll make you die a slow and excruciating death."

"No one will ever know it was me." He glanced around at the rushes and the kegs of oil. "For when I'm done with you, your body will burn as your long lost Lord Constable did. To this day no one knows what happened to the arrogant fool. That night in the Field of Cloth of Gold, he simply disappeared. And when this house goes up in flames, you'll disappear, as well."

Garnesche's back was to the door, but he heard it bang open as quickly as Elizabeth saw it. Whirling, the English knight thrust the dagger at Ambrose's chest with a single motion, and the weapon found its mark, sinking deeply into the Highlander's chest just below the shoulder.

Elizabeth screamed as Ambrose staggered back against the heavy oak jamb, the point of his sword dragging across the floor.

Peter Garnesche leaped triumphantly to the place where he'd dropped his belt, and whipped his long sword from its sheath. As the Englishman advanced across the room, Ambrose straightened himself, the hilt of the dagger still protruding from his chest.

"Come on, you filthy cur," the Highlander challenged. "It is time this world was rid of you."

The Englishman paused, and the two giants eyed each other.

"The only regret I have about killing you, Macpherson," Garnesche sneered, "is that you won't have the pleasure of watching me take your woman."

"Then save your regrets, Garnesche, for you aren't man enough to accomplish either."

With a roar, the Englishman swung his great sword and the sparks exploded as steel crashed upon steel. One arm hanging limp at his side, Ambrose shoved his foe backward, sending him reeling across the floor.

Following as quickly as he could, the Highlander spun hard, his long blade arcing through the charged air. Again a shower of sparks rained down as Ambrose's brand hammered at Garnesche's weapon.

The Englishman stumbled under the blow, but as he went down, Garnesche kicked out with his boot, sweeping the Highlander's feet from beneath him. With a sickening thud, Ambrose's wounded shoulder hit the floor, and in a moment the Englishman was looming over him.

Malevolence vied with triumph on the face of the brute, and he drew back his sword to finish the fallen Scot.

"What a pleasure this is—" he began.

Elizabeth leaped onto Garnesche's back, grabbing his hair and yanking it back as she slashed with all her might at his exposed neck. But the Englishman's head snapped forward, and her jagged shard of glass found only the side of his face, ripping open a gash on his swarthy cheekbone.

Reaching back, the giant tore the woman from his back, throwing her like a rag across the room.

But Elizabeth had given Ambrose enough time, and the warrior lurched to his feet.

Garnesche turned his bloodied face back to the Highlander and, with a shout, raised his weapon to strike. But Ambrose spun once again, his blade slicing toward the madman's ribs, and this time his sword found its mark, cutting the very breath from the Englishman's roar.

Before Garnesche's body had ceased to twitch, Elizabeth was at Ambrose's side. Sitting the warrior gently against the wall, she knelt beside him, easing the dagger from his shoulder and pressing her palm tightly against the wound.

"Are you hurt?" Ambrose whispered, clutching her hand, searching her face for any mark of injury.

"Nothing happened to me, my love. But you...you are bleeding."

He brought her fingers to his lips while reaching in and wiping the tears that rolled freely down her face.

"A wee cut, lass. That's all it is. I've survived much worse than this." Ambrose smiled weakly.

"I am sorry, Ambrose. I am so sorry."

"Hush, lass," he whispered.

"I never told you before. I should have. I thought it was over. But it wasn't. He came after me. In Calais at the Field of Cloth of Gold, in Troyes at the market, and now here."

"Garnesche."

"He killed the Lord Constable, and I witnessed it. I was running from my father's tent, and I happened on Garnesche and the Lord Constable talking treason. I saw him murder the Lord Constable in cold blood. And he knew I saw it. So he came after me. I am so sorry, my love. All this would never have happened if I—"

"Nay, Elizabeth." Ambrose tried to smooth back her hair. "You can tell me all about it later. But remember this—nothing that happened here was your fault. Garnesche was a madman. And he is now dead."

Ambrose smiled. "And I am proud of you. You have the courage of a Highlander. The way you fought. You saved my life."

She kissed his lips. "Nay, you saved mine. I was foolish earlier when I asked you to go. I never want to be anywhere without you again. Never."

"That's a promise." His deep blue eyes locked in with hers. "I love you, Elizabeth Macpherson. And I, too, am sorry for what you went through."

"Don't, Ambrose," Elizabeth replied, caressing his face. "I just thank the Blessed Mother you came back when you did."

"Jaime and I were just coming up the hill into town when your sister came riding out under a white flag, at the head of a troop of English soldiers."

"Did she see you?"

"Aye. She was looking for us."

Elizabeth stared at him.

"She told me that your life was in danger. That Garnesche had you at the point of his blade in here. She pleaded with me to hurry. And then she rode away like the devil was after her."

Elizabeth listened carefully to his every word. Moments. A few moments more would have meant certain death for her. Anne. Her sister had gone after Ambrose. After she had betrayed her. A change of heart? she wondered.

"Did she say anything else?" Elizabeth asked quietly.

"Aye, as a matter of fact, she did. She said, 'Tell her I've forgiven her. And tell her I hope that someday she might forgive me, as well.'"

Chapter 32

Benmore Castle, The Scottish Highlands
June, 1525

The Highlanders charged with wild cries across the cobbles of the castle courtyard, their swords raised.

At the far end, the warrior queen and her official guard stood their ground, their fearless expressions unchanged in the face of the reckless charge.

"Your Majesty," Malcolm MacLeod said, turning to the little girl standing beside him fully armed with her own wooden sword. "Would you allow me the honor of dispensing with this horde of ruffians and rogues?"

"Aye, Lord Malcolm," Jaime assented sternly. "But they are my cousins, don't forget. So spare their lives when you can."

As the whooping brigands swarmed around them, the sixteen-year-old Malcolm lifted the littlest one onto his shoulder and fought off the other two with exaggerated displays of swordsmanship.

Finally, after her guard had wrestled the assailants into submission and was lying on top of them, Queen Jaime sauntered over and placed the point of her sword on the chest of her eldest cousin, Alexander.

"Yield, villain!"

"Never!"

Malcolm tightened his hold on the eight-year-old, giving the warrior an opportunity to surrender with honor.

"I yield," Alexander gasped. "But next time, *we* get the giant."

"Perhaps, blackguard. But first promise to give up your plans to send my baby brother to the dungeons, and we will allow you to live." Her voice was commanding.

The young boy nodded grudgingly. "Aye, we'll leave him alone."

"Forever?"

"Until the bairn can carry a sword. But that's it. That's our final offer."

Jaime's eyes traveled to Malcolm questioningly. He gave a covert wink.

"We accept your offer, Lord Alexander," she announced. "And you may keep your holdings in the king's name."

Ambrose moved behind Elizabeth and gathered her and the baby into his arms. He smiled, watching the tiny infant sucking gently on a closed fist.

Following Elizabeth's gaze, the proud father looked out on battling armies untangling themselves in the yard below.

"Another victory for the queen?" he asked.

"Aye," Elizabeth whispered, smiling. "With the aid of her heroic knight."

Ambrose placed a kiss tenderly on the silky skin of her neck. She snuggled closer to him.

"Jaime is going to miss Malcolm when he returns to St. Andrew's," Elizabeth noted softly, watching the two cross the yard. The young girl's head didn't even reach the young warrior's waist, but she held his hand as though he belonged to her.

"His education at St. Andrew's is only a first step for him," Ambrose replied. "The lad has great challenges lying ahead."

Elizabeth turned in her husband's arms and gazed up into his deep blue eyes. "As we all do," She sighed happily.

Ambrose leaned down and placed a soft kiss on the black, silky hair of his sleeping son. Then, turning his attention once again to the mother, he met her upraised lips with his own.

He was the happiest man alive. Gathering her tighter in his arms, he whispered words of love. She answered with fervor.

The noises of the stirring bairn between them disrupted their moment together, and the two laughed as the infant stretched his tiny fingers upward toward their faces.

The sun shining on the Macphersons' carved stone coat of arms drew the young mother's gaze out the window, and she felt all around her the love and the strength of the family that was now her own. Then, her eyes traveling heavenward, Elizabeth's heart swelled with a happiness as infinitely vast, as infinitely deep, as the crystalline blue of the cloudless Highland sky.

Epilogue

Greenwich Palace, 1533

Anne Boleyn, Queen of England, snuggled the red-haired infant closer to her and, taking a deep breath, nodded to the physicians and the Lord Chamberlain. The massive door to her quarters swung open, and the king led his Privy Council into the room.

Wordlessly, Henry strode to the bed and sat beside the mother and child. His corpulent face folded into a wry smile as he poked a fleshy finger into the folds of the baby's soft covering.

The king didn't look up into Anne's face, but she hardly expected him to, considering his disappointment.

"Well, Annie," he growled. "I suppose the wind must have been from the south, eh?"

"She's a healthy girl, Henry."

"Aye. She has my mother's coloring."

"Perhaps next time—"

Anne's comment was left unfinished as King Henry rose abruptly from the bed.

"We've a country to provide for," the king stated shortly. "We'll look in on you later."

As the king reached the door, a thought struck him and he turned back toward the bed, his entourage scattering before him.

"If you have a name you want considered, Anne, let us know." Without another word, the monarch swept out the door.

Anne watched, her face a mask, as the room cleared. Nodding to the Lord Chamberlain as he turned to go, Anne looked down at the infant in her arms. Gazing at the wisps of red hair, the round little face, and the nearly translucent skin, the mother wondered at the sleeping child, so peaceful and unaware of the world she had just entered.

Huddling her even closer, the queen glanced up defiantly at the closed door.

"A south wind, indeed," she whispered bitterly. Anne's eyes lowered again to her baby. "Listen to me, little one, and learn this now. They will tell you it's a man's world. But take heart, fear nothing. You will carry the name of a great woman. You will carry her spirit."

In 1558, Elizabeth I, resplendent in her gown of cloth of gold, ascended the throne of Britain. For the next half century, she was to forge the glorious era of Sidney and Spenser, Jonson and Shakespeare, and in the end give her name to England's golden age.

Author's Note

What is it about those Highlanders that keeps us so enthralled with them? Their rugged strength and stamina? The fierce passion? Their indomitable integrity and sense of loyalty?

Perhaps it's the unconquered spirit born into them, the powerful energy that flows into them from their mountain streams and majestic peaks.

Whatever it is, we never seem to get enough of the Highlanders and the romance that they embody.

After writing the story of the eldest of the three Macpherson brothers in *Angel of Skye*, we were deluged with letters clamoring to know more about his brothers, Ambrose and John. *Heart of Gold* is our first response to those requests, telling of Ambrose's romantic pursuit of Elizabeth Boleyn, whose spirit matches his and whose passion for life is unrivaled. We hope you enjoyed *Heart of Gold. Beauty of the Mist*, the story of John Macpherson, completes the Macpherson trilogy. Of course, Jaime's story (*The Intended*) is the one that comes after that. We are currently writing a series of novels that begins with *Tess and the Highlander*. That series will follow the adventures of the next generation of Macpherson heroes. As we've said before, we cannot let our characters go.

As authors, we love feedback. We write our stories for you. We'd love to hear what you liked, what you loved, and even what you didn't like. We are constantly learning, so please help us write stories that you will cherish and recommend to your friends. You can write to us at NikooandJim@gmail.com and visit us on our website at www.MayMcGoldrick.com.

Finally, we need a favor. If you're so inclined, we'd love a review of *Heart of Gold*. If you loved it or hated it, please let us know. Reviews can be difficult to come by these days, so you, the reader, have the power now to make or break a book. And if you have the time, go to our Author Page on Amazon. You can find links to all of our books there.

Wishing you peace and health!

Nikoo and Jim

www.MayMcGoldrick.com

Preview of
May McGoldrick's Next Novel

The Beauty of the Mist

Prologue

Antwerp, The Netherlands
March, 1528

Let the Scots come.

Like the wings of a wounded raven, the black cloak fluttered madly about the running figure. Maria, Queen of Hungary, paused, pressing her exhausted body into the dark shadows of the shuttered, brick town house. The flaring light of the torch that lit the street glistened off the wet stone of the alley, and the young queen tried to melt even deeper into the blackness. Straining, Maria could hear no sound of pursuers in the cold, night air. Her jade eyes flashing, she peered back past the torch toward the gloomy walls of the Palace, towering above the roofs of the sleeping town.

Turning away, she could see the one finished spire of the cathedral rising before her. Unfamiliar with the twisting streets and alleyways of this town—or any other—Maria gazed up at the landmark she'd been told to follow.

The houses and shops crowded her on every side, and as she ran, the cold, damp air stabbed at her lungs. The sky above began to lighten, and she pushed herself onward, her feet flying over the slick stones.

At the end of the twisting way, she slowed before entering the open plaza around the cathedral. Beyond the stone walls of the huge church, black in the predawn light, lay the harbor. She had to reach it before life in the Palace began to stir, before the tide turned.

There, by one of the stone quays, a longboat waited. A longboat that would take Maria to her aunt. To the strong seaworthy ship that would carry them both far from the abhorrent marriage.

She ran across the empty plaza, hugging the walls of the cathedral. She would make it to the harbor now. She could smell the brackish water of the river already.

Let the Scots come, she thought defiantly. Let them come.

Chapter 1

Stirling Castle, Scotland
March, 1528

A gilded cage is still a cage.

John Macpherson, Lord of the Navy, stood with his back to the smoldering fire and watched in restrained silence as the young king with the fiery red hair halted his restless pacing at one of the glazed windows overlooking the open courtyard of Stirling Castle. Following the young man's gaze, he could see that the sixteen-year-old monarch's eyes had riveted on a solitary raven flying free in the gray Scottish skies that surrounded the castle walls.

Across the chamber Archibald Douglas, the Earl of Angus, smoothed his long black beard over his chest as he finished reading over the last of the official letters. Folding the document, the powerful lord paused and looked up at the black-clad young man by the window, before dripping wax onto the parchment.

John saw a smile flicker over the Lord Chancellor's face as he lifted the king's royal seal, pressing it into the soft wax.

"With these letters, Sir John should have no trouble fetching your bride, Kit...I mean, Your Majesty," Archibald corrected himself, seeing the king turn his glance briefly on him.

His face hiding the growing rage within, John Macpherson continued to watch the scene unfolding before him. The king had summoned him to court for instructions on a mission of the utmost importance. But after spending just a few short moments with these two men, John knew that the horrible rumors he'd been hearing were all true. Archibald Douglas, the Earl of Angus, chief of the powerful Douglas clan, Lord Chancellor of

Scotland, member of Regency Council, and the ex-husband of Queen Margaret, had King James, his stepson, under lock and key.

The Chancellor turned to the silent Highlander.

"Sir John, the Emperor Charles is expecting you at Antwerp before the end of the month. I don't think I need to tell you that it is quite an honor that he is entrusting his sister, Mary of Hungary, to our care for the voyage."

"Aye, m'lord," John responded, looking at the king as he answered.

"His Majesty will be spending Easter at Falkland Palace," Angus continued. "But if you need to contact me, I will be in the south, clearing vermin from the Borders."

The King turned his face to John and their eyes met.

Then John Macpherson saw once again the flash in the lad's eyes. The same fearless spark that the Highlander had first witnessed years earlier in the fatherless bairn. James had been only an infant when his father died fighting the English at Flodden Field. Entrusted to the safekeeping of one brave woman and a handful of loyal supporters, the Crown Prince had been whisked across the Highlands while a few stalwart nobles struggled to arrange for his safe return. And then he had come back to the arms of the Queen Mother. Still not yet two years of age, he had been crowned James V, King of Scotland.

That was the day John Macpherson had first seen him. The day of his coronation. A mere bairn sitting on the high throne of a country in chaos. But everyone who had knelt before him, swearing their loyalty before God, had been struck with the clear knowledge that the boy was a Stuart. Silent, serious, and steadfast through the course of the ceremony, Kit had shown them all that he had the blood, the courage, and the intelligence of his forebears. He was the one who would carry on. The new king who would rise to save Scotland from her enemies. The one who would save Scotland from herself.

John watched the king walk toward him, ignoring the Chancellor's continuing speech.

The Lord Chancellor. The man who had married the queen in her widowhood solely for the reason of filling the power void that existed in Scotland after the devastating loss at Flodden Field. Everyone in Scotland knew that the union would bring the Douglas family power, and it did. The marriage gave the Earl of Angus control over the young king, and eventually put him in a position of absolute power—to rule in his name.

And from what John had been hearing, since the Queen Mother requested that the Pope annul her marriage to the man, the Lord Chancellor had been tightening his control of the young king—and guarding him fiercely.

John knew, as did everyone else, that there was no one strong enough to challenge the Lord Chancellor. Little more than a year ago, several thousand men had tried at Linlithgow, but they'd failed. And as he cut them down in their blood, Angus had claimed that he was only protecting the Crown.

John straightened as the red-haired king halted before him. The Highlander towered over the young man, but their eyes never left each other's face.

"You think me weak, Jack Heart?" the King asked.

Jack Heart. John smiled. He hadn't heard the nickname for some time. Not since the days when the boy king had been under the protection of the Queen Mother. Then, James had been far less restricted in his liberties, and John had taught the lad to sail amid the whitecaps off Queen's Ferry. They'd spent a full summer in each other's company, and it had been then that the young king had learned the name that John had once been called by the sailors of the Macpherson ships. It had become a term of endearment between the two. Though few even recalled the name anymore, even fewer would have dared address the fierce Lord of the Navy in so familiar a manner.

Except Kit.

"Then you agree."

"Never," John answered. "You are not weak, lad. Only trapped."

"My father would have handled it differently."

"Your father was never separated from his people nor imprisoned at your age." John continued with more assurance. "And as much as I loved him as a king, he had his flaws."

"But he was a soldier. My father had courage. As you have courage." James stared at the commander's tartan. "If you were in my position, you would never have accepted this fate."

"But, m'lord—"

"Jack Heart," the young king cut in, "you were barely a year older than I when you stood your ground in the mud beside my father at Flodden Field. You have courage, John. You have determination. You have heart. I lack these things."

"Only in your own eyes, m'lord. In the hearts of all loyal Scots, you are our king and our future."

James gazed up at John, a wistful look flickering across his face. "I don't want to be a disappointment to my people."

"You won't be, sire." John answered in earnest, seeing the lad's distress. The young king almost reached his shoulder now. But he was so young. Too young, perhaps, to battle the evil that perched at his right hand. "You'll overcome this difficulty, and your triumph will win the heart of every Scot. You'll take your throne when the time is right. And then, the accounts of your bravery, the tales of your generosity, the recital of your acts of goodness will far exceed any standard set by your father and their fathers in this land. Always remember this, Kit. Your people see the promise. That is why they want you."

James looked up trustingly. "I will do my best not to disappointment them. I will slip this trap."

"Like the fox, himself." John's eyes shone with affection.

"Like my father." A perceptible change came over the young man's face. "Aye, Jack. Then you'll bring her to me."

"If that's your wish." John paused, casting a casual glance at the Chancellor, who was eyeing them suspiciously from across the room. "Of course, we could devise other means—other ways to bring an end to this...undesirable situation."

The young king smiled sadly, looking down at his untried hands. "If it were only that simple. But if we were to go that way, then it'd mean that others will need to fight my battle. Others like you, Jack Heart. But if I were free..."

John waited for him to continue, but Kit changed his course.

"He has given his word to me and to the Council that he will step aside after this marriage takes place." The young man gave a glance over his shoulder. "It's the best way. I don't wish that any more blood of innocent Scots be shed while any other way exists to settle this unholy affair. This is my responsibility, Jack. This is something I can do. This is the first chance for me to show my will, my strength. This means everything to me."

"But at your young age...you are willing to marry someone you've never known...never seen."

"For the good of Scotland, I will. And it will bring me one step closer to my people." The lad's eyes lit up at the thought. "Please, Jack, I need this chance."

John nodded in response.

"Bring her here, Jack." The young man placed his hand on the Highlander's arm. "I will wed her. It's God's will."

The Chancellor stalked briskly across the room, and John took the sealed letter from his hand. Archibald Douglas' voice was cool and his gaze steady.

"Keep her safe, Sir John."

John nodded curtly to the Chancellor and, exchanging a telling look with the young king, bowed to them both before departing from the chamber.

Read this swashbuckling tale of stolen love and adventure.

www.MayMcGoldrick.com

Made in the USA
San Bernardino, CA
05 March 2017